MOON ROAD

www.penguin.co.uk

Also by Sarah Leipciger

The Mountain Can Wait

Coming Up for Air

MOON ROAD

Sarah Leipciger

doubleday

TRANSWORLD PUBLISHERS
Penguin Random House, One Embassy Gardens,
8 Viaduct Gardens, London SW11 7BW
www.penguin.co.uk

Transworld is part of the Penguin Random House group of companies
whose addresses can be found at global.penguinrandomhouse.com

First published in Great Britain in 2024 by Doubleday
an imprint of Transworld Publishers

A CIP catalogue record for this book
is available from the British Library.

ISBNs 9780857526533 (cased)
9780857526540 (tpb)

Typeset in 11.5/15.75pt Adobe Garamond Pro by Jouve (UK), Milton Keynes.
Printed and bound in Great Britain by Clays Ltd, Elcograf S.p.A.

The authorized representative in the EEA is Penguin Random House Ireland,
Morrison Chambers, 32 Nassau Street, Dublin D02 YH68.

Penguin Random House is committed to a sustainable
future for our business, our readers and our planet. This book is
made from Forest Stewardship Council® certified paper.

For Alex
and for Meghan

CANADA

BRITISH
COLUMBIA

ALBERTA

SASKATCHEWAN

Jasper

Tofino • Nanaimo
Kamloops
Vancouver   Nicola Valley
Hope Merritt

Calgary
Cluny

Medicine
Hat

Swift
Current

Broadview

The
ROAD

MANITOBA

ONTARIO

Winnipeg

Kenora

Whiteshell ...... Thunder Bay ..... Marathon

Wawa

Sault Ste. Marie ...... Sudbury

Desbarats

Home

N

Rain

A WOMAN, SLEEPING in a tree.

Not like a lemur, nothing like that. She's not suspended in the branches by her toes. This tree, this red cedar, once awe-inspiring in a forest of awe-inspiring trees, is now dead. All that remains is a hollowed trunk with a triangular opening just big enough for a person to crouch through. The trunk rises about three and a half metres from the ground. Its open top is jaggy and covered with a blue tarp, which is secured around the wide circumference of the trunk with bright yellow nylon rope. Picture waxed paper secured with string over the lid of a jam jar.

This young woman is asleep under the tarp. She's warm and dry in a sleeping bag, on a bed of blankets and more tarps, and she's wandering through one of those dreams where you just cannot get to the place you're trying to get to. On her feet is a pair of cumbersome, flapping shoes that get caught on all the edges (there are edges underfoot) and she's taking wrong turn after wrong turn, destination blurring more and more. The dream hands her a peach. She takes a bite. It's rotten.

It starts to rain. Not in the dream, it is actually raining. The forest canopy is thick so at first the drops landing on the tarp are sporadic, but soon the rain comes down harder and the water begins to collect in little pools on the tarp and eventually finds its way to small tears in the blue, synthetic fabric. It drips on the sleeping woman. First on her forehead so she turns in sleep, then on her ear, and down her neck, and stipples through her thick hair.

She wakes up. The dark is so absolute that for a second she's not sure if her eyes are even open. She sits up and feels for something solid in the black, something she can touch. She pats the space beside her and feels the warmth and give of her sleeping friend.

The sound of the rain on the tarp is like the clop of a spooked pony and the woman is concerned that the collected water will get too heavy and the tarp will come down on them – it's happened before, while they were asleep. It was quite a shock, it was dreadful to be woken up that way, but they laughed about it in the morning and told the story over and over again.

The woman shifts her bedding away from the drip and lies back down but now she can't fall asleep. It's hard to trust the integrity of this shabby structure. She frowns because, well, come on, how did she end up here anyway? Having moved out of the path of the drip, she's now cramped in close to the inner wall of the cedar trunk. It smells dusty and musky and old. There are probably ants.

It is 11:28 p.m.

PART ONE

The Party

I

MANY YEARS AGO, Kathleen was told by a woman examining the mulchy tea leaves scattered in her empty cup that she would always be left by the people she loved. Kathleen didn't believe in tea-leaf reading but she didn't question the woman; neither did she ask her to elaborate. Kathleen knew what this tea-leaf reader meant, because she's always known it herself: she is the one who stays behind.

She encountered this so-called clairvoyant unintentionally while she was trying to fill several hours waiting for a ferry that was running very late. She was out west at the time, the other side of the country from where she lives now, from where she has always lived. When the ferry finally did arrive, she embarked with the other foot passengers and climbed the stairs to the top level and pushed through a heavy door to the outside deck, where the ocean wind pressed her clothes against her body. She wrapped her hands around the salty metal railing and looked across the cold water to where she knew the coastal mountains stood, though on this day the mountains were hidden in cloud. So she stared into the blank grey sky and thought, I will always be left by the people I love. Fine.

Kathleen was married, once. The marriage lasted only a few years, but they remained good friends for over two decades because of Una, their daughter. And because they never stopped being fond of each other. So, a lasting friendship, but then one day, they had an argument. The argument was bad enough that they didn't speak for nineteen years. Not a card, not a text message, not an email.

The argument played out on Kathleen's back porch. It was about Una, and other things, too. Kathleen told him to leave even though she didn't really want him to leave, and then she watched him go. She watched him stride across the weedy lawn and kick the folding porch table that lay with one fractured leg on its side. She watched him, the way he flowed like water, like dangerous water, so full of himself and oblivious to what he stirred up. To what he carried away and what he left behind. Yannick.

She watched him rip a dandelion out of the grass with all its green skirts, and she watched him mash the dandelion between his bloodied hands, then get angry at his own mashing hands. He tossed the mangled weed over his shoulder, white roots carving an angry arc in the air. For an instant, the tiny clods of black dirt that flew off the roots held in mid-flight. Long enough for Kathleen to consider calling him back so she could apologize for throwing the folding porch table at him. And the ashtray – she threw an ashtray, too.

It pissed her off, though, the way he pulled up that dandelion. Because it was her yard, and if she let a dandelion grow, so what? She let a dandelion grow. So she didn't call him back, and instead she watched him step up into his truck and start the engine and grind out of the driveway, hacking exhaust. For several minutes, she stayed on the porch, holding her shoe, which she had been about to put on when the argument started. She considered the lingering blue cloud of exhaust until she could no longer tell whether the fumes were actually there, or whether the blue smudge hovering a foot above the gravel was only the memory of fumes.

And it was such a fine day, the day they fought. Early September. Birds in the trees and a kitchen struck through with amber light and long shadows. All that.

Kathleen's kitchen. Her back porch. Her backyard. At the time of the argument, this yard was a barren swathe of not-a-lot, just unloved lawn gone to seed and dwarfish squirts of cat grass. But over the years, she began to dig and to build. She rented a back-hoe and turned over long strips of earth for planting beds. She built a hoop house, a greenhouse and a work shed. Bought a refrigerated shed. She raised market flowers from seed. Zinnias, lilies. Larkspurs, cosmos, dahlias. Celosia, like feathers, like fire, like tropical coral. Kathleen built a flower farm in this yard where her daughter Una had turned somersaults and played hide-and-seek as a little girl.

Nineteen years since Yannick left Kathleen's driveway amid the clatter and chuck of an old diesel engine. Not a word.

And then, half an hour ago, he called. Not exactly out of the blue, not entirely incidentally. Yannick isn't the first person to surprise Kathleen today with a phone call, and she's rattled. So rattled that she's just gone upstairs and walked down the hall, past Una's closed bedroom door and into her own room. On her bookshelf, which has never held a single book, is a little wooden box with a little hidden drawer that clicks open with the nudge of a finger. In that drawer there is a tooth. Not much more than a shard of enamel flecked with dry, brown blood at its craggy base, this was the first tooth to cut Una's bottom gum. Kathleen tips the tooth out of the drawer and onto her flattened palm to examine it. She remembers how it first felt on the pad of her thumb, how she could feel it in Una's mouth before she could see it, its eager knobs pushing up through Una's bone-hard, slippery gum. Later, this same tooth was the first to loosen, to cling to a tag of skin, bothered by Una's tongue until the socket bled and the tooth fell out and she presented it to Kathleen, dried to a wrap of stiff and bloodied toilet paper, when she got home from school.

Kathleen holds her palm up to her nose and smells the tooth. Odourless. She tongues her own tooth, a molar that has been warning her off and on for years, and has now, only a few days ago, cleaved down the middle, like an open book. She tastes the bitterness of pus.

She brings the tooth down to the kitchen and drops it into a clean jam jar, screws the lid until the metal wedges itself firmly against the glass, and takes the jar out to her Miss Pepper phlox. She gets down on her knees and digs under the phlox with her hand spade, digs deep into the rich, dark earth until the hole is as deep as her forearm. She stops, checks over her shoulder. The neighbour's cat, who is an asshole, coolly judges her from the top of the high wooden fence that divides the yards. His rickety tail hangs like an annoying little question mark over the edge of the fence.

'Scram, beast,' she spits, and settles the jam jar in the bottom of the hole. She refills it, and scruffs the surface of the earth with her shoe.

The reason Yannick called today was to tell her he's coming to town, whether she likes it or not. Tomorrow she'll meet him in a café, because she knows what will happen if she allows him into her house. He'll slide onto one of the tall stools in the kitchen and set his elbows on the island counter and ask for a coffee as if nineteen years haven't passed. He'll fill her space with his smell, the turps and the linseed oil, or the glue or epoxy resin or whatever it is he's got his hands into these days.

And that smell, that coffee cup with the grainy dregs at the bottom, it will sit there on the counter long after he leaves.

This isn't about love, no. It's much more than that.

Kathleen rises the next morning later than usual, having slept badly. She pours a cup of coffee and goes out to the beds with her clippers, not to harvest but to select a few stems for a personal arrangement for her friend Heather, whose birthday is today. Snapdragons and cosmos, and a few stems of lime-light millet as foliage will do, wrapped loosely in crisp brown paper.

Is Heather a friend, really? Still in her thirties, she's six years younger than Una and works part-time for Kathleen on the farm. She's a sweet girl but has no clue, like a dog. Her backyard sprawls over half an acre and whenever Kathleen visits, she thinks of the wasted potential, this open space that could be dug and planted. Filled.

Kathleen lays the bouquet on the passenger seat of her Toyota, thinking about what a good surprise it will be when she shows up with flowers, and about how much time this will fill before her meeting with Yannick.

Heather is on the lawn when Kathleen pulls up in front of her house. She has the sprinkler going and one of her kids is naked down to the underpants, charging full throttle through the spray like it's the best goddamn thing in all the world and not just a crappy sprinkler, the poor man's swimming pool. Heather is reclined in a lawn chair, eating something sloppy off a plastic kiddy plate. Probably, Kathleen thinks, all of her children have been fed and she's pecking at their leftovers with the few precious minutes she has before she has to clean blood and grit off a knee or tease bubblegum out of someone's hair.

The kid hugs her twiggy arms across her chest and squeals, and the sound of the sprinkler going schick-schick-schick, and the kid laughing the way she is, every muscle in her body tight with cold and uninhibited joy, makes Kathleen want to get back into her car and drive home. Too much noise and everything else.

'I brought you these,' Kathleen says, waving the flowers from where she still stands on the sidewalk. The sprinkler is dangerously close and she doesn't want to get wet. 'Happy birthday,' she says. Pain cracks through her split, infected molar and bursts across her jaw. She presses the side of her mouth with the heel of her hand until the pain subsides to a quiet throb.

'Oh,' Heather says, and waves Kathleen over. 'Come and sit,' she says.

'I can't stay long.'

'Just for a minute.'

Kathleen does a crafty shuffle and dance up the crumbling and weedy concrete walk, avoiding the sprinkler, and playfully sticks her tongue out at the kid. It's hard to tell which kid this is. Heather has a bunch of them, and a truck-driving husband named Dave. They've been together since high school, and as far as Kathleen can see, they aren't exactly in love, because how can anyone be in love after living together as long as these two have? What's easier to believe is that they were once in love and have come out the other side intact. Kathleen can appreciate this is a rare thing. She's witnessed it in the details: they still call each other 'baby', and he cups his big ugly hands around her face when he kisses her hello.

Kathleen slowly eases herself into the empty lawn chair next to Heather, which creaks and complains as it reluctantly takes her weight, and she passes Heather the flowers. 'Happy birthday,' she says again.

'Ah,' Heather says, murmuring, turning the bouquet to admire it. She looks embarrassed. 'Let me— Hold on.' She hops back up, knocking her flimsy chair onto its side, and takes the flowers into the house. She's very limb-y, Heather. Foal-ish.

Kathleen stretches out her legs, kicks off her shoes, and watches the kid. The girl executes a series of shitty somersaults through the spray of water, more of a sideways flop than a head-over-heels. Una was like that too, when she was this age. No sense of her own body, her centre of gravity. No good at gymnastics or any other sport. Heather's kid has tufts of yellow grass stuck all over her body and her undies have gone up her butt so that one of her little butt cheeks bulbs out like a peach.

Kathleen leans back and closes her eyes. The sun lies heavily, heavily on her eyelids. Like big, ugly hands cupping her face. A car shushes past. She catches a whiff of sun lotion, the smell of a child's skin in summer. Somewhere far off, the drawn-out whimper of a lonely dog.

Suddenly, the coolness of shade. Drops of water land on her thigh. She opens her eyes and the kid is standing over her, blocking the sun.

'What do you want?'

The kid holds her fist out, fingers down.

'What've you got there?'

She turns her fist and opens it slowly, dramatically. In her palm, a cricket. Dead as a doornail.

'Good for you,' Kathleen says.

She's covered in goosebumps, this girl. Violet lips and

chattering teeth. Her drenched hair is pasted in noodles to her neck and shoulders.

'Why do you keep saying happy birthday all the time?' she asks. Her words are all shivery.

'That's what you say when it's someone's birthday,' Kathleen says. 'Didn't anyone ever tell you that?'

The kid looks at her cricket, then looks back at Kathleen, nose and eyes scrunched tightly. 'Is it your birthday?'

'It's your mother's birthday.'

'She already had it.'

'That's right. You get one every year.'

The kid shuts her eyes so tightly that they disappear into mean little slits.

'Go bury that little guy somewhere special,' Kathleen says, pointing to the cricket, motioning to the far side of the yard with a nod.

Heather comes back out with her baby hitched onto her hip. The baby eyeballs Kathleen with the deranged and stupefied look of one who has been woken too soon.

'I put the flowers in water,' she says.

'A little sugar in the water,' Kathleen says. 'But you know that.'

'Yes,' Heather says, looking off across the lawn, and Kathleen knows she won't bother with the sugar. She'll mean to, but someone will need something, and then someone else will need something else, and she'll forget about the flowers.

The baby pulls the strap of Heather's tank top and Heather hauls out her tit, manoeuvring the child to feed.

'She found a dead cricket,' Kathleen says, pointing to the kid.

'Oh, that. Yeah.' Heather pushes her hair off her forehead and sighs. 'She's losing her friggin' mind over that bug. She thinks it's alive.'

'I told her to bury it.'

'She thinks it's just sleeping.'

The kid comes over and inspects the nursing baby, and the baby turns his head to his big sister, pulling at Heather's ravaged boob, and laughs. Kathleen tries not to look at Heather's nipple, but her eyes go there anyway, straight to it, now stretched out like an old sock.

Looking around the yard, trying to focus on anything else but this, Kathleen spies a collection of junk piled against the garage wall. A couch turned on its side, garbage bags and cardboard boxes, other pieces of furniture. 'You mind if I . . . ?' she says to Heather, pointing to the pile.

'Go for it. Dave's friend is moving. That's all the crap he doesn't want.'

'Why are you saddled with a bunch of crap Dave's friend doesn't want?' Kathleen says, timing her walk across the lawn to avoid the sprinkler. 'Don't be a sucker,' she warns.

Heather releases the baby into the grass and he sits where he's been placed, cross-legged and bewildered. 'Dave said he'd help drive it to the dump,' she says. Her face looks annoyed; it's got to be the heat and the baby.

'Dave's still helping me, though,' Kathleen says. 'I don't have any other way of getting those games to the hall.'

'Of course,' Heather says. 'He told you he would, and he will.'

Kathleen's annual party is in two days, and she's counting on Dave and his truck for delivering the party games to the hall. There's still a bunch of small jobs to tick off the list: paper plates to be bought, bottles of wine to be collected, gingerbread cake – Una's favourite and a party must – to be baked. Not that she isn't now grateful, however, for this unlikely treasure, this pile of junk. She loves sifting through other people's detritus. Some of her favourite furnishings – an ottoman, a hall table, a speckled oval mirror – have all been rescued from driveway sales or the side of the road.

One of the garbage bags contains old clothes, an unused wooden spoon and paperback books thick and wavy with damp. Kathleen flips through the books to see if any are in good enough condition to bring to Yannick, because she's pretty sure a love for reading never leaves you and he was always the voracious kind, but she decides they're all pulp. She digs through a soggy cardboard box and finds a broken desk lamp with a sturdy brass switch. Yannick likes to fix things and she wants to bring him some kind of gift. Something to pass between them; something to occupy her hands.

'Is it your birthday today?' she calls across the lawn to Heather.

'It was last week.'

'Ah,' Kathleen says. She avoids eye contact with the smug little girl, who's now digging in the sandbox, perhaps laying the cricket to rest.

2

YANNICK IS EARLY and his ex-wife, whom he has not seen or spoken to in more years than he can count, will be late. This man, sitting alone in a coffee shop, is seventy-three years old. He's bent over a book of cryptic crosswords, which is soft from being in his back pocket. He's using a blunt pencil that he found rolling around the passenger footwell of his truck this morning, and he likes the way the soft lead squeaks across the book's shiny newsprint.

He's pretty sure this coffee shop used to be a barber, but he can't remember. He lived in this town for a few years a long time ago. Nothing is familiar now.

He's chosen a table near the back because he's anxious to see her, to see Kathleen. His ex-wife. First ex-wife. He wants to see her before she sees him, wants to see what's coming. Birchfield is a small town and maybe he's also avoiding running into anyone who might recognize him. He's not a shy man. In fact, he's one of those people who will start conversations with strangers in bus stations, but today he's not in the mood for anything like that.

On the wall, by the door, there's a bulletin board tacked up with flyers for guitar lessons and boats for sale, dog-walking and house-cleaning. Yannick noticed it when he walked in because in the middle of the board there is a poster announcing Kathleen's annual party. Which happens to be in two days.

It's obvious that Kathleen cleared a space in the middle of the board for her own poster. There are a couple of abandoned staples in the cork, some with ripped corners of paper still attached, like sad bits of confetti.

Usually a crossword wiz, Yannick is finding it hard to concentrate. He doesn't know how Kathleen is going to be, or how she's going to look. Or how *he*'ll look to her. He suddenly feels very, very old. But he received some unexpected news yesterday and it feels like a big goddamn deal and it's about time they saw each other again. It was Yannick's boy Sunny, his eldest son, who said he should call Kathleen and go to her. And Sunny knows a thing or two about Kathleen. Out of Yannick's four other children, the ones he had with his other wives, the wives who came after Kathleen, Sunny is the only one who's kept in touch with her.

All these years.

Six down. *Damp fog hides nothing.* A cryptic clue and not a difficult one but he just can't see the answer. Five letters. Fourth letter is *s* if he's got seventeen across right. He scowls at the box grid, thinking hard, then looks up just as Kathleen is coming through the door. He knows that she knows he's there, that she knows he would be early, but she doesn't look for him. She stands at the counter and asks for a coffee, and that, there, is the old sound of her voice. Like a song you never forget the words to. Maybe a little smokier now, more of a grind, but this is her. Under her arm, she carries what looks like a lamp, and he watches her settle into a booth by the front window, studies her silhouette. She crosses her legs under the table, sets the lamp down and rests her chin in her hand.

He waits. The years, he sees, have taken more from him than they have from her – physically, that is. Her brown hair has gone coarse and silver, but still falls thick as it ever was, still the same style she always had, cut just at the shoulders. She's padded out around the cheeks and the tits and the ass and looks fit as a fiddle, back in fighting form. Big-toothed and big-boned, is Kathleen, and big-toothed big-boned women age well. She's the same height as Yannick, and she always told him that if he'd been a hair shorter than he was, she wouldn't have fallen for him.

Yannick always knew that, with Kathleen, he only made it by a hair.

He walks over to her table and here she is, this teenage girl doing cartwheels on the back lawn, and he the house painter her daddy hired, the house painter pretending not to desire this young thing from where he sits in the shade with his paper-bag lunch. He, Yannick, the roughneck with the buzzed hair.

'I thought you might want this,' she says, nodding to the lamp.

Yannick pulls out the opposite chair and sits down. He looks at the lamp instead of looking at her. It's one of those desk lamps with a neck like a grasshopper's leg. There's no cord.

'A friend of mine was getting rid of it,' she says, 'and I thought . . . since I was seeing you anyway.'

He finally looks at her.

'You still like to fix things?' she says.

He picks up the lamp and turns it in his hands, and puts it down again. If anyone were paying attention to them, he thinks, it would seem no time had passed since they last met.

The girl behind the counter brings over a cup of coffee. Yannick asks for a third. Kathleen turns her gaze to the window and he thinks of what to say. Tongue truly tied. He looks out of the window to where Kathleen's attention has gone, and across the street there is a hound with sizeable balls pissing up against the wall of the IDA drugstore. Kathleen used to work at the IDA, right up to being some kind of manager, but he knows from Sunny that she left that job long ago and now she grows flowers for a living. Growing flowers does not feel like a Kathleen type of thing to do, but this is what she does now.

'Sure, I can fix this,' he says, referring to the lamp – though he's doubtful.

She cocks her head towards the back of the coffee shop. 'Why'd you sit back there?' she says.

'You saw me?'

'Of course I saw you.'

'I wanted to see you before you saw me.'

'I bet you did,' she says, and sips her coffee. Maybe her hand is shaking. A little.

'I was nervous.'

'What for?'

'Well, fuck, Kathleen. How many years has it been?'

She shrugs.

'Twenty years?' he says. 'More?'

'Nineteen.'

'That's a long time.'

'How are your kids?' she asks.

Yannick leans back in his chair. This is safe territory. This is easy. 'Sunny married twice and twice divorced. Four kids.'

'Sunny I know about. What about the others?'

'Zachary married a little French gal from Québec City.'

'Your dad would have liked that.'

Another cup of coffee is placed in front of Yannick and he spoons it with one heaping sugar. 'They just had a baby girl,' he says. 'I got more pictures than I can count. They sent me about a thousand pictures.' He reaches into his back pocket for his phone but finds it unresponsive, all run out of battery. Which is its usual state. 'Devon I have not heard from in months,' he says. 'He's been working the oil rigs out in Alberta. Driven by cold, hard cash, that one.'

'Sounds like his mother.'

Yannick takes a gulp of coffee. It's too hot but he nurses it down his throat anyway. He says nothing: he does not speak ill of one ex-wife to another.

'And your youngest?' Kathleen says, looking out of the window again, as if asking about his girl Robin doesn't fill her mouth with dirt. Her leg fidgets under the table and he knows it will not be long before she says she has to go. She'll say she has too much to do for the party or make up some other excuse. Makes no difference how much time has passed between them, or how far he's driven to be here.

'Gone to the university,' he says. 'Motherfucking Queen's University. Getting some kind of biology degree.'

'You must be very proud.'

'I am.'

'That's good,' she says. 'That's good for her.'

'She earned it,' he says. He doesn't tell Kathleen how lonely they were, after Robin left for university. How empty he and his wife Leigh felt when Robin was gone. He doesn't tell Kathleen that Leigh has left, too.

Kathleen straightens her chair as if she's ready to get down to business and pushes her coffee to the side. Grasps her hands together on the surface of the table. 'Yannick,' she says, 'I haven't got a lot of time. I appreciate your coming all this way, but we could have done this over the phone.'

'No,' he says. 'It's about time. It's way past time.'

'For what?'

'To make friends again. What if it's her?'

'It's not her.'

This argument is pointless. Uninformed speculation at best. He says nothing.

'Can't be her,' she says.

'Why? Why can't it be her?'

'Well, what did they tell you,' she says, 'when they called?'

'If I took a wild guess I would say they told me the same thing they told you,' he says.

She rubs her fingers into her jaw and makes a sour face, winces as if in pain. Only together five minutes and he's already irritated her to the point of pain.

'Kathleen?'

'I've got a dicky tooth,' she says. She stops rubbing and closes her eyes tightly, and just keeps her fingers pressed into her jaw.

'You should get that taken care of.'

'I am.'

'Soon.'

She opens her eyes and there is warning there.

He gets to the point. 'I'm going out west,' he says. 'I'm going to drive out there.'

'You're going to drive out there? That's insanity. Why would you do that?'

'I want to see for myself,' he says. 'The place they found.'

'As I recall,' she says, 'the last time you were there, you couldn't get away fast enough.' She makes a big deal then of looking at her watch and gathering her things, muttering about him getting hyped up over nothing, over one phone call after years of nothing. Kathleen is no fool, Yannick knows. He wants her to come with him to the west coast and she knows he'll ask. She bends over to get her bag, doesn't look him in the eye, doesn't give him the chance.

They say goodbye in front of the coffee shop and he asks her if he can come to the party, the party Kathleen throws every year for their daughter Una. It's in a few days anyway so he might as well.

'Suit yourself,' she says.

He tosses that old lamp onto the back seat of his truck. It is beyond fixing.

The name Una means 'one and only'. For Yannick, this name is a smoking bullet hole. A hot, dead star. It is a diamond dug up from some deep shaft in the earth, dug up from oblivion, and it burns at the back of his head. That fucking kid. His first kid. He always wanted a kid and he's got five.

Una.

Minutes after she was born, pried by the head unceremoniously out of her mother's body as if she had no intention of leaving it, Kathleen looked at Yannick, who held this shiny new baby girl in his arms. She looked at him and said, 'We're calling her Una,' which was the name of her Irish grandmother, and he said okay.

He and Kathleen were on good terms for a long time after the end of their marriage. Una was three years old when they split and they managed to keep it civil, more than civil: they were good friends. Even when he got married a second time, and his boys Sunny and Zachary were born, Kathleen and he stayed friends. And when that marriage ended, it was Kathleen's couch he slept on for months until he figured out where to go. By the time he married a third woman, and Devon was born, Kathleen could see the humour in it. Made fun of his satellite families, as she called them. Implying she and Una were the mother ship, maybe, or the home planet. And when that calamitous union ended, the marriage to Devon's mother, after that he was on his own for a long time and Kathleen was still there. His good and stable friend.

And, finally, Leigh. He met Leigh and not long after that their lives were flipped all to hell and then Leigh got pregnant with Robin. By this time Kathleen was unable to see the humorous side in anything, so there was that big fight on her back porch and then there was nothing. Until now.

Damp fog hides nothing. Yannick has been doing crosswords for most of his adult life and knows the tricks. He's also okay with not finishing, with leaving some squares empty. But *damp fog hides nothing* is the last clue and he turns it over and over as he drives back to the Quality Inn hotel. He waits at a red light and wonders what it will take to convince Kathleen to drive west with him.

He was twenty-six years old the first time he saw Kathleen, this formidable woman who would be his first of four wives, his first real love. He was eating a ham and butter sandwich in her father's backyard. She came outside, wearing a yellow bathing suit and a pair of denim cut-offs, doing a string of cartwheels, and he was pretty sure it was a violation, the stuff he thought about her when he saw her doing those cartwheels. She knew it too. She manufactured that moment sure as shit. Yannick was working with a bunch of other guys on that particular job, and the net she cast, she caught all the fish, the one she wanted and the ones she did not. And they were rotten fish, those guys. An unruly, beer-guzzling pack of miscreants.

He asked her to get him a glass of water, and when she went back into the house, he followed her into the kitchen and told her she ought to be more careful.

'Careful of what?' she asked. She didn't bother to let the tap run cool and handed him a glass of warm water.

'Careful of what you attract.' He let his eyes run down her, thighs soft and a little belly paunch. Warm buttered bread, was his Kathleen.

'It's my yard,' she told him. 'I can do whatever I want.' Her cheeks were bright red and she was breathing heavily from the cartwheels. Her hair was all messed up as if someone just had their hands in it.

'How old are you?' he asked. He had to bite his lip against a smile that was pushing its way through. He wanted to scold her, to put her in her place.

'Eighteen.'

'You act like you're twelve.'

That pissed her off. She ignored him for the rest of the day, and for days after that, too.

But then one night she turned up at the place he was living, renting an apartment out on the concession road, a single room on top of this guy Cecil's garage, a guy he'd met in prison. Out of the clear blue sky, she turns up.

As she unbuckled his heavy belt, as she burrowed her warm, eager hand into his Y-fronts and wrapped her fingers around his cock, she told him her father would kill her if he knew what she was doing.

'Because I'm the guy painting the house?'

'No,' she said, putting her other hand on his neck.

'Why? Why would your dad kill you?'

'Because you're old,' she said, and pushed her groin up

against his and pulsed into him. Slipped her sweet tongue into his mouth like she was home.

When Una was five years old, maybe six, she came to Yannick where he was painting in the shed, dragging a picture book on the floor, dragging it by the corner of one page.

'You don't treat your books like that,' he told her, taking the beat-up book from her and closing it, and bending it gently back into its rightful shape.

'I wanted to show you the page,' she said. 'Give it back.'

'Excuse me, now?'

'Give it back,' she said.

'I think you're forgetting something there,' he said.

She mashed her lips together and looked up at him through her tangled hair (it was always tangled, her hair, when she spent the weekends with her father), apparently deciding between two options: trying to win this fight or showing him whatever it was she wanted to show him. She chose the latter.

'Give it back, please,' she said, one glinting eye visible between her thick weeds of hair.

'Close enough,' he said, and handed over the book.

She sat down and opened it importantly on her lap and turned the pages one by one until she found the page she wanted: a watercolour of a yellow moon shining on a green-black sea.

'Is that a road?' she asked, pointing to the picture, to the moonlight track on the water.

'It's the moonlight on the water,' he told her, leaning close.

'I know that,' she said, drawing her words out, like he was some kind of imbecile.

'So why'd you ask?'

She didn't explain her thinking but he knew what she meant. She was asking if the reflection was symbolic of a road, but she didn't have the words. She was so, so young. Her nose was still the characterless nose of a baby; her wrists were still fat. And, far as he knew, this was the first time she had expressed abstract thinking. Here was a kid who could do anything. Could *be* anything. All those good long years she had stashed in her back pocket. For free.

She didn't have the words and he didn't have the patience to get into it with her – she was still acting too fresh for his liking. He should have got into it with her, helped her complete the idea that was just there but not. Because she was right, it did look like a road. And she had brought this to show him. But instead he went back to his easel and took up his brush and forgot about her sitting there on the floor with her book.

Una moved out west to the province of British Columbia when she was twenty-two years old. Way the hell out to the west coast of Vancouver Island. She asked him to come visit, and it wasn't just that he hated to fly, which he did, deeply, but the cost of the ticket was more than he thought he could part with. And at the time he was deep in battle with Devon's mother over the sale of that blasted house they bought together. And there was the newness of Leigh. And all these bits of confetti that seemed important. So he never went.

He thought about her out there, though, other side of the country, and each time he did, he was surprised by the memory of that picture book, that moonlight reflection on the water. That moon road. Where it might lead and how far it might take her.

3

KATHLEEN IS WOKEN a few hours before dawn. This happens sometimes, not nearly as much as it used to, but she lives with it. Una breathes her awake, the girl broiling there (not there) in the dark, asking her, as ever, to keep up her end of an intricate bargain. Seconds later, Kathleen falls back to sleep, curled tightly into her blanket, content.

And in the morning, she is up with the sun. She gets dressed in her work clothes – old jeans and a long-sleeved, collared shirt to protect her neck – and goes into the kitchen to put on a pot of coffee. Her head feels tight and thumpy. She uncaps an erasable black marker pen, which rests on its own magnetic shelf at the top corner of the fridge door, and changes the number that has been written there, directly onto the door of the fridge, for twenty-two years. She changes the number from 7967 to 7968.

Seven thousand, nine hundred and sixty-eight days since Una disappeared. Since Kathleen knew where on earth her daughter was. She will repeat this routine tomorrow and the day after that, until the day she no longer has to.

Seeing Yannick yesterday wasn't as bad as she'd thought it would be; the pressure in her head today has nothing to do with him. It's all tooth. He's aged more than she was expecting. Always kept his hair cut short, but he's let it grow out, and now wears it tied back. Thin on top and mostly silver with a few dark strays, curled into a snug ponytail at the base of his neck, like a sleeping mouse. He was staring at some book when she came into the coffee shop but, then, he always was. He wears glasses now, and they were balanced at the tip of his nose, defying gravity. Sitting there with his legs spread under the table, like the world is a game he invented and the rules are all his own. Still broad across the shoulders. Strong and wiry. Kathleen always felt bigger than him. Her hands, her feet, her thighs. Bulkier. More dense. But he was always much, much larger than his physical size. Took up more space than a body should. Just like Una.

When Yannick sat across from Kathleen yesterday, she noticed a white scar, buried in the deep crow's feet fanning out from the corner of his left eye. It resembled a bird's wing, or a leaf, lifting upwards, so he looked like he was smiling even when he wasn't. She's never seen this scar before but knows she gave it to him.

Yannick, for the record, is not the only man Kathleen has ever loved. Okay, maybe she fell for him as soon as she saw him, his black hair buzzed neat and tidy. Flecks of white paint on his neck, on his smooth arms. And those ropes men get? Those veins that wrap around their arms? He had those. He was the foreman of the crew her dad had hired to paint their house and he slayed her without even trying.

And he rode a motorcycle. Whatever.

After him, there were others. There was Stevo, who owned the fleet of chip trucks. Real head for business that guy. A joker too, an absolute goof. But he wanted to have a baby with Kathleen, and she already had the only child she wanted, so that was the end of Stevo.

And maybe five years later there was Larry, originally from

Prince Edward Island. It was Larry who first got her interested in growing flowers, and she's always thanked him for that. She liked Larry, and possibly would have stayed with him, but he moved back to Prince Edward Island.

The men Kathleen cared for after Yannick were very different from Yannick. They had to be. Over the years there were fleeting encounters with sex, sparse and not always satisfying, but not always not (satisfying) either. Running her flower business, she came into contact with new people from time to time, it happened like that. Opportunities cropped up. Her friend Julius was always encouraging her to create more opportunities but . . . She was a single mother in her forties, her fifties, and now her sixties, living in a small town. She's done.

Yannick, though, he is dust. Visible only in a certain light, inevitable. As soon as you vacuum it up or wipe it away, it's back. Pull a couch away from the wall and there it is, collected in the corners, thick and furry. Open the curtains to the sunlight and there it is, drifting and flashing in the air. Clap a pillow and watch it rise. Yannick has a way of settling into her nooks and crannies. He always has.

Cosmos today for harvest. About two hours' work. When she's done, the stems stashed safely in buckets of water in the refrigeration shed, ready to be collected by her delivery guy later today, she still has some time to kill before her tooth extraction.

She puts an egg on to boil and opens her laptop at the kitchen table. Not a lot of traffic on the Find Una Facebook page but she still checks the comments every week, because you just never know. Each new message that appears, each blessed one, is like a heartbeat blip on a hospital monitor. She used to get messages from people all over Canada, and from the States, too. There was a time, early on, when she was hearing from folks in places she couldn't have pointed out on a map. Places like Burma, Moldova, Croatia, Uzbekistan. Una's friends sometimes post messages on the page too, sharing pictures of their children blowing out birthday candles or winning trophies or whatever. Look at our lives, the pictures say. See the way time passes for us.

Kathleen displays her appreciation with hearts and smiley faces. The instructor on the webinar she took, Growing Your Social Media Presence, said you have to interact with every post.

Every now and again Julius gets on her case. He tells her she is wasting her time on Facebook. He pooh-poohs the number she tracks on her fridge. What she doesn't explain to him – because self-justification is for the birds – is that sometimes, for her, the world feels as if it's made of glass. The glass is thin and pocked with air bubbles. It's webbed with hairline cracks. It's fragile. This is about maintenance.

When Una was very little, even when she wasn't little, even when she was fifteen, sixteen, seventeen, she used to climb into Kathleen's bed in the middle of the night and curl her body into Kathleen's. Press her cold feet against her shins. She would never stay – Una never stayed anywhere for long – and after she left to go back to her own room, Kathleen would feel her there still. Her child in her bed.

Now when Una visits in those hours before dawn, she is asking Kathleen to keep checking the Facebook page because if she doesn't, one of the cracks in the glass will split. If Kathleen doesn't respond to every message, even the long shots from Uzbekistan, or tally up the number on the fridge every day, or throw the party every year, one of the glass bubbles will explode. Each bubble and crack will set off the next until the world is nothing but a pile of fine sand.

You can't explain things like this to people.

Anyhow. There aren't any new posts on the Facebook page so she toggles over to email. She's got a message from Yannick's eldest boy Sunny saying, oh, I'm glad you and Dad are talking again, and oh, I think it's about time you made up, and oh, you have to go west with him, he can't do it alone.

She tries not to be angry at Sunny. He's a nincompoop, always has been, but he means well. She's pissed at Yannick, though. It's clear he's told Sunny what's going on, about the call from the coroner's office out west, and that he's serious about doing this thousands-of-kilometres drive for nothing. For absolutely nothing.

She closes her laptop and looks around the kitchen, the same kitchen where Una once came to her and said: 'Mom, I've been thinking I need to get out of here. I might move.'

Kathleen asked her why. Why did she think she needed to move? Kathleen was pulling a macaroni casserole out of the oven and singed the inside of her wrist.

Una didn't say anything but tucked her hair behind her ears. That unforgettable hair. Thick and long, dark brown. The soft hair at the temples was ashy, almost grey. The ends, in summer, turned that same ashy grey. Tie Una's hair up in a scarf, or a twist or a braid, and it just tumbles out. Too thick and slippery and abundant to be contained. Just like her father. Too abundant to be contained.

Kathleen asked her a second time why she was thinking of moving and Una looked out of the window, the same window Kathleen is looking out of now. It was winter then, the day

Una announced she was moving away. The view outside was blank and flat. The light on Una's face was pearly blue.

Kathleen asked Una if she was moving away because of Oliver Hanratty, her on-again/off-again boyfriend of many years. 'Never let a man run you out of a place,' Kathleen told her daughter, and sucked the rising welt on her wrist.

'I just have a feeling,' Una said. 'I want to go.'

'Go where? Where do you want to go?'

'I was thinking maybe Vancouver Island.' Una said this very coolly, in a tone that suggested the *thinking maybe* part was over. Decision made.

'Why on earth go there?' Kathleen said. 'What's even out there? Jesus, you cannot get further away from home than that.' She went on: 'We don't even know anybody out west. All your friends are here. Me. Your dad. What does your dad say? I bet he's heartbroken,' Kathleen said. 'I bet he's broken in his big, dumb heart.'

'I'm stagnating here,' Una said.

Kathleen felt utterly bamboozled by this: Una never stayed doing any one thing long enough to know what stagnation felt like. She'd tried university but dropped out. She wasn't academic and never went to class. All Una took from her university experience was a D in Psych 101 and a year's worth of student loan. Her next endeavour was waitressing at a Greek restaurant in Toronto, but she quit that within a few months. After that, it was a car rental place, which she loathed, complaining that she got headaches because everything in the office, including the T-shirt she was obliged to wear, was yellow.

'You're not trying hard enough,' Kathleen said. 'You never stick it out.'

'You say that every time.'

'It's true every time.'

'Harsh.'

'That's the game,' Kathleen said. 'Doing stuff you don't want to do. Get used to it.'

'I'm lost,' Una said.

'Life can feel that way.'

'I can't explain it better than that,' Una said. She went over to where Kathleen stood in front of the oven, with the casserole now cooling on the side. She plucked a piece of macaroni from the edge of the glass dish, the macaroni gilded with cheese and crispy brown at the edges, and crunched it. She put her arms around Kathleen's waist and coaxed her into a slow dance, chewing, enchanting her mother.

'You'll visit,' Una said. Her eyes, the colour of rich earth.

'Just tell me why you have to go so far away.'

'It's only down the road.'

'No point in me going way the hell out there to visit. You'll be back. You'll change your mind like you always do and you'll be back.'

'Have a little faith.'

'I go on experience.'

'Promise you'll visit.'

Kathleen shook her head, tried to twist away but her daughter held her tighter. Una: small and deceptively strong.

Before going to her dentist appointment, Kathleen swings by Julius's place with his blood-pressure medication. He is perfectly capable of picking up his medication by himself, but his driving is becoming a bit iffy, and she likes doing these small things for her friend.

She hasn't told him about the coroner calling her, slapping

her with the news that bones have been discovered and they could be Una's (and that this news has brought Yannick back). Julius has a freakish sense of intuition, and if he knows too much, he will have all kinds of sensible things to say. The party is tomorrow and she doesn't have time to listen to all the sensible things he will have to say.

Julius may well be the only person in Kathleen's life who doesn't irritate her. She met him a lifetime ago, when she was working the checkout at the IDA pharmacy and he was the new manager, just moved up from Toronto. He's the kind of person who looks you straight in the eye when he speaks to you, even if you've just met him. He's full of fancy talk, and he giggles at the worst times, like when people are upset or dissatisfied, which didn't go down well for him as the manager of the only drugstore in town.

Julius moved into town after some sort of mid-life crisis and quitting a career in law, and bought a farmhouse just outside Bobcaygeon on a farm that was, with much public resentment, being sold off in chunks after the death of the patriarch – an infamous local family feud. Being a Torontonian in small-town Ontario, and having scooped up this piece of land for next to nothing, automatically pitched Julius into a whole bunch of people's bad books, people who'd already chosen sides within the inheritance dispute. It was ridiculous and it was petty, and it attracted her to his friendship immediately.

Another endearing thing about Julius is that he's a very odd-looking man. His head is too big for his body; he has the proportions of a baby. As he gets older, into his eighties, this is only becoming more pronounced. His snow-white hair grows in a thatch that he combs into a kind of puff, straight up from his wide forehead.

And no one could accuse Julius of not loving his seven very pretty acres of land. He keeps chickens and wild guinea pigs, which he lets wander freely through the white birch and hazel trees behind his house. He grows tomatoes and squash, has an eye for what blooms together well.

This morning, Kathleen finds Julius at the back end of his property, spraying his Alaska roses with toxic store-bought chemicals that (if she's told him once) she's told him a thousand times not to use. He's dressed in crisp, midnight-blue Levi's that rise almost to his sternum, and an Edmonton Oilers' cap that barely fits over his hair.

'Acephates, Julius,' she says, pushing a low-hanging hazel branch out of her way. 'You know better.'

'Something has to kill me eventually,' he says. 'That other concoction you recommended is entirely ineffectual.'

She's told him that the safest and cheapest way to kill aphids is to use a mixture of ten parts water to one part castile soap. 'Persistence, you bugger,' she says, 'is the only way to get results.'

He soaks a tightly rolled bud that squirms with feisty green aphids. 'You got my drugs?' he says.

'Right here.' She shakes the paper bag at him.

'Leave it there,' he says, pointing with his pink knobbled elbow at a metal garden table.

'You're not even wearing gloves,' she says, and sighs.

He stops mid-spray, still aiming the bottle at the rose bush, and looks at her. 'There's something wrong with you,' he says.

'It's my tooth.' She rubs her jaw, for effect.

'No,' he says, and returns his attention to the roses. 'There's something else.'

'I let it go for too long,' she says. 'In fact, I've got an appointment. I can't stay for any of your chit-chat.'

He looks at her again, divining.

'Extraction,' she says.

'Come again?'

'I'm going in for an extraction.'

'You'd better hop along, then,' he says.

'Do you need me to pick you up tomorrow?' she asks. 'For the party?'

'Heavens, no, I'll drive myself,' he says. 'You'll be bitchy and short-tempered.'

'I will not.'

'You will,' he says. 'Happens every year.' He sprays three short bursts of poison at the rose.

The dental office is on the ground floor of a red-brick house at the corner of Maldern and Eastwood Streets, right in the east end. The house is what you might call Old Ontario. Wraparound porch and Canadian flag dangling from a flagpole mounted under the porch overhang. Lilac trees in the front yard. The dentist lives in the house with her family, which Kathleen believes consists of a husband and a pair of daughters who've flown the coop. Kathleen only half listens when people speak about their lives, about how their children are getting on. She likes her dentist, though, as much as one can. The woman moved over from England decades ago and Kathleen feels more comfortable with people who come from other places.

Kathleen arrives early, thinking she'll have a little time to browse out-of-date magazines, calm her nerves, before being called to the chair. But barely a few minutes after checking in with the receptionist she finds herself seated in the shiny white reclining seat. There's a new addition to the room: a television screen mounted on the ceiling above the chair. The dentist asks

Kathleen what she would like to watch during the procedure and Kathleen replies that she would rather the television stayed off.

The dentist explains the procedure: the anaesthetic; the possibility that the tooth may crumble during extraction, facilitating the need for a little unpleasant digging, which could take some time; the fact that Kathleen has, according to the X-ray, unusually long roots; aftercare (no smoking, no spitting, no foods with small seeds or sharp corners).

The anaesthetic syringe, which the dentist holds in one gloved hand a few inches from Kathleen's face, is a short, precise needle. The dental assistant, a face Kathleen doesn't recognize – and a feline, untrustworthy face at that – fastens a stiff paper napkin around Kathleen's neck with an alligator clip and hands her a pair of clear plastic glasses.

'Do you have any questions?' the dentist asks.

'What do you know about teeth and DNA?' Kathleen asks.

The dentist looks surprised. Kathleen feels a little surprised. She hadn't planned on asking anything like this. The dentist sits back on her stool, still holding the syringe aloft. 'In what context?' she asks.

'Can you identify a person by the DNA in their teeth?'

'I believe teeth provide very good DNA samples,' the dentist says.

'Like, you could use DNA from a tooth as comparison?' Kathleen says.

'If you had another source to compare it to, yes.'

'Right.'

'I saw it on *CSI*,' the dentist says.

'You saw it on TV?'

The dentist shrugs, smiles. 'Lie back and try to relax.'

Kathleen opens wide and the needle slides into the flesh at

the outer base of her gum. It's painless until the dentist pushes further, into the nerve, and further yet, into what feels like bone.

'Remember to breathe,' the dentist whispers, breathing out the word 'breathe'.

And Kathleen realizes she isn't breathing, so she closes her eyes and concentrates on that. The needle is pulled, sucked from her gum, and reinserted in another spot. Then injected again into the soft jelly under her tongue. The pain is minor but concentrated, like air whining tightly out of the mouth of a balloon. The anaesthetic tastes like aspirin.

'Go ahead and rinse,' the dentist says, and puts her hand on Kathleen's shoulder and squeezes. This touch is incidental; the woman probably thinks nothing of it, but Kathleen flinches a little, unused to being touched. When the hand is taken away, Kathleen still feels the pressure and aching warmth of her dentist's capable fingers.

The assistant hands Kathleen a plastic cup of mint-green fluid. Already the side of her face is going cold and a tingle spreads across her skin. Her tongue is also numbing.

'We'll wait just a few minutes,' says the dentist.

Kathleen clumsily gargles, and spits the green mouthwash into the clean white basin swirling with cool water. She wipes a string of spit from her chin and lies back down, and stares deeply into the silvery grey blankness of the television screen. In soft tones, the dentist asks her assistant to retrieve some unknowable instrument and issues other instructions that Kathleen doesn't understand. Her right eyelid feels heavy, as if it wants to close. Kathleen asks if this is normal.

'The nerve wraps all around here,' the dentist says, drawing a line on her face from her mouth, up past her ear and over her eye. 'Perfectly normal.'

'I thought maybe you gave me too much.'

'Nope.'

Kathleen's right ear is cold and thick. 'This is funky,' Kathleen says, without the use of her lower lip.

'I think we're ready,' says the dentist, and positions herself behind Kathleen, looming over her head, close enough that Kathleen can smell the detergent in her white frock and the latex of her gloves. 'Open wide,' says the dentist, and prods the middle of Kathleen's rotten tooth with her pristine metal hook. 'Any pain?'

'Nah.'

A tool resembling a ratchet passes across Kathleen's line of vision as it's lowered into her mouth.

'I'm just testing how loose we are,' the dentist says, clamping the tool onto the errant tooth. She nudges it back and forth a few times and Kathleen settles into however long this is going to take, how unpleasant it is going to be. She is used to settling in and waiting for unpleasant things.

There's a sucking, a vacuum pull at the base of the jaw, and the dentist nimbly pulls the instrument from Kathleen's mouth. And there, hovering just above her nose, the bloody root of Kathleen's tooth. No longer her tooth.

'Easy,' says the dentist.

'That's it?'

The dentist hands Kathleen a triangle of white gauze and instructs her to stick it in the new gap and leave it there for a few hours.

'I expected a lot worse,' Kathleen says, sitting up, relieved. The dental assistant, who, now that it's all over, looks a little less lynx-ish, unclips the paper napkin from Kathleen's neck.

'It can be a lot worse,' says the dentist.

Kathleen stands at the reception desk to pay what now feels like an exorbitant amount of money for not a lot of work. The dentist stands in the doorway of her examination room and calls the next patient.

'Are you coming to Una's party tomorrow?' Kathleen asks. Her voice is creaky and padded because of the gauze.

'Oh? Is that tomorrow?'

'Tomorrow, yes. I sent the invites in May?'

The dentist flicks her eyes to the wall. She looks cornered. 'What time was it again?' She steps aside to allow the next person to go through to the examination room.

'Three o'clock.'

The dentist nods.

'Same as every year.'

'I'll try,' she says, still nodding as she closes the door. She looks like one of those toys people put in the back windows of their cars, those plastic nodding dogs.

4

HOW DID HE end up here? How did he become that old man eating alone in a restaurant, staring, half focused, at the guttering candle on his table while he forks soggy lasagne into his mouth? That was one of Leigh's worst things, seeing old men dining alone in restaurants. Or in the grocery store, alone, befuddled by the shelves of pickled onions and beets. She hated the sight of that. She once came home from the store and told Yannick about this old boy who had half a loaf of white bread, one tomato and a can of pineapple slices rolling around in a shopping cart. 'You can't even make a meal out of that,' she said, her eyes shining. Yannick wonders if maybe she knew she was going to leave him long before she actually did it.

And here he is now, picking at his food, and maybe he looks familiar to people in this small town or maybe he doesn't. Who can be sure after so many years?

He will stay for Una's party tomorrow but after that he is gone.

The restaurant, the kind of restaurant that heats single portions of lasagne in boat-shaped dishes, is mostly empty tonight. There's this young guy, though, looks somewhere in the region of forty, who keeps glancing at Yannick. He's sitting at a table with a bunch of other guys. They've finished eating and are now sharing pitchers of beer. Guy has the soft, rounded shoulders of one who played hockey or football in high school. His hair and his eyebrows are dark and thick, and from underneath those impressive brows his curious eyes meet Yannick's more than once. When Una first went missing, Yannick was very well known in this town. He's accustomed to strangers knowing who he is, deciding whether or not they should approach and speak.

Yannick turns his attention to the dusty lamps on the walls, meant to look old-fashioned but, really, they just look old. He and Kathleen used to bring Una here when she was little because she liked the Shirley Temples they made. She liked chasing the maraschino cherry around the bottom of the glass with the long spoon that came with the drink.

Yannick pushes the tines of his fork into his food, which is rapidly congealing, and wonders again how in the hell he ended up back here.

Just like everyone else, he's got himself one of those phones they call *smart*. Ask him, though, if he can get a hold of any of his kids – he cannot. He would very much like to hear the voice of at least one of them. Just one would do.

The guy with the eyebrows comes over.

'Are you Mr Lemay?' he asks.

'I am,' Yannick says, and asks this man to call him by his first name.

The guy smiles and his demeanour changes from brutish to boyish. 'I thought so,' he says. He offers his big hand and Yannick shakes it. 'I'm Dave,' he says. 'My wife is Heather?'

He says his wife's name in a way that suggests Yannick ought to know who this Heather is, which he does not.

'She works for Kathleen,' he continues, 'on the flower farm. She helps with the party, stuff like that.' Dave looks off to the side and rubs the stubble on his chin in a way that leads Yannick to believe that, perhaps, he does not like his wife spending so much time with Kathleen. 'You here for the party?' he asks.

The truth is, until Yannick saw the poster in the coffee shop yesterday, he didn't know that Una's party was happening this weekend. 'Yep,' he says. 'I'll be there.'

'We go every year,' Dave says.

There's a wooden bowl on the table filled with thin slices of crusty white bread. 'You want to sit down?' Yannick asks. He gestures to the wooden bowl. 'You want some of this bread?'

Dave smiles politely and declines. 'Heather organizes a lot for the party,' he says, 'with the posters and all that. They're making decorations tonight back at our place.'

Yannick nods.

'I'm glad you're here,' Dave says. He rests his hands on the back of the empty chair across from Yannick. 'Last few years, the party has been . . .' He stops speaking and shrugs.

'I'm glad to be here,' Yannick says. He pushes his plate away and tries to get the attention of the waiter.

'I'll see you tomorrow, then?'

'I'll see you tomorrow.'

Dave shakes Yannick's hand and makes his way back to his friends. Halfway there he stops and turns, smiling. 'I remember your motorcycle,' he says.

'You do, eh?'

'You still ride?'

No, he does not still ride. He hasn't ridden for some years. He tells Dave he sold that motorcycle and prefers his truck, and Dave turns back to his own table.

This is what happened with the motorcycling.

Devon, being the most like Yannick of his five children, was born to love motorcycles. Dev graduated high school a year later than he should have, having failed most of his classes in grade twelve. He went straight up to the logging camps, just like his grandfather, Yannick's father. At nineteen, same age Yannick was when he himself saved enough to bring home his first Triumph, Devon bought what would be his first and last motorcycle, a Yamaha YBR. Midnight blue. A bit of an aggressive choice and not what Yannick would have gone for but, still, he was proud of his son.

One Sunday night, less than six months after Devon bought his bike, Yannick was reading the paper at his dining-room table when the phone rang. It was March, it was raining heavily, and on the phone Devon's mother was calling from the foyer of St Michael's Hospital in Toronto. Devon had been helicoptered there from where they'd scraped him off the 427 highway south of Barrie. Both legs broken in five places between them. Ribs fractured and subsequent pulmonary contusion. Lacerations to the liver. Broken hip, broken collarbone. Broken wrist on the left side. Yannick cannot remember his drive into the city, but he does remember being told that his boy Devon had been induced to a comatose state and was about to go into surgery to release the fluid that was building on his brain. Yannick remembers being told that Devon could die before the sun came up or he could live. And he remembers being told that if Devon did survive the night and the following days, the extent of the damage to his brain wouldn't be known for weeks. He was told to have a word in his son's ear before they rolled him away for surgery.

There are only two things worth saying into your son's bloodied ear at a time like this: I am here, son, and, I love you.

Other than that, there is nothing.

Organ donor on wheels. That was what Yannick's *tante*, his father's sister, who was a nurse back in Québec where his father was born, that was what she said to Yannick when he started riding motorcycles. 'That's what we call you, *totons*, you idiots, in the emergency room,' she said to him. 'Young and healthy. Strong and stupid. Best pickings for the harvest.'

Yannick waited all that first night with Devon's mother in a small room without windows. He bought her sesame snaps from the vending machine and she reciprocated with pretzels. They barely spoke but they were kind, and had not been kind to each other in a very long time. Sharing coffee-flavoured water in styrofoam cups and waiting to find out if the son they shared was going to live or die.

Devon did make it through the night, though, and in the morning, when the surgeon determined he was stable, Yannick did something he still doesn't understand: he left the hospital. Stayed away for days. He didn't go home to Leigh and Robin, Robin being about five years old at the time. Instead he slept on a buddy's couch, like a mouse crouched in a hole. After a few days, Sunny, who now had a brand new baby of his own to look after, knocked on the door and convinced Yannick to come back to the hospital, because Devon was fine, because Yannick was not going to lose another kid.

There followed years of surgery and physiotherapy. Devon lost the hearing in one ear, and his short-term memory has never been the same. He is scarred and volatile and clinking with metal, and one of his knees doesn't bend all the way. But he is here.

Both he and Yannick quit the motorcycling for good.

A Good Mother

OUR GIRL WAKES up in the tree around seven in the morning. Waking up might not be the right way to put it, because after what happened in the night, with the water dripping on her face, she never fell back to sleep, not deeply. Instead let's say, for now, she's given up on sleep, and is drawing her legs, unshaven and snagged with insect bites, out of her sleeping bag, twisting her long hair together at the base of her neck and tying it into a knot. She hasn't washed her hair in a week and it's coarse and tacky with sea salt and grease.

She could really use a hot shower.

Nobody else is up yet; she's got the forest to herself. It stopped raining hours ago, but cool water still falls randomly, dropping from the rounded tips of cones and the fine points of needles, and from the bud scars and knuckles on endless branches.

This woman shoves her bare feet into cold, damp sneakers and climbs away from the hollow tree – her home, for now. She climbs up past the tents and tarps of this woodland community, this illegal squat, clambering over muscular tree buttresses and roots, and landing ankle deep in spongy moss, water seeping into her shoes. When she's far enough away from the encampment, she balances herself against the trunk of a western hemlock, fern fronds tickling the backs of her knees and her thighs, and lowers herself to pee, and watches the pee splash on brown needles and absorb into the ground. For a moment the smell of her urine blocks out the smells of the forest, the damp earth and moss and wet bark. Old lichen, like fish scales, patterned onto rock.

A few metres above her head, silent, perched within a deep fissure in the rough bark of the hemlock: a mosquito.

The woman exhales and the mosquito catches a whiff of carbon dioxide. The mosquito detaches from the bark and floats lower down, towards the source of the carbon dioxide, searching for the blood meal that will provide protein to her developing eggs. She's a good mother.

The woman stands and shifts, tugging her underwear and shorts back up over her knees. This movement draws the mosquito even closer, as she detects a moving silhouette. There but not there. She lands again, lower on the hemlock trunk, alongside a hardened drop of glistening sap. The mosquito can smell the woman's sweat now, can sense the woman's heat, and the mosquito's abdomen, adorned delicately with brown and white stripes, twitches with anticipation.

When the woman moves again, she stumbles a little on the uneven ground. She presses her elbow against the hemlock for support and the mosquito alights, drifting, and settles on the woman's neck, on that smooth, warm plain behind her ear where the softest hair grows. She's a skilled mosquito, this one, deft with her proboscis, which she now slips into the woman's skin (with, it could be said, a lover's touch).

The mosquito's abdomen begins to grow. It looks pink at first, then, as it becomes more engorged, turns a deeper red, like a pomegranate seed. Like a jewel.

Sated, at last, she retracts and floats away, somewhat burdened, as she now weighs three times what she did before she fed. She will settle somewhere quiet and protected to digest, then search for a pool of still water to lay her precious eggs. Some will be eaten but the survivors will hatch in three days, and the larvae will mature into adult mosquitoes by the middle of next week. By which time finding our girl will be impossible.

But for now, she, not yet feeling the itch, not yet aware that she's been stalked and hunted, will slouch through the forest and down to the beach. She will sit on the damp and night-cooled sand, scooping some and letting it run through her fingers. She will try to build a cairn of smooth, flat stones, but they will insistently slip off one another and she'll give up.

And she will consider the smoky mist rising from the morning surf and will question, not for the first time, if this is where she's meant to be. Whether or not, maybe, it's time to go home.

5

THE HOLLY BUSH that grows along the south wall of Kathleen's house is being attacked by bindweed. The bush has nothing to do with her farm crop but, nevertheless, she has to deal with the weed in case it travels, this most audacious bastard of a weed.

Kathleen finds it satisfying to tease the rhizomes, roots like bootlaces, out of the earth. The only way to truly eradicate this weed is to go at the rhizomes with a fork, to gash into the dirt without mercy. There's something compelling about it: when she gets a good grip on a thick rope of rhizome, when she exposes the sallow root that's been slumbering quietly, unchecked, underground, she feels like she's excavating some kind of secret – something growing that she isn't supposed to see. This was how she felt when, years ago, Sunny shared with her some of Una's emails, messages she'd written to him when she moved out west. He thought there might be stuff in there that Kathleen needed to know. Words that might help.

Reading Una's emails, which were never intended for her, gave Kathleen that same sense of unearthing, of stumbling over something she wasn't meant to see. But most of what Sunny sent her to read was inert. Una wrote about excursions to the beach and coves and other wild places. Her writing, Kathleen thought, was flowery and a little melodramatic. The ocean couldn't be *that* haunting and moody, not every day, come on.

The trees couldn't be *that* big, or, and she really wrote this – otherworldly. Trees, for eff's sake.

One message, however, did catch Kathleen's attention. Una wrote about chartering a boat with some friends and journeying up the coast to a place called Hot Springs Cove. She wrote that the sulphuric water in the springs felt womblike, having travelled from deep in the earth, and in that water she felt like a baby suspended in amniotic fluid. Una wrote this schmaltz to Sunny, who would have been only fifteen at the time, and it pissed Kathleen off. It pissed her off that Una felt embraced in this way, by water that smelt like rotten eggs, and it pissed Kathleen off to read, also, that Una had never in her life felt like this – embraced, swaddled, whatever. Mothered in this way.

Una had never felt mothered.

If only she knew. If only Una knew how much Kathleen had wanted her. How much of a surprise she was and how, over the years, with every new idea or notion, every erratic choice of hairstyle or fleeting passion, she left Kathleen startled and awed.

Two months, approximately, was how long Kathleen and Yannick had been messing around when Kathleen got pregnant. When she told her father, he kicked her out of the house so she moved in with Yannick. He was renting a single room above a garage, you couldn't even call it an apartment, at the back end of a dilapidated country lane. It had a bed and a hotplate and a homemade shower rigged up in the corner.

Her father, son to Irish immigrants, kicked her out because she was pregnant and unmarried, and because she had accomplished this feat with a man who was too old for her and wasn't Catholic.

Anyway, whatever. Kathleen was in love.

They got married in November of 1971 at the city hall, by a bored clerk, in a beige corduroy suit, who had greasy eyeglasses and unforgettable coffee breath. The wedding, or whatever it was, was a week after Kathleen's nineteenth birthday so she didn't have to seek her father's consent. Una was born on the fifteenth of April 1972.

Never felt mothered, eh?

When Kathleen was eight months gone, ready to drop, Yannick ripped up strips of newspaper and mixed together a bowl of glue, wallpaper powder and water. He covered Kathleen's protruding belly with layers of papier mâché and when it dried painted it sky blue. While, inside her body, Una was curled in a ball, just as she would later curl up to Kathleen in the middle of the night, in the safety of mother's bed, when she couldn't sleep.

Kathleen prepared a basket next to the bed and lay beside it most nights, in the weeks before Una was due, patting her belly and looking down into the basket at the yellow blanket folded neatly across the empty cushion.

And Una, inside her, as close as she would ever be. There but not there.

They hung the papier-mâché cast on the wall next to their bed and brought it with them to the town house they rented when Una was two and Kathleen got a job at the IDA. It hung in the kitchen until, during a fight, Kathleen ripped it off its nail and tore it to smithereens. She did that when she fought with Yannick, destroyed the things that were precious to her. Things that were irreplaceable, that were hers. She thought it would hurt him more if she hurt herself. Because of this rationale she demolished some good stuff: a couple of Beatles albums, some family photos, a crystal perfume atomizer that had belonged to her father's mother in Ireland.

She can still remember the sight of white papier-mâché dust on her knuckles, and the flakes of sky blue paint and a little blood, too. She remembers the white dust in the air, and how it settled over everything and stayed there even after the fight had dissolved. She doesn't remember what the fight was about.

Kathleen is at Heather's house tonight. The sensation has returned to most of her face, though it still feels like part of her ear is missing.

While Heather deposits her kids in various cribs and rickety bunk beds, Kathleen waits in the kitchen, sipping a cold beer. Dentist said no booze, but surely one beer can't hurt. The second hand on the wall clock above the toaster silently circumnavigates its endless path and Kathleen settles into the buzz of light beer and codeine.

It was back in January when Heather came up with this year's theme for Una's party: life-sized games. When the idea was first mentioned it sounded pretty good. But now, the night before the party, Kathleen isn't so sure about life-sized games. They're so big that they have to be set up outside, and the weatherman is calling for rain. At the moment, the games are stored in Heather's garage: a towering Jenga and a gargantuan chess set. Also, inexplicably, a tug-of-war rope, which the party rental place threw in as a deal.

Heather comes into the kitchen and over to the table where Kathleen waits, and surveys everything Kathleen has laid out. The jam jars, the tea lights, the rolls of string. Heather plunges her hand into one of the plastic bags of pebbles Kathleen has brought from the creek and sifts through them. They make a soft, shifting, clopping sound as she scoops them up and lets them fall again from between her fingers. The sound is like rain. Kathleen worries again about the outdoor games.

'Do you think we've got too much?' Heather asks. She picks up a jar and turns it in her hands.

'We've got enough for fifty people,' Kathleen says. In the early days, they would have needed hundreds.

'Are that many coming?'

Kathleen shrugs. She doesn't know how many people are coming.

They're decorating candle jars, which they give out every year at Una's party, filling the jars to just under halfway with creek pebbles, then nestling the tea lights into the pebbles. Around the rims of the jars, they're tying laminated photos of Una with fibrous string.

There are five different photos of Una, which will be divided between the fifty jars. The thing about Una is, she has this uncanny quality of looking wholly different from photo to photo – and did so even when she was very little – yet always looking quintessentially herself. In those first weeks, when the police asked for more photos to help with the search, Kathleen sent them an album's worth.

She doesn't expect people to stick the photos to their refrigerators or anything like that. She only hopes that the guests will take the candles home and burn them in their front windows. Just for one night.

This isn't a memorial.

As this year's party centres around games, Kathleen and Heather are also putting together some prizes for the winners: six mini bottles of wine, tied with bows around their necks using that same rustic twine. Kathleen smoothes photos of

Una over the wine labels, which she's had specially printed on adhesive paper.

The two women work in silence for a long time, siphoning pebbles into glass jars, tying tight bows with string, settling the tea lights just so. Without any preamble, Heather lays her hand on Kathleen's arm and asks her how she's doing.

'What do you mean?' Kathleen doesn't know if Heather is asking generally, or if she's discovered Yannick is back, or if she's asking about Una. Heather's hand is firm and warm and unpleasantly heavy on Kathleen's arm.

Heather takes her hand away and taps her own jaw, and Kathleen realizes she's asking about the tooth. She's asking about nothing that matters.

Kathleen opens her mouth to answer and is cut off by the engine sputter of a baby fussing from somewhere in the house. Heather freezes, a loop of string dangling from her knuckle. She shushes Kathleen with a finger to the mouth and lifts her face to listen.

(Kathleen remembers what this is like, this midnight sputter, this moment of not knowing whether you'll have to attend to it or not.)

The baby whimpers and coughs. Kathleen and Heather stare at each other in this breathless moment until the house is silent once more.

'Thank Christ,' Heather says, exhaling. 'He's a restless bugger.'

'It's more of a throb than anything else,' Kathleen says.

'Huh?'

'More of a throb,' Kathleen says, 'than anything else.' She points to her jaw.

Heather tosses her a half-hearted wince.

The front door shudders, the clumsy scrape of a key looking for a lock. The door sticks a little on the jamb and then there are the sounds of the bustle and bump of a large man trying to go unnoticed in a cramped hallway after he's had a few. Heather brightens in a way that is both sickening and endearing. Dave comes into the kitchen.

'You're still here,' he says to Kathleen. His smile is partial, at best. His dark eyes rove over the mess in his kitchen, the loose curls of twine and stones scattered over the table. The punched holes of laminated photographs on the floor. It's time for Kathleen to go home.

'Are you drunk, baby?' Heather asks. She leans from her chair to grab his hand and he pretends to resist her pull while being drawn in close. She wraps both arms around his legs and he nuzzles the top of her head. Kathleen begins the process of packing the candle jars neatly into a cardboard box.

'Not drunk,' he says, and then announces, as if he's revealing some kind of bold headline: 'I saw Yannick tonight.'

Kathleen continues packing the jars in tight, tidy rows in the box.

'Kathleen?'

She looks up at Dave.

'Yannick's in town?' Heather says.

'Barely,' Kathleen says. 'He's leaving tomorrow.'

'After the party, though,' Dave says. And then repeats, for no reason at all: 'He's coming to the party.' He picks up one of the prize bottles of wine in his baseball mitt of a hand and frowns at the photo of Una.

Kathleen searches for her purse, her zip-up sweatshirt. Both items evading her.

'Why didn't you tell me he was here?' Heather asks.

It's not like Heather even knew Yannick. 'Because he's leaving,' Kathleen says. She nods to the mess on the table. 'You don't mind if I leave you with this? We're done?'

'Oh,' Heather says.

'What time can I expect you tomorrow?'

Husband and wife share a look. 'Early as we can,' says Heather.

With sweatshirt and purse finally in place, Kathleen holds out her arms, motioning for Heather to load her up with the two boxes of candles.

Walking out to her old car in the dark, struggling under the weight of boxes that are a titch too heavy, she can hear laughter as Heather and Dave close their front door. It's not mean, but neither is it laughter that includes her. She rests the clinking boxes of candles on the hood of the car and stands on the sidewalk, shaking the lactic acid build-up out of her arms, stretching the feeling back into her fingers. It's muggy tonight, and cloudy. Just one blinking star can be seen up there. Then another. And another one visible just over the crown of an old maple in somebody else's yard.

Driving home, Kathleen stews about Dave. And hates herself for caring about the way he makes her feel foolish, or like she shouldn't be where she is.

She rolls down her window and the late-night summer air brushes her face, and then she's hit by the oily smell of a skunk's spray. She rolls the window back up, struggling at the midpoint where the glass always sticks. She feels put out. Irritated. She never has liked how traditional they are, Heather and Dave, in their married roles. Kathleen has never fawned over a man, or needed a man the way Heather needs him. She and Yannick both lost their mothers young, and were both single children brought up by stern fathers. This childhood turned Kathleen into a solo flyer and it turned Yannick into a blathering romantic, but there you go.

The thing is, nobody ever taught Kathleen about traditional roles or whatever it is they're calling it these days. Nobody ever taught her how to be a fawner, a wife, a mother. Maybe even before she read Una's emails, the ones Sunny shared with her, maybe Kathleen already sensed she was a disappointment to her daughter. She never knew how to make things pretty, how to dress things up. She forgot about all the birthday parties and bake sales, and sent Una to school fundraisers with store-bought cupcakes. Didn't know how to iron a skirt or sew on a button and never volunteered for school trips. Said inappropriate things.

An example. When Una was fourteen, she caught Kathleen rummaging in her bedroom. The reason for the rummage was down to a tidbit of gossip Kathleen had picked up from the pharmacist at the IDA. Something about kids in Una's class who were, so the pharmacist said, having sexual intercourse. Something about the discovery of a pregnancy test in a bathroom garbage can. When Kathleen got home from work that day, she went straight to Una's room to look for condoms or a journal or some other evidence, carnal in nature. Una caught her with her butt in the air, half concealed under the bed, dragging out a shoebox.

'What the hell, Mom?' Una said.

Kathleen reversed out from under the bed and remained on her knees. 'Don't talk to me like that,' she said, peering up at Una. She pulled a dust bunny from her hair and looked at it.

'What are you doing in my room?'

'Checking to see if you're having sex.'

'Get out of here.'

'Don't be bold.'

'Oh, my God,' Una said, 'please get out.'

Kathleen picked at a feather boa hanging off the back of Una's desk chair. Fake feathers, fluorescent pink. 'Where did you get this?' she asked. The boa had been hanging innocently off the back of that chair for months, but now it gyrated where it was draped, raunchy and seductive.

'Darlene's birthday party,' Una said.

'You have a friend named Darlene? What is she, eighty?'

Una's eyes rolled to the ceiling, her whole body exasperated.

'How come I've never heard of this Darlene?'

'Mom.'

Kathleen pulled the boa from the chair and wrapped it around her neck. It smelt synthetic and cheap. 'Sex is a wonderful thing,' she said. 'Perfectly natural and all kinds of fun if you wait until you're ready. And I hope you have a lot of it one day. Just not now.'

'Oh, my God, ohmygodohmygod.'

'Say no as many times as you want. Any guy will be grateful for whatever you're willing to give, trust me.'

'Please. Mom.'

'And when you are ready, make sure you ask for what you want,' Kathleen said, rewrapping the boa around her neck. 'Nobody ever tells you this, but it's very important. You'll only be disappointed otherwise.'

Una yelling now, begging her to stop.

How could she claim she never felt mothered?

Kathleen cannot sleep. She rolls away from thoughts of Dave and Yannick and the party, pushing her face into a cool pillow.

She twists back the other way, dragging with her the phone call from the British Columbia coroner's office, dragging with her the bones they dug up.

She kicks the blanket off and swings her legs out of bed. It's two a.m. She presses both feet firmly onto the floorboards, the ligaments in her feet strumming and loosening. Sitting up causes blood to flow and the pulse in her wound jacks up. She can feel it all along her jaw and up around her ear, every beat. She pops another codeine pill from the bottle next to her bed.

She goes downstairs in the dark, turning on a dim lamp she keeps on the kitchen counter, to check the Facebook page again. There are several last-minute apologies, people backing out of coming to the party. Kathleen isn't stupid, attendance has been dwindling year on year, but some of these no-shows are, were – whatever – good friends of Una's. And their excuses are lame.

There's a new private message from ChairSleuth76. Whoever this person is, he or she has been following Una's disappearance for as long as the Facebook page has been up, at least fifteen years. Sometimes it feels like ChairSleuth76 is the only ally Kathleen has left. Kathleen hovers her finger over the click, worrying that ChairSleuth76 has somehow caught wind of the news from the coroner's office and is going to make a big deal out of it. The refrigerator fan whirs and the blue light coming from the screen warbles and Kathleen clicks on the message. ChairSleuth76 does not know anything about any unearthed bones. He/she has written with unsettling news of Oliver Hanratty, that confounded boy, that on-again, off-again beau of Una's.

Kathleen closes the laptop so hard that it zings, and that zing reverberates in her head as she drags her smokes and lighter off the kitchen counter and wrestles her arms into her sweatshirt. The zing follows her out to the yard and it follows her to the cosmos, the daisies, the snapdragons. Silent and colourless in the dark. The zing follows her to the Miss Pepper phlox where she sits on the dewy grass between the beds and presses her hand flatly on the dark earth, the spot where she buried Una's baby tooth two days ago. She taps a cigarette out of the pack and lights it, curses the dentist for her meaningless rules (*definitely no smoking*) and exhales a strong plume into the night.

Oliver Hanratty. What Una could never understand, as far as Kathleen could tell, was that if you wanted to be rid of a thing permanently, you had to dig it up by the root. Fork the rhizomes. Or maybe that wasn't it at all – maybe Una never really wanted rid of him.

Kathleen didn't pay much attention to Oliver Hanratty when Una first brought him home. It was the middle of June; Una would have been seventeen at the time. Kathleen was just getting back home from the creek with a muddy plastic bag of fiddleheads she'd picked.

This was the first boy Una had ever brought home. It was clear from the way she presented him as Kathleen came up the driveway, sandals sweaty, plastic bag swinging off the ends of her fingers, it was clear Una wanted this moment to somehow be marked, and to be remembered. She and this kid Oliver were sitting on the front porch steps drinking ice water with slices of lemon. Slices of lemon! Una sat up straight when she saw Kathleen, and nudged her body against his, knocking him a little to the side.

'Mom, this is Oliver,' she said.

'Okay.'

'He's staying for dinner.'

'Is he?'

'And then to watch TV.'

Kathleen slowly turned her head towards the little colt and asked him again what his name was. She wanted to play with him a tad, bat him back and forth, stand in for both Mom and Dad.

'It's Oliver,' he said, thrusting his hand out for a shake. He didn't look nervous enough. He was that grade of skinny where his body dangled from his shoulders, like a shirt from a hanger. His nose and forehead shone with grease and his Adam's apple, probably only newly bloomed, sparred up and down his throat.

There was a rite of passage happening here that was meant to be acknowledged, Kathleen understood this. But she wasn't one for ceremony and, besides, foremost in her mind was having to share out the fiddleheads between three people instead of two. The thing was, the best time for picking fiddle-heads was from May to June, particularly the second week of June, which was that week exactly, when the stems were at their plumpest and the heads were just about to unfurl into ferns.

She could have gone back to the creek for more, or sent the two of them. Instead, she sulked, she made it tense. She answered questions with as few words as possible and embar-rassed her daughter. And Una? She tried to make it special. She brushed the bird shit off the picnic table and covered it with a yellow cloth, and made a jug of lemonade from a can of frozen concentrate. She picked a spray of Queen Anne's lace from the side of the road and set it in the middle of the table in a water glass.

While they ate, Una told Kathleen that Oliver was teaching himself how to perform magic tricks.

And he didn't even eat any of the fiddleheads.

You only get these moments once.

In spite of herself, Kathleen grew fond of Oliver Hanratty. The boy spent an awful lot of time at their place. He was quiet, and thoughtful, and wove a kind of harmony into the chaos of Una and Kathleen, neither of whom were particularly harmonious people. He was also, surprisingly, very entertaining. A wonder at chess (which he played with Kathleen, Una not having the patience to sit in one place long enough to finish a game), he was passable with the magic. More than passable, he was good. Parlour stuff: card tricks, sleight of hand, pulling coins out of unexpected places. Some nonsense with plastic cups and red rubber balls. He was adept at making things disappear.

As summer cooled to fall that first year, he was the one out in the yard with the rake, without being asked. After meals too, Oliver did the dishes without being asked. And even though, when he was finished, there would still be parings of cheese in the grater, or a crusty film of egg on the rim of the pan, Kathleen appreciated this boy whose feet seemed to be so firmly planted on the ground. He thought about stuff that never occurred to Una, like he would ask Kathleen how she was feeling, or if she had plans on a Saturday night.

The week leading up to Halloween brought the first break-up. Una explained what had happened to Kathleen while she helped her decorate the front window of the IDA. It was hot there, behind the glass. The late-afternoon sun shone directly, and Oliver, it transpired, was not getting the picture.

(The thing about Una, she was one of those people who,

when her attention was on you, you were warm with it. You could burn with it. But then she would take her attention away and you would be left colder than you were when she first found you.)

'You're not a very sympathetic person,' Kathleen said, teasing apart a wad of cotton that was meant to be a cobweb.

'I'm being nice.'

'That's your problem, right there. Just leave him alone if you don't want him.'

Una put on a paper Frankenstein mask and her eyes glinted through the tiny eye holes. 'I am sympathetic,' she said. She picked up a waxy green gourd and tossed it coolly from palm to palm.

'You're not. You're not thinking about his feelings. Pass me that stapler.'

Una did not pass Kathleen the stapler. She lifted her arms limply in the air like a zombie and groaned.

'What did you actually say to him?' Kathleen asked. 'What were your exact words that meant "We're kaput"?'

Una shrugged. 'He should just get the message,' she said.

'That's not fair,' said Kathleen, 'and it's a shitty way to treat a person.'

'Why are you taking his side?'

'You don't need me on your side.'

Una dropped her arms. She pulled the mask off and let it hang from her neck by the elasticated string. Her cheeks were flushed and she looked so pretty. Fresh and plump and lovely.

'He leaves notes in my locker,' Una said, tracing her finger up the window. 'They're really sad. I think he followed me here after school.'

'What?' Kathleen said. She pressed her hands and forehead to the window and looked up and down the street.

'Kidding,' Una said.

'That's not funny,' Kathleen said. 'You shouldn't joke about things like that. You should be nicer.'

'Speak for yourself,' said Una.

'Eh?'

'You could be nicer, Mother.' She picked up a paper skeleton and dangled it from its head, jumped it up and down so that its arms and legs, articulated with tiny brass pins, danced a spirited, bony jig.

And then a few months later, in the new year, Oliver Hanratty was back in their lives, back at their dinner table playing cards after the dishes were done. And this is how it went between the two of them, off and on for years, until Una left for the west coast.

When Una went missing, Oliver was out there, out west, in British Columbia. This is an indisputable fact. He always claimed this meant nothing, that he hadn't gone out there for her. He was interviewed and cleared by the police, but Kathleen has always believed he knew more than he was willing to give up.

And now, according to ChairSleuth76, Oliver Hanratty is dead.

6

IN THE MORNING, Yannick waits for Kathleen on her back porch, a book at his feet that he hasn't even glanced at. Not much of a mind for reading, now that he knows about these bones. He's been waiting for half an hour, thinking if he came early enough, he'd catch Kathleen before she's consumed by the party today. The air smells weedy, humid, and the sky is yellow and low.

Eventually she appears, coming around the side of the house. 'You're still here, then,' she says, stepping up onto the porch. She settles into the chair next to him and fetches a pack of smokes and a lighter out of a flower pot, apparently reserved for this purpose, lights one for herself and passes Yannick the pack. Without hesitation he tips one out and she leans close so he can light his off hers. Like they used to.

'I quit,' he says, exhaling long and slow with his head thrown back.

'Is that so?' She expertly flicks ash onto a saucer at her feet.

He inhales again, deeply, with his eyes half closed. 'Yep. About when Robin was born. Leigh insisted.'

'Leigh made you quit?'

'I'm glad she did.'

She nods.

'Something about being with you on this porch, though.'

She looks away, her jaw set.

'You remember the last time we sat out here,' he says, 'the very last time.'

Her face, still turned. He knows not to push it any further than this.

They sit in silence for a few beats and he rests his eyes on this sweet little patch of buttercups in the grass, thinking that dog-eared thought about how so much time can pass and it's like no time has passed at all. Just how easy it is to sit quietly with this woman, on this sagging deck of wood, and open his lungs to the smooth, dry slip of smoke.

He looks again at Kathleen and, from this angle, he sees Una. Kathleen always said Una took after him, but he sees his daughter here, in the cut of the cheek, the top edge of the eye. In the coarseness of Kathleen's hair and the aggressive way it sprouts from the crown of her head.

Coming back here is, unsurprisingly, making him consider things he has not considered in a long time. Seeing Kathleen now, he realizes he'd forgotten what his daughter looks like, really looks like – not the photographs, not the remembering.

'You're really coming to the party, then?' she says.

'If you don't mind.'

'Why would I mind?'

'Your voice sounds watery,' he says.

'I had a tooth removed yesterday.'

'Don't they tell you not to smoke? You'll get that dry rot?' Yannick doesn't know what dry rot is but it sounds like something you do not want to get.

She sucks up the last of her smoke, shrugging, and mashes the butt into the saucer with one dedicated push. The pink roses on the saucer are blackened almost to oblivion by ash.

'I wanted to ask you something, Kathleen,' he says.

'Don't ask me to make this trip with you.' She looks halfway at him, shaking her head.

'That is exactly what I am asking you.'

'Well, don't.'

'I want to see where they found the bones.'

'Those bones,' she says, pushing herself up from the chair, 'are not her. They've got nothing to do with her.' She opens the screen door into the house.

He catches the door before it slams shut and follows her inside, into the kitchen. 'And you can do the DNA test out there too,' he says. 'Close to the people who are investigating this thing. They said you could do it here, but . . .'

She's got her hand on the fridge door and glares at him, confused. Maybe more angry than confused, it's hard to tell. 'What did the coroner tell you?' she asks.

'Like I said before, supposedly the same thing they told you. Parks guys dug up some bones when they were making a new trail. It could be Una. Gal from the coroner's told me they don't need my blood. Only yours.'

'What about my blood?'

'For the test.'

Her face registers nothing.

'They didn't explain it to you?' he says.

Kathleen leans back against the counter, barricades her arms across her chest. 'Yannick, she told me a whole bunch of shit. Just tell me what you mean about my blood.'

He explains what he was told: the investigators need DNA from the mother to compare with the sample taken from the bones. When he asked why they didn't want his DNA, it was explained to him in fancier terms than this that while mother can only be mother, paternity is no guarantee.

'Course you can do the test here,' he says. 'But why not do it there?'

'So they don't need something of hers,' she says, 'to make the comparison.'

'She didn't say anything about that.'

Kathleen looks out of the window and shakes her head like she has somehow been fooled. She's smiling in a queer way. 'If I can do the test here, I'll do it here,' she eventually says, returning to the fridge and opening the door. Yannick sees, in the top corner where it's always been since Una disappeared, that number scratched out in thick black marker. Seven thousand nine hundred and sixty-nine days. 'You want breakfast?' Kathleen asks. She's holding a loaf of brown bread in one hand and a jar of marmalade in the other.

Eyeing that tally on the fridge, Yannick tries a different tack: 'Maybe it would be good for you to get away from here. A week, maybe two.'

'Ah, shit,' she says, swinging the loaf of bread at her hip. 'I can't eat toast. Nothing with corners.' She tosses the bread onto the counter and opens the fridge again.

'Are you listening to me, Kathleen?'

'I am ignoring the BS that just dropped out of your mouth,' she says, in a muffle from behind the fridge door.

'If it's her, we should be out there,' he says.

She closes the fridge with a tub of strawberry yogurt tucked in her arm and gets a spoon, and eats the yogurt, gingerly, straight from the tub. After a few spoonfuls, she tosses the spoon into the sink where it jumps and clatters. 'I need a shower,' she says, walking out of the kitchen. 'There's coffee in the pot if you want it. And I've got the peanut butter you like. The sugary kind.'

'We can talk more about this, Kathleen,' he calls, following her down the hall.

Her feet are heavy on the stairs, and then she stops, looks over the railing to him. 'You remember Oliver Hanratty?' she asks.

'I do, why?'

'He's dead,' she says. They look at each other for a second or two and then she continues up the stairs.

7

THE INAUGURAL AWARENESS party was held two years after Una's disappearance, and has been going every June since. Always in the same venue: the community hall on Katherine Street. The space is convenient, has a bright, fully equipped kitchen and an outdoor area that backs onto the Otonabee River. For the first decade exactly, the municipality waived the fee for the use of the hall, their way of supporting the search for Una. But in March of the eleventh year, Kathleen received a call from a woman she didn't know, some newcomer who'd never heard of Una. This unfamiliar woman on the other end of the line was calling to ask if Kathleen wanted to book the hall early in order to be eligible for a 10 per cent discount. Kathleen told her she had made a mistake. She said: 'You can't take ten per cent off nothing.' This quip was met only with dumb silence and the same question was repeated. Apparently, sympathy has an end date.

Kathleen considered moving the party to another venue – the principle, not the money, obviously – but to move the party would have been tantamount to changing a set of lottery numbers you'd been playing for years. There are just some things worth repeating ad infinitum.

Now Kathleen crosses the hall, her arms wrapped fully around a stainless-steel bowl of macaroni and mayonnaise salad. The food table is at the back wall, next to the kitchen's entrance. Back in the early years, people contributed so much food to this party, she'd be sending them home with aluminum parcels and paper plates wrapped tightly in cling-film.

She rearranges some party-size plastic bowls of chips and popcorn so the table doesn't look so barren. She's done a fruit-and-veg platter, a spinach and cream cheese dip in a bowl carved out of pumpernickel bread, a cheese platter and two other pasta salads to go alongside the macaroni. She's also made a lasagne big enough to feed an army, which will go in the oven later.

It's muggy and hot and there's a lot to do. She's already set out the fifty glass jars of river pebbles and tea lights on the long table at the top of the stairs, where people will be coming in, and returns to the table now to straighten the photos of Una so they are each facing outwards.

It's been four days since the coroner's office called and she feels foolish because Yannick had to explain to her this morning what the call was actually about, the DNA test and all that: the fact that Kathleen's blood carries whatever information they need to determine whether or not the bones are Una, and, consequently, that there was no point in hiding Una's baby tooth.

She is not a stupid woman, nor is she easily shocked, but, when the coroner was speaking, it was like she was holding a conch to her ear instead of the telephone. In place of this woman's voice was the hollow, high-pitched wind you get when you put a conch to your ear. They say it's the sound of the ocean, but come on now. It's the raging howl of nothing. Nothing at all.

Sandra Hoffstead, current board member of the community hall and someone Kathleen has known since primary school, comes in through the kitchen, asking Kathleen if she has everything she needs. She's a rosy person, Sandra Hoffstead.

Overly. Her ample arms and cheeks are blotchy with the humidity. The soft silver hair at her temples is damp, and the fine white fuzz on her cheeks is dewy with sweat. She's like a glazed ham just out of the oven.

Most people call Sandra by her nickname, which is Sally, but not Kathleen, who sees no correlation between the two names.

Sandra's son is two years younger than Una; they went to the same school. Sandra was slopping drunk at the first party, and she cornered Kathleen in the kitchen just at the point when Kathleen was about to throw the coffee urn across the room because of its leaky spout. Sandra stood close, inches too close, breathing cheap wine into Kathleen's face. The wine had stained her lips, like poorly applied lip liner. She was compelled, in that moment, to seek out Kathleen in the kitchen and share with her that, since Una's disappearance, she had become more appreciative of her own son. More appreciative of time with her son, who was applying for a job somewhere overseas and would be miles away for who knew how long?

'You should never take one second, not one second, for granted,' she said, and was about to thank Kathleen; the words were unmistakably taking shape on those wine-tinted lips. She caught herself in the nick of time, though, did Sally Hoffstead. It would have taken at least one more plastic cup's worth of cab-sav to render her that tactless.

Now, though, *now, though*, Kathleen is able to concede that this is, after all, an awareness party. Why shouldn't people be more aware of what they've got while they're commemorating what she hasn't?

Whatever. Sandra Hoffstead has a bevy of grandchildren now. If life were a primary-school test paper, Kathleen would mark Sandra's with a 'Well done!!' underlined twice.

'Daniel has a soccer game this afternoon,' Sandra says, probably referring to one of her umpteen grandchildren. 'I can't make the party. He made me promise to come watch.'

'What position does he play?'

'Eh?'

'What position? Winger? Defence? What?'

'I don't know anything about any of that,' she says. Her cheeks flush even pinker. 'It's just that I promised.'

'Can't break a promise,' Kathleen says.

Sandra puffs up her chest, perhaps about to speak, but only nods solemnly.

At two o'clock, Heather and Dave pull up in a truck piled like a junkyard with the Jenga and chess pieces and the tug-of-war rope. The kids tumble out of the back seat one after another. They just keep coming and Kathleen is sure there's more than usual.

She says this to Heather: 'I'm sure there's more than usual.'

'More what?'

Kathleen nods to the frolicking children.

'We've got the cousins for the night,' she says, climbs into the back of the flatbed and starts untying the nylon lashing. The muscles in her arms bulge like tiny, unripe pears. She is, it has to be said, adept with the ropes. Kathleen tries not to be put out that Heather agreed to look after a bunch of extra kids today. Of all days.

Heather passes down a white pawn, which is lighter than Kathleen expected from the look of it. Heather passes down a black knight, a black rook. Kathleen doesn't have the arm breadth.

'You see what's happening here,' she barks, in the general direction of the children, who have dispersed. Scrawny, bruised legs dangle from a tree, shoes abandoned in the grass. One kid hops single-footed along the flowerbed wall and loses his balance, flattening an innocent marigold under his high-top.

Heather blows a shrill finger-'n'-thumb whistle, and the whole brood stop what they're doing and make their way over to the truck. They look impressed, like they didn't know she had the puff. They all form a sort of conga line from the truck, around the side of the building to the back.

The kids, directed by the eldest, set up the chess board, and it becomes apparent that a few pieces are missing: a black king and a white castle. Kathleen tracks down Heather and Dave in the kitchen. They're not doing anything useful, doing nothing really, just sharing a cup of orange pop.

'We have to run back home,' Heather says. 'We forgot the food.'

'You forgot half the chess pieces as well.'

Heather looks at Dave.

Dave shakes his big head. 'We brought everything,' he says.

'Are you sure?' Heather asks.

'The garage was empty. I checked.'

'It doesn't matter. We're going back to the house anyway,' she says, and drains the last of the pop, squeeze-cracking the plastic cup in a way that, to Kathleen, feels juvenile and aggressive.

'I wish you had counted them before,' Kathleen says. 'Before today. If the pieces aren't there, it would have been good to know before today.'

'Count them?' she says.

'Pretty busy around our house, Kathleen,' Dave says. He's standing directly in the middle of the kitchen. Taking up all the space.

'Dave's got a big trip coming up,' Heather says.

'Whatever,' Kathleen says. 'You're going back anyway.'

'For the food,' Heather says, again.

Kathleen follows them back out to the truck.

'Okay if I leave the kids?' Heather asks, yanking down on the chipped-chrome door handle.

'So, what? You're helping Dave get ready for his trip?' Kathleen says this very quietly, with a smile that's meant to show she's not being critical. She's just wondering.

'Excuse me?' Heather says. She's half in the truck. He's making his way around to the other side.

'Nothing,' Kathleen says, backing away.

Heather nods, and thunks the door closed.

Only a few things left to do. On the wall above the reception desk is a whiteboard with the week's activities written neatly in different-coloured markers – Kathleen recognizes Sandra Hoffstead's girlie, inoffensive penmanship. Monday: cribbage. Tuesday: Texas Hold 'em. Wednesday: whatever, who cares. Kathleen sweeps the eraser across the board and finds a thick black marker. With letters tall enough to fill the board, she writes: *Welcome to Una's Awareness Party.* She draws three little daisies next to Una's name. They turn out pretty good, considering how blunt and thick the marker is.

Worried she might lose one of the kids in the river, she's banished them to the basement rec room where there are board games and puzzles, and a retro Pac Man video game in the corner that takes actual quarters. She gave them every quarter she had and now all she can hear is the insatiable electronic uh-*wuh* uh-*wuh* uh-*wuh* of the Pac Man.

Next. There's a glass case beside the table where she's set out Una's candles. But when people come up the stairs from the front door, the case will be blocking the candle display. The top shelf of this distraction holds beaded jewellery made by Girl Guides. The two shelves below hold amateur ceramics.

Kathleen tries to move the case by pushing it across the floor, but it's too heavy, and its bottom edge catches on the tiles. She goes downstairs to the rec room and points to one of the boy cousins and says, 'You,' and curls her finger for him to follow.

On the way up the stairs he asks her if she has any more quarters for Pac Man.

'No.'

'Anyway, that game is for babies,' he says.

'Then why do you want more quarters?' she asks. This kid definitely looks strong enough to move the glass case. She tells him she needs his help. Explains that she wants to tip the case on its front edge, just a smidge, and pull it along the floor.

'Won't all the stuff break?' he asks. He screws his face sideways, sceptically.

'We'll be very careful.'

She pushes the candle table back a scooch so the kid can get in on one side of the case, and she gets on the other.

'Just hold tight,' she says.

She gently leans the case forward and the kid seems perfectly capable of supporting his end. One of the pottery mugs slides on the shelf and taps the front wall of the case. They stop, hold. All settles.

'You push, I'll pull,' she says. 'We're going to put it there, just by the other wall.' They inch along to the opposite wall, not quite two metres away. When they've made it to the right spot, they rotate the case and ease it flush against the wall. The beaded jewellery has collected in a heap in the front corner of its shelf, but other than that, all seems fine.

'You only get three goes in that game,' the kid tells her,

brushing his hands up and down his jeans as if he's just done hard labour.

'That's two more than you get in this one,' Kathleen says.

'Huh?' he says.

'You heard me,' she says.

'Whatever,' he says. 'Pac Man sucks. You only get three lives, then the game is over, and the music is all *wah wah wah*.'

'You kids are spoiled rotten with all your Nintendos and your whatnots,' she says. 'Endless lives. No consequences when you mess up. When my daughter was your age, she used to take her allowance down to the video arcade. Two bucks got you eight games. Do you know what a video arcade is?'

The kid takes his phone out of his back pocket and starts thumbing it.

'You asking the oracle?'

He holds up one finger to silence her (she's beginning to like him), and reads: ' "A video arcade is a place of entertainment where you can play video games on machines which work when you put money in them." '

'Exactly,' she says.

And then they hear it, the slide and inevitable smash of one pottery-laden glass shelf caving into another pottery-laden glass shelf. The shuffle across the floor seems to have dislodged the brackets supporting the middle shelf, and it's slid down. A mug is broken, as are a few bowls.

'I told you,' says the kid, hands deep in his pockets, bending close to the case and scrutinizing the damage. 'You're going to get in trouble.' Divorcing himself from this fiasco, he hops back down the stairs to the rec room. She hears him announce to the others that the old lady upstairs is in for it.

*

A few minutes past three, Kathleen goes out again to meet Dave and Heather in the parking lot. She looks into the back of the truck for the chess pieces, which aren't there.

A vibration of thunder in the far distance. So far away it's not even a rumble yet. So far away it's hard to tell if this is something heard or felt. The air smells like metal and the sky is yellow.

Heather hops out of the truck and proceeds to wrestle the baby out of his car seat, which is a surprise to Kathleen. She'd assumed the baby was downstairs with the others.

'What about the missing pieces?' she asks Heather.

'I guess they were just never there,' she says, struggling over the car seat.

'You don't seem very concerned.'

Heather's body stops moving. 'There's nothing we can do about it now.'

Kathleen peers over Heather's shoulder. The baby is fast asleep and it seems Heather can't pry his fat leg free of the strap. 'I just wish we'd known. Before today,' Kathleen says, standing just at Heather's shoulder. 'If you'd counted the pieces, we would have known.'

Heather lays her hand flat on the baby's belly, which is as perfectly round as a melon. Her shoulders heave with a long breath. It's frustrating, Kathleen knows. Babies are awkward and inconvenient. She remembers.

'Do you want me to try?' she asks, putting her hand on Heather's shoulder.

Heather backs away from the truck and Kathleen trips a little on her own feet getting out of the way.

'I'm just going to leave him,' she says. 'He'll be fine.'

'I'll stay with him,' says Dave, brightly, sliding back into the driver's seat. He nestles in and starts scrolling his phone.

Heather walks around to the other side of the truck and slides out a platter covered with tin foil.

'I'll get the rest,' Kathleen says.

'This is it,' says Heather. She moves past Kathleen, her eyes resolute, like she's already played this moment out in her head. 'We always make too much,' she says.

Kathleen glances at Dave through the windshield and, though he's holding his phone up in front of his face, his eyes are on her. This is all beginning to feel a bit like she's being flanked.

A mosquito lands on her upper arm and she lifts her arm closer to her face and watches the insect as it anchors itself to bite. She flicks the nuisance away.

It's time to, as they say, get this party started. She goes inside.

8

THOSE FEW HOURS before a thunderstorm hits? The air
waits. The trees, they wait. It is nearly four o'clock and Yannick
is late for the party.

He was there in the beginning, those first couple of years.
Back then he believed in the party; it seemed worth the effort.
And they were fun parties, in spite of everything else. Something loud and alive with music and stories, while every other
day without Una was either senseless or desolate. The parties
were festive. Kathleen insisted on it. People came with their
guitars and fiddles and drums. The food was rich and plentiful,
and Una's friends swam in the river and got drunk and sang.

He would have kept going too, but then, of course, he and
Kathleen had that fight out on her porch about his girl Robin,
and that was the end of the parties and the end of everything
else, too, to do with him and her. You don't think years will
pass without a word but they do. These things, they have a way
of thickening to gristle.

News of Robin, of another baby coming, this was a shock
to Yannick. He was fifty-five years old at the time, and he was
tired. You get tired. But Leigh wanted a baby very badly, and
he loved Leigh very much. Still does.

So the fight, the epic fight, happened a few weeks before
Robin was born. That day, he stopped by Kathleen's place on
his way down to Toronto, where he was picking up all three of

his boys for a weekend together. He knew Kathleen was preparing to go out west for the second time that year, to do her thing putting up posters and all that, and he thought he'd better see her before she went.

House was dark and locked when he got there, late in the morning, sometime in late September or October. He did what felt natural to him: he got the keys from under the stone planter by the back door and let himself in. He made coffee. No longer carrying his own tobacco, he pilfered her cigarettes out of the basket on top of the microwave. He hadn't exactly quit yet, officially, but his smoking days were numbered and now he was smoking whatever happened to come his way.

Yannick took his coffee and Kathleen's cigarettes out to the back porch and sat. He studied the various weeds swaying in the grass. Kathleen wasn't farming flowers at the time so the yard was unkempt, leaves beginning to drift.

Halfway through his second smoke, Kathleen came home, parked her car next to Yannick's and trudged across the grass carrying a cardboard box in both arms. She climbed the back steps and looked at the coffee mug in Yannick's one hand, and the smoke dangling between the fingers of the other, and said hello in a flat tone that had no hello in it whatsoever.

She opened the screen door and went into the kitchen and the door whined shut, slapping into the frame twice before it settled. As soon as it did, there was the sound of something dropping to the floor and Kathleen swearing roughly, straight from the back of her throat.

Yannick went inside and found her squatting down, sweeping both hands across the floor, rounding up glossy posters and flyers that had spilled out over the linoleum.

'Fucking box,' she said. 'The bottom wasn't . . .' she said.

And she wrung her hands in the air and looked over her shoulder at him.

'Folded together?'

She nodded. 'The bottom just dropped out,' she said.

Yannick got down to the floor to help but she told him she didn't need help and asked him why he was there.

'I'm on my way to get my boys,' he said. 'I wanted to see you. I know how hard it is for you going back west again.'

'Hard for me.'

'You know what I mean.'

She pushed herself up off the floor and set a stack of flyers on the kitchen counter. The stack slid out from underneath itself and the flyers fanned out across the counter. Una's face repeated many times.

'I can't do this right now,' Kathleen said. She pulled her hands through her hair and asked Yannick how he'd got in.

'I used the key,' he said. He bent again to the floor to pick up the rest of the flyers.

'Leave them.'

He ignored her and continued to sweep the slippery papers up in his arms.

'Leave them,' she said again, through her teeth.

He stood back up. 'What is it, Kathleen? Is it the trip?'

'You don't live here,' she said. 'And I just got home. And I'm tired.'

'I won't stay long,' he said. 'The boys are waiting. Have a smoke with me on the porch and I'll go.'

'You've gained weight,' she said, after they'd smoked and she couldn't likely think of any more reasons to be annoyed with him. On the folding table between them was a glass ashtray the colour of deep green water, and a cheerless, half-burned citronella candle that looked like it had not been lit in many years.

'Leigh goes in heavy with the butter when she cooks,' he said, looking at Kathleen without looking at her, gauging her own shadows and joints and edges, signs of thinness, of not enough food.

'I'm glad you're being well looked after,' she said, like she meant it. She seemed content in that moment before it all went wrong. She stretched her legs out and the porch boards sucked and creaked under them. She toed her shoes off her feet, one at a time. A flock of geese cut across the sky, their formation off kilter, one side of the V much shorter than the other and a few untidy stragglers fighting to slip back into the wake.

'Something I should've told you already,' he said.

'That Leigh's cooking makes you fat?'

'No. There's something I want to tell you.'

She looked at him, then looked out across the grass to the spruce trees. 'I knew it!' She slapped her knee, flicked ash off it.

The homing screams of the geese seemed to be getting louder, even as they grew smaller in the sky.

'What?' he said, smiling. He was smiling because she was smiling, and he thought maybe he was going to get away with this, without too much hurt.

'You got married again,' she said, with a considerable amount of glee. 'You didn't learn your lesson with the last one who took that house off you?'

Yannick didn't say anything then, just held her eyes with his own and very slowly, or maybe it was quick, he can't remember now, but when it happened it was unmistakable: her eyes jigged right into place. She knew.

'Ah,' she said, breathing out the 'ah' for a very long time, digging for another cigarette. 'Of course,' she said, nodding behind the safety of her thick hair. 'Right,' she said.

'I should've told you before now.'

She tucked her hair behind her ear and the side of her mouth wised up in an un-smile that she tried to hold back with her tongue. She shook her head slowly but didn't turn to him. '*Mazel tov*,' she said.

'It's happening soon,' he said. 'I'm so sorry I didn't tell you before.'

'You're calling it an it?' she said.

'She,' he said, realizing he had not wanted to say that, the worst part. 'It's a girl,' he said. 'She's a girl.'

Kathleen's face cooled to pale and her hand floated to her neck. Her mouth opened wider in that un-smile.

'I know there are things more important than this,' he said. 'You have got bigger fish to fry than this. But I couldn't leave it any longer. She's due in a few weeks.'

The sound that came out of Kathleen then was like a huffing – a breathy laugh without anything to laugh about. She laid her burning cigarette in the ashtray and bent for her shoes – soft, slip-on shoes, black with no laces.

'Say something, Kathleen.'

She pulled one shoe over her foot, which Yannick took as his cue to leave. Their visit on the porch, over.

'Okay, then,' he said, standing from his chair, smoothing the backside of his jeans. He would continue south to Toronto and see his boys, and she would leave for her trip. And in a few days, she would call him, like she always did, and they would talk about her progress, handing out flyers, talking to strangers in unfamiliar towns. Getting nothing new from the police.

'Maybe it's stupid,' he said, 'but I hoped this could be a

happy thing for all of us. We have not had happy news in a long time.'

Yannick knows now, he does, the folly of what he said and what he hoped for. But he was messy in those days too.

He dug around in his jeans pocket for the keys to his car. Kathleen stood abruptly and slapped his chest with her shoe, the one she hadn't yet put on. Yannick, confused and embarrassed, leaned back and smiled. He rubbed his chest in a way that was mocking, pretending it hurt even though it didn't, in the same way Zack would needle Devon or Sunny. Trying to turn whatever was happening into a joke. He raised both his hands in surrender and said, 'Heya,' and laughed openly, an invite for her to laugh too.

Kathleen told him to go – to fucking go, was in fact what she said. He stood in that position with his hands raised another second, another two or three. Waiting for the pressure to drop. But Kathleen's eyes didn't flinch. So. He went down the porch steps and headed for his car, but halfway across the yard he stopped and turned around, never good at walking away from a fight. She was there at the top of the steps, watching him go, one arm hooked around the porch-roof pillar.

'I didn't do it to make you angry,' he said. 'I did not do this on purpose, this baby. This is just life happening here.'

'You need to go.'

'Maybe she doesn't want to be found, Kathleen,' he said. 'Maybe she's not the one who is lost.'

She bent to the folding table for, he thought, her cigarette. But when she stood back up she was holding the glass ashtray. He didn't understand what he was seeing as he watched the ashtray soar, like a dead green goose, through the air. He didn't understand what was happening when the ashtray connected with his left cheek, striking the bone at the corner of his eye.

He pressed his face with one hand and stumbled a few paces towards her – this was instinct, he would never – but pain that sharp and sudden feels an awful lot like anger. Stars were going off. Maybe he yelled or maybe it was the look on his face, but whatever it was, she picked up the little folding table. The cheerless citronella candle rolled down the porch steps and disappeared in the tall grass. Kathleen held the table in front of her with the legs pointed towards him.

'You're stuck,' he said. 'You are stuck,' he yelled. His skin was split. Warm and tacky blood pooled between his fingers and he could smell iron.

She jousted the table towards him in frightened little stabs. If it were not such a sorry sight, it would have been funny.

He turned back towards his car, and as soon as he did, the little porch table came sailing past his face and landed in the grass, and jilted onto its side a few paces in front of him. He kicked that fucker out of his way and pranged his toe. Now he wanted to break something. To tear something up. This was his daughter too, who was gone. Just because he didn't staple posters to every mother-loving surface . . . He ripped a dandelion out of the grass, digging his fingers deeply into his own palm; the punch was strong in his fists.

Backing out of that long gravel driveway, half blind with blood and with his wet fingers sticking to the steering wheel, Yannick had no idea he would not see Kathleen again for so long. No idea at all.

There's a sign at the top of the stairs coming into the community centre with Kathleen's handwriting all over it. Big black brutal letters on a white sign. It feels more like a telling-off than a welcome: Welcome to Una's Awareness Party.

Under the sign there are the candles with Una's photo. All the photos are precisely lined up: the same photos, a girl from another time.

The few guests already here stand around like cardboard cut-outs of people and there is no music.

Yannick isn't hungry but is drawn anyway to the table of food – it's somewhere to wander to. He takes a paper plate and fills it with cherry tomatoes and pasta salad and a handful of potato chips. A cherry tomato rolls off his plate to the floor and he kicks it under the table so no one steps on it.

No wallflower, he moves from guest to guest, recognizing no one, yet they all seem to know who he is. He refills cups, cajoles people to eat more food. He finds a CD player in a cupboard in the basement and brings it up but the only CD he can find is the children's singer Rafi. He's not yet seen Kathleen.

There are some mini bottles of wine on the table where the food is, their labels covered with photos of Una. He opens these and empties them into people's cups, wondering why Kathleen would bother with such small bottles.

No one speaks about Una. What more is there to say? She's present only in the photos tied to the candles with brown string.

But for anyone who still remembers, these pictures are nothing more than relics from the early days of her missing-ness. When there was still hope. All those flyers stapled to wooden telephone poles and taped up in storefront windows. Warped by rain and torn up and stapled over by other, more recent, announcements.

So many of his favourite photos of Una were conscripted to this unwinnable battle. It's not her he sees. These are pictures of the girl who is lost.

Caught by a Bramble

NOT IN ANY kind of rush at all, or any kind of anything at all, she ambles and weaves down the gravelled shoulder of the highway. It's still early-ish, not yet nine a.m.; cars pass infrequently. Each time the burn of an engine approaches from behind, she sticks out her thumb and gives it a half-hearted wag. If she catches a lift, great. If not, it doesn't matter so much. She doesn't have anywhere she needs to be until later, when she's meeting an old friend.

Every now and then she stops and prods at the blackberry brambles that grow in abundance alongside the road, hoping to find a few gems. Stepping too close to the bramble, she's caught by a branch of thorns that impale the loose cotton of her knee-length shorts, expertly latching on. In trying to twist free, she's hooked at the shoulder by another overhanging branch. Blackberry thorns are wily, and the harder you fight, the deeper they clutch. She stops moving and, with nimble fingers and a bit of imaginative contortion, delicately pulls the branches from her clothes and steps back onto the road.

There's no point to any of this, this search for ripe berries. You could say it was a fruitless endeavour. It's much too early in the season, and the berries are uniformly bright green and rock hard. Coy, bitter studs, giving nothing away.

She continues to walk and eventually a truck pulls over onto the gravel. The tailpipe shudders and coughs as she approaches.

'Wickaninnish?' she asks the driver, a man she's not seen before. His face is plump and hairless and doesn't give away his age – he could be twenty or he could be forty. Across the eyes he looks friendly enough and the cab smells like bubble-gum.

He tells her he doesn't mind giving her a lift if she doesn't mind sitting in the back; his cab is packed with electrical equipment. This suits her just fine, so she climbs up and into the flatbed, grateful not to have to make small-talk.

He drives.

She settles against the back window of the cab and stretches her legs across the cold metal of the flatbed. The world passes by and the morning breeze pinches her skin, in a non-sympathetic but invigorating way. Kind of like her mother's touch.

Also in the back of the truck: muslin sacks of animal feed, the rusted frame of a bicycle, a heavy stack of loosely folded dust sheets tied with yellow nylon rope, and one black cork boot that has cracked and faded to chalky grey.

There's a tear in one of the muslin sacks and every time the truck goes over a bump, the tear burps a dribble of colourful seeds and dark purple kernels onto a growing cone of feed. She leans over and scoops some into her hand and, for a lark, presses her tongue into the seeds. The taste makes her think of goat's milk and barn and wool.

The wind blows from all directions and goosebumps rise on her arms, the sun not yet high enough to clear the trees on the side of the road. She zips open her bag and pulls out her towel, which she has brought in mind to find somewhere to shower today, and covers her legs with it. Unfortunately, what with living in a tree, the towel is never not damp, and provides little warmth.

The truck slows and, inexplicably, turns right onto a smaller road. This is not the way to Wickaninnish Beach. The forest is gloomy and thick on either side of this road, and they pass few buildings. Some houses fronted in cedar clapboard, sheds, a rank of post-office boxes, and a hand-painted Private Property sign nailed to a tree at an unfriendly angle. She twists around and peers through the window of the cab but can't see past the electrical equipment to the driver, so she raps on the glass with her knuckles, lightly, in a casual way – she doesn't want to embarrass either of them, but come on.

She leans over the driver's side of the truck and waves but can't see his face in the wing mirror. Looking over the edge of the truck, there's the road, passing fluidly, and she tries to guess how fast they're going. Soon, the pavement ends in an abrupt line and the road is now dirt.

'Hey,' she calls, 'hey!' She leans back and knocks again on the cab window.

Everything is rattling now as the vehicle grinds awkwardly over the uneven dirt road – her teeth, her eyes, her tongue. She sits back against the cab and presses her foot on the frame of the rusty bike. 'You could swing that at someone's head,' she says aloud, to feel less alone. She laces one end of the yellow nylon rope that holds the dust sheets together around her pinkie finger and considers its usefulness, in a defence scenario, and comes up with nothing. She chuckles weakly at herself, not truly believing she's in danger. 'You can't be stuck in a berry bush one minute and axe-murdered the next,' she says to the cork boot, now wondering exactly how sharp are its metal spikes.

The truck passes into a long stretch of sun that has made its way through the trees. Every single morning, at this time, she thinks, trying to rein in the skip to her heart, the sun touches here.

Her mouth has turned pasty and dry. She tongues a sharp seed that is wedged between her back teeth. 'Idiot,' she whispers.

9

YANNICK HAS MADE it to the party. A few minutes ago, Kathleen saw him pouring a drink for one of Una's old teachers. She also saw him greeting a neighbour at the top of the stairs, pointing out the candles. Playing host, like he's always been here.

And now Julius, at last. He plods up the stairs one by one. His strong, bony hand grip-slides up the railing, and in his other hand, a plastic shopping bag. She meets him before he gets to the top step and takes the bag, which contains a package of smoked-ham slices and a loaf of white bread.

'The dentist did a number on you,' he says, cupping his dry hand to her cheek. Julius has never touched her before. 'Is it painful?'

'It looks worse than it feels,' she says.

'It's gargantuan,' he says. 'You look like the Elephant Man.'

Only Julius.

She takes his elbow as they mount the last two steps. 'Look who's here,' she says, pointing with her chin towards Yannick, where he's talking to a group of women. 'Charming the pants off Heather's friends.'

Julius squints across the room. 'You kept that quiet,' he says.

She shrugs.

'He's still very attractive.'

'You can't see that far,' she says.

'Why didn't you say anything yesterday?'

'There's nothing to say.'

'After a thousand years,' says Julius, peering into her eyes like he's trying to see in the dark, 'he just comes?'

'Yep.' She has no intention of saying anything about the bones, not even to Julius.

The storm begins, as storms do, with wind. It comes knuckling up the river from the south, punching through the humidity. The temperature drops and the air expands and the sky billows into pea green. The rain isn't here yet but it's coming, fast, and Kathleen couldn't care less. She's coiling the hefty, whiskery tug-of-war rope around her midriff. A dozen or so children are outside with her and in this charged, dramatic light, where the blues are bluer and the reds are redder, et cetera, even she can appreciate how beautiful these rug-rats are, these random children. She is drawn to their vitality. Their *here*-ness. She challenged the group of them to a tug-of-war contest and the cousin who helped move the glass case earlier is the only one ballsy enough to take her on.

She glares at him now, poised opposite her as he encircles one arm with rope. She hadn't noticed before the flawless whites of his eyes, or that the irises are the silver-grey of pussy willow catkins in March. The summer-browned skin of this child, the thick splay of dark hair that plumes from his head. Even the buck of his two enormous front teeth. He sparkles. He radiates. Whatever. She's going to take him down.

A few of the smaller children circle and peck at each other like overexcited ducks, then waddle inside as the wind picks up even more and the sky darkens. Kathleen itches and sweats under the rope that binds her.

The river carries a bobbing chess piece away. She is unconcerned.

A silent gesture of lightning.

'One Mississippi, two Mississippi, three Mississippi,' slurs the cousin. It's a challenge for him to get his esses around those paddle-like teeth.

'Are we starting, or what?' she asks.

'Five Mississippi.'

'That's a myth, you know, counting how far away the storm is.'

The far-off rumble of thunder sounds like a heavy truck driving over an unreliable bridge.

'Five keelometres away,' he drawls.

'That's a load of BS,' she says. A heaviness clutches at her knees. The rope feels as if it's tightening on its own.

He takes a few steps backwards and stops, both hands gripping the length of rope between them, preparing his stance. He contemplates her with those silvery eyes. 'Where's your daughter anyway?' he says.

'Well, buddy,' she says, 'that's the whole point.'

He gawks at her.

'No one knows,' she says. She hasn't acknowledged this fact out loud for a very, very long time and it feels odd. Almost like when you repeat a word over and over until it loses all meaning and logic. Where. Where. Where. Where. Where.

He works his face back and forth, pondering. 'My uncle says you're unhinged.'

Dave. She knew it. She smiles and leans back until the rope is taut.

The kid mirrors her every move. You gotta give it to him.

'You ready for war?' she asks.

Digging his heels into the grass, he throws his body back, as does she. Knowing she must outweigh him threefold, at least, she thinks she's got it in the bag, but the power emanating down the rope is no joke. With burning hands, she tosses her head back, squeezes her eyes shut and gives it all her worth. An ugly grunt bores through her clenched teeth and she doesn't even care. She needs this win.

With each breath, her strength increases. She gains a little ground. He gains a little ground. Her toes mash into the front of her shoes. Palms hot, fingers ache and slip. She hunches her shoulders and prepares for the final blow, victory expanding from the bottom of her stomach up into her throat and then, pow! She is catapulted backwards and lands solidly on her coccyx. Her head bounces off the grass. She is stunned.

The sky churns and she watches a raindrop spiral earthbound.

The little twerp let go of the rope.

The raindrops increase, pattering her face. She waits, expecting the boy to come over and help her up.

'Boy.'

Nothing.

'Boy?'

The boy has abandoned her to the storm.

Blue forked lightning flashes, then once more. Its pattern lingers, burned into the dirt-grey sky. One Missi— Thunderclaps. So much for five kilometres.

She raises herself up onto her elbows and keeps her head tilted to the sky. The lightning and thunder are exhilarating and she is overcome with the sort of peace that can only exist when one is completely powerless.

She closes her eyes and feels the water kiss her face, the creases of her cheeks, her lips and down behind her ears. She could just stay here, forget the party, give herself over to this water that snakes down her scalp.

Hands grip both her shoulders, shaking her. Heather's face, crooked with alarm, cuts into view.

'You need to come,' she says. She's shivering, trying to unravel the wet rope from Kathleen's body.

'Stop. You're making it worse.' She bats Heather's hands away. 'Help me up first.'

Heather is quivering like a Chihuahua puppy, and everything is wet and clumsy as she struggles to yank at Kathleen with scrappy hands, pulling her in all directions. Kathleen tells her, more sharply than necessary, to stop.

'What the hell is wrong with you?' Kathleen jerks at the rope until it's loose enough that she can step out of its coil. She rubs the sensation back into her tailbone.

'We had an accident,' Heather says.

Kathleen abandons the rope in the wet grass and trots behind Heather, through the side door and into the kitchen. A food bomb seems to have detonated. Ribbons of pasta and tomato sauce, ricotta cheese and ground beef on the floor and walls, dripping like something eviscerated. Chunky shards of glass are splayed across the counter and the floor, and there are also pieces embedded in the walls. Heather has blood on her arm.

'What happened?' Kathleen asks. 'You got cut?'

'I did?' Heather inspects herself, apparently unaware she's bleeding. She finds the contrail of blood on her arm and twists it at the elbow to find the source. 'I took the lasagne out of the oven. I put it on the counter and . . .' Heather appears to be at a loss for words.

'And what?'

'Don't yell at me.'

'Did you throw it at the wall or something? Did Dave do something?'

'Stop yelling.'

'I'm not yelling.'

'You are,' says Heather. She licks her thumb and rubs at the cut on her arm.

'Did you throw it?'

'What? No.'

'So what happened?'

'Why would I throw a lasagne?' Heather says. 'Why would you even ask that? The dish just exploded.'

A few people crowd the kitchen door and Kathleen notices for the first time that there's music playing in the other room. Something twangy. Yannick appears with a broom and dustpan and an earnest look that Kathleen would like to slap off his face.

'Everybody out,' she says.

'The dish exploded,' says Yannick.

'So it would seem.'

'I have never seen that before,' he says.

'This is impossible,' says Kathleen.

Yannick peels a shredded string of lasagne sheet off the wall and slings it into the garbage. 'Clearly it is not,' he says.

Kathleen opens drawers aggressively enough that they jerk and clop against their bearings, until she finds a neat stack of blue J-cloths and tea towels, and drifts into the middle of the kitchen, wondering where to start. Heather pries pieces of glass out of the wall with the edge of a butter knife and drops them one-by-one into an aluminum pie plate, each piece of glass tinkling off the aluminum in a minor key.

Dave comes in and asks if everything is okay, but Heather

sends him back out, tells him to make sure no children come in. He goes without comment.

'You've got him well trained,' says Kathleen, trying to make light. Trying to make friends again. Because it's true, she wasn't yelling, exactly, but neither was she speaking calmly.

Heather doesn't respond. And then, several minutes later: 'Do you even know how many chess pieces there are in a set?'

Kathleen is on her knees, wiping mushy pasta off the floor, wary of potentially hidden shards of glass. 'Eh?' she says.

'You asked me why I didn't count the pieces, to make sure they were all there, but do you even know how many pieces there should be?'

'Thirty-two,' says Yannick. He's at the sink, filling a bucket with steaming water.

Heather looks over her shoulder to him and smiles gratefully.

'That's not the point,' Kathleen says.

'It is,' says Heather, working at a stubborn bit of glass.

Kathleen gets up off her knees, ready to argue this point. To drive home how in the wrong she is not. But then an unfamiliar voice yells from the other room for someone to call an ambulance.

What now?

Heather, ever a mother, eyes wide, drops the butter knife to the floor and dashes – really dashes – from the kitchen. Some mothers are like that, Kathleen knows, assuming everything bad that can happen will happen to their own kid, the world full of sharp corners and long falls. Without knowing what real terror is, these mothers appropriate the unthinkable: they hoard it, possess it until it orbits them.

The few party guests who remain – several took the exploding dish as a cue to leave – are crowded around a big easy chair in the corner of the main room. At first glance, Kathleen sees a manikin sitting stiffly in the chair, which makes no sense. Rod straight, face lifeless and white as paper. It's not a manikin, of course, it's Julius. Julius taut and fragile.

'Is he breathing?' someone asks.

Yannick is knelt low between Julius's knees, holding his wrist. Kathleen bends down next to Yannick and leans in close to Julius, so close she can smell this morning's coffee on his breath. His eyes, dark and stunned, lock on hers. His skin is like wet dough, and his neck is blotchy and red. She gently undoes the top two buttons of his shirt. He belches softly.

'Is it indigestion, Julius?' This is something he suffers from, she knows.

He crinkles his eyes slightly, a strenuous yes.

'You look like shit. You need to go to the hospital.'

'I called an ambulance,' comes a voice from the huddle.

'So did I,' comes another.

Julius whispers, 'God, no. Call them back.' Sweat drips off the tip of his nose.

The paramedics determine anaphylactic shock, and strap him onto a gurney with a white sheet tucked over his legs. Yannick offers to ride to the hospital with him, but Julius warns him off, so Kathleen promises to drive over there as soon as she's cleaned up here.

The party, as the storm, is over. It lasted barely two hours. Kathleen counts the candle jars. There are thirty-nine left.

She suddenly feels heavy and drenched with exhaustion.

Dave and the kids load the wet, ridiculous game pieces into the back of his truck while Kathleen, Heather and Yannick finish up in the kitchen. An old CD player sits on the kitchen counter wheezing out a Willie Nelson song. Yannick says music will make the work go by easier.

'Couldn't you find better music?' Kathleen asks him.

'I thought you liked this.'

'It makes my teeth hurt.'

'Your teeth make your teeth hurt,' he says.

'Pah.'

'We could play it in the truck,' he says. 'Good music for the long road.'

Kathleen doesn't bite. She wrings out a J-cloth slimy with cheese and tomato sauce, and refreshes the cloth with scalding water. Yannick has got another thing coming if he believes she'll tolerate five thousand kilometres with him. She scrapes stubborn cheese off the counter with her fingernail.

Willie Nelson can't wait to get back on the road again.

'You must have something more upbeat than this,' she says.

Dave leans in through the side door. 'We're done,' he says, looking directly at Heather, as if there's no one else in the kitchen.

'I'll drop her home later,' Kathleen says.

'Or,' he says, 'she comes with me now. We're done.'

Heather abandons on the floor a brown paper bag grinding with pieces of glass. 'Time to go,' she says.

Dragging the cooling cloth across an already-clean counter, Kathleen mutters something about Dave's orders being followed or else.

'Sorry?' Heather says.

Kathleen stops and leans against the counter, and twists the cloth tightly in her fingers. 'You two,' she says.

Heather is poised, unmoving, in the middle of the kitchen. Dave is in the doorway with his beefy shoulder wedged against the frame. One small pair of arms is wrapped around his leg, trying to coax him outside.

'You two, what?' she says.

'You just. It's like, come *on*.' Kathleen, caught now, not even sure what she wants to criticize. Just itching for a fight, any fight. Yannick is looking at her with a face that's telling her to shut the hell up.

'What are you trying to say, Kathleen?' Heather asks. Her chin is raised.

Dave's face hardens with pride. Evidently this is something he has been waiting for.

'What I am saying,' says Kathleen, wholly unsure of what she is saying, 'is that you, you married people—'

'You married people? You married people, what?'

'You wouldn't understand,' Kathleen mutters.

Heather stares at her a second longer, words in her mouth, for sure, just lapping there at the edge, but then she just kind of gives up, deflates. She moves to Dave and puts her hand on his chest. 'I want to go home,' she says.

'No,' Dave says, 'I want to say something.'

Kathleen turns to him. Here's her fight, at last. 'So?' she says.

The arms around his leg pull harder, nearly dislodging him from the doorframe, but he holds fast, his eyes on Kathleen's. 'We've had it. She's had it with you, taking advantage.' He looks to Heather, who's looking at the floor. 'You're an asshole, Kathleen,' he says. 'And you ask for too much.'

What can she say to that?

'And this,' he says, waving his one free hand around.

'What, this?'

He frowns. 'This *party*,' he says, with no party in the word 'party'. Now he's looking at the floor too. Fightwise, this isn't shaping up to be one for the books.

The child is now leeching up Dave's back, pulling herself up by the collar of his shirt. Dave twists and takes the little girl into his arms, cradles her. Swings her high then pulls her back into the protective shell of his body, engulfing her so all Kathleen can see of her is some tangled brown hair, a tiny clutching hand and one sandalled foot. She's giggling maniacally, gulping for breath. This giggle, secure and confident and totally oblivious, is a horse's swift kick to Kathleen's gut.

'Bye, Yannick,' Heather says flatly.

'Bye, now,' he says.

'Bye, Kathleen,' she says.

Kathleen turns away.

No one left now but Kathleen and Yannick. And also Willie Nelson, woefully and straight from the back end of the nose, warning mamas not to let their babies grow up to be cowboys.

'Please turn that fucking music off, Yannick.'

Which he does, mercifully. He picks up the bags containing much of the uneaten food and unused paper plates. 'It's going to be okay, Kathleen,' he says.

He packs the bags and boxes of candles into the trunk of her car with careful logic, so that everything fits snugly and doesn't jangle around, as if he's neatly pencilling letters into one of his crossword puzzles.

There's something about a man packing the trunk of the car for you.

There just is.

Julius is tucked up in one desolate bay of the Emergency Department, hidden behind a pale yellow curtain. He's not in the bed, but instead sits up in a tall-backed vinyl chair, a starchy hospital sheet folded over his knees. An IV taped to his inner arm means he no longer looks like a dead person.

Kathleen sits on the edge of the bed, facing him.

'I ruined Una's party,' he says. He picks delicately at the corner of his nostril with his pinkie finger. The air smells sour, and Kathleen is pretty sure it's him.

'Let's face it, Julius,' Kathleen says.

'There wasn't much to ruin,' he says, looking at her warmly.

She nods, and then, 'They're keeping you overnight?'

'One of these people – you can't tell who's the doctor who's the nurse these days – has insisted. In case of further reaction.'

'Do you know what caused it?' she says, and pours him a cup of water.

He lifts his shoulders in a faint shrug, refuses the water and inhales deeply. He lets his eyes fall to half closed and exhales a weak little yodel.

A small scratch, inconvenient as a fishbone in the throat, jabs at Kathleen: the knowledge that this dear man, the only friend she has left, will, sooner rather than later, leave her too.

She asks him where his glasses are. Another shrug.

'How strange,' he says, his eyes now fully closed, 'to have seen Yannick today.'

'There were plenty of people there today that we haven't seen in a while,' she says.

He opens his eyes. Binds her with them. 'He's incredibly lonely,' he says.

'That man has never been lonely a day in his life.'

'Incredibly lonely.'

Julius has always had a soft spot for Yannick, Kathleen knows. A crush.

'He told me,' he says, 'about what they found out there. The bones and everything.'

'I thought he might.'

'Why didn't you?'

'Tell you?'

He nods.

'Because it's not her.'

'And you're certain of that, how?'

'Julius.'

He raises his hands, an apology. One of the reasons he is such a good friend. Lines even he won't cross.

'He wants to take me on a wild-goose chase out west.'

Julius sits up straighter in his chair, interest piqued. 'Oh?' he says. 'He didn't mention that.'

'It's ludicrous.'

'Says she,' he says, referring, no doubt, to Kathleen's many trips out west in the first decade-plus of Una's disappearance.

She tells him about the DNA test and the buried tooth. She tells him about Oliver Hanratty. She tells him that, even though it's irrelevant, she's leaving Una's baby tooth where it is, under the Miss Pepper phlox, where it's safe.

Julius says nothing for ages. It's possible he's fallen asleep, so Kathleen lifts her purse from the end of the bed and hooks the strap over her shoulder as she rises to leave. This day has taken everything out of her, as she suspected it would, and she wants to go to bed.

'Did Una ever do one of those helium balloon fundraisers at school?' he asks. His voice is croaky.

'Eh?' She sits back down.

'It's a charity thing. School children go door-to-door, begging sponsorship for helium balloons. They tag the balloons with their names and addresses and send them off into the sky. The idea is to see how far the balloons travel, to find out where they land. The hope is someone far away will find a grounded balloon and get in touch.'

'I don't know, maybe she did something like that.'

'I heard the most peculiar story recently, on the radio,' he says, 'about a little girl who took part in this fundraiser. She sent a bunch of balloons off, they all did it together at school, and a few weeks later she receives a letter from another little girl who lives hundreds of kilometres away. A balloon snagged in a tree in her backyard.'

Kathleen nods. The image of a balloon swirling up into an endless sky fills her head.

'Both girls, sender and receiver of said balloon, have the same name. Born in the same month of the same year. Both have brothers named Ted, or something like Ted. Maybe it was Brad. Anyhow, there are other, less impressive, similarities. They both favour the colour red, and kittens over puppies, what-have-you.'

Kathleen continues to nod.

'They've decided they're going to be best friends for ever.'

'That's what little girls do.'

'They think they've been chosen, singled out,' he says. 'They believe that they're special. Only the thing is, they're not.'

'They're not?'

'They're not. No one is.'

'On that point, I would agree.'

'You're not listening. You agree because you happen to dis-like most people, but this is a matter of statistics. Anything you can think of, from the mundane to the absurd, is bound to happen to someone somewhere. No one is special.'

'Julius, I'm tired. I'll pick you up in the morning.'

'Stay five more minutes. And pass me that water.'

A man pushing a cart pokes around the curtain and asks Julius if he would like a cheese sandwich. This man has the wormy look of one who only works the nightshift.

Julius closes his eyes, slowly, considering the sandwich, and finally tells the man no, thank you. With his eyes still closed, he continues: 'If you're standing at the side of a field of grass, and a single raindrop lands on a single blade of grass, you would think nothing of it. The drop has to land somewhere, right?'

'Are you asking me?' says the man with the cheese sandwich.

Julius opens his eyes. 'Sorry, no.' He looks at Kathleen and the man pushes his cart away. 'It has to land somewhere, right?' Julius repeats.

'Sure.'

'But what if you are that blade of grass in the field, among countless others, and that one raindrop, the only one, lands directly on you? You would conclude that Fortune has chosen you – for good or bad. And who could blame you? Of course you would think that you were special.'

'Why are you talking like the wise best friend in a movie?'

'Go on your wild-goose chase,' he says.

'You're delirious.'

'Bring me back a souvenir.'

'Shut up,' she says. And gives his bony knee a squeeze, a good and loving squeeze.

It could be that the party was a flop, or it could be that she's fresh out of painkillers, but Kathleen flounders through another bad night's sleep, and pours herself out of bed at five a.m. There's a new flavour to the pain in her empty socket, something novel, possibly something to be worried about. She ignores this.

A quick slurp of hot coffee as she changes the number on the fridge from 7969 to 7970, the thick black marker squawking at her, and she's out of the door by five thirty, preparing for the day's harvest. A patch of cockscomb celosia are ready for the clippers, as is a section of zinnias. She has an order to fill that includes black-eyed Susans, delphiniums and cosmos, and she'll have to push the zinnias hard so they don't go to waste. She needs Heather today, but is damned if she's going to pick up the phone.

This time of the morning? At this time of year? Bliss. Everything is washed out and lemony, soft. The birds are supremely birdy. At the wash station, Kathleen rinses her buckets in a solution of water, liquid detergent and bleach. If bacteria are present in the buckets, where the flowers will sit in water until they're delivered, the bacteria will be absorbed by the freshly cut stems and they won't draw water as efficiently. To this end, she also sterilizes her clippers. Every detail.

She scrubs everything with a rough brush, then rinses and scrubs again. As much as she scrubs, and rinses, and repeats, here is Yannick, taking up space in her head. He didn't say when he was leaving – she assumes today – and she just wants him gone. And wonders if he'll call to say goodbye.

When her business began to grow, when she quit the IDA ten years ago so she could grow flowers full time, she invested in the wash station and the cool house. Her cool house is no great shakes, just a ten-by-twelve-foot refrigerated shed she bought second-hand from a grocery store, and the wash station is nothing more than two industrial sinks and a wooden counter underneath a lean-to against the back of her house, but it's a set-up that works. It's clean and orderly. Her tools are well looked-after and the cool house keeps her flowers fresh for at least a day and a half before delivery. Over this, she has total control.

She looks around at what she's built and feels a sense of protectiveness that she hasn't experienced in a long time.

A house sparrow is warbling louder than the rest. He sounds worried, like a rusty swing getting faster and faster.

Even if she wanted to go on this . . . trip she cannot leave her farm.

She wraps the middle and index fingers of her left hand with white medical tape and begins with the delphiniums, selecting the stems where the bottom quarter of the flowers have opened. These particular blooms are an eye-catching, metallic periwinkle with shots of deep cobalt blue. They're practically luminescent and their pistils look like bees.

Sometimes, when she's doing this work, sometimes this is all there is. Colours so pretty you almost can't believe it. The smell of the dirt, the worms and the bugs and the mulch and the flowers, and the reassuring sun settling on her shoulders. This work binds her to the earth when the loss gets too big. When, like one of Julius's balloons, she's in danger of floating into oblivion.

Loss can do that. Cut the tether. Watch it go.

It's failing to help, though, this morning. The work isn't helping. She's distracted. Instead of pretty colours and whole-some smells and all that, the only things on her mind are Yannick and these stupid, stupid bones. It's not going to stop her, though; the flowers don't care. She goes in for the del-phiniums. It took her years to perfect the harvest cut. She cuts each stem with her dominant hand, while holding it with the other, then flips the stem upside down, pinching it between her ring and pinkie fingers. She then strips the foliage with the thumb and index finger. She can hold up to twelve stems in her two fingers and still strip foliage, and this way she doesn't have to stop with each cut to put a flower in the bucket. She used to drop flowers and damage them, wasting time. She used to get flashing cramps in her fingers, and get angry, and be covered with sores and minuscule, painful slits, like paper cuts, but now harvesting is an act that is both thoughtless and all-consuming. Perhaps a different kind of oblivion, then.

She's dropping stems today, though. And splitting them. Her wrists feel achy and vulnerable. She has to stand and stretch more than usual, her lower back and shoulders and neck. Even her sunhat, a dozen years old, soft and faded to no colour, feels tighter than it should.

She grinds through the delphiniums and carries the buckets, one at a time, to the cool house. Maybe she'll have a quick smoke before moving on to the cosmos. Ah, cosmos. The flower farmer's bread and butter.

She comes out of the cool house, lighting up, and Yannick is standing there, picking at the peppergrass patch. He pulls out a long stalk and rubs the seeds between his fingers.

'Smoke break?' he says.

'I thought you would've left already,' she says.

'I'm dropping the truck at a garage for a once-over,' he says. 'Then I'm gone.'

It's irksome to her, how well she knows this man, how much he has changed and how exactly the same he is. The bow to his small legs, almost childlike in a pair of faded jeans, which are probably the only pants he owns. The long slope of his fore-head, the angle of his neck and shoulders, still strong and broad, a little out of proportion to the rest of him. And just the way a person stands. This is how Yannick stands.

'I guess I wanted to say goodbye before I leave,' he says. 'You got time?'

She's got rows of flowers ready to be cut, that's what she has. Not time. Not a second, not for this.

'And I wanted to check you're okay and all that,' he says. 'I figure yesterday did not go the way you wanted it to.' He runs his fingers through the tall peppergrass, pulling and releasing it into a reluctant sway.

She is suddenly aware of how sweaty her hair is, how it falls in greasy hanks from under her sunhat, or of how fat and pale her knees are, like undercooked bread rolls.

He picks another stalk of peppergrass, snaps it in two, chews on the end, winks at her and does a little chuck-chuck sound out of the corner of his mouth, like he's spurring a horse. 'Tastes good,' he says, 'sweet.'

'It is,' she says.

'How's Julius?' he asks.

'He'll live.'

'How's the tooth?' he asks.

She tongues the gap, which aches very badly. 'The tooth is gone,' she says.

'Kathleen, you know what I mean. How is the pain?'

'Painful.'

Yannick puts his hands on his hips and takes a few steps alongside her perennial beds. She waits for him to make some sort of comment about how surprised he is, or impressed, by how well she's done, considering. Look what you've built, he's going to say. Something patronizing like that.

'What are those ones over there,' he says, pointing, 'those

yellow ones down there that look like my grandmother's swimming hat?'

'Zinnias.'

'Zinnias,' he says, puckering his lips. Nodding. The peppergrass still bobs from his mouth.

'Yannick. I'm sorry I'm not going on this trip with you.' She means this; she's not just saying it.

'Why the hell not?' he says. 'Why wouldn't you?'

Jesus. She walks back across the yard to the house, up the porch steps and into the kitchen. She plucks an apple out of the fruit bowl by the window and scrambles in the drawer for a paring knife. Peeling the apple at the sink, she lets the peel fall in one long and jerky spiral, hoping maybe he will just leave. Knowing he won't.

Back outside, Yannick is sitting on the bottom porch step so she sits there too. She slices a translucently thin white disc off the apple and eats it with the same hand that holds the knife, letting the slice fall apart on her tongue because she can't chew it.

'I could get us there in six days if we only stop to sleep,' he says.

'Why not just fly?' This is unfair to suggest (Yannick is afraid of very little, but he will not get on an aeroplane), but she's not in the mood to be fair.

'I've got a tank full of gas,' he says, ignoring her snark.

'Uh-huh.'

'It would do you good.'

'Don't do that,' she says.

He stares at his hands, worries at the cuticles of his thumbs with his middle fingers. This too, this tic. This is what Yannick does. 'You will do the test?' he says, looking at her with his face downcast, his eyes raised over the top rim of his grubby glasses. Either she is being scolded or warned. Neither is okay.

'I will,' she says. 'I promise.' She taps out the sign of the cross with the knife, and slices another crescent off the apple, claps it onto her tongue with the blade and lets it kind of fizzle there.

He's still looking at her.

'I'll call and make an appointment,' she says. 'Wherever it is I'm supposed to make an appointment, I'll call. Tomorrow.'

'Aren't you even curious?' he says. 'I would be there right now if I could, right now, today.'

'Where they—?' She stops, doesn't know what to call it.

'The bones place. I thought you might feel the same.'

'I don't.'

'Well.'

'Anyway, I can't leave my farm,' she says. She can, though, leave. It's nearly August, and August is a slow month. Wedding season is virtually over. People have flowers growing in their own gardens and the florists and grocery stores keep their stocks to a minimum. If she were to go away at any time of the year, this would be it. 'It's impossible,' she says.

'What about your gal? Your girl Heather?'

She gives him a look.

'Fair enough,' he says.

She comes to a bruise in the apple, begins to cut around the gamey flesh. 'Why don't you ask Sunny?'

'Because I am asking you. You've still got that number on the fridge, Kathleen. There is something wrong with that.'

'Driving across the country won't fix diddly-squat.' She flings the excised pulp into the grass.

Yannick looks a little heartbroken. A little hope-dashed. He has always been a sensitive man, a real empath. He takes things, other people's feelings, that don't belong to him, and he feels them too. But he will not take the number from her fridge. It belongs to her.

'I'm losing half a day here, Yannick. My cosmos are beginning to senesce.'

He looks at her with one eyebrow cocked.

She heaves herself up from the porch step. 'They're dying.'

He gets up too, brushes the seat of his jeans and smoothes his thin hair back from his ears. Pats his jeans pockets searching for his keys. He looks at her again and his eyes behind the drugstore old-man glasses are looming. 'Okay, then,' he says.

'Okay, then.'

'We'll keep in touch, though, eh? About the test?'

'You'll turn back, won't you?' she says.

'Eh?'

'Well, what if I do the test and you're halfway to wherever and it isn't her? You'll turn back.'

'Right,' he says, still patting his jeans pockets, still looking for his keys. 'Yes.' He hovers there just one moment longer, too long, then goes, crosses the lawn back towards where his truck is parked. She must have built him up in her mind, over time: he looks smaller than he should. Something is missing from him.

He stops in the middle of the yard, roughly the same spot as nineteen years ago, if, Kathleen thinks, memory serves. He turns back to her, raises both hands up by his face defensively, feigns a dodge, like she's about to throw a glass ashtray at his head. He chuckles, sadly, and she does too. He can be pretty funny, Yannick.

A can of mushroom soup for a late lunch. Kathleen is tired; her hands are tired. Even opening the can of soup feels heavy and seems to take an age.

Julius calls from the hospital to tell her they're keeping him for at least another day because he still has, in his words, the shits and dehydration. Minutes after she hangs up, the phone bleats again. All she wants to do is heat up her soup and eat it, but she could never ignore a ringing phone. Could be anyone.

'Hi, Kathleen. It's Sally,' says Sandra Hoffstead.

'I've already paid what I owe for the hall,' Kathleen says. Fine silver steam wisps up from the pot of mushroom soup.

'That's not why I'm calling.'

'Oh?'

'We're wondering what happened to the display case? Why it was moved?'

'That glass box thing?'

'Several irreplaceable items have been destroyed.'

As much as she would love to challenge Sandra's notion of irreplaceable, she thinks it smarter, at this moment, not to. 'It was in the way.'

'You didn't see the damage? All the broken pottery?'

'I didn't expect it to be so flimsy. I'm sorry.'

Sandra's shallow, indignant breaths beat down the phone line. Kathleen stirs her bubbling soup so it doesn't stick to the bottom of the pot.

'We also have to discuss the damage to the walls in the kitchen,' Sandra says.

'Uh-huh.' Kathleen stirs.

'And to the whiteboard by the front desk.'

'Give me a break, Sandra.'

'What the heck happened in the kitchen? There are all these gouges in the walls? This morning I picked cheese off the ceiling fan. It took me half the morning to get that cheese off.'

Kathleen explains how Heather exploded the lasagne and asks what's wrong with the whiteboard by the reception desk.

'You wrote on it in permanent marker.'

'Oh.'

'The kind that doesn't wipe off.'

'I know what permanent marker is.'

'Apparently you don't.'

'I'm sorry.'

'I had to throw it in the garbage.'

The mushroom soup suddenly comes alive, bubbling and foaming and blurbing over the edge of the pot like something primordial. Kathleen slides it off the heat.

'We haven't worked it out yet formally but the cost of repairing the walls alone is going to run us – you – upwards of a thousand dollars, with the painting and everything. There's also the replacement and mounting of a new whiteboard, and replacement of the shelving in the display case.'

'I thought you said that was irreplaceable.'

'The pottery. The pottery, Kathleen, not the case. I knew you'd be like this.'

'Like what?'

Sandra doesn't answer.

'I'm not giving you a thousand dollars,' says Kathleen. 'You must have insurance for this kind of thing. It was a party. Things get damaged.'

'You're paying for this, Kathleen. You're not talking your way out of it.'

With the phone tucked under her ear, Kathleen pours the soup into a bowl, spilling half of it on the counter, slopping some on her hand. 'You know what?' she says. 'This is real community support here. I can really feel the love.' She goes to the sink, turns on the cold water and thrusts her burning hand into the stream.

'Please, Kathleen, stop.' Sandra's voice is exhausted.

'What?' she says. 'Stop what?'

'We've all had it.'

'We who?'

'And wherever Una is,' Sandra says, and sighs, 'well, I'm willing to bet she's had it, too.' Sandra is silent, her silence as heavy and thick as liquid concrete pouring from the spout, the sound of someone realizing they've gone too far. And then she hangs up.

Kathleen lets the phone fall from her shoulder to the floor. She turns her hand under the water, the red welt now appearing on the web of skin between her thumb and forefinger. Her pulse hammers through her body, mostly in her mouth. She holds her hand under the water until it's numb, then turns and leans against the sink, holding her hand in a loose fist against her chest. The number on her fridge throbs as if it wants to suck her in.

She goes upstairs to Una's bedroom door. She does this on occasion, less now than before, but still. She opens the door, stops and leans against the frame, doesn't pass the threshold. She opens her eyes widely to the dim and sees that nothing is different. The dust is abundant and the air is stale. The bare mattress sags on the bed, the curtains are half closed. In this room, it's always twilight. Most of Una's things were packed into boxes in the basement years ago but the full-length mirror remains on the wall; some loyal books still hold each other up on the bookcase, painted purple, which Una did herself. You can still see a line of purple paint in the carpet if you know where to look. The lamp she'd had since she was a baby is still on the desk. Nothing special about it other than that it's still here. Maybe it works and maybe it doesn't. Kathleen has that feeling again of repeating a word over and over, losing its meaning.

IO

THE THING IS, Leigh is finished with Yannick. After twenty-some years of a life together, harmonious for the most part, she is gone. Not by design or conceit, Yannick has always been the one to do the leaving. And now he cannot see the road ahead without her.

His *grandmère*, the first woman of many he was to disappoint in his life, used to say, on the rare occasions he called, *tu me manques*, which is how Québeckers say *I miss you*. What it means, literally: you are missing from me. This is how it feels to be left. A piece of you taken; something tangible is gone. This is contrary to the action of *doing* the missing. Something has been cut from you, lifted away from you, and this way around is so much worse. He's not going to say this is like Una all over again: this is a different thing entirely. Hurts, though.

What happened was, he had been staying out of the house for a few weeks, finishing the final snags on their latest investment property, a two-bedroom town house three hours' drive from home. It takes him longer now to turn a place around, and he's become pernickety with the finer details. So maybe Yannick was gone for longer than he'd said he would be. And maybe he's not one of those people who turn their cell phones on every living second of the day.

One thing's for sure: an empty closet like the one he came home to last week, or the gaping drawers that once held her balled-up pairs of socks, her tangled underwear, emptiness like that has got its own gravitational pull.

Now, then. West is west, but you have a choice to make before you hit that straight shot across the country, and that is, which way are you going to get around the Great Lakes? There is no quick fix. No shortcut. Yannick can follow the northern shore of Lake Superior, but the roads up there are long and lonely, deep in the woods like uncharted rivers, nothing for days but trees, rock and water. Alternatively, he could shoot in between Superior and Lake Huron at Sault Ste Marie and into the United States. This route could be fifteen hours quicker but it would mean going through the border, which could be a problem.

His small bag is packed and flung into the back seat of the truck. Tank is full, and this should get him as far as Sudbury, a good stopping point for fuel. He knows of a roadside eatery there, or at least there once was, with picnic tables right on the bank of a pretty little creek.

His phone rings from deep in his bag, and he can't reach it. By the time he unbuckles his seatbelt, he's missed the call. Before he can look at the number, it rings again. He swipes the screen and puts the phone to his ear.

'Have you left?' Kathleen says.

'Pretty much,' he says.

'Can you wait? Just until the morning?'

'You coming?'

'I'll do the drive out, but I'm flying back.'

He doesn't ask. A U-turn like this, you don't ask.

PART TWO

The Road

11

EACH STEP LEADING up to Heather's front porch bows and
sinks with Kathleen's weight. The porch is scattered with toast
crusts and crayons and mismatched patio furniture. One white
hula-hoop with a red barber-shop swirl, bent out of shape.
Busy Lizzies crowd together in a hanging plastic pot.

Kathleen squints through the screen door into the day-dark
house. She smells coffee and burned toast and cleaning prod-
ucts. Can hear a series of thumps from somewhere upstairs.
She yoohoos, calls Heather's name. She is not a yoohoo person
and does not yoohoo a second time. She can see straight down
the front hall, through the kitchen to the back door, which is
open to the bright yard. She calls Heather's name again and
this time Heather answers, her voice carrying through the
house from out back.

Heather is sitting in the backyard, cross-legged on a blanket
with the baby. The baby is pulling at his sunhat, pulling it so
hard that he forces his head to the side, mashing his ear into his
shoulder.

'You're pulling in the wrong direction,' Kathleen informs
him, as she approaches. In one fist, she grips by its neck a bottle
of wine from the party.

The baby is purple, enraged, but eventually manages to
wrench the hat off his head, leaving his downy blond hair

furiously spiked. He looks at the infernal hat with disgust and throws it at nothing.

Kathleen tests the ground with her palm, finds it still damp from yesterday's deluge, and lowers herself to sit stiffly on the edge of the blanket, with her feet and legs out over the grass. She already feels enough of an interloper, and thinks it wise to take up as little space as she can. She has, after all, come begging.

'Is Julius better?' Heather asks. She reaches for the sunhat and jams it back on the baby's head.

'Fully recovered,' Kathleen says. She called Julius just before coming here, to arrange to take him home, but he had already taken himself in a taxi.

'I never saw anybody go that white before,' Heather says, putting her hand to her chest as if she's shocked by this all over again. 'I thought he was dead.'

'Indigestion,' says Kathleen, shrugging.

Heather nods, eyes to the ground, absentmindedly kneading the baby's milky thigh. Is there anything in the world harder to resist than a baby's milky thigh?

Kathleen takes a deep breath and begins to speak. Tells Heather everything, as well as Yannick's decision to drive to the other side of the country. 'I'm going to go with him,' she says.

'I've never been to the west coast,' says Heather. 'I've never really left here, come to think of it.'

'I can only go if you'd be willing to manage the farm on your own. I'll be gone ten days, tops.' Still strangling the wine by the neck, Kathleen holds out the bottle to Heather, like a baton in a relay race. 'I'm sorry about yesterday,' she says.

Heather accepts the bottle and looks over her shoulder, back at the house. Kathleen looks too, expecting to see Dave's smug face looming in one of the windows.

The baby, only now realizing the hat is back on his head, goes to battle with it again. He pulls and yanks, his sharp eyes glinting and pleading with Kathleen. She leans over and plucks the hat from his head, and frisbee spins it over the grass.

'He'll burn,' Heather says, and gets up to retrieve the hat.

'I couldn't bear to watch him suffer.'

The baby bellows and raises his arms to his mother, who dared to leave the sanctity of their blanket.

'You can manage the farm?' Kathleen asks. 'Will you?'

Heather, baby in arms now, runs her tongue over her teeth, sucks like she's trying to loosen something caught, and in that gesture Kathleen reads that nothing is yet forgiven.

'I would pay you more, obviously.'

'I know,' Heather says.

'It's just watering and deadheading. There's a van coming tomorrow for a delivery, and another again on Tuesday. Nothing complicated.'

'No, that's not complicated,' Heather says, maybe sarcastically. Maybe not. 'I'd have to talk it over with Dave,' she says. Her chin, perhaps, is raised just a little in defiance. It's hard to tell.

The baby, one hand clutching Heather's shoulder, turns his round face to Kathleen and shudders, his eyes full of contempt.

'Of course,' she says. 'You have to talk it over with Dave.' And to the baby, she says: 'Little man, I was only trying to help.'

He drives out his lower lip and cries.

And a few hours later, Heather calls Kathleen at home and says she would very much like to look after the farm on her own.

*

One thing Yannick and Kathleen could always agree on was an early start. In the morning, he picks her up at ten minutes to six, ten minutes earlier than they'd agreed. She's already waiting outside, one small bag packed so tightly it's rock hard, enough clean underwear for ten days. In fact, she's been outside since five thirty, standing in the yard. Smoking, obviously. Nothing happening but the birds singing at the tops of their lungs, competing for stage. A white sky, wet grass, honeyed air. In the front window of the house, one of Una's leftover candles from the defunct party. And in Kathleen's pocket, a battered, spiral-bound notebook she uses for grocery lists. She's torn out old lists and written Una's number on the first page, today, this last Monday of July, being 7971 days since Una disappeared.

An hour and a half into the drive, Kathleen feels she's made a mistake.

Even the way Yannick reclines in his seat and guides the wheel with one hand, stroking the wheel with his thumb, the way he rests his other hand just at his crotch, even this irks her. Seventy-three years old and he's still running on hubris. Here they are, hurtling at a hundred and twenty klicks an hour, and there he is, looking like he's going thirty. Of course, when she first met him, when everything was fresh and everything was alluring, like a thickly iced chocolate cake all for her, it was marvellous to sit next to him at dangerous speeds, those arms, those nimble hands on the wheel. She would look at his fingers and think about where they'd pressed into her, maybe minutes before. Oh, the backs of his hands, how smooth they were, and the colour of sand.

Kathleen looks at him in a way, she hopes, he cannot tell she's looking at him. As if she's looking past him and out of his window, as if the scenery were different on his side of the road.

Here is this man, again.

A soft blue unimposing sky lies over crisp, golden hay fields, which are buzzed down to stubble. Hay bales are deposited here and there, reminding Kathleen of life-sized games, the bales like discarded playing pieces.

Other fields are dotted with cows all ignoring each other.

Una, after summer camp one year, gleefully asked them in the car on the way home, from the back seat: 'You know how to tell which way the wind is blowing?'

Yannick and Kathleen, front seat, in unison: 'How?'

'From the cows.'

'How, baby?' Yannick had asked.

'They stand with the wind behind their butts because they like the smell of their own farts,' Una said.

Now, looking out of the window, Kathleen says: 'Whenever I see cows I remember what Una told us about cows.'

'I don't remember,' Yannick says, a half-smile on his lips.

'You do,' she says. 'The fart thing.'

He tilts his head, thinking. His smile widens and he nods.

For a few kilometres, they say nothing. Yannick, always the more talkative, the more sociable between the two of them, is just as comfortable with silence. He is, Kathleen thinks, just about the gentlest person she has ever known. And he loves harder than anyone she has ever known. She's always believed this is because he never had much in the way of parental love: what he missed out on growing up, he wanted to create for himself.

She met his father only a handful of times, never his mother, who died when Yannick was a teenager. About his mother, of whom he spoke very little, Kathleen knows this: she had a problem with booze and with staying put.

His father, Guy, was born in Québec, brought by logging to Ontario when he was twenty, which was where he met and married Yannick's mother. Kathleen doesn't remember much but she liked Guy a lot. Every third word was 'fuck' or '*plotte*', which apparently is very bad, and he ate raw onions as a side to his dinner. Not slices of raw onion, but whole. He would bite into an onion as if it were an apple. And she remembers that, while he wasn't very loving, or vocal, and though he had sunken eyes and a face like old bark, nicked and scarred, he wasn't an unkind man.

You can have a face like old bark, nicked and scarred, and be kind. You can be the gentlest of men, but still harbour a kind of darkness.

The first time Kathleen went to see Yannick, in the apartment over that ex-con's garage, she brought a six-pack because she thought that would impress him. But he didn't touch it. Told her he stayed away from booze, which he mostly did. They kept none in the apartment and later, when they had Una, they never went out. The rare times he did drink, it would be with the guys he painted houses with, especially in the summer. A cold beer at the end of a sweaty day. Those few times after drinking, he came home and his face was dark and slack. He looked old. He would want sex but wouldn't look Kathleen in the eye. It turned her on, to be treated like an object, to be desired with no trace of love . . . it was hot. But it wasn't him.

As a kid, Yannick was a schoolyard rumbler and, when he was older, fell into a couple of harmless fistfights in bars. And then there was the big one that happened in the ravine in Toronto, which was – there's no way to sugarcoat this, Kathleen knows – an assault. This one landed him in Mimico Correctional Centre for eighteen months.

Kathleen only ever saw one fight. They were in a bar called Shawnigan's; it was somebody's birthday. She can't now remember whose.

Shawnigan's was a dark hole suited only for drinking cheap, watered-down beer and dancing to songs you would never admit to liking when you were sober. It had a parquet dance floor with a real bounce to it, and in those days, Kathleen loved to dance. You wouldn't think it to look at her now, but she did.

Pitchers were half-price and everyone was having a good time. Kathleen was dancing with a couple of girls she hardly knew, passing between them damp cigarettes. The cigarettes tasted like the other women's lipstick. The room was all smoke and beer logos in neon and Bruce Springsteen, when someone burst in the door yelling about a fight in the street. Kathleen looked to the booth where Yannick had been sitting moments before, which was now empty.

By the time she pushed her way outside, a circle of braying fools had already formed around Yannick and the other guy in the middle of the road. Yannick had the guy, who was twice his size, in a headlock, and the man was bleeding heavily from his nose.

Kathleen begged the men around her to break it up, but they were fizzing. In the bar, everyone had been beautiful, but out here, they were greasy and ugly.

Finally, the bartenders came outside and deputized some meatheads to break it up. Yannick's T-shirt was stretched and ripped at the neck and Kathleen remembers thinking she'd pulled that shirt out of the dryer in the laundromat that very day, folded it carefully and piled it with all her husband's soft clothes while Una slept in the stroller.

Yannick didn't speak until they were in bed. She'd asked him to take a shower, to wash off the other man's blood, and his skin was still soft and warm from the hot water. His thick, bristled hair was damp. He told her he'd been introduced to the other man a bunch of times, and that each time, the guy acted like they'd never met.

'So?' she said.

'It's rude,' he said. 'It's ignorant.'

She worshipped him, she was so young. She didn't know what to do with the shame so she tried for sex, but he turned his back to her.

Alcohol, she realized, inspired either fucking or fighting, but never both.

Drive a solid four hours north on Highway 400 and you get to a mid-sized town called Sudbury, which Yannick has deemed will be their first stop. This highway is two lanes of nothing, with Georgian Bay to the west. It's not the first time they've driven this stretch together. In fact, this is the very road that leads to Una's old summer camp in French River. They used to deliver her to camp, then go back to their separate homes and wait for the letters she would write, sometimes pencilled on silver scraps of birch bark, so they would be illegible, with only the odd, just-about-readable word: *fire*, *spidery*, *itchy*, *friend*, *sick*. Then they would pick her up two weeks later and she would be brown as a berry, hair smelling of lake. Her ankles swollen with insect bites, her knees speckled with scabs and her wrists wrapped in embroidered bracelets. All the colours. And she would be just there, right there, singing in the back seat, crooning about country roads taking her home and fixing holes in buckets and darling Clementines.

The windows would always be wide open because Kathleen and Yannick both chain smoked, even in the car. Especially in the car. And maybe they even joined in on the songs, what words they knew.

They were lousy at being married, Kathleen thinks, but pretty good at being divorced (until they weren't).

This road hasn't changed, up here; not a lot changes up here. Trees and more trees and endless lakes. Stout roadside pines and wild grasses, bone-white deadfall and tall birches fluttering. Every now and then a lone single-storey house, or a washed-out gas station and variety store with a bleached, cardboard ice-cream-cone-shaped sign in the window.

Kathleen is not going to make it as far as Sudbury without stopping. 'I need the bathroom, Yannick.'

'Are you kidding? We've barely hit the road.'

She gives him a long look.

He sighs, deeply.

There's nothing for several minutes, and Kathleen feels a dangerous, wet prickle. 'Yannick.'

'Can you make it to Parry Sound? There's nowhere to stop.'

'Just pull over.'

He slows the truck on the gravel shoulder alongside a high wall of granite and she gets out. Some long-ago rebel has graffitied a message on the rock with blue spray paint but the lettering is so old the markings no longer say anything. There is no shelter for a sixty-five-year-old woman to drop her drawers and pee.

'You picked a great place to stop,' she calls.

He rolls down his window and sticks his head out. 'Eh?'

'There's nowhere to go.'

'You told me to pull over.'

'Yes, but . . .'

'I'm not looking,' he says,

'I do have a scrap of dignity.'

He laughs.

She repeats this quietly to the apathetic rock face: 'I do have a scrap of dignity.' She walks the length of the granite wall until it tapers to the level of her shins, when she can clamber over its shoulder into the cover of trees. Kicking off her sandals, she shimmies her shorts and underwear down to just above her knees, grips the smooth neck of a young birch for support and squats. She hasn't done this for decades. There is the *shoom* of a single car passing on the highway and then there is nothing. And then the sounds that spring out of nothing: the cricks of insects with articulated legs inching across dry leaves. The chirrup and echo of birds. Heat beats on rock that is scaled with silver-green lichen. Stems of wild rye graze the undersides of her bare thighs. When she stands, her pulse drums in the empty hole in her mouth. It hurts a little more than it should.

'When was the last time you did that?' she says to Yannick, when she gets back into the truck. 'When's the last time you peed outside?'

He pulls out sharply, directly in front of an approaching car. The driver swerves, an irate face in a passing window, followed by the receding scold of his horn.

'Yannick. You couldn't wait?'

'The last time I pissed outside,' he says, accelerating so fast that her head bounces off the headrest, 'was this morning.'

*

They drive twice around the outskirts of Sudbury because Yannick is inexplicably determined to eat at this one place where he once ate a hundred years ago. Nowhere else will do.

'I don't see why it matters, Yannick. We'll just get some fast food.'

'I know it's somewhere,' he says. He's hunched solid over the wheel, peering ahead for some known landmark. Some *aha* turn-off.

Finally, down a nondescript road, he finds it, and grins at Kathleen, either relieved that it's still there or that he hadn't remembered wrongly in the first place. It's just a greasy chip truck, propped on cinderblocks on a weedy gravel lot. Next to the truck, a dark brook cuts deeply through scrubby brown meadow. Couple of peeling picnic tables. A skulk of teenagers commands one, ignoring this old couple utterly and completely.

Food is good, though. They have grilled cheese sandwiches and thick-cut chips, even though it's not yet eleven. Kathleen chews with gusto on the side of her mouth that doesn't hurt; Yannick barely touches his meal. She considers asking him, because they have a very, very long way to go, why he insisted on this place if he isn't even hungry. But it's obvious why, because he remembers it from some other time; it would be unkind to ask.

When they finish eating, Yannick takes a short walk alongside the brook, saying his knees and lower back lock up if he stays in the same position for too long.

Between her bladder and his joints.

A Plan

IT'S NOT POSSIBLE to judge distance travelled on a forested and erratic dirt road, so our girl has no sense of how far she is from the main highway. The truck bounces across a low, rickety bridge over a noisy river and, not long after that, swerves into a driveway concealed behind a curve in the road.

Our girl has a plan. As soon as the truck stops, she's going to jump and run.

She feels a little bit foolish, but more afraid of where this stranger is taking her than foolish, so . . . She's secured both of her backpack straps over her shoulders, and has even clicked together and tightened the chest strap that runs between the two. She's braided her hair. Tied it into a thick bolt at the base of her neck.

The driveway falls into shadow under shaggy, closed-in hemlocks, and at the end of it sits a tidy white house. Unexpectedly perfect as a toy. A stalk of sun shines down on the house and on the lupins and hydrangea that grow in abundance in well-kept beds.

Some kind of leggy, wire-haired dog comes cantering out of the open front door, barking hoarsely. The truck pulls up in front of the house and before its wheels stop turning, our girl is hurdling her body over the tailgate. Right leg over first, and then left. But what she doesn't know is that, as she raises her left foot, it hooks into a loop of yellow nylon rope. When she throws her weight over the back of the truck, the loop tightens on her foot and instead of a clean catapult to freedom, her body seizes like an emergency brake has been pulled. Then she is dropped, hard, to the ground. First, her right palm and then her forearm skid across the packed dirt, leaving behind a microscopic trace of skin and blood; then her chin pangs into the ground and her teeth clack percussively. As she pushes herself up, dazed and tasting blood, her left knee collapses because of the awkward twist enforced on it. She limp-runs down the driveway, shaking the fall out of her head, pushing the back of her hand against the raw welt rising on her chin. Her braid uncoils and flumps against her shoulders, a dead weight.

Two wet paws land on her shoulder blades and scrabble down her backpack. Humid, meaty breath on her neck.

'Dog! Get the hell off her!' Our girl turns around and sees a woman about her mother's age coming across the lawn, clapping her hands at the dog, which is now running in slanted circles and yapping its tiny head at nothing.

This woman, of clementine-orange hair with silver roots, wears a housecoat over thin pyjama bottoms. Her feet are bare. She is apologizing for the dog, saying he's just a big old love-bear, as our girl continues to back down the driveway, now unsure as to whether this is comedy or horror.

The driver, the man with the soft face who could be twenty or could be forty, is unloading the electrical equipment out of the back of his truck.

He calls over his shoulder. 'Figured I'd offload some of this stuff,' he says. 'So you can sit up with me. Thought you might be getting cold.'

'I don't need the ride any more,' our girl calls to him, almost tripping on her own feet as she walks backwards.

He stands there with his arms cradling an indeterminate black box, which has wires noodling from its exposed back to the ground. His bready face has collapsed a little. 'Course you need the ride,' he says. 'I didn't mean to scare you. I just wanted to . . .' He lifts the black box to illustrate what he just wanted to do.

'You didn't scare me. I just don't need the ride any more.'

'Well, that's no good,' he says. 'I've left you worse off than I found you.'

'You want some breakfast?' asks the woman, coming towards her, her hand proffered for a shake. She introduces herself, gives a name that our girl doesn't bother to register. Says something about nettle tea, kippers and homemade cheese scones. Her eyes are very blue – sun-on-the-water glinty blue.

'I don't eat breakfast,' she says. At this point, the only move seems to be to turn and keep walking. She can't run: all she can do is create distance between herself and this house. The dog accompanies her down the darkened, hemlock-lined driveway back to the road, ignoring completely the calls of his mistress. He stops at the spot where the driveway meets road, and gallops back.

Ears cocked for the rumble of the truck coming from behind (which doesn't happen, and won't, because the driver is now ensconced in his mother's sunny kitchen with a plate of cheese scones lathered in butter, having refused the kippers and the nettle tea), she continues down the road, now patched with more sun. As she walks, the screw of pain in her knee tightens. At the bridge, she crabs down the bank to the noisy river and washes the blood and dirt off the palms of her hands, finger-tweezes the few minuscule stones embedded in the skin. She can't be seen from the road here, and feels safe.

She cups cool water into her hands and splashes her face generously, and leans back against the bank, resting her head on the ground. Scratches the mosquito bite behind her ear. Up through the thickly coated coniferous boughs (some branches as stiff and orderly as soldiers, others like the soft, drooping arms of her father's old parka) there are geometric fragments of blue sky. The water caresses her face on its journey down her cheeks and over the border of her jawline to her neck, and continues to soothe her in this way until it warms and runs out of itself.

12

WHEN YANNICK TELLS Kathleen that driving through the US could save them a day she says, 'Well, why don't we do that, then?'

They discuss this as they're passing a nowhere town called Desbarats. Kathleen argues that American gas is cheaper, which he cannot deny.

'There could be problems for me at the border,' he says.

'Oh, get off it, Yannick.' She laughs. 'Like you're some kind of outlaw.'

'I don't know how long these things stick,' he says. 'I'm pretty sure it's permanent.'

'Why would they even check? It was a thousand years ago, outlaw.'

Kathleen was always a bit of a bully.

Yannick doesn't do so well with bullies, or with threat. There was a time when threat would rouse him to fight.

Summer 1964, he is twenty-two years old and living in Toronto, working a contract on a construction site downtown. End of the work day, he and a couple of the guys from the site sprawl back against pallets of masonry and pass around a brace of 26ers until they're empty. He hadn't realized how far gone he was until he stood up, and then fell over, determined to go back to where he was staying, sleeping on a couch belonging to a friend of a friend, for fifteen bucks a week.

He's only got snapshots of what happened next. It was buttery light, middle-of-summer evening light. So humid you could take a bite out of the air and suck on it. Yannick doesn't remember getting on the Carlton streetcar but he does remember pulling the stop cable to get off it. Walking north up Parliament and wandering first into St James cemetery, and then into a ravine. He remembers the pale pink granite of a gravestone and how it sparkled, and how it made him think of his own mother's gravestone because of the asymmetrical cut of the stone. He remembers the sun setting in a puddle. He remembers a glass vase with dead flowers rattling around in it.

The ravine was a deep gash of forest right there in the middle of the city, steep-walled and dark. He remembers being dragged into it, stumbling down the path. Much darker inside the ravine, and slightly cooler. Nothing but trees and the ground covered with dead leaves.

He saw a guy sitting on a log, just where the path levelled out. At first he thought it was one man sitting alone, but then the guy seemed to writhe and to split into two, and it was two people kissing, a guy and a girl. But Yannick was confused. He was staring, ogling, trying to work this out in his rye-soaked brain. His eyes would have been dark and unpleasant as he stumbled closer to get a better look. She stood up and called him a pervert. Her voice clanged with fear.

The guy moved on him fast. Yannick remembers the mammal heat, the unexpected intimacy, the body smell of a stranger standing close.

He remembers kicking the guy's head, twice. The unstoppable momentum, the weighty swing of his steel-toed boot.

Yannick ran until he knew the way home, tripping over his

own feet and bloodying the palms of his hands. The guy he was staying with took him to the police station and stood by him as he turned himself in. For a couple of hours, Yannick believed he had killed that boy, and when it turned out he had not, everything after that was easy. The boy spent two months with his jaw wired shut and saw double out of his left eye for many months more, but he was alive.

In court, the couple testified that it was all Yannick's doing, that he had jumped them from behind, pounced out of the trees, like some kind of wildcat. That was not what happened. But what did happen was eighteen months in prison.

Now, Yannick has to make a decision fast, pulling into the town of Sault Ste Marie. The signs point either south to the international bridge and across the border to the US, or north, the long road up and around Lake Superior and Thunder Bay.

'Come on, outlaw,' Kathleen teases, hitching her thumb to the left, to the bridge.

'The border line could be hours,' he says.

'Saves us a whole day, Yannick, and a lot of money.'

He flips his indicator to the left and follows the signs to the border. They pay the bridge toll on the Canadian side and hit the bridge, which takes them up, up into the windy sky, the expanse of this old steel town spreading out behind them, a power station and steel factories to the west and beyond that Lake Superior. Directly below them flows St Mary's River, industrious with rapids and locks.

Yannick was expecting a dead line of vehicles but the bridge is free of traffic, the expansion joints in the tarmac beating steadily under their tyres. They come up and over the suspension bridge and eventually get to a wall of Customs bays. They wait ten, fifteen minutes, and Yannick feels an increasing grip down his neck and across his chest. It's the reproachful no-nonsense signage and officialdom of flashing lights. It's not being believed in a court of law. When it's their turn at the window, Yannick passes their IDs into the chubby hands of a Customs agent. With a vacant expression, as if he's barely paying attention (but clearly is), he asks the particulars: what is your purpose of travel, how long are you staying, et cetera.

Wound up and fidgety, Yannick begins to explain what they are actually doing, why they're driving across the country. In his peripheral, Kathleen is shaking her head.

The Customs agent squints at Yannick's photo and squints at Yannick and then back at the photo.

'You're driving across the country to see where they dug up your missing daughter?'

'We don't know yet.'

'You don't know what, yet?' Monotone.

'If it's her or not.'

The agent stares at him. 'And you say you're passing through the United States just to save time.'

'That is what I said, yes.'

'No need to be rude with me, sir,' he says.

Yannick stares ahead, both hands still on the wheel.

The agent considers his identification a moment longer. Leans closer to the window and squints at Kathleen. 'Park your vehicle over there, please, sir.' He points with a pole-straight finger, the fat bunching white at the knuckle, to a long, single-storey building with mirrored windows.

They pull into a parking bay next to the building and Yannick, not wanting to let go of the wheel, turns his face to Kathleen. 'I told you,' he says.

'You didn't have to tell him the whole bleeping story, did you?'
He says nothing.

'Oh, come on,' she says. 'He doesn't know you have a record.'

Yannick and Kathleen are asked to vacate the truck while three agents circle it like hornets, checking the glove compartment, the back seat, the contents of their bags and the few items in the covered flatbed. Yannick is asked to explain why he has a fishing rod.

'For fishing,' he says.

And why he has a toolbox.

'For when things break.'

One of them, a bald kid with a razor-burned neck, flowery with acne, flips slowly through an old sketchbook that Yannick didn't even know was abandoned under the back seat. He turns each page as if pulling back a private curtain, his eyes landing on whatever it is he sees with no emotion at all – Yannick has no memory of what is drawn in that book.

They're brought into the single-storey building and made to sit side by side against the wall while their credentials are checked. A uniformed man at a long counter ignores them with well-practised proficiency.

Eventually, the pimply kid who manhandled Yannick's sketchbook comes out to where they're waiting and hands them their IDs, and tells them they will not be crossing into the United States of America today due to Yannick's criminal record. Thank you very much and you may take the bridge back to where you came from.

'There must be a statute of limitations on something like this?' Kathleen says, standing up. 'That was fifty years ago.'

'He needs to apply for a waiver, ma'am,' he says, pointing them to the door.

Yannick drives back across the bridge to the Canadian side in silence, and there is a lot more of that same silence while they are made to wait another hour in an almost identical single-storey building once Yannick explains why they were denied entry. The Canadian agents check to see if there are any warrants out for his arrest.

'I'm so sorry, Yannick,' Kathleen says, when they're finally on the road they should have taken, up the north-eastern shore of Lake Superior. There is genuine sorry in her tone. About fifteen minutes later, she knuckles him lightly in the arm. 'On the bright side,' she says.

'Yes?'

'Outlaw. Confirmed.'

It is seven hours give or take up Highway 17 towards the city of Thunder Bay, where the road will eventually take its leave of the mighty Lake Superior. Because of the time wasted at the border, they won't make it as far as Thunder Bay and have decided to spend the night in a town called Wawa. Kathleen is at the wheel. Twenty years ago, she was a nervous driver. Yannick can't remember her ever volunteering to drive on the highway. She doesn't seem so nervous now.

It is awfully pretty up here. Pine trees and spruce and white birch, grey and pink granite with black tiger stripes.

The water is vast and the sky is immeasurable and the insult at the border is fading into the south. The lake is so calm it's got that look of thickness to it, like warm milk. There are those clouds, Yannick doesn't know what they're called, but the ones that look like they've been spread across the sky with a spatula. The sky is saying: 'Look how big I am.'

For hours there is nothing but this water, this cloud, this

rock, this tree. How deep, how wide, how plentiful. How easily a person could get lost in this country. How misguided to think a person could ever be found.

The tarmac rushes underneath. They are stationary and the world speeds by so fast, it doesn't even notice them.

They are missing from the world.

Of course, the first time they went west, they flew. Kathleen had received a phone call from a girl called Mariella, a friend of Una's, telling her she had not seen or heard from Una in two days. She was wondering if maybe Una had just gone home, because she, Mariella, had the feeling Una was thinking of doing that, of going back home. Kathleen told her to call the police, then she and Yannick, along with Sunny, got the first available flight, which was the next day. This was only the third time Yannick had flown, the first two instances being an impromptu trip to Calgary with a bunch of guys to watch a play-offs hockey game, the return-flight turbulence putting him off flying for life. He spent this flight to find his daughter with his eyes firmly on the seat in front of him.

The plane coasted down into Vancouver and Kathleen stood and opened the overhead baggage flap before the seatbelt sign flickered off, and was flatly reprimanded over the intercom. They drove onto a ferry bound for Vancouver Island, and once the ferry churned across the Strait of Georgia and berthed and the ramp came down, they disembarked and continued straight across from the east coast of the island to the west. Stopping only once for the necessaries, where they all, Yannick included, experienced their first giant cedars.

Those colossal trees? Ancient, watchful. Awesome trees blanketed with thick and shabby moss, trees that drew your eyes up, up, up. Yannick approached one and stood as close as he could and held it. He stood there, like a fool, embracing a tree, and he could feel it, something deep in this place. Something bigger than him and something even bigger than the daughter who was not in any of the places she was supposed to be, something bigger than his fear. He pushed his face into the bark. Bark that smelt sweet and pulled away from the trunk in soft, meaty strings. He pushed his face into the bark and he felt the pulse of that tree, and he asked for help.

Pretty much the edge of the world, out there. You do things you normally would not.

They didn't get to Tofino until after ten o'clock that night so there was not a lot they could do other than check into their motel, which was on the main highway into town. Yannick didn't sleep that night and neither did Kathleen, and with the time difference, three hours earlier than home, she was knocking on his door at four thirty in the morning. The three of them sat together and brewed undrinkable coffee from the packets you find in cheap motel rooms. They were to meet the police at eight a.m. so they had hours to stare at the walls until then. With bad coffee coating his tongue and the tick of the clock in his head, Yannick suggested they get back in the car and go somewhere else. Anywhere else. He could no longer wait for time that was unwilling to do them the favour of passing quickly.

This was the in-between time. No shape to this thing yet. There was still a high chance that Una was somewhere they hadn't considered. They got back in the car and turned down roads at random, but in Tofino, a tiny fishing town clinging to the edge of a peninsula in the Pacific, most roads spit you out at the coast.

And so there they were, wandering the biggest beach Yannick had ever seen. Air thick and distorted with spray and salt. Sun just coming up over the hills to the east. The sound of the edge of the world was like the rush of blood heard through a stethoscope. Even the sound of the motherfucking Pacific Ocean heaving itself up onto the sand, pulse after pulse after pulse, was kind of far-away, surreal. Nothing on that beach at dawn but Kathleen and Yannick and his boy Sunny, and some deflated purple jellyfish drying on the sand. Bone-white driftwood logs cross-hatched one over the top of another. Bunch of birds. Yannick picked up a gummy strand of kelp and twisted it between his fingers as they walked across that tide-rippled sand. These were the last numb and merciful hours before Una was truly missing.

They went straight from the beach to the Royal Canadian Mounted Police detachment in the central part of town, and were met at the door by a woman, forty-ish in age and tidy as a pin in uniform, who introduced herself as Sergeant Zoric.

Barely enough room in her office, and a tinted view of the boats in the harbour and the mountainous islands of Clayoquot Sound. Sunny put himself directly behind Yannick's chair, and leaned against the wall. Yannick could feel on his back the heat of Sunny's fingers curled tightly around the frame of his chair. He reached behind himself and gripped Sunny's calf; maybe he was making sure that Sunny, at least, was real. Was there.

Sergeant Zoric had a long face and prominent jaw, alarmingly blue eyes (*surprise blue*, if you had to give the colour a name) and thick, dusty brown hair balled neatly in a bun. She spoke in a low, hardened voice.

This was day four. The last time anyone saw Una was the Saturday, the second Saturday in June, and now it was the Tuesday. The problem was, as far as Yannick could tell, Una was an adult with no fixed address, so the police were not out pounding the streets with guns blazing. Sergeant Zoric felt strongly that Una would resurface within a few days.

'She tried to call me,' Kathleen said. 'It's on the machine, the operator. She was trying to make a collect call.'

'When was this?' asked Zoric.

'On Saturday. I'm three hours ahead, though, so . . .' Kathleen looked up, her eyes fluttering as she tried to remember. 'It must have been about four o'clock her time.'

'Can you get me the exact time? You still have it on your machine?'

'Yes,' Kathleen said.

'Your daughter is currently unemployed?' Zoric asked.

'She has a job,' Kathleen said, shifting in her seat.

'At a grocery store,' Yannick said.

From behind him, Sunny spoke, his voice unsteady: 'She quit that job.'

Yannick turned to look at him. 'No, she didn't,' he said. 'She never said that.'

'She quit, Dad. Like a month ago or something.'

'How would you know?' Kathleen asked.

'Email,' Sunny said. He looked at Sergeant Zoric. 'She told me not to tell them she quit,' he said, his voice high and apologetic.

'Did she tell you why?' Sergeant Zoric asked him. 'Why she wanted to keep it a secret?'

Sunny started to jig his leg; Yannick could feel it through the chair.

'This is important,' Sergeant Zoric said.

'She knew Kathleen would be pissed,' Sunny said.

Kathleen sighed. 'Well, I . . .' she said. She twisted in her seat so she was facing Sunny. 'She said that? What exactly did she say?'

'I can't remember exactly.'

'Approximately, then.'

'Basically that you were always pissed at her about changing her jobs and that.'

Kathleen took a rough breath and shuddered it out, and settled back into her chair.

'Sorry,' Sunny whispered.

'This is helpful,' said Zoric. 'If she's – I'm not saying this is what you said – but if she tends to be a little unreliable? Frequently changes her mind? This is good for us. She has no commitments here. Nothing to get back for right away.'

'She's not unreliable,' said Kathleen.

'Does she like to go to parties?' Zoric asked.

'Sure,' said Kathleen. 'She likes parties. She likes being with people.'

'Would she, say, party for a few days? Go on a bender?'

'She isn't like that,' Kathleen said.

'You sure?' Zoric looked between Kathleen and Yannick, and up to Sunny.

'Kathleen is right. She wouldn't do that,' said Yannick.

'And nothing like this has happened before?'

'No,' said Yannick.

'She could have gone fruit-picking over in Penticton,' the sergeant said. 'Popular job this time of year for people like Una. Good money.'

'People like Una?' Kathleen said.

'Transients,' said Sergeant Zoric.

Kathleen shifted in her seat again, bumped her knee against the sergeant's desk. The fingers of both her hands were dead-white and folded into a tight weave. 'That seems like a shot in the dark,' she said.

'Not around here, it isn't,' said Zoric. 'It's very common. People head out that way to pick peaches.'

'Peaches?'

'It's very common.'

'You said that already,' said Kathleen.

'She would've told us,' Yannick said. 'She would've told us if she was going somewhere else.'

'As far as I can see, she didn't say anything about quitting her job at the Co-op, either,' Sergeant Zoric said.

Another police officer shuffled sideways into the office and set down three plastic cups of water, spilling a little on the desk.

'What's being done, exactly?' Yannick asked. 'What should we be doing?' He picked up one of those cups of water and it buckled between his fingers, the plastic was so flimsy.

Sergeant Zoric explained that they were interviewing Una's friends, and talking to people in town. Mariella, the friend who had initially called and who, it turned out, lived with Una, had told them that Una got an email from an old friend at home, and she had been surprised to hear from him, and she was meeting him that Saturday evening at a restaurant called the Nootka.

'I've been to the Nootka,' Sergeant Zoric said, 'and no one saw her there on Saturday. Nor was anyone waiting for her.'

'This is unreal,' Kathleen said. Her eyes were red and wet, and her voice trembled.

'Any idea who she could have been meeting?' Zoric asked.

'It could have been Oliver,' said Kathleen, wiping the bottoms of her eyes. 'Her old boyfriend.'

'He lives on the other side of the country,' Yannick said.

'He can get on a plane,' she said. 'You said old friend, didn't you?' Kathleen asked Sergeant Zoric. 'You said she was surprised to hear from him?'

'What's his full name?' Zoric asked, pen poised over notebook. 'Have you got a number for him?'

Kathleen delivered a number, rote, as if she dialled it every day.

Yannick looked at her, surprised.

'So what?' she said. 'Una slept over there a lot. I know his number.' She put a hand on the desk and said: 'Oliver is a bit, you know . . .' And she swirled her fingers at her ear.

'What do you mean by that?' Zoric asked.

'He was a little obsessed with Una,' Kathleen said. 'For years, you know, puppy dog at her heels.'

'I don't think that's fair,' Yannick said.

'It was like that,' Sunny said.

Again, Yannick turned to him. 'She tell you this in an email?' he asked, the words coming out harsher than he intended.

'Una told me he was hard to get rid of.'

Zoric looked up at Sunny. 'When did she tell you this?'

'Bunch of times.'

'When was the last time she said something like this? That he was hard to get rid of?'

'I don't know,' he said. 'A long time ago. Like a year or something.'

'Do you hear from your sister much?' she asked.

'Not really. A bit.'

'She ever call you?'

'Only email,' said Sunny.

'Me too,' said Kathleen. 'She uses a computer at the library.'

Sergeant Zoric wrote all these things down, nodding as her pen moved across her notebook, gathering, Yannick thought, these pieces of his daughter, like cryptic clues.

'How often is she in touch with you, Kathleen? You said she tried to call on Saturday?'

'That was rare,' said Kathleen. 'She doesn't usually call.'

'That was unusual? For her to call?'

'Yes.'

'But you didn't speak?'

'I wasn't home. She called collect. The machine picked it up.'

Zoric scribbled in her pad. 'So how often do you usually hear from her?'

'Every few weeks,' said Kathleen.

'And you?' she asked Yannick.

'I don't like computers,' he said. 'I give her money for a calling card. Maybe she calls once a week or something like that.'

'And the last time you spoke?' Zoric asked. 'When was that? Did she call you on Saturday too?'

'Monday,' he said. 'Last Monday.'

'Did she tell you she was meeting anyone?'

'No.'

'What did you talk about?'

That phone conversation? Well, it meant nothing until it meant everything. They spoke about the situation with Devon's mother and they spoke about Una's employment, which he now realized she was no longer in.

'Did she say anything that concerned you? Anything out of the ordinary?'

'Well, I guess she lied,' he said, 'about her job.'

'Is that out of the ordinary for her? To lie?'

Yannick and Kathleen looked at each other. 'She doesn't lie to us,' he said, his eyes still on Kathleen.

'Unfortunately, that's the thing with lies,' said Sergeant Zoric. 'You can never be sure if you're being told one.'

This woman was only doing her job, but Yannick felt like . . . like he was grasping a lid he could not unscrew: he couldn't find the right words to convince her, to unlock this. You know your kid, who was by now twenty-three years old but still your kid, you know she would not lie about anything that mattered and you know she would not leave the place she was living without telling you. If she were heading off somewhere to pick peaches or pears or whatever it was, she would have told them. She would have told someone.

Yannick asked the question again: 'What should we be doing? Should we be out there driving around or what?'

The sergeant put her notebook on the desk and laid her pen across it, and the pen rolled off the notebook and across the desk, and they all watched her chase the pen and plant it along the crease of the notebook like it had better do what it was told.

'This is awful for you,' she said. 'But I have seen this before, many times, and I am confident she'll be back, soon. Chances are she and this ex-boyfriend have gone off somewhere.'

'Are you even looking for her?' Kathleen asked.

'Like I said, I've got constables making enquiries.'

'What about one of those lines of people,' Sunny said, 'like on TV. All walking up a field.'

She smiled at him, said something about not having the information to suggest a ground search, or where one might be performed. Sunny held his face sideways to her, unconvinced.

She stood up, thanked them for coming in. Asked them where they were staying and how they could be reached. She said she was going to track down Oliver Hanratty, and asked if they had brought any photographs of Una to use for canvassing, if it came to that.

And here Yannick dropped his face into his hands, where the smell of salty kelp still clung, and he felt hollow. A strong hand gripped his shoulder – either Kathleen's or Sunny's – real as rock.

Coming off Highway 17 into the town of Wawa, there is a statue of a Canada goose, comically large, perched on a block of cement by the side of the road. Its long neck thrusts forward and the wings are flexed as if it's about to take flight over Lake Superior. Thinking he's seeing things that aren't there, Yannick twists in his seat to get a better look as they drive past.

'What are you looking at?' Kathleen asks.

'You didn't see that?'

She shrugs.

'How could you miss it?'

'How could I miss what?'

'We just drove past a goose twice the size of this truck. Three times the size.'

'That's a big goose,' she says.

'It was a statue.'

She nods, looking to the road for complicity: check out this old fool. She shakes her head and chuckles.

'It was there,' he says. 'Wild goose,' he says.

Yannick used to know a guy who came from here, Wawa. Wild Goose, Ontario. And now he can see why he left. The main road into Wawa is derelict, mostly boarded up. A few restaurants, a video store. A furniture showroom showing only a web of cables dangling from the ceiling. They pass a littered field with nothing but a swing-set frame missing its swing and a seesaw pointing in condemnation to the sky. One kid tossing a ball for a grubby white dog; even the dog looks like it cannot be bothered.

'Here?' Kathleen says, pulling into the parking lot of the Outpost motel.

'Good a place as any,' Yannick says.

Kathleen parks in front of Reception and sends Yannick for a walk and a stretch. He doesn't argue. It's late, after nine, but they are far enough north that the sun won't fully set until eleven. The sky, where it meets the horizon, is the red of oxide powder. Nothing is happening. Dickey-town Ontario is Yannick's world entirely but there is small and then there is small.

They get adjoining rooms on the ground floor, and as soon as Yannick's kicked off his shoes and fallen into bed there's a knock on the door that separates the two rooms.

'I'm hungry,' she says, when he opens the door. 'Let's go out.'

'Nothing will be open.'

'Let's try.'

They find a place called the Trading House, just another beige brick box next to the defunct video rental store. Kathleen pushes the bar handle on the door, but it doesn't budge.

'Let's head towards the lake,' she says. 'There'll be something.'

'This is it, Kathleen. This is town.'

She crosses her arms and sighs, a little dramatically. He suggests the Mac's Milk and she nods her reticent agreement, and there they load up with cheese sandwiches wrapped tightly in plastic, a few bags of chips and a box of Oreo cookies. At the counter, Kathleen asks for a carton of Export As.

'Are you kidding?' Yannick asks, as the girl behind the counter unlocks a rolling metal door and pulls out a long, cellophane-wrapped box. 'How many packs in a carton?'

Kathleen and the girl simultaneously answer: 'Twelve.'

'You're not going to get through twelve packs of cigarettes. And I am not smoking with you.'

'Cigarettes are cheaper in Ontario,' she says. 'As soon as we cross into Manitoba, price'll shoot up. And it'll just keep rising. You watch.'

'You just invented that,' he says. 'That is made up.' He looks to the Mac's Milk girl for confirmation, as if this kid knows shit about anything other than Wawa, Ontario.

She holds in her bottom lip tightly, trying not to laugh.

Yannick sits on the edge of his bed and Kathleen sits in the upholstered chair opposite, and together they dine on Mac's Milk's finest at a little round table. He watches Kathleen hungrily pinch off morsels of food, work them tenderly in her mouth, masticating like a farm animal before swallowing.

'It's killing me,' she says. 'But I am so frigging hungry.'

He is envious of this appetite, this vibrancy.

'Did you notice that girl was missing a finger?' Kathleen asks. She's now eating an Oreo cookie the way Dev used to, licking the dry, white icing off the coal-black cookie. Not even eating the cookie. 'The whole finger down to the hand.'

'What girl? The Mac's Milk girl?'

'She was missing her pinkie finger.'

He wonders if they are going to talk about anything that matters, if they are going to talk about Una and the bones, and what if the bones are her? And what if they aren't? 'Left hand or right?' he asks.

13

IN THE FIRST few seconds of waking, Kathleen stares hard at the murky blue light pushing through gauzy curtains and a too-small window, which is on the wrong side of the room, before remembering she's not at home. She stretches out of bed, splashes through her ablutions and, before leaving the room, crosses out the number in her notebook, 7971, changing it to 7972.

They barely get going and Yannick pulls over to the side of the road, next to a ludicrous goose statue. The size of it. Engine idling, he looks at her and grins. She recognizes the lean and crook of his teeth, and what this does to her. The way his left eye squints more than his right when he smiles.

'Why are you smiling like that?' she says. She grins right back at him. 'Why'd you stop?'

'Last night I told you this was here, and you thought I was wacko.'

'So?'

'Well?' He shoots his finger at the statue. Bam bam bam.

'Well, what?' Of course she remembers him getting excited last night about something along this stretch of road, but maybe now this is too much fun, him getting all worked up. Taking jabs. She can't stop smiling.

'You,' he mutters, knuckling the gearstick into reverse.

'Me?'

'You.'

She wasn't going to say anything, but the gap in her mouth is becoming a real problem. She's been protecting it, chewing only on the good side, gargling saltwater like she was told. Last night, she googled *dry socket* on her phone. Dry socket, it turns out, is unpleasant indeed. The throb, like a strobe light, kept her awake for several hours.

She's smoking a lot, even for her.

She tries to distract herself from the pain by focusing on this repetitive landscape, this northern wilderness, but she's getting desperate. The next town, Marathon, is seventy klicks up the road. She comes clean. 'We need to find a walk-in clinic. Pronto.'

'What's wrong?'

She gingerly taps her jaw.

Yannick shakes his head. He thinks she's an idiot, she knows it. She waits for him to say something virtuous about smoking, but he doesn't.

They pull into Marathon just after eight a.m. It's quaint, if anything in northern Ontario could be considered quaint. A pretty town, directly on the shore of Lake Superior. They find the hospital in the east end and there's a walk-in clinic on its grounds.

After explaining her issue to the receptionist, she and Yannick settle with their backs to the plate-glass front window, baking. Kathleen stares at a mason jar on the reception counter that holds wild asters and goldenrod, and one sad dandelion hanging its wilted head. She moves her attention from that to the ceiling fan, which is not on. Current tooth-socket pain: gusty.

'You're not going to like me saying this,' says Yannick.

His need to talk, to get real, dangles like water collecting at the mouth of a leaky faucet. She asks the receptionist to turn on the ceiling fan.

'Kathleen.'

She turns her head to him. 'If you know I'm not going to like it, then why say it?'

'Because I have seen you do this before and it's no good. This thing you do, hurting yourself. It's not only that you smoked even when you were warned not to smoke.'

'You don't make any sense,' she says, in a whisper. The receptionist clackity-clacks her keyboard.

'You have this idea that you cannot be hurt,' he says. 'But you are always hurting yourself.'

'What do you know about always?' she says. 'It's been twenty years.'

'Not a lot has changed,' he says. His eyes are serious with affection. The scar she gave him smiles sadly.

A bland man in bland shirt and bland tie, presumably the doctor, lopes in from the back of Reception and summons Kathleen, saving her from this inconvenience. This affection.

Back in the car, one phial of strong antibiotics and another of painkillers in a crinkly paper bag tossed onto the back seat, Kathleen closes her eyes. Yannick remains, mercifully, quiet.

Back when they were married, it would frustrate Kathleen, the way that Yannick was always the one to accommodate, to make room so that others were comfortable. It frustrated her, that first day in Tofino, when the police were convinced that Una had gone off to some fruit commune or whatever it was. She wanted to kick and scream, and Yannick had been so calm.

On the second morning, Kathleen was in the shower, in their hotel, when the phone rang. She stood naked and shivering next to her bed, pressing a starchy hand towel to her breasts, while the RCMP cop who was in charge of their case, a sergeant, explained over the phone that there had been two major developments: a local fisherman named Abner Francks had seen Una that Saturday night on the marina jetty, and there was CCTV footage to prove it.

Kathleen asked her – the sergeant's name was Patricia (please call me Patti) Zoric – what this man Abner Francks had seen.

'Not a lot,' Patti said. 'Just that Una was on the jetty.'

Kathleen asked her what the video showed.

Instead of answering, Patti asked if Una had a history of psychological issues.

'That's a strange question,' Kathleen said.

'Her behaviour on the footage is concerning.'

'What do you mean?' Kathleen said, speaking through clacking teeth.

'She seems agitated. Confused.'

'What's she doing?'

Patti Zoric was stingy with the details but asked that Kathleen and Yannick come right away to the marina. Things were happening.

Kathleen remembers forcing uncooperative clothing onto her body, cotton and denim resisting and catching and tugging at her wet skin. She remembers pounding with an open palm on Yannick and Sunny's door, her unbrushed hair dripping down her neck, dampening the collar of her shirt. The hallway smelt of cold toast and vacuumed carpet. The hotel cleaner wheeled her cart out of the elevator, a bunny in ill-fitting slacks who grinned at Kathleen as if nothing were wrong in all the world.

Yannick opened the door. In the window-drape stillness behind him there was the slumbering mound of Sunny asleep on the cot bed. Yannick's eldest son, accounted for.

'They've found a video,' she said, and told him about the jetty.

'Give us two minutes,' he said, and was about to close the door but she asked to be let in. She would cover her eyes if they wanted her to while they pulled on their jeans or what-have-you. She was not going to be left alone.

She has no memory of getting to the marina, but she does remember that it was already hot in the early morning, and that the thickly forested islands in the sound cut cleanly into the blue sky. Deep summer, delphinium blue. The perfection and clarity of the morning unsettled her. Felt awfully final. As they walked down the ramp onto the cement jetty, Kathleen couldn't feel the ground under her feet. Of course she walked alongside Yannick and Sunny but she has no memory of them in that moment, where they were in relation to her. She was looking for what she was looking for, what she was trying to pick out from the expanse of heavy water shifting under that flawless sky, and the boats, and the birds. What she was looking for: a daughter, dead on the jetty. These were – are – the only few seconds, in all these twenty-two years, when Kathleen believed Una was dead.

What she found instead was Patti Zoric. Recognizable by her broad shoulders and tidy ponytail, she was talking to a group of proficient-looking people in navy blue T-shirts and bright orange lifejackets. They all stood on the jetty next to a sturdy red and white boat, a rescue-looking vessel with various radio antennae and a many-windowed bridge at the top. Patti Zoric skipped the hellos and spoke quickly: the Coast Guard was already out searching and the boat at the jetty belonged to the Tofino Lifeboat Service. Something else about a helicopter. One of the men in lifejackets put his hand on Kathleen's shoulder and told her they would do everything they could to find Una.

'Find her where?' she asked.

Patti Zoric explained that a sea kayak had been stolen from one of the local outfitters on the same day Una had gone missing, and now, what with the CCTV footage as well, they had to consider that perhaps Una had stolen the kayak, and got herself into trouble out on the water.

'Yesterday you said peaches,' Kathleen said, the words somersaulting out of her mouth. 'This is a joke,' she said.

Yannick, it seemed, in his Yannick way, was taking all this in. Asking questions, his face inexplicably, infuriatingly calm. It was windy out on the jetty, a wind that was brash and tacky with salt. Kathleen's hair whipped her eyes, infinitesimal slashings. Territorial birds seemed to fill the sky, diving and screaming.

More information, delivered to them in brief. This was being coordinated by the Coast Guard now. This was a Search and Rescue Operation. An International Distress Call had been broadcast on Channel 16. Every boat with a radio would have heard the call, which meant that all the sailboats, leisure craft, water taxis, commercial fishing boats, ferries – every boat in the area – were looking for this stolen sea kayak. Or for a girl, stranded. Marine law demanded it.

A man approached them. He was wearing a square-headed baseball cap with a flat peak, and it was clear this man was rarely without his cap. It was also clear from his clothes, even if you had no prior knowledge of this: fisherman. Canvas pants tucked into rubber boots that were grimy with scales and dried fish guts, plaid flannel long-sleeve flapping loosely over a light grey T-shirt. This man introduced himself as Abner Francks, and was the last person to have seen Una. To have *seen* Una, a tangible body taking up tangible space. Not a photograph, or a closed-caption video. Not a dream. Not the sucking, yawning hole of the left-behind.

Kathleen remembers Yannick's hand on the small of her back while Abner Francks explained that he and his wife sometimes stayed in a little apartment just behind where they now stood, on the drive leading down to the marina, within eyesight of the jetty and where his own boats were moored.

The tufted hair that curled up from under Abner's cap was black and silver and he had the cured look of someone who spent more time on the ocean than off it. He also swore like a champion, reminding Kathleen of Yannick's father. Sometime later he would tell them that he was a Tla-o-qui-aht hereditary chief from Opitsat, just across the water on Meares Island, and he would be the person both she and Yannick trusted more than any others in those first few weeks.

'The wife woke me up around midnight,' he said, 'falling out of bed. She sprained her knee and doesn't move too good, like sleeping with a lame horse. I said to her, "What are you doing, woman?" and she tells me she's getting up because she can't remember if she locked the door. Couple of break-ins around here recently, so. I told her, "You go back to sleep and let me check the door."'

At this point in his story, Abner took a few steps up the jetty, past the lifeboat that was now chugging white water at its stern, preparing to depart, and up to a fenced cage that housed a rack of kayaks. Kathleen, Yannick and Sunny followed him, watching him closely, like ducklings. He pointed to a spot next to the cage, then drew his arm up and indicated a length of the jetty a few metres long. 'She was just fucken wandering up and down along here,' he said. 'Rubbing her arms, like she was cold. It was blowing pretty hard that night, so.'

'Did you talk to her?' Yannick asked.

'No, no, I saw her from my place,' he said, gesturing over his shoulder.

'Was she with anyone?' Kathleen asked.

Abner shook his head. 'She was walking funny? Like with a limp, I think? It was hard to tell. I didn't watch for long.'

'She was hurt?' Yannick asked.

'It was just a bit funny,' Abner repeated, 'like a limp.' He adjusted his cap by the peak, a swift and concise adjustment, like a man clearing his throat to stop himself crying, and looked out across the water. 'I should've gone out to her,' he said. 'She was alone. But I thought, these kids, you know? They come out here for the summer. They like to party. I thought she was just . . . I don't fucken know, eh?' He rubbed his hand back and forth across his stubbled jaw, and then he looked Kathleen straight in the eyes. 'That was my mistake,' he said. 'I should've gone out to her.'

'You didn't know,' Kathleen said. Or maybe it was Yannick who said this. Maybe she turned away from him because a voice in her head was hissing, *Yes, why didn't you?*

'We'll find her,' Abner said. 'That's mine over there,' he said, nodding to a fishing trawler that rocked solidly in the water, a white deck and green hull with weeds of rust creeping up the paintwork. Masts and booms and a network of cables and coils of rope, those orange plastic bobble things, Kathleen didn't know what they were called, dangling over the side as buffers against the jetty. Even looking at the boat, hearing the gallumpy sucking noise of its weighty up-and-down, the base of Kathleen's stomach did a little flip, a little throb, a nauseous little heave.

A young woman with a blue bandana tying back her hair was on deck, leaning over the side of the boat smoking a cigarette with an elegance that was wholly out of place. She waved at them and exhaled smoke into the summer air.

'Our daughter,' Abner said.

She could be Una, Kathleen thought. Right here in the flesh. Right where you can touch her.

'We're waiting for the Coast Guard to tell us where to go,' Abner said. 'Then we go.'

'I don't understand,' Kathleen said. 'Why suddenly all this with the water?'

'You search the water first,' said Abner Francks.

The bitter reek of salt and fish settled in the mid-point of Kathleen's head, that un-clearable space between nose and throat, and the birds, well, they just would not shut up.

14

YANNICK DRIVES THIS long road and thinks about his children. He thinks about the last time they were all together, the Christmas of 1995, the last Christmas before Una disappeared. Yannick was renting a cottage up on Kushog Lake and was going to spend that holiday week alone with his three sons until Una called mid-December and said she wanted to come home. Asked Yannick if he could buy her an airline ticket.

'Finding a ticket now?' he said. 'I can look but, you know, it won't come cheap.'

'It doesn't matter,' she said. 'I don't need to come.'

'I said I'd try.'

She started to say something else then but ran out of credit on her calling card and the line clicked dead.

He did get her a ticket, though, went halvesies with Kathleen, which meant all of them spending Christmas together.

The place up on Kushog was what he could afford at the time, still being ensnared in a dog fight with Devon's mother over the sale of their home, and not working as much as he would have liked. It wasn't nearly big enough for all those people but he got busy preparing the couch for Sunny to sleep on, straightening his room for Kathleen and Una to share. He was using the second bedroom for making his art because it had a big window facing the lake and the light was good. Not much in that room but an easel, desk and stool. He was doing mainly charcoals at the time and on the desk were the soup tins he used to store pencils, willows and shammies. Stacks of paper. He pushed all that aside, out of the way, folded up the easel and tucked it against the wall behind the desk. This left just enough room for the second-hand bunk bed he'd found for Devon and Zack.

Yannick was not accustomed to hosting his children together. Not because he didn't want to, but he was never in the same house for very long, having got deep into the business of buying houses on the cheap, renovating them and selling at a profit. Wherever he did happen to be living was likely to be short on hot water, or heating, or stair rails.

He put up a scraggy little tree, tacked some lights around the fireplace and filled every bowl he had with peppermints and nuts and those silver-foil drops, those Hershey's Kisses. He hid Leigh's things away in the bathroom closet, things she'd started leaving behind: her housecoat and hairbrush and toiletries. Wasn't ready to share her just yet.

Sunny and Zack were the first to arrive, having taken the bus up from where they lived with their mother in Toronto. What Yannick saw when he pulled up to the Mercantile and Feed on Bobcaygeon Road, where the Greyhound bus dropped off his two sons, was his boys in some kind of stand-off on the hard-packed snow. Sunny's face was screwed up tight and Zack was bent over, laughing. The thing was, even though Zack was the younger brother by almost three years, he was always stronger and wilier, better-looking. A faster runner, a bigger eater, a louder voice.

'What's this about?' Yannick said, as he got out of his car. The sun was shining so keenly on the snow that his eyes ached, and the air was so cold, the hairs in his nose froze dry.

'He's such a fucking pussy,' Zack said, laughing.

Yannick had not seen these boys since they'd helped him burn piles of leaves in the late fall. Zack's voice had dropped and his laugh was creaky and mean.

'You don't talk about your brother like that,' Yannick said, cuffing Zack on the top of his head. He put his hand on Sunny's shoulder and Sunny shrugged it off, unable to look his father in the face.

'You guys fight on the bus? Did you embarrass yourselves?' Yannick asked.

Neither responded.

Sunny shuddered and took a deep breath and he went for Zack, and this only made Zack laugh harder. The new pierce and crack to his laugh echoed sharply over the snow. Even though he was taking a pummelling from Sunny, Zack continued to laugh, a high-pitched, staged *haw haw haw*. It did the trick, and Sunny was out of control, flailing on Zack across the shoulders, his thick ski gloves doing a whole lot of nothing. But then Sunny landed a good clop across Zack's chin and they were at it, bear cubs scrapping in the snow, their winter coats riding up their young torsos all stretching and ebbing with muscle, their skin turning blotchy and pink.

A few bright drops of blood in the snow quickly ended it. Zack's lip.

'You done now?' Yannick asked. He pulled a wad of tissue from the deep pocket of his parka and tried to dab at Zack's mouth. Zack jerked away and then both boys wavered on their feet, steaming like cows in a field, not knowing what to do with the weight of their own bodies. Both glaring at Yannick like it was his fault.

166

In the car, on the way home, both of those boys cried privately, faces turned to their respective windows.

Devon's mother dropped him off a few hours later and he got all wound up and wild when he saw Zack's lip. Couldn't believe it was Sunny who gave it to him. Devon was ten years old at the time and back then he believed his two big brothers were the beginning, the middle and the end of everything that mattered or would ever matter.

In the morning, Devon was the first up, needling Yannick to take him out on the Ski-Doo. It wasn't Yannick's Ski-Doo, but borrowed from the next-door neighbour in return for Yannick checking on his place once a week over the winter.

Out on the frozen, snow-covered lake that morning, Yannick and Devon were alone. They sped north, crossing the tracks of other Ski-Doos, like signatures in the snow, grinding over thick black ice that showed itself only in the old tracks and the bare patches raked by the wind. Yannick had swaddled Devon in a thick coat and snow pants, helmet and goggles, and settled the boy between his legs for the ride. This kid, his youngest son, his heart beating wildly and his body curled into the shell of Yannick's own.

Yannick and Devon arrived back at the cottage to find Una and Kathleen sitting at the kitchen table, drinking cups of coffee. Dev marked his territory in that small house, parading from the front door to the bathroom, discarding along the way his gloves and toque et cetera and telling anyone who would listen that he drove the Ski-Doo himself (untrue) and that he needed to take a dump. Yannick watched Kathleen eyeing Devon as he took up the space he took up, making his kingly way through the living room.

The coat stand next to the door looked like it could not take another garment, so he folded his parka neatly over the back of the couch. Neither was there room on the rubber mat for his boots, so he left them outside the door. Didn't want snow melting on the carpet.

'Pour me a cup o' joe, Una,' Yannick said. To get around the kitchen table, he had to move Sunny out of the way by his shoulders. He sat, waiting for a hot cup to wrap his itching, thawing fingers around.

'You going to say hi first?' she said.

'Come here,' he said, pulling her over for a hug.

'Could we get a little more heat in here?' Kathleen asked. She was still wearing her coat and complained that it wasn't much warmer inside than out.

So while Yannick's coffee went cold, he brushed the ashes out of the fire grate, started a fire and kept it going all day. Devon topped up the wood basket, carrying in chunks from the shed out back, tramping snow on the carpet every time. Perfect little diamond cut-outs of snow from the tread of his boots.

Wasn't long before he came to Yannick, who was dozing on the couch with a book, his wrist held up, displaying a sliver deep under the skin, long and severe at the base of his hand.

Yannick took hold of Dev's hand. 'That looks like it hurts an awful lot,' he said.

As soon as his suffering was named, tears rolled plumply down the boy's cheeks.

'We'll let Una do it, eh?' Yannick said. 'This is a Una job if ever there was one.'

Devon shook his head. A hot tear landed on Yannick's hand.

168

'She's the best at slivers,' Yannick said. 'Done mine a hundred times.'

'You never had a hundred slivers.' This was Zack, bored, peering over Devon's shoulder. 'Holy crap, Dev,' he said. 'That looks deep. That looks like a minnow swam up in your arm.'

'It's not that bad?' Devon said, eyes shining and wide, looking up at Zack. He turned his face to Yannick. 'It's not that bad?' he said again.

'Can't even see where it ends,' Zack said, dropping this little gift as he cast off, back down the hallway, chuckling.

'Don't listen to that gearbox,' Yannick said. 'Look, you can see for yourself. It's not as bad as he says.'

Kathleen perched herself next to Yannick on the couch – she'd come over from where she had been sitting on the other side of the room in his reading chair. Next to the chair, an untidy pile of his charity-shop paperbacks that she'd selected from the shelf.

'Let me see,' she said, in a tone half the distance between caring and sceptical.

Devon raised his wrist limply and Kathleen squinted at it, nodded as if she were impressed.

'Una can get that out for you,' she said. She ruffled his hair awkwardly and he jerked his head away. That was his one chance gone, and Yannick knew she would not try again.

'Why do I keep hearing my name?' Una said, coming out of the bedroom, where she'd been for most of the day.

'Surprised you could hear it,' Yannick said.

Una stopped and looked at him.

'You've been behind that door since this morning,' he said.

'What's the problem?' she said.

'Dev's got a sliver,' Yannick said. 'Show her, Dev.'

Devon shook his head, no.

'Have you got tweezers?' Una asked Yannick. She went down the hall to the bathroom and Devon looked swiftly around the room, trapped. Yannick lifted him into his lap, and his small boy forgot how tough he was and rested his head on Yannick's shoulder. The smell of his son's hair, not clean but not dirty, either.

'I'm telling you, son,' Yannick said, 'Una will have this out of you lickety-split. She's got the magic touch.'

Una came back from the bathroom and nudged Yannick on the shoulder, gave him a queer kind of smile. He remembered the collection of Leigh's odds and ends that he'd stashed in the back of the bathroom closet.

Una knelt on the floor in front of Devon and put her hand on his leg, and he pressed his body stiffly into Yannick's.

'Let me show you,' she said. She held up the tweezers and pinched them together a few times. 'Not even sharp.'

'Come on,' Yannick said, nudging Devon. The injured arm was tucked protectively between their bodies – Yannick had to push his away so Una could reach. She barely touched the points of the tweezers to Devon's pale wrist before he pulled away and yowled like a wet cat. Told her to get the hell away. She reached for him again and he slapped her hand. She peered up at Yannick, clearly displeased that he was letting the boy get away with this jack-assery. Well. She was twenty-two years old and Devon was ten and Yannick's refereeing days were over.

Una shuffled on her knees to the fire and knelt there, one baby toe sticking out of a hole in her sock. She took the poker from where it was propped against the wall and stabbed at the wood. A spark landed on her jeans. She flicked it away and it nestled into the carpet.

'Una,' said Yannick, shifting Devon off his lap. 'You are burning a hole in the carpet.'

Una ground the spark into the carpet with the poker, leaving behind a black smudge.

'Una,' Yannick said again. 'You see that burn mark you made?'

'Leave her,' said Kathleen.

Una remained at the fire, poking half-heartedly until a log that was nearly burned to coal toppled over the grate and broke into pieces on the hearth tiles.

'Una,' Yannick said. 'You, girl.'

'Jesus,' she said. Got up, closed herself into the bedroom once more.

Sunny was now going at Devon's wrist with the tweezers and had managed to break off the exposed tip, that minuscule nip of a chance, gone.

Sometime later that day, Yannick laced up his boots to trek through the snow to his neighbour's place to run hot water through the pipes. Keep them from freezing solid. The temperature was dropping to twenty below. Una wanted to walk with him but all she'd brought from out west, where the climate was warmer, was an oversized wool sweater and an old pair of tattered sneakers. So he gave her his parka and toque, and she pilfered Sunny's heavy goloshes.

'Already forgot what real winter is like?' he said, maybe more cutting than he meant to. He couldn't figure it: she had come all this way, and now she seemed surprised to find herself at home. She and her flimsy sneakers and holes in her socks. She, keeping behind a closed bedroom door.

It was a short hike to the neighbour's place, a traverse through a patch of woods. It was so cold that you could feel the air going down your throat and the path was buried under a foot of snow.

'Dad.'

'Yup?'

'Why haven't you come out to see me?' She was walking directly behind him, following the collapsing trough he carved with his legs.

'You know why,' he said.

'Do I?'

He stopped and turned. 'You know why,' he said again.

'Because of flying? Seriously?'

'Part of it, yup. And I don't have the money and I can't lose the work days.' He turned and continued to plough. 'I work and I work but it doesn't matter how much,' he said, 'there's only ever just enough.'

'All that child support must be tough,' she said, not kindly.

He stopped again and turned to her. 'You sure you want to say what you're saying?' The ground was steep, where they stood, and his feet were slipping under the snow. It was a struggle to stay upright.

'I don't think money has anything to do with it.'

'I don't get it,' he said. 'You're out there doing your thing. Why does it matter if I come?'

'You would love it,' she said.

'I am not arguing that.' He turned and started again towards the neighbour's.

After a few more minutes, her voice again, feeling sorry for itself, which, by this time, was pissing him off. 'I think I made a mistake,' she said.

He didn't stop walking, only raised his voice. 'Give it more time,' he said. 'If you come back now, that would be the mistake. These things happen in their own time.'

'Uh-huh,' she said.

'You'll figure it out.'

'Whose stuff is that in your bathroom?' she asked.

He stopped again. And turned only the top half of his body, his feet anchored. Held himself in a twist with one arm wrapped around a birch tree. The snow was blue now with the sun dropping behind the trees on the other side of the lake, dragging the temperature with it.

'The tampons and slippers and stuff,' she said.

'That is Leigh's stuff,' he said.

'Who's Leigh?'

'Leigh is Leigh.'

'Will you get married again?'

'Hold your horses, girl.'

'I don't care,' she said. 'I just don't think you have the space.'

'Eh?'

'Devon would shit his little pants.'

'That is not your problem.'

As if they'd conjured him up, the cacophony of Devon came racketing through the trees, branches cracking and echoing, his insistent 'Hey, you guys, hey, you guys!' He danced towards them, shouting between deep, cloudy breaths about how he was a hunter and they were the elk, and he'd tracked their hoof marks in the snow.

It got titchy with all of them in that small house. That evening, he drove the three klicks up the two-lane highway to the liquor store and convenience grocery run by the Korean family who were there in those days. Jug City, it was called. He parked directly next to the payphone in the parking lot because he wanted some privacy to call Leigh. His Leigh. Those early days. Those easy days, soft and unfocused in brand new love.

'How's you?' he said, when she answered.

Her voice was surprised but also low and throaty with affection. 'Missing you,' she said. 'More than I thought I would. More than I should.'

He let that linger until she spoke again.

'How's your clan?' she asked.

'There are a lot of people in my house,' he said.

'They driving you around the bend?'

'No,' he said, and then: 'Yes, they are. A little. The cottage is small and the people are many. The boys are all arms and legs and hair and stink.'

She snorted, and asked where he was calling from.

'Payphone,' he said. 'I wanted you all to myself.'

'And your daughter? You were so happy she was coming. How is she?'

'I'm not sure,' he said. 'She's keeping herself to herself.'

'Oh,' she said. 'It's normal, I guess. For her age.'

'She's not a teenager,' he said. 'She's a grown woman acting like a child.'

'You told me,' Leigh said, 'that sometimes she forgets about the people around her. Goes about her own stuff and that.'

'I said that?'

'I'm not inventing it.'

He did not want to talk about Una. 'What are you doing?' he asked. 'Right now, what are you doing?'

'Thawing out a turkey.'

'That's sexy.'

'My brother and his wife brought me a frozen bird.'

'You alone?'

'No, I am not.'

'Can I call you tonight? Can I call you tomorrow?'

'Baby. You can call me anytime you want.'

'I will, then.'

That night, Kathleen made her signature dish, which was passed on to her by Yannick's father: tourtière. Her cooking filled every room in the cottage with the fat-rendering smells of minced pork and beef frying in the pan with the onions and potatoes, cinnamon and cloves and nutmeg and mounds of black pepper. After dinner, while everyone sat idle, picking at bowls of nuts and candies even though their stomachs were full, Una came out of the bedroom and pulled on Yannick's coat and said she was going for a walk. Soon as Sunny heard this he sprang up off the living-room floor, leaving Devon alone at a board of checkers, and asked her if he could come along. Una waited by the doorway, looking as comfortable as a mouse in a trap, while Sunny laced up his boots.

'I want to come too,' said Devon, carrying the foldable checkers board in a V to the kitchen table, dropping pieces as he went, his socks half off his feet and in danger of tripping him.

'Absolutely not,' said Una.

'Take your little brother,' said Yannick, trying to catch her eye for a smile.

'Please,' Devon begged, pulling on Sunny's arm.

'It's freezing out there,' Sunny warned him. 'I don't want to hear it from you.'

'He'll get cold,' Una said. 'He'll be a pain in the ass.'

'I won't, I promise,' Dev said.

'I don't want any complaining,' Una said. 'Or any storytelling, or wars, or burping out the alphabet. This is not the Devon Show. It's just a walk.'

Devon got his boots and coat on so fast Yannick had to chase him out of the door with his toque and mittens.

A doze by the fire, maybe sleep but probably not, and Sunny and Una came back inside, laughing together. Yannick noticed this, Una laughing, and was grateful for it, and watched her shrug her arms out of his large coat with a smile on her face. He got up to put a pan of milk on the stove as Una was closing the door behind her.

'Dad,' she said, 'you have to go out there. It's magical. You can hear the snow settling in the trees.'

'Where's Dev?' Yannick asked.

Una was pulling a woolly black scarf from her neck and stopped mid-pull. 'He already came back,' she said. 'Like twenty minutes ago.'

Yannick stared at her for a moment, then called Devon's name down the hallway.

'He's not here,' Kathleen said, pushing herself up from her chair. A book fell from her lap to the floor and slowly fanned open.

'I sent him back,' Una said, wide-eyed. 'He was bitching about the cold.'

Yannick pushed his feet into his boots.

'We were only up the road, Dad,' said Sunny, already heading back out of the door.

'He'll be close, Yannick,' Kathleen said, fumbling her feet into her own boots.

So there they all were, criss-crossing each other's paths in twenty degrees below zero. Laces trailing alongside loose-tongued boots that no one took the time to tie, snow melting in their boots, calling out the name of their youngest. The snow continued to swirl from above, slowly and directionless, ignorant of gravity. There was half a moon and the light was an empty light, and Devon's name echoed through the bony black trees that creaked under the weight of that new-fallen snow.

When he didn't come, though, when the calling of his name was met with nothing more than the pitched *tchue-tchue* of a red cardinal high up in a tall birch, the ground began to shift under Yannick's feet.

(How could he have known that this would not be the last time he called for one of his children in the woods? How could he have known that the time after this would be so much worse?)

Eventually they found him when Zack heard his laughter ricocheting through the trees, up from the lake. And there he was, making snow angels on the ice, winged bodies scraped black out of the blue snow. Dozens of snow angels connected like paper dolls.

Later, when Devon was sniffling in bed, quietly crying after the mother of all tellings-off, Una joined Yannick in front of the fire and rested her head on his shoulder.

'We could see the house, Dad,' she said. 'We could see your lights from the road when I told him to go home. I didn't just send him off into the woods.' Her voice vibrated into his bones.

'You cannot trust that boy to do what he is told,' Yannick said. He held his shoulder stiffly under the weight of her head. Didn't relax into her touch.

'Hardly my fault,' she said, and sat up, leaving his shoulder cold.

His cold shoulder.

'Yannick,' Kathleen said, 'she didn't know he would run off like a lunatic. And look, he's fine now. Safe in bed.'

'Yep,' he said, his eyes on the chattering fire. Una sat next to him a little longer. Some utter foolishness, the need to make a point, stopped him pulling his daughter close even though all he wanted to do in that moment was to pull his daughter close. She stood up, eventually, and went to bed. And he did not see her again.

Yannick woke next morning with Devon's foot in his face, Devon climbing over the back of the couch where Yannick had slept, Devon scrabbling for his Christmas stocking.

'You have to wait until everyone is up,' Yannick said.

'Everyone is up,' Devon said, and jumped on Sunny who was asleep on cushions on the floor.

Kathleen came out of the bedroom and went straight to the coffee-maker. 'Who wants a cup?' she said, spooning grounds into a paper filter. 'Where's Una?' she said.

Yannick, on his knees in front of the fireplace, trying to revive the fire from the heart glow that still pulsed in the pile of black coal and white ash. 'She's not in bed?' he said.

'No.'

Kathleen went down the hall and knocked on the bathroom door, eliciting a grumble from Zack, and went back into the bedroom mumbling about Una having gone for another walk or something like that.

The fire was just starting to smoke and lick at the underside of a dry block of pine when Kathleen sat heavily on the couch and said, 'Una's gone.'

'Eh?' Yannick said.

'Her bag's gone.'

'You sure?'

Kathleen shook her head, rubbed her hands up and down her thighs.

'Why are you surprised?' This came from Sunny, still on his cushions on the floor, wrapped tightly in a blanket.

Kathleen, bewildered, looked to Sunny, then to Yannick. 'Where would she go?' she said.

'She wouldn't.'

'She did,' said Kathleen. 'And it's freezing out there.'

Yannick, denying Una would do something so stupid, continued to poke at the wood.

'Idiot girl doesn't even have a good coat,' said Kathleen. She got up and went to the back window that faced the driveway. 'Truck's still here,' she said, wiping condensation off the window.

'Better be,' he said. He pushed himself up from the floor and stood in the middle of the living room. 'Go ahead and open your stocking,' he said to Devon, and Devon tore right in.

Una called two hours later from a payphone in Minden. Explained that she left early in the morning because she didn't want to upset anyone, and walked the three kilometres to Jug City. She thought she could call a taxi from the payphone there but neither of the two local companies were operating, it being Christmas morning, so she stood out on the highway and hitched a lift to Minden with a guy who was out looking for his runaway dog.

'You walked that road in the cold and the dark,' he said to her.

'So?'

'You don't even have a coat.'

'I took Mom's.'

Yannick turned his face from the phone and said to

Kathleen, who was perched tensely next to him at the kitchen table: 'She stole your coat.'

'I didn't want to wake anyone up,' Una said.

'You are playing a game, Una,' he said.

'There's a bus back to the city this afternoon,' she said. 'I can change my flight, so. I'll be back by tomorrow night.'

'Back where?' he said, fending off with his shoulder Kathleen's attempts to grab the receiver.

'Where I live,' she said.

'What am I supposed to tell your brothers?'

'They won't give a shit.'

'Safe flight then, I suppose,' he said.

'Right.'

He hung up, and left the kitchen with Kathleen at his heels, arguing that if he'd let her speak, she would have changed Una's mind. Probably she would have, probably that was all Una wanted, for them to change her mind, to ask her to come back.

15

FACT: DAYS BEFORE Una disappeared, Oliver Hanratty sent her an email. Kathleen knows this because it was in the police report. He was going to be in Vancouver, on the mainland and only a few hours' travel from where she was living, and wrote that he wanted to see her. Later, in an interview, the police learned that Oliver was applying to graduate schools, one of them being the University of British Columbia in Vancouver. He was there touring the campus and meeting faculty. He provided the message he wrote to Una, asking her if he could come to the island, and his email account showed no response from her. But Una's account proved that she had written back, suggesting a day and time to meet at a restaurant in Tofino.

The police ruled him out too quickly, in Kathleen's opinion. Something about an alibi dinner with a professor from the university, which didn't allow enough time for travel to the island the day Una disappeared. But they didn't know Oliver the way Kathleen knew Oliver, that he had been one very heartsick boy. They didn't know about the time he split his chin open crashing his bike into a parked car, drunk, riding to their house after midnight to beg Una back. The end of that episode had Kathleen plying him with ice chips all morning in the Emergency Department waiting room. The blockhead's bottom lip was so fat he could barely speak.

They didn't want to hear any of this, the police. Oliver Hanratty had been crossed off their very short list.

Over the years, Kathleen has kept one eye on that boy. She knows that he got married in 2005 and moved to Toronto, and was working as some kind of engineer, which was a relief, after what happened, after what she, Kathleen, did to him. After learning of his death the other night, she looked up his obituary. He rests with his father and is survived by his mother. He was a devoted husband and loving father to one and another and another. Loving uncle to, et cetera, et cetera. Died at the age of forty-seven after a three-year battle with melanoma.

When Una went missing, Kathleen stayed out west for two months, returning home only because she needed to work, and raise money for a reward. It was late September, and one morning, Kathleen wandered back to that same creek where she had picked fiddleheads the first day she met Oliver Hanratty. It was a pretty spot: frog spawn and bulrushes – what you would expect. The sun reflecting off the endless ripples in the water and finding and lighting up each fibrous silky strand of milkweed pod floating on the breeze. Metallic green dragonflies screwing in mid-air, silver birches fluttering, balsams shivering. A hint of peace when Kathleen had none. There had been more rain than usual that autumn and the water was high, forcing her up the bank into the browning bracken and the thistles. The ground was mulch, each footstep releasing the smell of mud and rot. The mud was so strong it sucked one of Kathleen's shoes off.

With wet shoes and slimy socks, she climbed up out of the creek ravine at a different spot than usual, ending up near Francis Street, from where, it so happened, it was a quick right turn to Oliver Hanratty's house. She hadn't left home that morning with the intention of going to his house, but she took this as a sign.

Oliver Hanratty's mother Susan, who had never really liked Una, still lives in that same house. A bungalow on a dead-end street at the north-east end of town.

Walking up to the house, Kathleen could smell the thick egginess of the creek mud coming from her shoes and socks, so she stopped, and took them off. Continued barefoot up the porch steps with her muddy shoes and socks dangling from her fingers.

Maybe, in those early days and months, her mind was a little blown. Her judgement, a little off.

Kathleen knocked and waited, switching weight from foot to foot, angry for not having had the strength to come sooner. And then the door opened and there Susan Hanratty stood in a terrycloth robe with her hair strangled in a twisted towel on top of her head. Her face was pink-fresh and eyebrows arched high on her shiny, freckled forehead.

'Oh,' she said.

'Hi,' said Kathleen.

'I was in the shower,' she said.

'I can see that,' said Kathleen.

Susan hung in the space between the door and the frame, head cocked and one arm crooked protectively around the edge of the door, waiting for Kathleen to state her business. Kathleen asked if she could come in.

'Kathleen,' Susan said, 'you put the police on my kid.'

'I did no such thing. I just want to talk. Just for a minute.'

Susan glanced at the pair of wet and muddy sneakers, then at the dirty bare feet, then again at Kathleen's face. 'You want to talk?' she said.

'Just for a minute.'

Susan shrugged.

'I won't stay long,' Kathleen said, and put her shoes and socks down neatly, side by side next to the door.

Susan's house, the place where Oliver had grown up, was small and simple. Old couch draped with afghan blanket in the living room, TV in the corner, remote on the floor. Big front window and kitchen at the far end of a short, dark hallway. The smell of decades of nicotine but also the smell of cooking, laundry detergent, the shampoo from Susan's recent shower. Home. Life going on as normal. It occurred to Kathleen how much time Una had spent in this house over the years, mainly in Oliver's bedroom, mainly out of Susan's reach.

In the kitchen, Susan took a pack of cigarettes from the top of a breadbox, shook one out for herself and offered Kathleen the pack. She cracked open the window over the sink and they both lit up. She made no move for kettle or coffee-maker, which was fine. The cigarette was hospitality enough. Instead, she leaned against the counter and blew smoke out of the side of her mouth towards the open window. On the fridge, a magnet that said: Fuck Cancer.

'When did you get back?' she said. 'I heard you were still out there.'

Kathleen wasn't entirely sure when she got back. Time is hard to follow when you're not able to sleep. 'I think I've been back a week,' she said.

'I was just getting ready for work,' Susan said.

'You won't return my calls.'

Susan shrugged. Looking at the floor, she asked, 'Have you heard anything?'

Kathleen shook her head, no. She had not heard one single thing. The ash on her cigarette was about to topple and Susan thumbed an ashtray down the counter for her.

'This is kind of a Una-type thing to do, though, eh?' Susan said. Without putting her cigarette down, she undid and retied her terrycloth belt, which was frayed to ribbons, pulling the whole robe more tightly around her avian frame. She did this, it seemed, so she didn't have to look Kathleen in the eye. 'I'm only saying,' she went on, smoke curling out of her mouth and nose, 'this whole thing could be something Una's just cooking up. You know? Maybe she isn't thinking about you or her dad or anybody. One thing's for sure, that girl is not thinking about my son.'

'She wouldn't do that,' Kathleen said. 'It's been months.'

'She could be anywhere,' Susan said, and again pushed her mouth to the side of her face, drawing the skin on her neck into many folds, and exhaled out of the window. 'Una does what Una wants,' she said.

She was right, Susan was right. Not about Una being off somewhere, running away somewhere, but about Una doing what she wanted. That's not what this was, though. Not a chance.

'It would really help me,' said Kathleen, 'if I could talk to Oliver. I've called so many times.'

'You certainly have.'

'So, can I? Can I talk to him?'

'The cops talked to him already. Lots.'

'I know.'

'You sent them.'

'Don't be ridiculous,' Kathleen said. 'You can't tell the police what to do.'

'He was supposed to have a scholarship, did you know that? And now they're saying they might take it away.' Susan lit another cigarette off the first, inhaling so deeply the burning paper squeaked.

'I didn't know that.'

Susan stared at Kathleen for a moment. 'Why?' she asked. She looked over Kathleen's shoulder to the clock on the wall. 'Why would it help you to talk to Oliver?'

'He was in touch with Una when she disappeared. I want to know if he noticed anything. If she said anything.'

'He was not in touch with her,' Susan said, fiddling again with her robe, making no effort to hide the fact that she had one eye on the wall clock. 'There was no contact,' she said. 'The police know it. Just accept it.'

'Is he even here? Is he okay?'

Susan sighed, deeply and grievously, and hammered the butt of her smoke into the ashtray in concise blows. 'He's up with my sister in North Bay,' she said. 'This is messing with his head.'

'I'm sorry.'

'Hours,' she said. 'The police interviewed him for hours. More than once. He's very upset.'

Kathleen was going to say, wanted to say, that they must have had a lot to talk about. That the police must have thought Oliver had something important to say. This was Susan's home, though. This was her kitchen, where she cooked for her kid, and that was her Fuck Cancer magnet on the fridge.

'I'm going to be late,' Susan said. She started back through the house towards the front door and Kathleen trailed behind. On a bookshelf in the living room there was a photograph of Oliver that looked like it was taken in grade four or five – that age when the hair starts coming in more coarse and the baby face begins to harden. The way his hair stuck up on one side; the way he was sitting up straight and smiling firmly with his mouth shut because he'd just been told to sit up straight and smile; the way one eye was open a little wider than the other – Kathleen got tight-throated and misty right there in Susan Hanratty's living room. Not just somebody's kid in the photo, but this kid. She knew this kid. Had fed him. Seen him cry. Wiped blood off his face. Now she was losing him, too.

She picked up her shoes, headed down the front walk and turned for home, still barefoot. A deep shiver spread from her middle and she pulled her sweater tightly around her body, though it was mild and the sun was out. Fiery September sun hitting every single leaf, lighting up windows.

She got to the end of the street and stopped, and pivoted, confused as to the best route home. She chose to go left and, as she turned, mashed her toe into the fractured sidewalk, catching it on the inside edge of an escarpment in the pavement, a slab that had been forced up by weeds and winter. The blood ran thickly and impressively and, looking for something to wrap around her toe, she realized she'd forgotten her socks on Susan Hanratty's front porch. She turned back to get them because she was ashamed, because her socks were swampy with mud.

As she approached the house, a car was reversing out of the driveway and she assumed it was Susan, late for work. Kathleen waved to get her attention, but it wasn't Susan driving the car. It was Oliver, with Susan in the passenger seat. Time paused, Oliver's pale face seeming to take up the whole of the window, a full, cratered moon. With a crunch of gears and rubber, Oliver cut a wide, panicked arc over the kerb and across his own front lawn. Kathleen chased the car down the road and stopped only when she scoured her already-mangled toe on the cement. The pain was beyond sound.

16

YANNICK HAD HOPED they'd be crossing the provincial border today, over into Manitoba but, thanks to Kathleen's dry rot, they won't make it that far. He won't say this aloud, but it wouldn't bother him one bit if the trip took longer than it should. What is there to get back to but an empty house and all Leigh's stuff gone, her clothes and bits of cheap jewellery and the discombobulating assortment of creams and oils from the medicine cabinet?

Hurts a lot more, the things she did not take.

But now there is something easy about slipping back into the familiar with an old friend, a friend who was once your wife even.

Kathleen's tooth, no, the hole the tooth used to occupy, the business of letting the wound get so bad she needed antibiotics, this is something Kathleen does. Has always done. Yannick looks over at her, frowning and asleep in the passenger seat as the world blurs past the window. To wilfully do the one thing she was warned against doing, this is what she does. Personal neglect. The way she has waited for Una all these years. Same thing.

He turns on the radio but the reception here is the pits. The highway is now inland from Lake Superior and they are ensconced completely in thick bush.

After two days of driving, he and Kathleen remain, in a sense, close to home, but the feeling dwindles with every passing kilometre. The lake is to the south-west of them, still, still. It cannot be seen from the road but it's there, the weight of it is there. The space it takes up. Big water.

You don't appreciate how big the ocean is, or how indifferent, until you're searching for someone you have lost. That second day they were out there in Tofino, Kathleen came banging on Yannick's hotel-room door, and the next thing he knew, they were all down at the marina, and there he was with his feet firmly on the jetty where his girl Una had stood less than a week before.

Was an Indigenous guy who last saw her there, guy called Francks. He was upset for the part he played or the part he did not think to play that night she disappeared, and he apologized to Kathleen. She said nothing, just stared at him until he looked away. It was a bad time for everyone.

The jetty that morning was busy with volunteers, more than half of them Indigenous guys, mostly fishermen, and men who yelled with clear voices and carried radios and megaphones, who walked briskly and with confidence alongside the jetty's edge. The fella in charge of the local lifeboat crew gathered everyone together for a briefing before sending crews out to search. Yannick burrowed into the outside edge of the crowd and listened to this man speak about what the conditions would have been like the night Una went out on the water, if indeed that was what she had done. It had been a spring tide that night, which Yannick gathered was very bad news as the word 'treacherous' was used more than once. That particular spring tide, it would seem, meant there was two, three metres' difference between low and high tide, which was, this lifeboat man said, a shitload of water moving into the sound and lapping around the islands. Strong currents, he said. Whirlpools and eddies. Swell travelling up the sound and bouncing back off the islands and overlapping into itself again and again in all directions. This was how the water was behaving that Saturday night, whether Una was out there or not.

The people around Yannick listened to all this talk of treachery and hazard and didn't bat an eye. They conferred among themselves and it was obvious that they knew every inch of that water, in which direction it flowed and when that flow shifted around the point of a certain island over there, or over there, or over there. Theories began to bounce around and overlap into each other as to where the water may have carried a girl in a kayak, and Yannick could see this was not just a chuck-your-ball-in-the-court-and-see-where-it-lands kind of deal. He began to believe that if she was out there, these people would find her.

Yannick caught up to the lifeboat operator, who was now heading to his boat, and asked if he could tag along. This man served him a very quick and definitive no, and assured him there would be constant radio contact, et cetera.

Not good enough. Yannick retreated to Abner Francks with the same request and Francks stretched out his hand to help Yannick aboard, telling him to lie low and keep his trap shut because if the Coast Guard guys found out a family member was on the water they would have a conniption. Sunny also hopped on and even Kathleen tried, for what it was worth. Abner Francks's daughter brought out a metal folding chair and set it square at the back of the boat, and Kathleen pinned herself in that chair and settled her eyes hard on some distant landmark, and you could see she was willing herself to be okay. Like she was trying to transform herself into stone, something with weight and density that would smash through the water rather than be swayed and tossed by it. To lead the dance rather than be dipped or twirled.

Put that woman on a boat, even a canoe on a calm lake: forget it.

Yannick knew it and Kathleen knew it, and as Francks's daughter was untying thick ropes and tossing them onto the deck, Kathleen stood up from that chair and asked Yannick to help her off: she would wait on dry land.

'You're not going to find her out there anyway,' Kathleen said, as Yannick took her hand and helped her back onto the jetty. 'That's not where she is.'

'We don't know where she is.'

'She's not out there. She wouldn't do what they're saying, steal a friggin' boat.'

'She might,' he said.

The stolen kayak, they were told, was faulty. It had been stowed, unlocked, with a collection of others that were waiting for repair. The missing kayak had a loose steering cable and a rudder that stuck to the left, causing the boat to veer forever to the right. Leave it to Una, Yannick thought, to pinch a boat that didn't work.

After helping Kathleen off Francks's boat, Yannick followed him into his wheelhouse where Francks unfolded a maritime chart on a wooden table and explained what they had been assigned to do that morning, drawing a line with his finger up and down the map to illustrate what he meant.

'Tides are treacherous around here,' he said.

'You guys use that word a lot,' said Yannick. 'Treacherous.'

Francks grunted through his nose. 'Your daughter got any real boat experience?'

'Lakes,' Yannick said. 'Canoeing.'

'So, none then,' he said.

You look at Vancouver Island on a map and you see that the west coast is like a comb, an endless series of prongs and inlets. Who knows how many islands? Taking into account the wind and the currents and time passed, the Coast Guard had a general idea of where Una could have ended up. But to look at the map. The possibilities.

When they motored out of the marina that day, north up Clayoquot Sound, it didn't take long for Yannick to feel himself shrinking against the size of their task. And it didn't take long for him to lose his sense of direction among all those islands. All that water. Making their way to their designated search area, Francks explained to Yannick that the big Coast Guard vessels were searching the open ocean to the north, because that was the direction the main currents flowed, and that the volunteers would cover the inland waters of the sound. Some crews were searching the water; others were searching the islands' shorelines in the event Una was sitting on a rock, waiting to be found.

There were so many overlapping islands, Yannick could not always tell where one ended and the next began. They were steep, and entirely covered with trees. Rocky bases the colour of ash, of willow charcoal, like the rock had been burned and cooled. The black was chalked over with the salt mark of the tides.

The missing kayak with the faulty steering was bright yellow, so this was what they were looking for, either out there in the waves or hauled up onto a beach. This wedge of yellow fibreglass burned in Yannick's eyes like the after-image left by a camera flash. He was fooled more than once by the sun's cruel play on the water, thinking he'd found her, thinking the glint of light on the water was the kayak, his need for it to be her playing tricks with his eyes.

Francks's daughter piloted the boat while Yannick, Sunny and Francks stood on either side of the deck under a hover of diesel fumes. At first, Sunny called out Una's name but Francks told him not to waste his energy: if the kayak was out there they would see it well before they were in earshot.

So they did not speak a lot, just put their heads to the grim job as the boat pushed sluggishly through the water, which, to Yannick, seemed to be breathing. It was a deep and shifty green, mottled here and there by tangles of kelp and whitened on its surface by the breeze and the churning wash of their boat and all the other boats that were looking for Una.

They found fuck-all that first day. Same as everyone else. They worked until the sun slipped down behind the islands to the west. On their way back to the marina, they motored around this rocky point and ended up crossing the mouth of a small cove. Yannick spotted a pack of otters, maybe a dozen, floating on their backs in a pod, drifting together as if there were no trouble and never had been any trouble and never would be any trouble. Stubby paws crossed over their bellies, like they were indulging in a post-lunch stupor, their shiny black noses and keen whiskers twitching skywards. A single black eye turned his way and then another, and the otters engaged him with half-lidded stares, and seemed to decide he was A-okay. One of them slipped under the surface of the water and popped back up much closer, wiry fur slick as paint on its hard head.

Yannick, both hands gripping the boat's gunwale, called: 'Have you seen her?'

*

The officials who were involved in the search, the Coast Guard and lifeboat people, they all dressed in reassuring gear with many pockets and zips and Velcro attachments. Their talk was full of lingo, most of which Yannick has now forgotten except one thing that stuck: Point Last Seen. The search in those first few days fanned out from one precise spot on the jetty where Francks had seen Una, where a security camera had captured her movements before she walked out of the frame for ever. The more time that passed, the further the search moved away from the Point Last Seen; the area of uncertainty grew while the possibilities multiplied.

Yannick has come to learn that when a thing like this happens, a thing as horrific as losing your daughter off the edge of the earth, when it first happens it starts off sharp. It starts off, in its way, pure almost to the point of perfection, like a drop of black ink on white paper. It's undiluted. It's the truth. Even if there was no one to witness it, even if no one ever finds it, there is a truth. Indisputable.

But with time? The ink gets soaked up by the paper and fades. All the thousands of possibilities that are not the truth spin you senseless, unless you stop the spinning yourself.

Of course, Yannick was not thinking in those terms on that first day of the search. This all came much later. That day, though, he must have had some intuition because when they got back to the jetty, he stood again on the spot where Francks had spied Una. Point Last Seen. He kicked off his shoes and pulled off his socks and pressed his bare toes against the rough concrete. Dusk was rolling over into night and everything was losing its edges. Sunny stood there with him and they watched a seaplane pivot into position and take off towards the open ocean before it banked right and disappeared behind a headland to the north.

Yannick closed his eyes and quietly called her up, his Una, he called her up.

A whole lot of nothing happened, those days on Abner Francks's fishing boat. Four days, they spent. On each, they were allotted a new patch of water to search, further away from the marina. They worked their way up the westernmost islands, towards a place called Hot Springs Cove, as one of Una's friends had suggested she could have been trying to get there: a gang of them had chartered a boat there recently and apparently, according to this friend, Una had been deeply moved by the experience.

Yannick was grateful for the monotony of those four days, the repetitive *doing*. Hours of leaning into the hard boat gunwale and scanning with his whole head, not just the eyes, from right to left (opposite to how you read, Francks taught him, to ward off the search blindness).

On the last day, they drifted in close to a beach and Francks turned off the engine. With the sudden absence of its drone and gargle, the world was at first numbly quiet and then it was all birds, and wind in the trees, and the lap and suck of a steel hull nestled in the ocean. Francks came out of the wheelhouse and lit up a smoke, and poured coffees out of a Thermos for himself and Yannick. Sunny opened a can of pop and Yannick was digging his fingers into his own cigarette pack, chasing the one goddamn smoke that was left in there, when Francks stopped and held his hand up, head cocked. Yannick and Sunny stopped too, and were all eyes on Francks.

'You hear that?' he said.

Yannick and Sunny turned their heads to listen and Yannick heard nothing, but then Sunny's eyes went bright and he said: 'That clunking?'

'Yup, that's the ticket, boy-o,' said Francks. 'Over there,' he said, and pointed towards a fallen cedar tree that lay where the beach curved into an elbow of rocks. Francks ducked back into the wheelhouse and revved the engine. The boat turned sharply towards the rocks and when they got around to the other side, Yannick saw something bright and yellow, and this was not the sun playing tricks on the water. This was a solid, man-made thing. It made him sick, that up-and-down swell of the ocean, that up-and-down swell of hope and hope dashed. It was a second, less than a second, before it was obvious that they were not looking at a yellow kayak, but instead just an oil drum trapped between the rocks, pushed rhythmically by the waves.

Francks gripped Yannick's shoulder. 'This is better,' he said. 'We don't want to be finding an empty kayak half fucken sunk.'

Yannick stared at the oil drum until Francks went back into the wheelhouse and the boat turned away. The drum looked like it had been there for ever and would stay there for ever. Una had never been more *not here* than she was in that moment.

A Prank

THE SUN HAS gone again. That's just the way it is around here. There's no telling. Our girl has made it halfway into town and the wrench in her knee has turned bad enough that, half a kilometre back, she foraged by the side of the road for a walking stick. It's not a bad stick, as sticks go.

She'll phone her mother today and confess to the humiliating hitching blunder. Her mother will probably tell her she acted like an idiot, which she did. (Her mother is very good at calling a spade a spade.)

Just up the road from here is the place where she lived for the better part of a year before she moved into the tree. (Say it again: moved into the tree.) She's headed that way now, to the house, to beg a shower and maybe a cup of coffee and some toast with peanut butter. Maybe a lift the rest of the way into town.

She is greeted, before she even gets to the front door, by the next-door neighbour's dog, which she remembers fondly from when she lived in this house.

'You're a good boy, aren't you? Aren't you a good, good boy?' she coos, ruffling his ears, thinking of that other hound from a few hours ago and his wet breath on her neck. The dog raises his head to her and breathes a kerfuffly kind of snort.

She knocks. Trent, the man who lives here, is a pleasant enough person. A little weird, but he let her stay, for free, in a kind of tacked-on room at the back of his house. So she put up with the weird. She knocks again, no answer. She steps back from the door and looks up at the inexpressive second-floor windows.

She picks her way around the side of the house to the back, and opens the gate to the backyard, remembering, as she does so, the piece of wire you have to twist to set the gate free. Dog at heels. Tall grass flowing around her calves.

Trent never used to lock his back door, and this proves true today. Absentmindedly scratching the new mosquito bite behind her ear, she lets herself into the house and goes into the kitchen. The reason she felt safe living with this odd man was because, though he was slovenly (never cleaned up after himself, rarely washed his clothes other than the clothes he wore to work, where he was her manager at a grocery store), he also tended towards the obsessive, the compulsive. She trusted that. It reminded her, quite distinctly actually, of the guy she's meeting later today. *The guy* hardly seems fair. The person she's meeting today is her closest, oldest friend. Her first love, if we're being honest. A piece of home is coming here, at last.

Anyway, Trent: at work, the shelves had to be meticulous. The money in the cash register counted at regular intervals and the bills all facing the same way, the Queen and the prime ministers lying face-up at the top.

At home, he insisted on keeping his toaster on the floor as a fire-prevention measure (don't ask). He ate his dinner at seven thirty every night. Breakfast at six. He displayed a collection of animal statuettes, which he carved himself, on the windowsill over the kitchen sink, each statuette equidistant to the next.

Soapstone, purchased directly from a quarry further up the island.

While the coffee percolator percolates, she inspects the soapstone animals. Among many, a tuft-backed grizzly bear. A cougar flexed to pounce. A contemplative kestrel. In the middle of the row sits a Chinook salmon, arched, which she has always coveted. She picks it up for a closer look, then drops it into her pocket, justifying this theft as a prank; she's only jerking around with the mathematical accuracy of the display. She'll give it back. Maybe. It feels good to rub her thumb along its scaled body. Its muscled arch. She likes the weight of it in her pocket.

There is not a crumb of food in the house. She has to drink her coffee black and forgo the toast. She rinses her cup and dries it, puts it away, and goes back outside, as there's no access through the house to the little backyard room where she used to stay. This room is also unlocked; the door isn't flush with the floor and makes a dusty, scraping sound when she pushes it open. She props her bag on the single bare mattress and takes out her towel, her comb and nearly empty bottle of shampoo. The shower is a rigged-up deal around the back of this small room, in a breeze-block outhouse built for purpose. She used to love how wild this felt, but now pines for the shiny tiles, the heat vent, the spider plant hanging in the window of her mother's bathroom, trailing its baby spiders to the floor.

The dog, Jimi, follows her to the shower and plays sentry at the open entrance while she lathers and scrubs and shivers under the meagre flow. Her knee is alarmingly swollen. The soap slides down her body, taking with it almost two weeks of dirt and sweat and salt residue from the ocean.

Jimi follows her back into the room, where she lowers

herself to the bed and stretches out her bad leg. She lies there until she is completely dry, then gets dressed and combs her hair at the mirror. Dabs amber perfume oil between her breasts and behind her ears. Stares at herself for a little while.

She pulls the salmon out of her pocket and holds it up to her face. 'You know your way home, don't you?' she says.

17

KATHLEEN AND YANNICK have settled into adjacent rooms on the first floor of a motel in the town of Kenora. The pain medication has made Kathleen feel a little nauseous so she's declined dinner with Yannick and locked herself into her room. Yannick seemed relieved to go to bed early. He's tired: she can see it in his face. This drive is already harder than he'd thought it would be.

She relaxes onto the bed with her phone. One text message from Julius that just says: hi. One message from Sunny letting her know that Yannick isn't responding to anyone's calls or messages. Asking her if she knows where he is.

Yannick has gone missing from his children.

She replies to Sunny that she and Yannick are together, heading west. Tells him not to worry.

She sinks her head deeper into the starchy pillow and phones Heather. Maybe she should have been more apologetic the other day in the backyard, nicer, but apologies stick in her throat.

Heather isn't answering so Kathleen lets it ring. She'll leave a message, even better. A few recorded words of remorse. A word or two about there being a lot going on right now. Heather answers, though, and Kathleen bellows, 'Hello.'

There's not a lot of intonation in Heather's return hello.

'Just wanted to see how it's all going,' Kathleen says.

'It's only been two days.'

'A lot can go wrong in two days.'

'Everything is fine,' Heather says.

Kathleen asks her about today's delivery, which, Heather replies, was also fine. 'I did most of the weeding yesterday and today,' she says. 'I'll finish tomorrow if it's not pouring.'

'It's raining?'

'Supposed to.'

'Well, it's good you got it mostly done.'

'The kids helped.'

'Huh.'

'I put Angus on the wheel hoe. He picked it up fast.'

'Angus?'

'My oldest son, Kathleen.'

'As long as he didn't damage my annuals.' Kathleen says this with a little chuckle, to show she's not actually worried. Neither of them says anything for a second or two. Here, now, this is where Kathleen can say sorry, properly, for being unkind. For taking advantage.

'Where are you guys?' Heather asks.

They are east of where they should be by now. They're on a fool's errand. They are nowhere. 'Kenora,' she says.

'Kenora.'

Another few beats of silence. Kathleen knows she's being punished, but she's never been very good with the cold shoulder. 'Anything you need to ask?' she says.

'It's fine.'

If Heather says *fine* one more time, Kathleen is going to hang up. 'You sure?' she says.

'Kathleen.' Her voice is softer now. 'I've got it.'

'I know you do,' she says, which is as much sorry as she can manage.

They say goodbye, though she still feels unsatisfied. She is thinking about her growing debt of apologies. She scratches at the raised pattern of the hotel bedspread and thinks about how it seems so much easier for everyone else to just . . . be nice. She is not always nice. For such a weak word, 'nice' now seems, as she takes short stock of the people in her life whom she hasn't pissed off, something she ought to try to be better at.

In her grief, she has done unkind things. She continues to softly scratch the fabric and she thinks about that poor, goofy kid, that dope, that Oliver Hanratty.

The media, in the beginning, were taken with Una's story. She was in the newspapers a lot. Kathleen said yes to every interview, and not long after she faced Susan Hanratty down in her kitchen, she voiced her suspicions about Oliver to a radio journalist over the phone. It was no better than gossip, but it caused a lot of damage.

After that she heard snippets about what happened to Oliver Hanratty. Media on his back. Hate mail. People pointing him out in the street. Apparently he dropped out of graduate school, left the country for a while. And this was all before the whatsit, the Facebook.

Now she thinks about that boy (all lanky shoulders and plummeting Adam's apple) raking the leaves on her front lawn, or standing at the sink doing a hack job of the dishes after dinner or, oddly enough, lining up the condiment bottles in her fridge door by height, and puts her phone face down on the bedside table. Turns off the lamp.

(For the record: She does know that Angus is Heather's eldest child. The next is Cory, and there's one called David, named after Dave, and the sassy one, the Keeper of Birthdays and Dead Grasshoppers, is April. The baby who hates her is called Jake. She is not totally oblivious.)

Tonight, she gets little sleep.

Their aim the next day is the town of Medicine Hat, over a thousand kilometres and twelve hours away. It's probably a big ask, but it's already day three and they've only just crossed the provincial border between Ontario and Manitoba. Yannick is giving it hell on the pedal.

They stop for gas at an Esso station in a place called Whiteshell. Yannick's knees and back are already feeling tight so they leave the truck at the gas station and walk up the road towards a cute log-cabin restaurant called the Point. There's an orange Volkswagen van in the parking lot covered with stickers. Volkswagen vans remind Kathleen of cheap narcotics and unprotected sex.

'How's your pain?' he asks, as they approach the restaurant.

'How's your pain?' she asks.

'I asked you first.'

'It's manageable,' she says.

He stumbles on a rock and grabs her shoulder to steady himself. She has to get used to this version of Yannick, this Yannick who is not as mighty as the one she remembers.

There are a few other diners at the restaurant. A lone old-timer in plaid, carving into a stack of pancakes. A couple sitting by the window, thumbing their phones – a young man and a woman, barely adults. Around her bare neck is a drape of necklaces and beads, drawing down to the smooth valley between her breasts. The array looks simultaneously random and carefully curated. Like she doesn't have to try to be beautiful.

Kathleen remembers how Una changed from Little Girl to

Young Woman. The transformation was, oddly, both gradual and sudden. She remembers how her nose changed from baby round to narrow and slanted, and the darkening, the thickening of her eyebrows and hair. The heaviness to the bum and thighs, the swelling of her breasts and the new fullness in her voice. Everything becoming more substantial, more entrenched. And then later, when Una was entering her twenties and Kathleen her forties, when Kathleen began to notice changes in her own body that were as surprising as those experienced in puberty, she would look to Una, this spectacular, disastrous young woman, and feel held, somehow, preserved in her daughter's youth.

She is ravenous. This will be her first solid food since the Oreos in Wawa, and even then, she only licked the icing. She orders oatmeal, brown toast and home fries, and a mint tea. Yannick orders black coffee and something called a granola harvest bowl with yoghurt.

Kathleen can't stop looking at the young couple, who are now stroking each other across the table, heads bent close together. The girl catches her looking and Kathleen blinks her gaze in another direction. 'I'll take the next shift at the wheel,' she says, for something to say.

Yannick nods.

'Why aren't you eating real food?' she asks.

'This is real food.'

'For a bird.'

He smiles. She's bullying and he doesn't care.

'You see that couple over there? Don't look.'

'Well, if I can't look, how can I see them?'

'Don't make it obvious,' she whispers.

Yannick very obviously tilts his head and has a look.

'Should we tell them it's not worth it?' she says, smiling sideways. 'Save them years of trouble?'

Yannick looks at her sadly.

Sheesh.

The young couple get up and as they walk away from their table they gravitationally attract, two bodies orbiting together in space, and when they connect, their baby fingers link. As if this small, almost involuntary, act is meaningless, as if this were something you wouldn't miss terribly when it was gone.

The food arrives and Kathleen tucks in, though carefully with the toast. Yannick dips at his granola.

Once they've paid the bill, Yannick makes a stop at the toilet, and Kathleen takes this opportunity to go somewhere private for a sneaky puff. She finds a spot behind the garbage bins next to the restaurant, and lights up with the intention of only having a drag or two, or three, out of respect for the dry rot. Pacing in small circles, she takes a stiff haul and throws her head back to exhale. As promised, she drops the cigarette after three – four – puffs, and grinds it out with the toe of her shoe. Some small knick-knack on the ground next to the bin catches the sun and glints for her attention. She picks it up: a wind-up music box, no bigger than a matchbox. Its mechanics exposed: tiny brass screws and the row of thin, needle-like keys alongside the rolling drum, which is pimpled with a braille-like pattern of minuscule spikes. She rotates the little elbowed handle but the toy is broken. The drum doesn't turn. It's still a good find, though, interesting, and now that she's seen it, she can't leave it there on the ground. She tucks it into her pocket.

Since she's here, and hidden by the industrial bin, she might as well pee, so she unbuttons her shorts and pulls them down, then lowers into a solid squat. With all the harvesting and weeding, the digging and hoeing, her thighs are balanced and strong.

Just as she's letting go, she hears crunching footsteps on the gravel. It all happens very quickly: she's still squatting when the necklace girl comes into view, swinging a plastic bag. As the girl draws back her arm to toss her garbage into the bin, she makes direct eye contact with Kathleen, who hasn't moved an inch, displaying to the girl whatever she's got to give.

The girl does not throw her garbage away; instead she turns quickly, and goes. Kathleen's pee backs up, like a dormouse.

She meets up with Yannick at the front of the restaurant and hears the revving of an engine, which she assumes belongs to the Volkswagen van.

'Walk,' she says.

'Where did you go? You were smoking. Jesus, Kathleen.'

'Just walk, please.' Without waiting for him, she heads back towards the truck, moving fast. She goes into the toilets at the Esso station to finish the job and, while she's in there, digs through her purse for her notebook and a pen. Sitting on the toilet, the silenced music box pressing against her thigh through her pocket, she changes the number from 7972 to 7973, having forgotten to do it first thing this morning.

At the beginning of Una's disappearance, they measured time in days. Three days missing, four, eleven. Each day more significant and complex than the last, like the development of a brand new baby. For everyone else, the days very quickly lost their relevance and soon the count was measured in weeks, then months and years.

But to count a day is to ensure urgency. Kathleen stares at the number she's just scrawled, trying to milk it for meaning. For so many years, it's been written on the fridge in the same spot. Written in this notepad, it doesn't seem to belong to anything.

That first day they searched the water, which was also the fifth day of Una's disappearance, Kathleen was angry. She was angry that everyone seemed sold on this stolen-kayak theory, and she was angrier that she couldn't stomach even five minutes on Abner Francks's bulky oaf of a fishing boat.

Instead, she watched the boat reverse away from the jetty, boiling and chewing the water, then watched it splice off and away. Yannick standing there on the deck, grasping the railing with two hands, and Sunny next to him, his face set and grim. Looking much older than his sixteen years. Kathleen watched until the boat got smaller and disappeared behind an island, and she remembers a pair of massive birds, albatrosses maybe, diving exuberantly above the water. Having a lovely time.

An alarming yellow helicopter, cumbersome as a bus and with two sets of rotor blades, whomped overhead, further out in the sound. Kathleen asked the man standing next to her if the helicopter was for Una and he said it was, and the sight of the powerful machine, agitating the air, scattering the birds, made Kathleen feel sick.

Patti Zoric brought Kathleen back to the detachment so she could be shown the CCTV footage. She had set up a television in a staff room of sorts – no windows, not a lot of air. Kathleen sank into a natty couch and watched a red light on the VCR flicker at abrupt intervals.

Patti Zoric took out her notepad. 'We spoke briefly on the phone,' she said, 'about the possibility of Una having psychological issues.'

'You asked me if she had any and I told you she didn't,' Kathleen said.

Another officer came into the room. He introduced himself and pulled a chair close to the couch, so that he was next to the television, facing Kathleen. He asked Kathleen how she was doing and if she was ready to watch the tape.

She shrugged, unsure.

'We hope you can help us understand her behaviour,' Patti Zoric said.

For this initial viewing, Kathleen was shown only a few minutes here and there, the sections the police specifically wanted to discuss with her. But now, having watched the video umpteen times, Kathleen knows it by heart.

All dirty tones of grey, the footage is captured from a static position by a camera affixed to the top corner of the kayak cage. Una enters the frame for the first time at 9:32 p.m., dressed in a sleeveless top and long shorts. Her hair hangs well past her shoulders and she has a backpack secured tightly to her body. Her movements are eerie, but that seems to be because the light is eerie, and there is a stop-start quality to the tape. She is limping; this is clear. She stands at the edge of the jetty with her hands deep in her pockets, then takes her hands out and rubs her arms vigorously. She collects her hair into a bun at the top of her head and winds it with a lock of hair around the bun to secure it. Then, without any intent in her movement, she walks, with that limp, out of the frame. This happens six times in the first hour, wandering back and forth, in and out of the frame. Hair up, hair down, hair up again. The last time she returns, she sits on the jetty so that her feet hang over the edge. Here she remains for twenty-nine minutes, until 11:05 p.m. Within this twenty-nine-minute period, she lies back a few times and dances her hands in the air. It looks a little like she's making shadow puppets, though of course there is nothing on which to cast them.

At 11:17, she looks sharply over her shoulder as if she's responding to something. Perhaps her name. She listens with her head turned, then relaxes forward again, looking down into the water.

At 11:23 she turns her head again and cocks an ear. Then she turns half of her body, pushes herself up and stares at something down the jetty. At 11:28 she steps, with absolute intent, out of the frame. She is going towards something. This time, she doesn't return.

This is how Kathleen has always interpreted those last few minutes, even from the first time she watched them, and the police have never agreed with her – that there was purpose in her gait at the end. That she was responding to something or someone.

When they finished watching the tape that first time, Kathleen said this to them: 'There's someone there with her.'

'Why do you say that?' Patti Zoric asked.

'Look how she turned her head. It's obvious.'

They rewound the tape and watched the last six minutes. And then they did this again and again. Neither Patti nor the other officer could see that there was anything obvious about Una's behaviour.

'It does look like she heard a noise or something,' the other officer said.

Patti turned off the television. 'Does any of this seem characteristic to you?' she asked. 'The way she's behaving?'

'I don't know why you're asking me,' said Kathleen.

Patti and the other officer glanced at each other.

'Because you know her,' Patti said.

'I already gave you my opinion and you didn't agree.'

'The rest of it, though,' said Patti. 'It was cold that night, you know? And she's out there for hours. Does this feel normal to you?'

The truth was, it did not. It was weird. And she looked agitated. Her shoulders were tensed in a way that was not Una. Her hair was too long and she looked like she'd lost weight; her arms were too skinny. Kathleen wouldn't say this aloud, though. She could see where this was going and thought they wouldn't look so hard for Una if her mother confirmed her behaviour was off. They would think Una had taken herself away.

Patti Zoric began, thus: 'Your daughter has never been diagnosed with a mental illness?'

'I already told you, no.'

'Has she ever needed treatment of any kind? Counselling?'

'No.'

'Would she have sought counselling without your knowledge?'

Kathleen wagged her head and admitted, 'Maybe.'

'Is she on any medications?'

'No.'

'Does she use recreational drugs?'

'Only grass, far as I know.'

This line of questioning crept into even darker corners. Does Una experience hallucinations? Has her mood changed recently? Is she depressed? Does she suffer delusions? Have there recently been any stressful events in her life? Heartbreak, job loss, threat of criminal prosecution? Unwanted pregnancy?

Is she impulsive? Does she have difficulty adapting to change? Has she ever tried or expressed a desire to take her own life?

Kathleen's answer to all: 'No.'

In truth, she couldn't be completely sure.

And this is something she will never admit.

18

HOW SAD IT IS, Yannick thinks, that poor boy, that boy
Oliver, dead. The nonsense with him and his mother got out of
hand quickly, and Yannick has always felt partly to blame. At
the time, Kathleen was on her own, and this made her desperate, and Yannick should have done better.

Susan Hanratty could have pressed charges over what happened, and she didn't. Kathleen was lucky. She was never able
to explain to Yannick why she went over to their house that
day, but the first he knew of it was when she called him around
ten that night.

'I need you to come get me,' she said.

'Come get you where?'

'Police station,' she said.

First thought, Una. And it was a dark thought. The worst.
Kathleen must have known, though, that his mind would go
there because she spoke quickly, telling him it had nothing to
do with Una. 'Not in the way you're thinking,' she said.

'What's it to do with, then, Kathleen?' he asked.

She sighed. Her whole body sighed through the phone.
'Just come, please,' she said. 'I'm injured.'

An hour's drive from where he was living, he picked Kathleen up from the police station and took her to Emergency.
Her foot was mangled and gashed from where she'd stepped on
broken glass. Her big toe of the same foot was also broken and

swollen purple, with its meaty end scraped off. Kathleen had stepped on broken glass in the Hanrattys' kitchen. There was glass on the kitchen floor because Kathleen had thrown a stone garden gnome through the back-door window to break into their house.

The biggest pieces of glass were relatively easy to extract from her foot. The small ones proved a little more difficult.

'These little guys cause all the trouble,' the nurse said, in their close, curtained-off cubicle. Kathleen was on the examination bed and Yannick stood with his back against the wall and his hands thrust deeply into his pockets, his jaw tight. The nurse placed herself on a stool at the end of the bed and pointed a bright light at the sole of Kathleen's bloody, filthy foot, and got down to business with a scalpel.

Dawn, just surfacing, silent and cold, as he drove her home. Too tired now to be angry, Yannick helped her with her crutches into the house and settled her on the couch.

'You hungry?' he asked her. 'You want a coffee or a sandwich or something?'

She agreed to coffee but had no appetite. He hadn't seen her in weeks and she looked dragged down and thin. In the kitchen, there was one plate, one fork and one glass drying in the rack, and he thought about Leigh waiting for him at home, and he felt awfully, awfully sorry for Kathleen. While the coffee percolated, he snooped. Una, only two months missing, so much hope still, was very present in this house. Mail addressed to her in a pile left on the table. A shoulder bag she used, bunch of tassels and sequins, hanging off the door that led to the basement. One dangly earring, too beady and flamboyant to be Kathleen's, in a basket of odds and ends next to the telephone.

He brought the coffee and a glass of water for the

painkillers and sat with Kathleen until she was ready to talk. She told him this: Oliver Hanratty was hiding from her, and she had caught him, red-handed. She'd had no choice but to break into the house.

'It was instinct,' she said. 'I didn't even feel the glass. I was that focused.'

'On what? Focused on what?'

She stared at him with eyes that were hollow and shadowy from lack of sleep. 'On Una,' she said.

'What did you expect to find in that house?'

'Specifically?'

Yannick nodded and the room drifted. Sleep was pulling at him, too.

'There was nothing specific,' she said.

'So what did you do?'

'I can't really remember. I called for her. I looked in closets, I looked under the beds. I opened drawers.'

'Why go through their drawers?'

'Freezer, too.'

'Kathleen.'

'There has to be something, Yannick.'

'Una was hundreds of kilometres away,' he said. 'I don't understand this.'

'Nor do I.'

Yannick asked her why in the hell she wasn't wearing any shoes when she decided to commit her first B and E.

'Jesus Christ, Yannick, my shoes and socks were wet from the creek,' she said.

He did not ask her how it came to be that her shoes and socks were wet from the creek.

'Anyway, I stopped as soon as I heard the cops pulling up

outside, the sirens and the lights and everything. Some good-for-nothing neighbour must have called.'

'What'd you do?'

'I sat at the kitchen table. One of them came to the back door and I told her I'd broken in.'

'You're in deep shit, Kathleen.'

'Cops said Susan Hanratty isn't pressing charges. I just have to pay for the window. And the living-room carpet.'

He raised his eyebrows in question.

'I got blood on it,' she said.

'Do you believe them now? Do you believe Oliver?'

Kathleen rubbed her hands up and down her face and sighed. She spoke through her closed hands. 'She lied to me about where he was. Why would she do that?'

'Why would she want to keep her tormented kid away from you?' he asked, nodding at her foot.

'It can't not mean something, Yannick, that he was out there when she disappeared. It has to mean something.'

'You are acting desperate,' he said.

'You're not acting desperate enough,' she said.

People in this country tend to believe that the prairies are a never-ending drone, nothing to see but antelopes and grass, but now that he's here, Yannick does not agree. There is something about the simplicity that is not simple at all.

Before now, the landscape was all rough edges and overlapping curves. Thick bush and the inability to see what was coming. But the world unrolled and emptied out somewhere around the city of Winnipeg, in the province of Manitoba. Now, you take all 360 degrees of this flat horizon and you'd better believe you can see what's coming.

There's the old joke that goes: if your dog runs away in the prairies it's no problem – you'll still see him running two days later.

The road hurtles away from them, stretching with geometric precision to the most distant point, where it shivers and disappears. Far ahead is an oil tanker. The tanker seems to hover at the wavery vantage point, as if it's driving through heat, as if it's going to drive off the edge of the world into nothing. They've just passed a hand-painted sign propped in the grassy verge and it made Yannick chuckle, red letters painted on a white sign not much bigger than a paperback, and all it said was: 'Potatoes here'. In this forever landscape, this comically small sign: 'Potatoes here'. And no *here* in sight.

Not long after crossing the provincial border into Saskatchewan, they stop for gas in a place called Broadview. The old boy who fills their tank has nicotine-white hair and no top teeth and makes a big deal about their Ontario plates. He tells them they are going in the wrong direction if they're trying to get back to Ontario.

'Not even sure I should be selling you my gas,' he says, most likely assuming they're from the hated Toronto, rather than a small town, same as him. He giggles and winks at Kathleen, who is currently at the wheel, clearly unimpressed with the flirting. Refuses to humour him.

'Why wouldn't you sell us gas?' she says, straight-faced.

'Onterrible,' he says, gesturing to the rear licence plate, the air coming out of his flirt as he realizes she's not playing ball. Even so, he winks again.

Kathleen turns her head to Yannick and shakes it. Half an eye roll.

'So where the heck you running to anyways?' he says.

'Vancouver.'

'Oof!' he says, like he's been punched in the gut. 'Enjoy the gap.'

'Eh?'

'Nothing between here and the Rockies but nothing. That's the gap.'

As they're pulling away, Yannick pinches her elbow. She slaps his hand.

'What was that for?' she says.

'He liked you,' he says.

'For Pete's sake.' She scowls.

Without turning his face, Yannick checks out Kathleen's hands on the wheel, gripped confidently at ten and two. She wears a ring on her right pointer finger, a rounded, thick silver band. Buffed and scratched and hunkered into the roughened flesh of her finger, as if she's been wearing it for years. He wonders for how many years, and if someone gave it to her. He's curious about how long it is since she's been with a man. This is not jealousy but there is some goddamn thing burrowing behind his ribcage as he thinks about the man who (maybe) gave her that ring and he thinks about what those hands of hers are capable of when they're full of a man.

He jerks his head towards the passenger window. The sky: as expected, there's a hell of a lot of it.

They drive on.

Some point later they pass a sign saying: 'Look after Saskatchewan's Waterways. Stop Invasive Species. Remove Boat Plugs. Dry Boats Completely.'

'I guess we're in Saskatchewan,' Yannick says.

'Even flatter.'

The Canadian Pacific Rail line periodically drifts in close enough that they're driving parallel to cargo trains, hundreds of boxcars long. A little company where there is little company, the trains visit for a few kilometres, then are gone again. An inconstant companion. Yannick senses loneliness here, a loneliness that has got used to itself, maybe a bit like how it must be for Kathleen.

He watches a flock of birds rise from a cropped field and fall together in a low cascade, then land in this solitary, perfectly tree-shaped tree. An hour ago, or maybe it was two, three antelopes sprang together out of the tall grass. A loneliness that has got used to itself.

And there are power lines running alongside the road, perfect all the way to the horizon as if they were drawn on the sky with a ruler. He suspects that in a winter storm, when the road is obliterated by snow, you would be grateful for these power lines. Some kind of authority to follow, something rigid and functional to help a person find his way.

Yannick and Sunny spent four days with Abner Francks on his fishing boat, and on the fourth and last day, when they motored into the marina, approaching the jetty, Yannick could see Kathleen waiting there with her arms wrapped tightly around her body and her face all dark shadows.

'They're quitting,' Kathleen called, as soon as the boat was in earshot. By this time, Yannick had figured out how to be of some use to Abner Francks, and when they drifted in close enough, he hopped over the water onto the jetty with the bow rope coiled over his arm.

Kathleen said it again: 'They're quitting.'

'Eh?' he said, looping the rope around the metal cleat on the jetty.

'The Coast Guard, the search and rescue guys,' said Kathleen. 'They're leaving us.' She still had her arms wrapped around her middle and she looked small. It was a mild evening and she looked like a woman locked out in the cold.

Francks leaped expertly off his boat, as sure-footed on terra firma as not. 'This is how they do it,' he said. He lit a cigarette for Kathleen and passed it to her, and she dragged on it like it was the last cigarette on the planet, the paper squeaking tightly as it burned.

A lurching somewhere deep in Yannick's head, an off-kilter queerness from being back on land after hours of sleepy motion on deep water. Sometimes out there, it was like he could feel the entirety of the Pacific Ocean rolling and swelling and dropping under his feet. Back on land, the world continued to shift.

'What do you mean, this is how they do it?' Kathleen asked.

'This is what they do,' Francks repeated. 'They work off what they think is probable, eh? They look at the situation and they say, "Okay, the water is so-and-so cold and she was wearing this or that, and it's been this many days." They tally it all together and make a decision.' Francks went on to explain that if the danger to the crew became greater than the chances of finding a person alive, or if their resources were needed somewhere else, they would halt the search.

'It's fucken shit,' he said, his eyes on Kathleen's fingers, trembling as she brought her cigarette to her mouth.

Sunny shuffled to the edge of the jetty and sat with his legs over the side. His shoulder blades looked like the stumps of wings poking under his T-shirt, and Yannick wondered what must have been going through his head.

Francks lit a cigarette for himself and squinted the smoke out of his eyes. 'If they think it's got worse than what a person could survive, they call it,' he said.

'But they haven't found anything yet,' said Kathleen. Her face was pale and twitchy.

'Coast Guard doesn't search for bodies,' Francks said softly.

'She's not dead,' Kathleen said.

Francks drew deeply on his smoke and nodded, and spat into the water.

Yannick held Kathleen's face in both his hands. 'Maybe this is better,' he said. 'You didn't think she was out there anyway.'

'But all those people, Yannick,' she said, pulling his hands off her face. 'The helicopter. They're leaving.' She explained that the case was being handed back to the RCMP, and that instead of this being a search and rescue operation, Una was now considered a missing person.

'*Now* she's considered a missing person?' Yannick said.

'I know,' said Kathleen. 'They said she was lost. Now she's missing.'

'I do not understand that.'

Kathleen flicked her cigarette butt over the edge of the jetty and stood there, watching it sink.

'I guess lost is lost,' Yannick said. 'Missing could mean anything.'

'We won't stop looking,' said Francks. He took his cap off, ran his fingers through his hair and jammed his cap squarely back on his head. Smoothed the wings of his hair behind his ears. 'I got a lot of cousins and I got a lot of friends. People with boats. Fishermen. Guys who run the taxis from Opitsat

and Ahousat. Those guys'll all keep looking. We aren't so interested in probabilities,' he said, 'and we won't stop. You want
your girl back so you can do it right.'

'Do it right?' Kathleen said.

Francks looked at her hard, his eyes lively, looked at her as if
he were thinking about what to say. He took another pull on his
cigarette and said: 'We won't fucken leave her out there alone.'

Yannick doesn't now remember how the arrangements were
made, but early the next morning, a wet and dreary morning,
he and Kathleen were back in town, meeting up with Mariella,
the friend who'd called Kathleen in the first place. Yannick
trusted this Mariella right away, a nice kid from Saskatoon
with boy-short, dirty-blonde hair that looked like she cut it
herself with garden shears. She was wearing Dr Marten boots
and stringy jean shorts and a red raincoat, glossy vinyl, like a
kid's raincoat, and she had this kind of cross-eyed look behind
a mother of a pair of Coke-bottle glasses. Tattoos all up her legs
before the whole world was tattooed.

They met her outside a bakery with only a meagre selection
of sweaty baked goods in its window, and she hugged them
both as if she'd known them for years, greeted them with a
hefty hello and inexplicably called them chickens. They crossed
town to the other side of the peninsula and she told them she
had already been living in Tofino for a year before Una turned
up. She said that because Una had arrived in February the year
before, in the middle of winter, she'd been lucky to get a job as
quickly as she did.

'That was the job at the grocery store?' Kathleen said.

'That's the one,' Mariella said. 'She found a gig at the Co-
op. Moved in with her boss.'

'She didn't tell us that,' said Yannick.

'He had this little shack behind his house,' said Mariella. 'Una lived there rent free.'

'She ever tell you why she quit that job?' Yannick asked.

They were walking, three abreast, along the grassy shoulder of the road because there were no sidewalks. Just a cracked-pavement road and dusty, scraggled bushes crowded with unripe blackberries.

'No biggie,' said Mariella. 'She didn't want to live at Trent's place any more, too much of a mission getting into town, too far, so she quit and moved into my digs.'

'That's the boss's name?' Kathleen said. 'Trent? Was he getting fresh with her? Do the police know about him?'

'He's harmless,' Mariella said. 'Maybe a little strange but strange in a good way, eh? Kooky,' she said, blinking rapidly behind those glasses. 'You could probably go see him yourself.'

This set Kathleen off. She wanted to turn back and go straight to Sergeant Zoric, but they had just come to this set of rickety wooden stairs leading down into a cove, and where they were going now was important, too.

Yannick said as much to Kathleen. 'One thing at a time,' he said to her. 'This is what we're doing now.'

Kathleen looked around. 'Where the hell are we?' she said.

They were now standing on the sand in a very small cove, a horseshoe beach with tough, knuckly coniferous trees growing close, some dipping into the water.

'I thought we were going to Una's house,' said Kathleen. 'What are we doing on this frigging beach?'

'This is the way home,' Mariella said.

They followed her to the far end of the beach and up onto a path that you would never find if you didn't know to look for it. Scrambling up that path, Yannick could see that for Kathleen, every step was taking her further away from her familiar. It was the way she kept looking back over her shoulder, her eyebrows frozen halfway up her forehead, or the way she moved, tentatively and not one bit Kathleen-y, with her hands out as if she were trying to find her way in the dark.

They followed this path for several minutes, then stepped down into an even smaller cove that was more foamy surf than beach. They crossed to the other side through cold water sluicing up their calves, and then again up into the trees, another scramble over roots and moss and a path that almost wasn't there, until eventually Mariella stopped walking and said, '*Voilà.*'

'What are you *voilà*-ing about?' said Kathleen.

'Home,' she said.

Yannick looked around more carefully and now he could see that there were tents hidden in the trees, going up the slope from the beach, tarps tied at wonky angles to the ground and hammocks everywhere. No trees or bush had been cleared away to make room, the forest just was and the tents just were.

'Totally illegal,' Mariella said.

'This is where you live?' Kathleen asked.

'Every few weeks the cops come to chuck us out, but we just pop back up like those gophers in that game where you . . .' She made the motion of knocking gophers' heads with a mallet.

'Which one is Una's?' Yannick asked.

'Follow me,' Mariella said, and carried on up through the woods. No path now, and they were dodging branches and ploughing through stick and thistle and fern, crashing through the bush. The slope eventually levelled out and Mariella stood in front of the trunk of a great old cedar long dead, about the width of a car. The trunk was hollow and covered at its top with an old tarp. Mariella unlaced her boots and kicked them off, then ducked inside a triangular opening in the trunk, and Kathleen and Yannick followed her.

Inside, the scant light was murky blue because of the tarp. The ground was lined with more tarps and old scraps of carpet and two sleeping bags. The air smelt of damp clothes and sleep. Mariella stood in the middle of all this and said, 'Home sweet home, chickens!'

'What is this?' Yannick said. He ran his hands over the concave wall of dead wood, smooth and ridged and knotted.

Kathleen picked up the corner of a sleeping bag and let it drop.

'This is where we lay our heads,' Mariella said.

'This is a dead tree,' Kathleen said.

Mariella put her hand on Kathleen's shoulder and turned her around to show her a shallow niche carved out of the trunk. On this uneven shelf: a toothbrush and hair elastics and the waxy drippings from nights and nights of candles. Black soot on the wall. Kathleen took a Ziploc bag from the shelf and passed it to Yannick. It contained photos of him and Kathleen and Una's friends from home. Una's big backpack was propped against the wall, open. Yannick knelt to it and started pulling clothes out, severely wrinkled cotton shirts and jeans, scarves and single socks and the smell of Una.

'The police already went through all that,' Mariella said.

Kathleen looked at Yannick and said, 'Why the hell would they think she went off to pick fruit if all her stuff is here?'

'Good point,' he said.

'She has another bag,' said Mariella. 'A small one. It's not here, so.'

'You sure?' Yannick said. 'Do you know what else she took?'

'It's hard to tell. Most of her things are here.'

Just then, a girl not much older than Sunny appeared at the opening in the tree. She shouldered a hefty backpack, and a loose sleeping bag spilled over her arms. She looked a little cock-eyed. A little unsure.

'Come on in, chicken,' Mariella said.

The girl took a step forward and saw how crowded it already was. 'I'll wait,' she said, reversing out.

'She moving in already?' Kathleen asked Mariella.

Securing her glasses with a solid push at the bridge of her nose, Mariella said, 'Nobody wants to sleep alone just now.'

'I don't blame you,' said Yannick.

'Well, we'd better make room then,' said Kathleen. She collected the things from the small shelf and stuffed them into Una's backpack, along with all the clothes that Yannick had just taken out. She pulled the tie tightly and fastened all the buckles, hoisted the whole thing into her arms and bungled her way out of the tree, stumbling sideways under the uneven weight of the carelessly packed bag.

'I'll see you later, though?' Mariella said, following Kathleen back outside. 'For the search party?'

'We'll see you in a few hours,' Yannick said, 'and thank you.' He took her big hand in both of his and shook.

Kathleen insisted on carrying the bag. They were toeing carefully down the slope when she tripped and fell, and her body rolled into the underbrush, like a car without an engine or brakes, a thing with no control. Yannick hopped down to where she was just as she was sitting up, not bothering to brush the dirt from her elbows or the hair from her face. She slid her arms out of the straps and leaned back against the bag, most of her body swallowed by thick ferns. The set of her face, the square of her lips made it clear that this was not a time to offer help or to say a word. Yannick waited until she was ready to move again.

They did see Mariella a few hours later, at the bakery where they'd met before. She was friendly with the owner and he offered his premises as a kind of headquarters for the ground search, which was beginning that afternoon. This was to be a wholly volunteer effort, with only one RCMP officer to get them organized.

Dozens of people showed up to help. The plan was to split up into three groups: one to comb the area fanning out from the tree where Una had been sleeping, one to search the local beaches, and another to knock on doors and hand out flyers.

Kathleen and Sunny went off with the door-to-door group and Yannick followed one of Abner Francks's cousins into the woods.

First thing the cousin said to Yannick: 'Your daughter know how to start a fire?'

'I guess so if she had a book of matches, but she would not be sparking a stick with flint or anything like that,' said Yannick.

There were probably thirty people that first day, moving slowly, poking at the underbrush with sticks, looking for anything that didn't belong. Probably feeling, as Yannick did, that they had suddenly found themselves in an unreal situation. A place they never thought they would be.

There was a guy with a news camera. This guy from the

news asked Yannick some questions to which he gave some answers. Made it all the more unreal.

As they covered ground, this old guy who'd asked if Una knew how to start a fire, this cousin of Francks (Yannick has lost his name to the years), explained that a girl lost in this kind of bush, bush that was dense and wet and on steep ground, would most likely follow running water or the path of least resistance, which would take her higher as it's easier to move up a thickly wooded incline than down it. The man had a lump on the side of his neck the size of an apple and it played on his vocal cords so that he spoke with a dry, whispery rasp. Scratchy and tight.

They called Una's name. Called it and called it, like tossing pennies down a wishing well. They crawled deeper into the bush, away from the coast, bent over low to the damp, mossy earth, their fingers in the rich dirt. They weren't on any kind of trail, there were no trails, and the ground under their feet was either solid rock or tangled roots or moss. The moss grew in many forms. It engulfed the rocks and entire trunks of trees and it draped itself in long, swaying ropes from high limbs.

It might have rained a little.

It was strange for Yannick to hear Una's name coming off the tongues of all these strangers. In their tone he could hear the futility he himself felt. Not a soul had been through that bush anytime recently and Una was not there.

They searched this area and others too, for several days, and they found, among other meaningless articles: the metal cap, bent and rusted, off a Coke bottle; a handful of cigarette butts; a broken wine bottle; a nickel; the casing of a ballpoint pen packed with dirt where the ink tube once would have been.

On the morning of the last day, one of the volunteers found a blue T-shirt on the beach half buried in the sand, which everyone who knew Una agreed was the type of shirt Una would wear, what with the V-neck and short-short sleeves, but no one could say for certain if they'd ever seen her wearing it, so it meant nothing.

Late afternoon on that last day, when all (except Kathleen) agreed that the search area had become too big and it was time to stop, the remaining volunteers came back together at the bakery. Kathleen reported that, all told, they'd knocked on hundreds of doors, including those in the next town further south on the peninsula.

'People around here are different,' she said.

'These people are helping us,' Yannick said. 'Keep that thought to yourself.'

Every table in the bakery was taken up by volunteers who were wet, tired, dirty. The man who owned the place served coffee and doughnuts and wouldn't take a cent for any of it.

Sunny sat with his hands around a cup of coffee and his face to the window, and didn't turn his face when Yannick sat next to him.

'How're you doing, kiddo?' Yannick asked, stirring sugar into his own coffee.

'She's not here, Dad,' he said. Kept his face to the window.

'No,' Yannick said. He pushed other people's crumbs around the table with his thumb and tried to remember if he had eaten anything that day.

'I think it's my birthday,' Sunny said. 'What day is it?'

Yannick's mind snapped shut, like a trap. He could not recall the day or the month. A woman sitting across from them, with a doughnut halfway to her mouth, paused and told them the date.

'Ah, shit,' Yannick said. 'Happy birthday, my boy.'

The woman offered Sunny her doughnut and asked him how old he was.

'Seventeen,' he said. He turned the doughnut in his hands, took a bite, and left the rest. It was time to take him home.

19

A PERSON, KATHLEEN thinks, could veer off the road around here out of sheer boredom or madness or both. At least the long, flat straight suits Yannick's driving style; he can top a hundred and forty klicks and it feels like nothing. And he seems very content at the wheel.

By Kathleen's reckoning, they've travelled over two and a half thousand kilometres from home.

With not much to look at, her eyes are drawn to roadkill, tufts of fur and ribbons of pelt, and bright pink scraps of bone scattered over the dull cement. She could almost guess how long the animal has been dead by the colour of the blood or the flatness of whatever is left of the carcass. The flat of this landscape flattens her.

They pass splintery barns, more peel than paint, and rickety, defunct grain elevators that lean and buckle under the unfathomable weight of this empty sky. Kilometres and kilometres of salt flats, like crusty snow, rimmed with deep purple algae. Unexpected and otherworldly and, it has to be said, very pretty. As are the black-eyed Susans that bob merrily along the side of the road and have done from wherever they were two hours ago to wherever they are now, which is somewhere east of the town of Swift Current.

Kathleen reaches over and switches on the radio, toggles the knob left and right until something melodic and familiar parts the static. Gordan Gano of the Violent Femmes is singing to her directly, telling her that she was born too late and he was born too soon, and every time he looks at that ugly moon, it reminds him of her. She bobs her head a little to this song that she's always loved. Mouths along silently.

There was a time when all she wanted was to dance. Knew how to lose herself in punk rock. It didn't matter – she could dance alone or she could dance with a man, or she could dance with her daughter, high volume and bare toes mashing into the living-room carpet.

'You love this one,' says Yannick, winking at her. 'I remember this tune.'

A sign warns of dangerous wind gusts. Another sign warns of crossing elk. An eighteen-wheeler oil tanker passes and they rock in its wake. The song ends and is replaced by an aggressive advertisement for car insurance, so Kathleen flicks the radio off.

She's better when she's at the wheel. Doing something. Anticipating the road.

Those days in Tofino when Yannick and Sunny were out on Abner Francks's boat, searching for Una, Kathleen had had nothing better to do than mope around town.

Tofino. Almost too beautiful to be believed. Those untamed Pacific beaches, misty with salt spray that was so thick and disorienting you couldn't see where a beach began or ended. Nothing on the sand but stacks of smooth, bleached driftwood. Rainforest and wild rhododendrons growing everywhere.

Okay, it was very pretty, but the town itself was also rough. There was a jumpiness to it, this layover for loggers and fishermen. Unshaved men with greasy wool coats and sturdy boots who were only in town for a few days, hungry and thirsty and probably wanting sex. One day, in the middle of the afternoon, Kathleen watched a clumsy wet fight outside a bar where both opponents were so drunk neither was able to land a punch.

At some point Kathleen asked Patti Zoric if this was a factor in her investigation, these roughneck out-of-towners who fed their families off fish and lumber.

'Are they being questioned?'

'We're talking to as many people as is humanly possible, Kathleen.'

So she wandered. She once found herself in a titchy, messy store that housed racks of second-hand clothes and soaps wrapped in brown paper, and jewellery made out of copper wire bent around sea glass. The store smelt of soap – lavender and waxy – the kind of smell that travels right into the back of the nose and settles there.

On the walls, a series of prints done by a local artist. Totem poles and eagles and orcas. And all the different ways you can think of that moonlight reflects off the surface of the ocean. All the different ways you can think of that rain falls on trees. An artist at home in this place.

Kathleen must have been staring at the art for a long time because the woman behind the counter approached her and began to speak about the prints and the person who made them.

'I'm looking for my daughter,' Kathleen said, cutting the woman off, assuming this should be obvious to everyone.

'Are you meeting her here, honey?' she asked.

'No. I'm looking for her,' Kathleen said. 'Her name's Una?' she said, yanking her hair. 'Long brown hair,' she said, 'like mine.'

The woman put a hand to her mouth. 'You mean the girl they're looking for? The helicopter and the boats and every-thing?'

Kathleen tried to nod, but realized she was trembling. Really shaking.

'You need to sit down,' the woman said, dragging a chair out from behind the counter. 'Jesus Murphy, Mama Bear,' she said. 'Take a load off and I'll get you a glass of water.'

Kathleen refused the chair and the water. The reek of lavender soap was curdling up into her sinuses. She was probably rude. As she left, as the door was drifting shut behind her, she heard the woman promise to keep an eye out, as if Una were a runaway dog.

People don't always know what to say.

There was a shitty playground across the street from the Nootka, the restaurant where Una was supposed to have met with Oliver Hanratty. Kathleen ended up there. Not much to it: a gritty sandbox harbouring a half-sunk Tonka truck; a derelict, wooden merry-go-round that was rusted to a standstill; a single swing. She sat in the swing for long enough that the light changed, and she deepened the groove in the black dirt beneath it with her bare heels.

She watched oblivious, happy, normal people going into and coming out of the Nootka.

She replayed again and again that moment at the end of the CCTV footage, when Una reacted to something out of shot, when she turned her head that certain way.

You think about something too many times, it loses its meaning.

A hot, tight crick developed between Kathleen's shoulders and wired its way up into her neck, but she would have stayed in the swing indefinitely. She only left because some sun-browned brat with long, tangled hair and no parents in sight stood aggressively close, eyeing her, waiting for his turn.

*

After the border hold-up two days ago, and then the tooth detour yesterday, Kathleen is proud of how far they've come today. They've torn a huge chunk out of this road and are now driving into a remarkable sunset. Fiery pink clouds striate the wide sky – a gift, just for the two of them.

There is sagebrush, acres and acres of sagebrush, not as much nothing as there was before. A train travels alongside, then tucks behind a series of hills to the north, and Kathleen thinks: This must be it. Prairies finished. Made it through the gap. But then the world flattens again and it seems this will never be finished.

Twenty klicks east of Medicine Hat they pass an orange VW van parked diagonally on the wide shoulder. Kathleen says nothing.

Yannick checks the rear-view. 'That's those kids from this morning,' he says. He slows and pulls over onto the shoulder, and reverses.

'What are you doing?'

'They might need help.'

'They're probably just having sex,' Kathleen says.

'At the side of the road?'

'Why the hell not?'

He stops in front of the van and the thought of facing this girl again spreads a hot itch up the back of Kathleen's neck. Yannick gets out of the truck and she watches him through the rear window, crutching himself hand-over-hand along the length of the truck bed, using it for support.

For heaven's sake, she is sixty-five years old. What does she care if this nubile child saw her peeing behind a garbage bin? She sighs, straightens her T-shirt and steps out of the truck into tall, dry grass that immediately irritates the backs of her knees.

'I think I should do the rest of the driving,' she says to Yannick, who's only just made it to the back of the truck.

He ignores her.

The driver's side door of the VW is gaping open and the girl is just getting out. She's wearing a faded green hooded sweatshirt with the hood up so that half her face is in shadow.

Yannick says hello. 'You kids okay?' he asks. Without any truck to lean against, he stands gingerly, with his thumbs casually hooked on the hips of his jeans as if he's in no pain at all.

'Absolutely,' she says. She won't look at Kathleen. Presumably she is just as embarrassed.

'Engine trouble?' Yannick asks.

'It overheats,' she says. 'I just need to let her cool.'

'You want me to check it out?'

'No. It's really okay,' she says.

Yannick looks away, northwards, and it's like all the light of the day, the last light of this long, long day, is focused on the side of his face. His ear, his cheek. His handsome nose. Kathleen turns her gaze away so he doesn't catch her looking.

'She says it's fine, Yannick,' Kathleen says.

'We saw you this morning, remember?' says Yannick.

The girl nods, slowly, as if she's only recognizing them now. She winks at Kathleen, and all at once Kathleen feels grateful and sheepish. That this child could so confidently put her at ease.

Yannick continues: 'In the restaurant, in, uh . . .' He glances to Kathleen for assistance.

'Whiteshell,' she says.

'Whiteshell,' he repeats.

Yannick continues to look at the girl, angling for more of her story. He thinks he's intimate friends with everyone he meets and ends up charming most of them into agreeing.

236

'Where's your fella?' he asks.

The girl jabs her thumb behind her shoulder to the east. 'I dropped him off in Regina,' she says.

Yannick waits. He should have been a counsellor. Or a cop. 'You got tired of him?' he jokes.

She laughs again. She's not going to explain why she dropped her fella off in Regina, or where she's going now.

As Yannick is telling the girl that he can't just leave her alone by the side of the road, it occurs to Kathleen that maybe the music box she found belongs to her. She reaches into her pocket and feels it there, the spikes and the needles and the handle. The metal is warm from being next to her leg.

Nope, she's keeping it. She pulls her hand out of her pocket.

Yannick limps towards the back of the van and lifts open the little engine hatch with a loud *oof.*

'Yannick, she said it's fine,' Kathleen says, following him. She doesn't know what he thinks he's doing. He used to tinker with motorcycles but he's not a mechanic, and even Kathleen knows: a hot engine is just a hot engine. Nothing you can do but wait.

Kathleen stands with the girl while Yannick pokes and prods under the hatch. It's getting darker by the second. The girl lifts her arm to pull the hood off her head, and when she does, Kathleen notices the pregnant swell of her belly.

'So, where you guys from?' the girl asks, resigned to this old lady who pisses in public and that incorrigible old man with his head stuck up the ass of her van.

Kathleen tells her, Ontario.

The girl nods slowly and asks more polite questions about where they stopped today and how far they're going, et cetera, and Kathleen sees that these are inevitable questions on a road like this, in the middle of all this empty space.

The girl flits worrying looks towards Yannick, and Kathleen would not blame her if she suspected they were planning to murder her, that at this very moment, Yannick was dismantling her engine and that Kathleen's role in the plot was to keep her distracted with small-talk.

'Honestly,' she says, taking a step closer to Yannick, 'I can take care of it.'

'Yannick,' says Kathleen. She presses a finger on his shoulder.

He backs away from the van and straightens up, like he's resurfacing from underground. He squints closely at the oil dipstick he now holds between his fingers. 'Oil's fine,' he says.

'I just topped it up,' the girl says. 'We've got a leak.'

'That would be your overheating problem,' he says.

'Yes, thank you.'

The clank of the hatch closing radiates out from the van and over their heads, and carries on, it seems, as far as the horizon in all directions.

'Why don't we see if it'll start?' says Yannick. 'We can't just leave you here.'

'This happens all the time,' she says. 'I know she'll start. She just needs time.'

'We'll wait,' Yannick says. He looks at Kathleen. 'We'll wait, eh?'

'She doesn't need us to wait,' Kathleen says. A curt nod and casual salute to the girl, and she heads back to the truck. Yannick stays put. Kathleen steps up into the driver's side, closes the door, adjusts the seat and mirrors. Yannick is still speaking and gesticulating. The girl stands with her back to Kathleen and nods politely.

Kathleen would like to go over and offer this girl some help she actually needs: tell her that having a child is a reckless and insane thing to do. It is to lob your raw heart out into this spinning world. It is to try to survive without skin. Kathleen would like to tell the girl to stay in her van and just keep driving and stop for no one.

Yannick finally looks Kathleen's way and shrugs, and shuffles back to the truck. The look on his face, the pull of it. Oh, Yannick.

'She was only humouring me,' he says, as he pulls the seatbelt across his chest. Fumbles with the buckle.

'I know,' she says. She turns the key in the ignition. The friendly grumble of truck fills the space between them.

Yannick sighs. 'I am thinking about her more than I have for a long time.'

'I know,' she says.

The last time Kathleen laid eyes on Una was that goddamn Christmas when they all stuffed themselves into Yannick's draughty shack on some godforsaken frozen lake up near Minden, or wherever it was.

She and Una had been sharing Yannick's bed, and on Christmas morning, before dawn, she felt Una get up. She felt the shift in the mattress, the empty spot cooling beside her, Una's body heat no longer there. She assumed Una was going to the bathroom so she fell back to sleep. When she woke up hours later, Una was gone. Telling no one, she'd left.

Kathleen was hurt that Una had left like that, but also, in a way, didn't blame her. Yannick's younger sons, Zack and the other one, Devon, were behaving like jackasses. Scuffling around and farting all over the place and pissing in the snow.

Fighting and bickering and eating all the food. They pillaged Kathleen's tourtière, her Christmas speciality, before anyone else could get any.

Una'd had enough. She didn't care about what day it was. She simply didn't want to be there any more, so she left.

There's freedom in that.

Yannick is slumped into his seat like wax that has melted and then re-solidified. He grunts in response to Kathleen's questions: what do you feel like eating tonight? Highway motel or something in town? How's the back pain?

Suit yourself, she thinks.

Medicine Hat is a much bigger place than she was expecting. They pass five off-ramps leading to the town centre and pull into a Holiday Inn just off the highway at the town's western edge.

'Meet me back here in ten minutes,' Kathleen says to Yannick in the lobby, once they've taken their separate key cards in stiff paper envelopes. 'I'll shout you a dinner.'

'I'm going to bed,' he says.

They share the elevator, which smells faintly of chlorine and clean towels, in cool silence to the second floor.

It's nearly ten o'clock and Kathleen should be exhausted – she is, really, but she's antsy too. She's got road fever. Truck fever. This is the furthest she's ventured from home since she got serious about her farm and now she's standing in a hotel bathroom in Medicine Hat, Alberta, unwrapping the miniature soap and smelling it. She digs her fingernail into its pristine, waxy edge and slices away a thin crescent of butter-coloured soap.

There are two missed calls from Julius showing on her phone, but it's too late to call him back. They've crossed time zones and he's now two hours ahead of her. She is moving backwards in time.

She stands under the hot shower, then gets dressed in a set of clean clothes. She swipes her hand across the steamy mirror and, in the window of the cleared and dripping arc, brushes her hair into a neat bun. Forces into her earlobes a pair of small silver hoops, which she found tucked into the pocket of her toiletry bag. It's a battle, getting the earrings in, but she persists.

Her fingernails are clean, which is unusual for the middle of summer. She feels moderately guilty for having left the farm. It's been only a few days but she has a hankering, would like to be smelling her flowers instead of cheap hotel soap.

There are over one hundred species of rose. Kathleen feels secure in this fact.

Or this: the benefit of the flowering garlic chive is that it attracts the soldier beetle, which feeds on aphids. This is also a good fact.

When she told Julius she was going to turn her flower hobby into a business, eleven years ago, he said to her, 'Oh, Kathleen, you're not romantic enough to grow flowers.' He dipped his head in a way Kathleen didn't like. It was condescending. He said: 'You're not a nurturer.' It's unusual for Julius to be wrong, but in this he was – he is – wrong. Growing is a passion, of course, it has to be, but it's far from romantic. There's the tilling and the weeding, the fertilizing and the harvesting. Stripping, deadheading, hauling buckets heavy with water and crop. Hauling tools.

This is cumbersome, time-consuming labour and it has transformed her body. Her fingernails are forever black and her hands are thickly calloused. The skin of her right hand is stained chlorophyll green from stripping stems. She wears a wrist brace when she's harvesting to protect against carpal tunnel syndrome, which will probably be her eventual end, and she's pretty sure a mole on the back of her neck is flirting with the idea of becoming cancerous. Her fingers have swollen and split nearly to the bone because of an allergen found in tulips, okay? Romantic? Pah.

Maybe it moves her a little, maybe a lot, to witness that bright green seedling pushing its pointed head up through crumbling soil, like a hatching bird, discarding its husk. Maybe she walks alongside her beds and touches those first embryonic leaves, the cotyledons, which will shrivel up and fall off like umbilical cord knots on an infant, as the turgid new stem follows the sun. Maybe there is an appeal to the nurturing side of farming, protecting her crops from infestation, or testing the soil for nutrients and feeding, if feeding is required.

But when the time is right, she takes her sharpened, oiled clippers in her strong hands and she cuts.

For most types of flower, the time for cutting is just after the blossom unfurls but before the appearance of pollen. You cut the flower in its prime, before it has the chance to reproduce. This is crucial, to get to the plant before the bees do, because once pollination occurs, the plant puts all its energy into the production of seeds and the flower fades. It is obsolete and begins to senesce, which means it begins to die.

Not good for business.

On her way down the hall to the elevator, she pauses at Yannick's door. She can hear the television and imagines him sprawled on the bed, one booted foot hanging off the edge. Asleep with his mouth wide open.

Outside, summer dark. It's grim, here at the edge of town.

Her choices for something to eat on this side of the highway are McDonald's, White Spot or Taco Bell – none of which she wants. Or she could risk her life crossing four lanes of traffic for Kentucky Fried Chicken.

This is silly, and she's hungry. In less than two minutes, Medicine Hat has defeated her. She ducks into a 7-11 for Pringles and beer, and skulks back to her room.

Second beer in and halfway through the Pringles, there's a knock on the door. She freezes, a lone scimitar of Pringle held at her lip.

'Kathleen?' Yannick's voice through the door. 'You up?'

Maybe it's the beer but she can't deny it: something without a name lifts in her chest and throat.

'I'm sorry,' he says, as she opens the door. He comes in and sits on the edge of her bed, takes a look around the room.

'Sorry about what?' she says. She sits on the Holiday Inn armchair. Its cheap upholstery sizzles against the backs of her calves.

'I didn't know if you'd be up,' he says.

'Well, now you do.' She eats a Pringle and brushes her fingers together to get rid of the salt.

He raises his tired eyes and looks at her for the first time. 'It's pretty,' he says. 'Your hair tied up like that.'

Her ears have gone hot around the silver hoops she bullied through them earlier.

'Kathleen,' he says. 'It's all opening up for me again.'

'I know.'

'And I'm sorry.'

'Stop saying sorry.'

'But I am. All those years you spent.'

'Don't be. It won't do either of us any good.'

'And I am surprised by your life. Your flowers and every-thing. And just. You look good. Healthy. You got so frail after.'

She passes him the tube of Pringles and he takes it, then looks at it as if he's surprised to see it in his hand. He gives it back. 'I don't want this,' he says.

'Why don't you ever eat?' she asks.

'Lost my appetite.'

She eats another chip and again brushes off the salt. 'You imagined me sitting by the window for twenty years,' she says. 'Planning parties that no one wants to come to.'

'Yes, I did.'

'Maybe I have, a little. Maybe I don't care.'

He crosses his hands behind his head and lies back on the bed, puffs his cheeks and makes a quiet whomp-whomp noise. She'd forgotten about this habit, his way of soothing him-self. 'And my Robin,' he says to the ceiling. 'I'm sorry for that, too.'

'Come on, Yannick, you can't apologize for the birth of your daughter.'

'Well.'

'You're being stupid now.' She removes the earrings and pulls the elastic band from her hair, setting her entire head free. She hoists herself out of the armchair, collects her pyjamas from where they're crumpled into the top of her bag, and heads to the bathroom. He turns to look at her; she feels his gaze as she crosses the room. She doesn't ask him to leave.

It's a queer thing to stare into her own eyes, brushing her teeth at the mirror and knowing what she really wants. When you're looking in the mirror, you can't pretend you don't want what you want.

She combs her fingers through her hair, still a little damp at the roots. It falls around her face the way she likes it, with a bit of a kick because it was twisted tightly as it dried. Pulling her pyjama top tight to her body, she examines her folds and contours, and sucks in her paunch. Failing to muscle it into a more pleasing shape, she lets it drop and jiggle. Whatever. She angles her face to the side, always more alluring than the frontal mugshot. It's something about the jawline (not that she has much of a jawline any longer, more the suggestion of jaw), and the hair falling over one eye. Not giving it all away. Before she goes back to him, she sets each foot on the toilet seat, one and then the other, to check her toenails aren't overly haggish.

He's still lying on the bed, on top of the covers, staring up at the ceiling. He sits up and draws his hands over his face, making creaking noises like he's about to get up and leave.

'You don't have to go,' she says. She sits down on the other side of the bed, behind him.

He turns his body partway to look at her and there is the curve of his back, his strong profile, just a corner of eye, glinting, and she is transported. 'I would like to stay,' he says. He takes off his glasses and lays them on the bedside table.

'What about your wife?'

'Walked out,' he says, and turns his whole body to her.

'That explains a few things.'

'Shut the hell up.'

'Come on, then,' she says, and reaches for him.

She hasn't undone a man's belt in a long time, and has to stop kissing him to wrestle the metal prong out of the leather notch. She undoes the buttons of his shirt and helps him pull off his jeans, aware of the weakness of his back. They make jokes about geriatrics. They are who they have always been, joking about other people who are old, who aren't them, and laugh into each other's mouths. He apologizes for his pain, and for his underwear because he only brought a few pairs and they're all pretty thready, and she tells him no apologies.

She could almost cry, just to be touched. His hands on her shoulders, his arms around her, gathering her up. And his hands on her face, cupping her face, his fingers tangled in her hair and curled up behind her ears. They clack teeth like teenagers and she apologizes, and he pinches her chin hard and says, 'No apologies.'

It's been over forty years and she remembers how to kiss this man. Every kiss is unique between two people and she remembers this kiss. His crooked tooth and the measure of his tongue, and how much of her tongue he wants. What he responds to.

She's self-conscious of her wounded mouth and her kiss feels unnatural. She's embarrassed she's not doing it right, so opens her eyes to laugh, the spell temporarily broken, and finds that his eyes are closed. She remembers what the bridge of his nose looks like this close. His face out of focus.

'Should we turn off the lights?' she asks.

'If you want to,' he says heavily, drugged already. He takes her earlobe in his teeth.

'Do you want to?'

'I want to see you.' He pulls his head back and smiles, and licks the tip of her nose.

She remembers this exactly, the long slope of his forehead when he's above her, his breath filling her ear. The goosebumps that rise on his shoulders, or the sound he makes when he's particularly aroused, a kind of *huh*, like he's just getting the punchline of a subtle joke. Everywhere he touches her lights up. She's surprised by how easily she falls back into this, and evidently this goes both ways because his fingers find her, exactly where they should, and he's very patient. When she's ready, she rolls him over. She wants to be on top, to use just that part of him for just that part of her. She checks she's not hurting him, his back; he smiles and moans and she takes that as a no.

'You are not hurting me,' he confirms.

Yannick.

'Yannick.'

'Yes.'

Maybe she cries, a little.

20

THE LIGHT IS tinted dirty orange when Yannick opens his eyes in the morning, the room hazy with the drapes that are pulled most of the way across the window. Kathleen is still asleep, and Yannick? He barely slept at all.

What happened last night was, they screwed, and he had not expected that. He had not. Even when it began, when she pulled him down to her, he was waiting to be pushed away. Kathleen is like a cat, how it is when you pick up a cat that isn't so sure it wants to be held; the vibration in its throat could be either a purr or a growl. But she always wanted sex, if it can be put that bluntly. Whatever problems they might have had as man and wife, sex was not one of them.

Her back is to him now, and has been all night. Oh, the loneliness of lying awake when the person next to you is deeply, tranquilly asleep and doesn't reach for you.

Her thick hair falls over one cheek and folds into her neck. The pale tip of her ear pokes through the grey. He doesn't remember her being as solid as she now is. Her frayed bra strap cuts deeply into the ample flesh of her strong, freckled shoulder and he wonders what would happen if he hooked his little finger under that strap and dragged it loose. If he kissed those freckles and the elastic dents that would be left behind on her skin. He wants to bite that nub of ear. He doesn't want sex again, God knows he couldn't anyway. He only wants to fill the gap between them.

'I can feel you breathing on me,' she says.

'Eh?'

She turns onto her back, easily, without the creaking and wincing he has to contend with every morning, crosses her arms over her chest and stares at the ceiling.

'Don't look at me,' she says. Her voice is morning thick. 'I look like shit.'

'You do not.'

'I do.'

'Well, then, we both do.'

'Close your eyes,' she says.

'I will do no such thing.'

'Have it your way.'

The mattress shifts as she sits up and swings her legs like a goddamn dancer over the edge. She stands and steps away from the bed, retrieves her underpants from the floor and pulls them up. She flicks on the bathroom light and it hums meanly.

'I might be a while,' she says. 'Maybe shower in your own room?' She closes the door.

Okay, then.

But he needs a minute. He digs for his Y-fronts, which are under the covers, abandoned way down at the foot of the bed. He has to lie on his back and hoist one leg off the bed, then the other, to get them over his feet and up his legs. His jeans lie discarded on the floor, one leg inside-out from when Kathleen pulled them off. He bends to pick them up and pain jacks deeply into his lower back. A cry, a wet little bark, escapes him, and he's grateful Kathleen has turned on the shower and won't be able to hear. This old man who can barely get himself dressed.

As he leaves, he is confronted by the closed bathroom door

and the smell of her shampoo. He fears they may have been careless with this new calm they've found.

His room is only a few doors down. There is the bed that was not slept in. There are the shoes side by side next to the bed. He splashes his face with hot water and puts on his last clean shirt. Takes his time gingerly with socks.

At some hour before sunrise, Kathleen had sat straight up in bed like she'd just remembered something important. He asked her what was wrong and she told him to go back to sleep. He rested his hand on her warm back but she didn't touch him after that, and his sleep, he's sure, was fitful because he so badly wanted her to.

He's hungrier than he has been in a long time. At least there's that. Breakfast is included with the room and he goes down to the restaurant, hoping to find Kathleen there, but as yet, she is not.

His hand shakes as he presses a glass that is still warm from the dishwasher against the grapefruit juice tap. He swallows the whole glassful standing right there at the tap, can feel the cool liquid work its way down his pipes, and fills the glass again. He puts two slices of white bread on a conveyor machine that seems like a colossal waste of parts and electricity when a regular toaster would do. While his bread makes its journey, he coasts up and down the breakfast counters, politely avoiding other early-bird diners who also coast with plates in hand, locked in the intimacy of spooning food out of communal stainless-steel trays. He loads up his plate with watery scrambled eggs, baked tomatoes, an oily, dripping knot of bacon and some triangles of soft cheese wrapped in foil.

He sits down to eat and remembers that he has forgotten to

retrieve his toast, but decides toast is not worth the pain of standing up again. And sitting down again.

He felt wholly comfortable in the bed of his long-ago wife, mother of the daughter who is lost. She was beautiful last night, maybe they both were, two fools bumping knees and elbows, a little sweaty and tangled up in starchy hotel sheets. Weary skin clinging to weary skin, hands anywhere you can put a hand. Appreciation, rising deep and smooth from the bottoms of their throats, like singing. Now he pulls this bacon apart and he can still hear her song.

Kathleen's hair, the way it falls from where it parts naturally down the middle, the way it sprouts from her head in these two uneven cowlicks, there is a shape to it that a man only gets to see if he is up close. That shape, that kink where the two cowlicks meet, it's like a signature. The form and *Kathleen-ness* of it are undeniable. Or the black freckle in the dent at the bottom of her neck, in that little bone cup there, the familiar freckle and skin that is deeply tanned and softly wrinkled. Or the shape of her fingernails. The look on her face when she gets off. Decades since he's been intimate with this woman and these are details he did not know he'd forgotten.

Kathleen now comes into the restaurant looking flushed and clean and attractive. Gallingly youthful. He watches her as she stands impatiently behind an old man, a real old gramps, at the coffee machine, and he watches her as she trawls with her tray in much the same way Yannick did. He shifts in his chair, trying to find a position that eases the pain in his lower back, and feels a little like he's been compressed. A little shattered. He does not – *does not* – want to need this, to need her.

She comes over and sits, and rearranges the food on her plate. Messily unfolds the golden foil from a pat of butter and spreads the butter across her toast. Pours two of those plastic thimbles of cream into her coffee and stirs.

Finally, she looks at him. 'You're eating,' she says. 'I'm glad you're eating something.'

'You want to talk about what we did?' he says.

She rests her elbows on the table and folds her fingers together under her chin and looks to the other side of the room. She smiles like she knew this was coming.

'You woke up in the middle of the night,' he says. 'Like you were bothered or worried or something. I don't want you to—'

'No,' she says, wagging a finger. 'No, you don't have to worry.'

'You didn't let me finish. I don't have to worry about what?'

She selects a single-serving square of honey out of a bowl of single-serving condiments, peels back the covering and dribbles it in circles over her toast, not even bothering to staunch the flow when she moves from one slice to the next. Honey all across the rest of the food. (Was a time this would have driven him berserk. Today it's endearing as all fucking hell.)

'I'm not bothered and I'm not worried,' she says. 'I won't make trouble for you.'

'That is not what I meant.'

'It's fine, Yannick.'

'Why'd you wake up like that?'

'No, no,' she says, shaking her head at her plate.

'What? Please tell me.'

She puts her knife and fork down, finishes chewing. 'It was perfect, Yannick. All of it.' She shrugs. 'Didn't you think so?'

'I did.'

'So that's it then, okay?'

'Whatever you say,' he says, and gets up after all to claim that toast, cold now.

The rain fell lazily and endlessly the day Yannick, Kathleen and Sunny drove up the peninsula to meet Trent, the manager of the Co-op who'd let Una live at his place. This was the day after Sunny's forgotten birthday, and was the last thing Yannick intended on doing before taking his boy back home.

As Mariella had said, Trent did seem easygoing when they called him up and asked if they could come by. He lived in a little bungalow mostly hidden from the road behind a row of trees.

He was a peculiar-looking guy. Hair so blond it was white, and soft, like a baby's. His mouth remained on the verge of a smile, whatever he was talking about. Yannick guessed he was in his late thirties, and he told them he had been living in Tofino for ten years. He seemed worried about Una, and apologized over and over again for not knowing where she was. For not being there to help. It seemed he had just returned from a salmon-fishing trip up in a place called Campbell River, way up the other end of the island. He hadn't even known she was gone until he was contacted by the police.

They drank coffee in his kitchen at a small table that was bare except for a stack of unopened mail. He didn't have enough chairs for all of them, so he brought in a damp one from outside and dried it with his own T-shirt. Yannick felt a little on edge there. It was the domestic details that did it, like how this man's toaster was on the kitchen floor, next to the garbage. Or it was the pictures on his fridge, not real pictures, but people cut out of magazines, like what Una used to tape on her bedroom wall when she was a kid. Yannick didn't like to imagine his daughter living in this place.

On the windowsill over the sink there was a tidy row of small figurines, the colour and texture of bad teeth: a bear, some kind of prowling wildcat, a sharp-beaked bird. Yannick got up from his chair to look at them.

'You like them?' Trent said. 'I carved them myself.' He launched out of his chair, plucked the cat off the windowsill and handed it to Yannick. It was cool in the palm of his hand and heavier than it looked. Trent hovered at the windowsill, poking at the figurines. 'One's missing,' he said.

'Eh?'

Trent carefully moved each animal along the sill until they all stood equally apart. 'It doesn't matter,' he eventually said, smiling, reaching for the coffee pot. He refilled Yannick's cup, splashed coffee on the table and didn't bother to wipe it clean.

'You want a glass of milk or something?' he asked Sunny, who hadn't touched his coffee.

'I'm fine,' Sunny said, and drank a little from his cup.

'We're grateful you gave Una a job,' said Kathleen. 'And that you let her stay here.'

'I like Una,' he said. 'It was easy having her here.'

'Did she ever say anything to you about wanting to leave town?' Yannick asked.

'We didn't see each other after she moved out,' he said. 'She quit working for me, so.'

'Why'd she quit?' Kathleen asked.

Trent shrugged. 'She just quit,' he said. 'My best guess is she got bored.'

'Did she seem unhappy?' Kathleen asked.

Trent turned his coffee cup around on the table a few times.

'No,' he said. 'She seemed bored.' He looked back and forth between Yannick and Kathleen and smiled, and there was a big gap between his two front teeth. 'She didn't tell you, did she,' he said, 'that she quit?'

'Apparently she didn't want to disappoint us,' Kathleen said.

'That's how it goes with parents, though, eh?' Trent said.

Yannick asked if they could see where Una had slept when she was there, and they followed Trent out of the back door into the yard. A scrappy terrier dog came yipping out of a border of cedar trees and Trent shovelled the dog up in one meaty hand. He roughed its head and tossed it back the way it had come. 'Jimi lives next door,' he said. 'He runs away a lot.' He looked at Sunny. 'He was your sister's buddy when she lived here,' he said. 'She used to feed him cheese sandwiches.'

'This is where she stayed?' said Kathleen, with a warble in her voice. 'This is where Una lived?' She was standing with one hand planted on the wall of a wooden shack tacked onto the back of the house. It looked like it had been assembled by a child, without so much as a spirit level.

Yannick hadn't thought it could get worse than the tree, but this was somehow worse than the tree.

'At least it's not a tree,' Sunny said.

Trent scraped open the door and stood by it, and they went in. The smell must have hit Kathleen first because she sank to the bed, into the single bare mattress, her legs buckling. She lowered her head into her hands. Una. Una's hair, it smelt like that. And the dark, woody oil she dabbed behind her ears.

'But when was she here?' Kathleen asked. She looked up and her face was twisted and wet.

'She hasn't been here in months,' Trent said. He stood in the doorway, as if he didn't want to come all the way in.

Sunny sat down on the bed next to Kathleen, close, without touching. Just right.

'Room smells like her,' Yannick said. 'Like she's standing right here with us.'

'I never come in here,' Trent said. 'First time was yesterday, to show the cops.'

'And you didn't notice?' Kathleen said. 'It's so strong.'

That half-smile was still crouched on Trent's mouth, but his body was square in the cockeyed doorway. 'The police already talked to me, eh? I was up in Campbell River. They called up my cousin to verify and he verified. My aunty too.'

'That's not what she means,' said Yannick.

'I don't know what Una smells like,' said Trent. 'We weren't close like that. I told the cops already.'

'It's okay, son,' Yannick said, scanning the room. Not much to it. The single bed and a standing wardrobe, a full-length mirror opposite the door and one grubby window over a sink.

'Is there a bathroom?' he asked.

'Around the other side,' said Trent. 'I hooked up a shower out there too.'

'This is enough,' Yannick said. 'Kathleen, come on. This is enough, now. Let's go.'

She breathed deeply and rubbed her hands roughly up and down her thighs several times. As if she were trying to erase herself. 'Just give me a second,' she said. 'I'll be out.'

They waited outside for her in the gloomy drizzle. The dog Jimi sprang back out from the trees and raked its muddy paws all up and down Yannick's legs, and he wanted to kick it into oblivion.

'So the police came for a talk, eh?' he said.

'Yesterday.'

'They think she got herself lost out there on the ocean,' Yannick said.

'That's what they told me,' Trent said. He darted for the dog but missed, and the mutt ran circles around them both, yapping.

'This dog does not give one cold shit,' said Yannick.

'No, he don't,' said Trent. He put his hand up to his chin, kind of gripped it, and spoke: 'When stuff is really bad,' he said, 'I wish I was a dog. Or a cat or a fish, eh? A cat or a fish, they don't feel nothing. They don't know about when things are bad.'

'Maybe they've got their own bad,' said Yannick. He watched Jimi's irritating sprint, the animal's tiny legs lost in the grass. Fool dog.

Trent nodded thoughtfully. 'Go on and pick some,' he said to Sunny, and pointed up to a raspberry bush. 'Careful of thorns.'

Kathleen came out then, her eyes red and her face rubbed dry.

'Sorry,' she said, her arms wrapped around her middle and her eyes roving in line with the dog.

'You don't have to be sorry,' Yannick said.

And Sunny, eating raspberries. Both of his arms were scratched with the finest scratches. The smallest beads of blood.

Yannick drove back to the hotel and Kathleen stared out of the window for a long time before she said anything, weakly tracing her knuckles in an arc across the wet glass, like somebody lost. Nothing to look at but a wall of grey sky and mist and wet cedar.

'Smelt like she was with us,' she said. Her voice stuck in her throat.

'That was messed up,' Sunny said.

'I had a look around,' she said. 'When you went out. I had a look.'

'Find anything?' Yannick said.

'Nothing,' she said, and then: 'I did not like that guy one bit.'

'He was different, all right, but I don't think there's anything to it.'

'I have never been so scared, Yannick,' Kathleen said. 'I don't know how to do this.'

'I know,' he said.

Later that day, Yannick and Kathleen were using the photocopier in the library, making copies of Una's flyer. The librarian, as Yannick recalls, did not charge them for the use of the photocopier.

They must have printed over two hundred copies and the machine ran out of paper, and Kathleen asked the librarian for another stack.

'I think we have enough,' Yannick whispered, angry that she would ask, because the copies were free.

'So we'll pay,' said Kathleen.

'We have enough,' he said.

'It's not nearly enough. You don't know what enough is.'

'I meant for now. It's enough for now,' he said.

Outside, the rain was heavy, and the library, which was not much bigger than a boxcar, seemed to sink underwater with the sound of the rain pelting its aluminum roof. Because they had been running the photocopier for so long, it ticked with heat, and there they stood beside it, staring each other down. A ticking machine and the sweet smell of ink on warm paper.

'It will only be enough when we find her,' said Kathleen.

'I know that,' he said. 'I know. But whether you have a thousand of these right now or a couple hundred, you can only put them up so fast. That's all I meant. And the whole town is plastered already.'

'So we cover the whole island. And we keep going.'

Looking out of the window, Yannick felt trapped by the mist. It pushed up against the glass and fiddled with the latches, trying to get in. They had sprinted to the one place in the world Una no longer was, and it was time to go home.

'I'm taking Sunny back,' he said.

'What?'

'He needs to go home. Back to normal.'

The bitter smile on her face told him what she thought about normal. And Sunny's ability to go back to it.

'It was his birthday yesterday.'

'He's fine,' she said.

'He's not.'

'So send him home then,' she said. 'He's old enough. Just had a whole new birthday and everything.'

'I am not sending that boy alone,' he said.

'You worried about your kid?'

'Course I am.'

'You worried about losing your kid?' she said. Her nostrils did an angry little flare, like a struck match.

The librarian came over and opened the flap where the paper went in the machine and loaded the empty tray with a stack of mint green paper. 'It's all I have left,' she said. 'I hope it's okay.'

'We're grateful,' Yannick said. 'Thank you.'

Kathleen was ready for more fight, but instead she opened the lid of the copier and took her time to square the flyer on the glass, and pushed the lid down and held it there. She jabbed the necessary buttons with the flat pad of her thumb.

'I'll come back,' he said. 'Soon as I can.'

Kathleen held her hand flat on the lid of the machine, while the components inside shifted and stuttered and jarred.

'Maybe one of us should be there anyway,' he said. 'In case she comes home.'

'The green is going to ruin the photo.'

And there, in the tray, Una's face again and again and again.

Abner Francks arranged a ride for Sunny and Yannick back across the island, where they would catch a ferry to Vancouver, and from there, fly home. The morning they were leaving, Yannick knocked on Kathleen's hotel-room door, but she was not there. Wherever she had gone that morning, she had taken the rental car, so he and Sunny walked along the highway into town to say goodbye to the people who had helped them.

They found Abner Francks on the jetty, standing astride a dismantled array of oily winches and chains, spraying soapy water off his boat deck with a powerful hose. He looked a happy man. 'Kathleen came down here this morning sniffing around for a lift,' he said, as Yannick and Sunny approached. 'I'm taking her up to the hot springs later today.'

'The Coast Guard already looked there,' Yannick said.

'She wants to see for herself.'

'You have to go by boat?'

He nodded. 'It's blowing the tits off a dog out there today,' he said. 'She's not going to like it.'

'That is an understatement,' Yannick said.

Francks dug out a pack of smokes from his back pocket and offered them to Yannick and Sunny both. 'You ready to go home, Sunnyboy?' he said.

'I guess,' Sunny said. He slid a cigarette from the pack and immediately fumbled and dropped it.

'Well, you have got to be joking me,' Yannick said, swiping the cigarette from the jetty before Sunny could get it.

'Dad.' Sunny held his palm out flat.

Yannick stared him down for a few seconds before pressing the now damaged cigarette into the boy's palm. 'Dirty habit,' he said.

'You didn't come down here to thank me or nothing like that,' Francks said, and tossed Sunny a lighter. He squatted down to his haunches and tinkered with a length of chain.

'Thank you for what?' Yannick said, smiling.

'I meant what I said. We won't stop looking.'

'I appreciate that,' Yannick said. He looked out over the water, at the frayed white caps on curt waves. 'I do not think she's here,' he said.

Francks looked up at him and nodded. 'Still,' he said. And grinned. It was the first time Yannick had seen him smile and it was a bright, sad smile, and he's never forgotten it.

They crossed the road from the marina to find Sergeant Zoric at the RCMP detachment, where she was waiting for them wearing a pretty T-shirt with a collar, tucked into a pair of jeans. Her hair hung loose and bouncy past her shoulders. Clearly off-duty but had come in anyway to say goodbye. They stood outside on the grass where she made promises of keeping in touch whether there was news or not.

'It's still new, Yannick,' Zoric said. 'It's still possible she'll come home on her own.'

'And you are absolutely sure about that old boss of hers? That Trent?' he said.

'He was out of town. Absolutely.'

'Kathleen called you? About how his place smelt and all that?'

'She did.'

Yannick nodded thoughtfully. 'She might surprise us all, eh? Come back on her own,' he said.

'It's okay to go home, Yannick.'

'I don't know what else to do,' he said.

They called the hotel to see if Kathleen had gone back there, but she had not, so they headed to the marina to try to intercept her en route to the hot springs. Soon as they got to the ramp that led down to the jetty, they could see Francks's boat was already gone. They walked to the end of the jetty and there she was, out on that boat, motoring north into the sound. She was all statue except for her hair, which whipped in the wind.

She was too far away to see them and this was better, Yannick knew. It would have taken guts for her to get on that boat in the first place, and she did not in that moment need to be reminded of him, he who was abandoning her and Una both.

Love Too Easily

WHEN SHE WAS seven, her father told her about the animals that use the earth's magnetic field for navigation. He told her that he read this in a book. He told her that she should try to read as many books as she can.

(Her father also told her not to believe everything you read in books. That there are ways of knowing that aren't in books.)

Her father refurbishes houses for a living but he also makes art, from which he has earned very little.

Her father has been wearing the same winter parka for decades. It's roomy enough that she can snake her arms into it, even when he's wearing it, to keep warm. She hasn't done this for a long time.

Her father learned how to play gin rummy and euchre in prison, taught by a man from Moose Factory named Cecil.

Her father falls in love too easily.

Her father falls out of love too easily.

Her father has been mortally afraid to fly ever since the aeroplane he was on encountered severe turbulence, causing it to drop four hundred feet.

Her father smells of turpentine and cigarettes.

When she was very small, her father rested his chin on the top of her head and sang her happy birthday, and his deep voice rumbled like an engine all through her body and down into her toes.

Her father graduated high school in 1958 with a D in every subject except biology, for which he received a B+.

Her father recently mailed her a package c/o the post office containing: a Nestlé chocolate bar (disfigured, having melted and re-solidified en route), a calling card worth twenty dollars, three packs of Wrigley's spearmint gum, forty dollars in cash, two new pairs of socks and, without explanation, a newspaper clipping about a Minnesota man who specializes in carving Elvis Presley busts out of butter.

Her father is punctual.

Her father does not believe in God.

Her father sometimes forgets to call her on her birthday.

Her father is not afraid to drive on the highway in a white-out blizzard.

Her father can crack a walnut shell without cracking the nut.

And, like her father, she falls in love too easily.

She has loved the same man since this man was a boy.

They met in the weeds behind the school gymnasium, where this boy uncurled his fist for her and in his palm hunched a frog not much bigger than a Hershey's Kiss.

From sharing a bed with this boy she learned that, if some-one is snoring in your bed, all you have to do is jig your leg against his leg and he will stop.

This boy's fingers, fumbling and persistent as a moth.

This boy, this man, always knew when she was wrong and was claiming to be right (and he would tell her so).

This skinny boy with few friends has grown into a man with

a broad smile (having still few friends, which now feels more like a choice than an affliction).

This man, whom she has let down more times than she can count, has ignored her for two years.

This man is coming today.

21

KATHLEEN AT THE wheel, worrying her right thumb hard against the plastic as she drives, as if she's trying to rub a stain off a shirt collar. Could have been three or half past three when she jolted awake this morning. Una, again. She won't call it a dream because it wasn't – it isn't – a dream.

It was startling enough that she sat straight up in bed, wide awake, like how it used to be when this happened in the early days. She opened herself to it. By *it* she means Una. The living girl with hair the colour of ash. How she was, how Kathleen understood her to be when she was by her mother's side, when there was no gap between the two of them. Before time took the living girl and left Kathleen with the fossil.

So, last night in the dark, Una pulsed at her shoulder. The air closed in and shuddered against her skin, and she felt as if she had no bones to hold her up. She was vulnerable again to the raw truth, that perfect pinprick to the tip of the finger: your kid is gone.

Una's presence – it only came out of sleep, in the pit of night – was once so strong that Kathleen had to force her mouth open by gripping her teeth, bottom and top, pulling her jaw wide to let the scream out. A silent scream, obviously, she's not crazy, but her jaw ached all the next day, and so did her nose from where she pushed down on it with the heel of her thumb, and she was ashamed of having hurt herself.

As distressing as these visits (or whatever you want to call them) are, Kathleen needs them. Because when it happens, Una is close, and once again belongs to her mother. Kathleen falls back to sleep full of her and promises of her, and when she wakes up in the morning, Una will be there but not there, lingering in some parallel place. Like how it was, staring into the empty basket in the months before she was born.

A bargain has been struck, okay? Kathleen is allowed to have Una for those few seconds in the night, and the resonance of that hums for days or even weeks. In return, she keeps looking. Candle in the window and all that.

So it happened again last night. Only this time, Kathleen wasn't alone in the bed. Yannick woke too and put his hand on her back and spoke, and Una dissolved in the way a dream does as soon as you try to describe it. Kathleen attempted to curl back into her, but she was aware of the weight of his warm hand on her back, the smell of him, the pull of his breath.

When she woke up this morning, she looked for Una, first in the middle and then at the edges, but saw only an empty beer bottle tipped over on the floor. Dear, frigging Yannick was in the way so she got into the shower and turned it on as hot as she could stand it. Hotter than she could stand it. The steam built up quickly and then she turned it even hotter, to really feel the water on her skin. But the thing that happens with really hot water is that you stop feeling it. The sensation turns cold and sharp. She looked and looked, but where Una had been, there was nothing to find but close, tiled walls and steam. No bargains or promises. Her skin was burning and she was hurting herself again. She tried to cry, because she thought maybe she should. But there was nothing to cry about.

*

Now the world blurs past the truck's windows, like the rapidly flipped pages of a picture book, and she shifts her eyes sideways to look at Yannick. Yannick. Sex with him last night was glorious, it was delicious, and what a thing it is, to be reminded of your own desire after believing for so long that it had burned out. Today, she feels her breath rising from a deeper place in her body and there is better agility in her fingers.

But sleeping with him was also a stupid thing to do – though that's sex generally, a stupid thing to do. She worries that she hurt him, not just the stress to his old bones but inside, too. Last night seems to have pushed him even deeper into himself. She rolls down the window a crack, to give both of them some blessed air, but the pressure drops. The wind buffets and flaps, and her inner ears seem simultaneously to expand and shrink. She rolls the window back up.

The boundless horizon continues to bamboozle her. Prairie flat and then, suddenly, a bunch of hills or a series of ravines and she thinks: Finally, we're getting somewhere. And then it flattens again as if they were only ever running on the spot. She rearranges herself in her seat, slides her hands to different points on the wheel.

'You want me to drive?' Yannick asks.

'Nope.'

There's a distant ringing, which could be her phone. They're running on a little less than half a tank, which makes her feel uneasy. Since Winnipeg she's had gas anxiety, thoughts of two old fools stranded, empty and alone under this vast sky.

'We need gas,' she says.

Yannick leans close to squint at the gauge. 'We're fine.'

Her faith in Yannick's judgement isn't absolute the way it once was. She looks for the gas-pump symbol on every sign they pass. Finally, she sees one: next station in forty-five kilometres. That'll do.

They pull into an Esso at a pitstop town called Cluny, while Yannick gruffles under his breath about the unnecessary stop.

Kathleen peels her hands from the wheel and expands and contracts her aching fingers. 'You hungry?' she asks him. Her knuckles pop and crack.

'I'm still dealing with breakfast.'

'Well. I'm hungry.'

Again, the ringing. Definitely her phone. She reaches through to the back seat for her purse and hauls it into her lap, and rummages for the phone, which slips like a harried fish among her wallet and a lighter and a package of tissues. She scrabbles more, and her fingers find the notebook, reminding her about the number she forgot to change, again, this morning.

She has two missed calls from a number she doesn't recognize, area code 604, which means the call came from Vancouver.

'Do you think it's the coroner's office?' she asks.

'Did they leave a message?'

'What if they've already identified the bones?' she says.

'They need us for that.'

'Yes,' she says. 'They need us for that.'

She calls the number. It is indeed the coroner's office, and she is put through to someone who sounds extremely young and inexperienced. (Most people in the world are extremely young and inexperienced; the world has been this way since Kathleen reached the age of fifty.)

The girl on the other end of the line apologizes for bothering Kathleen.

'You're not bothering me,' Kathleen says.

The girl tells her that she's following up on their case and asks if she's had a chance to give her sample yet. Which, Kathleen supposes, is a gentler way of demanding: why haven't you given your sample yet?

'We're en route,' Kathleen says.

'You're going now? That's fantastic,' she says, and Kathleen can hear the tapping of a keyboard. The girl asks for the details of the clinic to which Kathleen is now fantastically heading to give her sample.

'We're coming to you,' Kathleen says.

'Oh,' she says. And apologizes a bunch of times, her voice flustered. 'You know that's not necessary. You can do it locally.'

Kathleen looks at Yannick. His expression is impatient and tense and this makes her feel tense. 'I realize that,' she says, her eyes still hard on him. 'Una's father wanted us to come out there, out here, so we just thought, two birds, you know? I'm assuming he spoke to you?' She cups her hand over the phone and to Yannick, in a rough whisper, 'You told them we were coming?'

He shakes his head.

Kathleen sighs and apologizes into the phone.

'That's a very long way to come,' she says.

'Yes, it is.'

'All the other families are local,' she says.

'Other families?' Kathleen shoots another look at Yannick.

His mouth spits silently, asking, what what what?

The girl on the phone is stuttering again, and ploughs her way through a load of gibberish, but the upshot is that other families have also been contacted about the remains. She thought Kathleen and Yannick had already been told. She is so sorry they have not.

'I don't understand,' Kathleen says.

Yannick has planted both hands flatly on the dashboard

and is looking off to the fucking horizon now, his shoulders squared and resolute.

'How many others?' Kathleen asks.

The girl tells her that she doesn't have the details but someone who does will call. She'll make sure that happens today. 'Where are you staying,' she asks, 'when you get here?'

'I don't know,' she tells the girl, and it feels like a confession. 'I don't know where we're staying.'

'It'll help,' the girl says kindly, 'if you can figure that out. Then I can make an appointment for you at a hospital clinic. For the sample.'

'Right,' Kathleen says, feeling now like this young and inexperienced girl has got it all under control. All Kathleen has to do is whatever she is told to do. 'Okay.'

She drops the phone back into her purse and explains to Yannick what she's just learned about the other families, but all she can think of is Julius's story about the blade of grass in the field. How, suddenly, it makes a lot more sense. Perhaps she has not, after all, been singled out. Or even if she has, it no longer means anything.

That there are other families should not have come as a surprise to Kathleen. This country is full of missing women, and this is something she understands completely: to be full of something that is missing.

She stayed on Vancouver Island for another month after Yannick and Sunny left, but quickly began to run out of money. She had to go home, back to work at the IDA, to pay the bills and the mortgage. Raise cash for a reward. She returned to a house that was so empty there was nothing to hold it up. She couldn't eat, could barely sleep. It was at this time she broke into Oliver Hanratty's house. It was at this time she slandered him with that journalist.

(How grateful she is, now, for the larkspur. How grateful for the red yarrow, the dahlia. Her home no longer empty.)

She didn't last long at home and by that first winter without Una was drawn to go back west. Beginning of December, she flew to Vancouver with a suitcase full of posters and very little warm clothing, and from there boarded a Greyhound bus. It made sense that she canvass a different part of the province so she chose to go to the biggest town in the north, a city called Prince George, which was eight lonely hours on the night bus from Vancouver. She spent the whole ride stiffening with cold and cramp, staring into darkness.

The bus pulled into town around six a.m. and she bumped her wheelie suitcase over gritty, salted sidewalks to the first hotel she could find. The girl at Reception blinked thick, electric-blue mascara as Kathleen explained to her that she was there to hang posters of her missing daughter.

'I'll show you where to go,' was all she said, unfolding a city map and smoothing it over the counter. With a sparkly pen she drew a route that bordered downtown, including long sections of the two main highways that converged a little further south of where they were: the Caribou and the Yellowhead.

'How far you want to go?' she said.

Kathleen had no idea, okay, at the time, where she was. How much empty road there was. How full of missing.

'You could take your posters all up the Yellowhead,' the girl said. 'There's towns and reserves all along there you could do them, all the way to Prince Rupert if you wanted. You got a car?' she asked. 'You need a car.'

'Is there a bus?'

'Not one that stops along the way,' she said.

'Maybe I'll hitch a ride,' Kathleen joked.

The girl looked startled, possibly pissed off.

She walked into town. She stopped in gas stations, corner stores, restaurants. A bike-repair shop, an army-surplus store, a pet store. Very few people were out walking; this was a town of hefty trucks and utility vans. Wide roads dry-white with crushed salt, and towering Sitka spruce trees, and sun glinting painfully off high snowbanks. The town sat in the hinge of two large rivers, the Fraser and the Nechako, and she encountered both of them that day, winter brown and roiling, chunky and threatening with flowing ice.

It was bitterly cold and she wasn't wearing enough layers. Her gloves were insufficient and she kept losing the edge of the tape because of her dopey fingers. A few hours into the walk, she found herself in a part of town that was mainly strip malls and parking lots. Head down in the wind on barren, icy sidewalks. Berating herself for being an idiot. Not many places to stop and hang a poster, and what was she doing in this town anyway? She went into a grocery store that had a bulletin board in the entrance space where the shopping carts were lined up, and this was where she saw the first poster of another missing girl: sixteen years old. Height. Weight. Indigenous. Last seen three years before this; the date was old but the poster brand new.

After this, she saw posters everywhere. Not just this girl but others, too. Nineteen years old, fifteen years old, twenty-one years old. All First Nations girls. Last seen, last seen, last seen. All from towns along or close to the Yellowhead highway. Many of the posters were brittle with age and weather, curled at the edges with the corners ripped away. Awkward, smiling girls in high-school photos, or standing in front of a cabin in the summer, or grinning at a birthday cake.

The next day, mid-afternoon, she was at the back of a Husky gas station, taping a poster to the wall next to the coffee machine, just by the little corridor for the toilets and the Staff Only room. The first poster, the one she had seen the day before of the sixteen-year-old who'd been missing for three years, was there on the wall, taped securely along each edge.

An old man approached. He wore a thick parka, unzipped, and a grizzly wool sweater with holes in it and tattered cuffs that hung to his knuckles. His short grey hair was plastered sideways across his forehead from where he'd just pulled off his toque. He looked like he knew how to keep warm in cold weather.

He leaned against the coffee machine and took a careful sip from a steaming styrofoam cup of black coffee, and gestured to the poster of the other girl, with the same hand that held the coffee.

'My buddy's niece,' he said.

'I'm so sorry,' Kathleen said.

He looked at Una's poster. 'She was all over the news,' he said. 'Your daughter?'

'Yes.'

He nodded slowly. 'Nothing worse,' he said.

'No,' she said. 'There's nothing worse.'

'Even better to know the worst than not knowing, eh?'

Something like anger dripped in her. 'I'm not there yet,' she said.

A woman excused her way between them to get to the bathroom.

'Your daughter was on the news,' he repeated.

'Yes.'

'Our daughters don't make the headlines so much,' he said, as he leaned closer to Una's poster to squint at the finer print. 'Why're you way the hell up here?' he said. He took another sip from his cup and winced the coffee down his throat. He was kind enough not to say what he was probably thinking, that Kathleen was just as lost as Una was.

She tried to think of an answer that made sense. 'I don't even know,' was what she eventually said.

He nodded slowly.

'It beats sitting at home,' she said.

'You don't know what to do,' he said. 'It makes you crazy. My buddy, it's got to where he can't pass a dirt road he hasn't seen before and he's turning up it and looking. He's been down every road. He looks under rocks.'

'I broke into someone's house,' she said.

The man chuckled, looked her up and down. 'You got someone helping you?'

'I'm not from here, so no.'

'You give me some of them,' he said, nodding to her shopping bag. 'I've got deliveries in places you'll never get to.'

A toilet flushed behind the women's bathroom door.

'Really? Are you sure?'

'You give me some of them,' he said again.

She would have liked to say, now, that she offered to help in return, but she didn't. She wouldn't have refused, if he'd asked, but the thought didn't even enter her mind. And the following day, when the Greyhound bus taking her back south pulled into a gas station in a place called 100 Mile House, she would have liked to say that goodwill occurred to her then, when, buying an orange juice and a bag of M&Ms, she again saw the poster of that man's friend's niece. She would have liked to say that she carefully peeled the poster off the wall in that gas station and made stacks of copies when she got back to Vancouver, and plastered them all over the city while she was doing Una's. Fighting for a little bit of space on telephone poles and bulletin boards where there were yet more posters of women, all those young women, missing from the city. She didn't do anything like that. She was drowning, okay? And a drowning person is the most dangerous, single-minded kind of person there is.

Patti Zoric stuck with them for a long time. Kathleen has to give her that. When Una's case was officially suspended, three years after it began, Patti Zoric called to tell her. Kathleen stood in the middle of the kitchen, same spot she stood when Una told her she was moving to the other side of the country. This was back when phones were attached to a cord and the cord was attached to a box on the wall.

'You're closing the case,' Kathleen said.

'That's not what I said,' Patti explained. 'Solved cases are closed,' she said. 'We're suspending Una's case.'

'I don't see the difference.'

'We won't be actively investigating.'

Kathleen might have sworn at her.

There was a second's silence when Patti was probably, Kathleen thought, considering whether or not to end the call. 'We'll be doing periodical reviews,' she eventually said, 'and if new evidence surfaces, we'll look into it. And obviously we'll respond to tips. If any come in.'

'How the hell will new evidence surface if you're not looking for it?'

'We've exhausted all lines of enquiry, Kathleen. I'm always here. You can call, anytime.'

Kathleen hung up.

Nothing new for several months: miles of flat and unchanging prairie. And even after the uncalled-for hang-up, Patti Zoric always took Kathleen's calls. Then, maybe a year and a half after the case was suspended, Patti got in touch to tell her about a retired logger who had been picking mushrooms on some small island tucked tightly into the northern tip of the Strait of Georgia. He claimed to have seen a girl, deep in the forest, who seemed to be living there on the down-low, as the logger told it. He spoke of a tent and a thrown-together shelter made of tarps and driftwood. He said she had what looked like a larder, with pots and crockery and cans of soup.

When this man told his daughter about whom he'd met in the forest, she told him to call the police. The local RCMP dispatch searched the entire island and there were no signs of the mysterious woodland fairy. No sign of a shelter or campfire in the spot to which the retired logger directed them.

'I guess it wasn't chanterelles he was picking,' Kathleen said to Patti Zoric, over the phone.

Patti laughed at that.

Anytime there was a tip that seemed halfway legitimate, Patti would let her know. A woman with hair like Una's in a bowling alley in Powell River. A woman with no memory in a homeless shelter in Salmon Arm. A woman begging on a street corner in Red Deer.

Or there was the young woman who called to say she'd dropped a hitchhiker in Tofino around the time Una went missing. Could have been Una, she wasn't sure. When asked why it had taken her so long to report this, two years, in fact, she said she'd been out of the country, and didn't make the connection until her return.

This sort of thing happened again and again, and every single time Kathleen believed this might be the end of it.

Patti Zoric was transferred out of Tofino in 2003 so that was the end of that. Very little communication with anyone official from then on. Years passing by the window at a hundred and forty klicks an hour.

Somewhere around 2004 or 2005 Kathleen got wind of this thing called Facebook and she set up Una's page. This was where the armchair detectives got involved, devouring the CCTV footage frame by frame. For a long time, many years, Kathleen believed this would be the thing to bring Una home. Hundreds of tips and theories about what could have happened. Possible sightings all over the world. Rumours and theories galore.

Kathleen saw abductors everywhere. A man in a hard hat choosing a bottle of bourbon at the liquor store, a man on a bike waiting to cross the street, a man with his arm in a sling, slouching in line at the post office. She would watch them and wonder if they were following her, to see how close they could get to the mother of the girl they had taken. This happened hundreds of times over the years. Hundreds of men wearing hats walking dogs buying toothpaste throwing baseballs talking on phones stopping at red lights biting into burgers on restaurant verandas.

You can only imagine the disappointment on repeat. The ringing phone. The unexpected knock at the door. The handwriting on the envelope lying in the front hall. Even the sound of mail hitting the floor. Every single time, hope burned to ash. And Kathleen is exhausted. She is exhausted by hope. (She's fucking sick of it, to be frank.) This unpromising glimmer in the dark. This false lifebuoy, mirage, call it what you will. Pah.

Hope is as dangerous and addictive as her Export As. Something has to go.

And she's not giving up her Export As.

In trying to bypass the city of Calgary, Kathleen screws up. She takes an off-ramp, or something, and now they're embroiled in the spaghetti system that edges the city's southern limits. In an instant, she's been plunged from driving at perpetual speed on a single unchanging lane, which required zero thought, into multiple lanes of traffic and underpasses and discombobulating ramps. Yannick has the satnav going on her phone (his phone is dead, as usual) and barks at her to cut across three lanes of traffic to avoid exits they don't want to take.

By some miracle they are eventually spat out at the west side of the city, and ahead, Kathleen sees a ragged darkness hovering at the bottom edge of distant clouds. 'Look at that storm,' she says, pointing. 'That's not good.'

Yannick leans forward, squinting, as if that will make any difference. 'Not a storm,' he says. 'Mountains.'

She looks harder, telling herself what's ahead isn't storm-laden cloud but instead solid rock, rising from the ground, and sees that Yannick is right. Huh. They've done it.

They drive, and the mountains grow. They look like they've been painted on the sky, rising in a series of sharp peaks all leaning in the same direction, as if the wind formed them that way.

It's not long before the mountains cease to be a dark jag on the horizon to become something that rises and juts all around them. The volume of sky has halved and they are surrounded by rock, and this is just the foothills.

The view changes with every curve of the road. Lakes and tall pines on either side of the road, a moose crossing, a weedy train track, a series of peaks to the north the colour of wet sand. In fact, these peaks look just like sandcastle turrets, like the kind you make on the beach when you dribble waterlogged sand from your fist, layering it in dollops.

Ahead, the true Rocky Mountains, the real deal. Sheer, crisp cuts into the sky. Kathleen feels the air getting drier, thinner. Nothing to distort the view.

And so what if she didn't change Una's number this morning? Those sandcastles to the north? Still standing. Nothing crumbles, or cracks, or turns to dust.

They drive.

22

THEY HAVE TAKEN a detour. It will add hours to the drive, which means they won't get as far today as they figured they should, and Yannick can feel Kathleen's frustration in the bullish way she brakes hard on the tight turns.

The kid pumping gas at their last stop advised them to carry on north, keeping to the route that cuts up through the middle of the Rockies instead of heading due west, which is what they were going to do, because of a rockslide that happened a few days back in that direction.

So, really, this detour could save them time, but Kathleen's face is pursed and she glares ahead because she just wants to get to the end of this. The plan now is to head north until they come to the town of Jasper, and from there they'll turn west and curl back south, last shot into Vancouver.

These mountains have been crunching into this sky for millions of years, something along those lines. They are flawless, and something this old should not be flawless. It looks to Yannick like when you tear a piece of paper and you can see every detail at the edge, every fibre. And with the air so clear? Nothing here looks old.

This clarity is not what interests him, though. What he's thinking about is that all this stuff, Una, Kathleen, all this worn-down stuff, is starting to feel new again.

All that hurt again.

'When I left you there in Tofino,' he says, 'that was the wrong thing to do. I should've stayed.'

They pass a yellow sign warning of a sharp bend and Kathleen hits the brakes without subtlety and gears down, grating metal. Yannick's body is thrown side to side. A muscle in his lower back spasms. It's like being bitten by dull, hot teeth.

'I'm trying to apologize to you,' he says, when the pain has subsided.

'We said last night, no apologies.'

To the left is a wide riverbed of bleached white rocks and hardly any river in it.

'You didn't hear what I said to you just now? About when I left you on that fucken island?'

Again, she doesn't respond for a whole minute, which is a long time, and all he can do is stare out of the window at this unfathomable beauty. There's too much of it.

'Yannick. Why do you always have to make things so . . .' she makes an angry little fist and shakes it in the air '. . . blah blah blah.'

'You were furious,' he says.

'When?'

'When I left. When I took Sunny home.'

She sighs. 'I understood.'

'We saw you out on Abner Francks's boat.'

'You did?'

'You were way out, far out, but I could see how angry you still were.'

'I don't remember it like that.'

'You had the right to be furious,' he says.

'There was no room in me for fury,' she says, sighing. 'We only just lost her.'

282

'We did,' he says.

They pass a mint-green lake held in the palm of yet another godlike peak. Not long after, they drive through a grove of poplars, leaves like moths' wings.

'You had the right to look after your kid,' Kathleen says, after a while.

'I thought I would come back,' he says.

'So? Now you have.'

'Now I have.'

When Yannick and Sunny left Kathleen and flew back to Toronto, they were met at the arrivals gate by Zack and the boys' mother. They became furiously scrambled trying to locate the car in the multi-level parking lot and it was humid as all hell. Tired and moody, they hauled their bags between hot cars, none of which was the right car, and Zack, without any warning at all, asked Sunny if he thought Una was dead.

'That's a stupid question,' said Sunny.

'But what happens now?' said Zack.

'I don't know,' said Sunny. 'I just want my bed.'

'Why didn't I get to go?' said Zack, his voice echoing queerly off the metal and the tarmac and the low, concrete ceilings.

'You can help next time,' said their mother, combing Zack's sweaty hair across the top of his head. 'And she is not dead,' she said, and lifted Yannick's bag from his shoulder and strapped it over her own.

It took them another half an hour to find the car, having been on the wrong level all along.

Once Yannick had dropped them off, he drove straight to Kathleen's, two hours away. They'd been calling the house every day and letting it ring, but as he got closer he could feel some kind of hope itching his fingers. Of course there was a chance, just like Patti Zoric had said. Una'd had an episode or some kind of queer breakdown. She was at home in bed with the phone off the hook and the lights out.

He pulled up the long driveway, parking the car at an erratic angle, and started calling her name even before he turned the key in the front-door lock. Continued to call her name, tripping up the stairs and flinging doors open to dark and fathomless rooms. Checking closets. Every space a person could fit into, you know? He went into her bedroom and switched on the bedside lamp with dusty yellow frills on its shade. He sat at her desk and touched the girlhood paraphernalia and pinched his nose against crying, and then he cried.

Listen. All these kids he's got. All this love he's got. The weight of it. Life has shown Yannick that you can just as easily grieve the kid you haven't lost as the one you have. Even now, especially now, when he looks at pictures of his kids from when they were still fat and plush at the edges, and bubbling with all that chaotic jumping around, silky messy hair bouncing, happy spittle on those red lips, or if he watches a video (he's got a bunch on his phone in his back pocket, mostly of Robin, all of Robin), well, it can feel an awful lot like mourning, like grief. Because when they grow up, your kids, they are different. Growing up is, in its way, a little bit like a death. Your kid is two people: the one that belongs to you, needs you, and the one that does not. Una, she is neither and she is both.

All her things in that bedroom were covered with dust. The meaningless things he remembers: an AA battery in an ugly ceramic bowl she must have made herself. The battery had leaked and was scabbed over with crusty acidic residue, and crystals of it stuck to his fingers. A black film canister with someone's hair in it. A glass box with a little brass hinge where she kept odd earrings and those woven bracelets from summer camp, and a dried-up cornflower that fell apart when he touched it. None of this crap told him anything. He stared at his tired reflection in a full-length mirror that wasn't even hung properly, was just leaning there against the wall. He was pissed at Kathleen for not hanging that mirror, or for not asking him to come over to hang that mirror. He did not recognize himself: he looked disproportionate; he looked like a man lost.

Mainly bric-a-brac in that room not worth the inventory except for one thing, on Una's bedside table in a cheap frame: a snapshot of his own mother and father together, rare as rare. He had forgotten that picture existed. Una would have had to go to oblivion to find it. Yannick Senior, the Québecker, the logger, the hairy man twice the size of his woman, which did not take a lot of doing as she was a small woman. Yannick's mother, her dark hair combed and falling around one side of her neck so it covered her shoulder and spilled onto his father's burly arm; he only ever remembered her hair being short and badly permed. His mother wearing a pretty little cardigan over a blouse. His mother, looking straight and sober right into the camera lens and smiling like the cat that, whatever it had done, swallowed something it wasn't supposed to? His mother tucked into the crook of his father's big logger shoulder.

Yannick did not recognize himself, his mother, his life, in that photo either.

He pulled the tiny cord on the dusty yellow lamp and fell asleep in his daughter's childhood bed.

'I need a walk,' Yannick says, eyes ahead to the road.

'Can't we just keep going, Yannick?'

'I'm seizing up.'

Kathleen glances at him. 'I need you not to break,' she says. 'Then pull over.'

Kathleen would drive through the night if she could and he can see she's done with this whole thing. They drive to the next rest stop, exiting onto a dirt track into some tall, lanky old pines. Bunch of picnic tables and some fancy shitters built in the style of ski-resort cabins.

'Look at those fancy shitters,' he says.

'I'll wait in the truck,' she says. She doesn't even take her hands off the wheel.

The smell out here is new to Yannick. It's coniferous but it's sweet and dry, with a cold edge to it. The smell of ice, even though there's no ice in sight. He hobbles down an embankment to the same broad riverbed from before, with the smooth white rocks. But here the river is resurrected in a shallow rush of freshly soft, aquamarine water.

A woman, a mongrel dog and a small toddling boy are nosing about by the water. He smiles at them as he shuffles past and the old dog circles him, sniffs his fingers and trots off, apparently satisfied that this old man is not a danger to his people.

Everything here belongs here. This is what Yannick would call a balanced composition. There's the foreground of river, then a wavy layer of verdant pines, and just beyond that, the mountains rise up brown and grey into the sky. And the sun, it just kind of glazes the whole scene.

These rocks underfoot, however, are shifty and smooth and exactly the wrong size for a foot to find grip, but still he walks upstream. After a few minutes, he lowers himself down to his haunches and cups his hand in the water, and the cold, maybe only a degree or two above freezing, strikes right up his arm and into his shoulder. He has to do a kind of crab dance to get himself upright, and again, a new pain tears through his lower back, into his backside and down one leg. He sits awkwardly, one ass cheek higher than the other. Just for a few minutes to absorb this new sensation.

He could just stay here.

Turns out, he can't stand up in the normal way, so he turns to all fours, wedges his knees into the rocks and pushes. He feels foolish and broken. Without any grace whatsoever he pushes himself to his feet, but to balance on these rocks, it takes all the muscles of his back. He looks for a stick but there are no sticks. Each bungling step, each slip of a foot causes pain to shine down his legs. What sort of idiot is he? The path he took down the embankment is only a few hundred metres away but he can't make it there on his own.

It would appear he cannot make it very far on his own in general.

Woman, boy and mongrel dog are walking downriver, away from him. He calls a feeble hello but the river is louder than he is. He calls again. The boy notices him this time and stares blank-faced for a second or two before throwing a rock into the water and carrying on. He tries once again, this time calling for help, and discovers that 'help' is an ugly old word when you are the one calling for it.

Kathleen soon appears at the lip of the embankment, yelling something to him, but all he can hear is the constant reprimand of the river. He points to his ears to gesture that he can't hear her.

She makes her way over.

'Why are you just standing here?' she says.

287

'Threw my back.'

'You already did that.'

'Well, it's worse now.'

'I've got those painkillers,' she says. 'I don't need them any more. Can you walk?'

'Yes, I can walk. Just not on these rocks.' He points.

She looks up and down the riverbed, hands on hips in an assessment kind of way. 'I would call these stones.'

'You must be joking me.'

'Why the hell did you come down here? Perfectly good walking trail up there.'

'You going to help me or are you going to keep asking questions you already know the answers to?'

She shuffles in next to him and he anchors his arm over her shoulders and she grabs his wrist, pulling him in tight. She puts her other arm around his waist and they begin to move forward. But they're both unsteady, and the pain is bad. He holds his breath and moves with her, and tries not to whimper or wince.

'Four days,' she mutters. She's breathing heavily.

He just wants to make it back to the truck. If he lies across the back seat, he'll be tip-top in a matter of hours. Sweat drips down the side of his face with the effort, yet he's not able to lean on her entirely. What that means is: he doesn't want to.

They get to the foot of the embankment and stop for a rest. This rocky shoulder seems much higher and steeper than when he came down it. Kathleen untangles herself from him and looks across the river to the craggy mountains on the other side. 'It's very pretty,' she says, frowning. 'You could just stay here.'

'I thought the same thing.'

'Eh?'

'Nothing.'

She turns to the embankment and surveys it, then looks him up and down. Those hands on those hips again. 'Can you get up it?'

'Well, I have to, don't I?'

'Why are you being so pissy?'

He stares at her.

'You've been pissy since before Medicine Hat,' she says. 'Since we stopped for that girl.'

'I wasn't pissy in your bed last night.'

'Yannick, please.'

There isn't a single thing he could say right now that wouldn't come out sounding needful or childish. Damn her.

'Come on,' she says, offering her arm. 'Let's get this over with.'

He doesn't take her arm. Instead, he tests the slope with his foot. Painful, but not impossible. Even better if he leans into it and uses his hands too. He manages a few feet, then rests on his knees. His arms are shaking. The smell of moss and warm dirt reminds him of how close he is to the ground, to falling.

'For the love of Pete, Yannick, let me help you.'

He looks up at her. 'I don't need help.' He leans back into it and builds up a rhythm that works. It gets even steeper close to the top and he sits up on his knees to look for the easiest line. As he starts to climb, Kathleen shovels her hand under his armpit, trying to haul him up, and he topples forward. Mashes his chin into the dirt and scrapes his knuckles.

He turns and sits, wipes blood and dirt from his chin with the back of his hand. Barely any blood to tell the truth; it feels like there should be more. Feels like you've been cheated when a wound hurts more than it bleeds. 'You trying to kill me?' he says.

'You were falling,' she says.

'No, I was not.'

'You were going to roll right to the bottom.'

'Hell I was.'

'Can we just get going?'

'Shit,' he says.

'Shit what? Four days, Yannick, and look where we are.' She nods at the rocks and the river. 'I don't even know where we are.'

'Two days ago it was your tooth.'

She glares at him.

'And this is a big country.'

She looks up the slope and she looks across the river, shielding the sun from her eyes. Her body relaxes a little. 'I just want this to be over, Yannick.'

'End this trip as fast as you can.'

'You're being a baby.'

He dislodges a stone with the toe of his shoe and regrets this for the pain it causes. He watches the stone pinball to the bottom. Kathleen offers her hand again and he ignores it, and when he's good and ready, he shambles to the top of this heap of dirt.

23

LAST NIGHT THEY stayed in a motel in a ski town called Jasper, deep in the belly of the mountains. This morning, Kathleen woke up feeling possessive about the bones. She would like to know how many other families are involved, and it would appear she missed several calls from the coroner's office yesterday, there being no reception up in these mountains.

No more farting around. She's driving today and she's not stopping until they reach Vancouver. Ten hours, eleven, doesn't matter. Yannick, who has barely spoken to her after some fool escapade down by a river yesterday, reluctantly swallowed two of her painkillers and is now dozing in the back seat, legs up, suffering. Poor dear man. Kathleen misses the silence of her life, though, and she's grateful to have some road hours alone.

Up in these mountains, the horizon confronts her. With the air being so dry and pure, and with the stark, uncomplicated beauty, it's impossible to be full of shit up here, where everything is absolute.

She's been thinking again about her accidental tea-leaf reading. It happened on her last trip west, winter, nine years after Una disappeared. She was in Nanaimo, back on the island. There was some kind of problem with the ferry and she was stuck with a four-hour wait.

Not wanting to hang around, she left the ferry terminal and stepped out into the cold drizzle, hiked up to the main drag and followed it south until she got wet and hungry. She found a teahouse, cute enough, white clapboard and violet trim on the windows. A deep, creaky porch.

She was seated at a table with a white cloth, near an electric fireplace that roasted the left side of her body. The only other customers were a group of three women who leaned towards each other earnestly over their teapot.

Kathleen ordered tea and a chicken salad sandwich with mayonnaise. The tea, loose-leaf, came in a pretty pot with a delicate, fluted cup, a saucer and strainer, and an embroidered napkin.

The waitress asked her if she'd made a booking.

'Eh?'

'For Renata,' she said. 'For a reading.'

Now the three women at the other table made sense. Two of them, young girls, were rapt, all eyes on the other, a punky woman in her sixties with buzzed grey hair, wearing large, heavy-framed glasses and gesticulating gracefully. Renata, Kathleen presumed.

'She has an opening in twenty minutes if you want it,' the waitress said.

One of the tree urchins, one of those kids who'd lived with Una on the beach in Tofino and helped with the search, had suggested they consult a psychic. She wasn't the only one. Patti Zoric had also called a psychic, some woman down in Florida the police had used before. Nothing came of it. And even pragmatic, hard-headed Julius was in on it. He'd offered, more than once, to take Kathleen to someone he knew in Toronto.

But now here she was, and with a full pot of tea, and she thought it would be amusing at the very least. And she had time to kill.

So Renata's schtick was to get you to drain your cup, turn it around three times while making a wish, then place it on the saucer. She put both her hands around the cup and considered it for a few weighty seconds before speaking. Kathleen can still remember the chiming of Renata's bulky silver rings against the china. She remembers feeling embarrassed because she'd dropped crumbs and a shred of mayo chicken on the pure white tablecloth.

Renata spoke for half an hour, often picking up the cup and tilting it to the side, or dribbling some of the dregs into the saucer. Sometimes, mid-sentence, she would stop speaking to Kathleen and raise her head to the side and listen, and nod, and say things like: 'Yes, okay, uh-huh, yes, thank you. I will, yes, thank you.'

Kathleen kept her expression neutral.

But then again. Renata knew both her parents were dead, that her mother had been gone a lot longer than her father had. She also described Kathleen's hands digging in the dirt, which caught Kathleen's attention, considering her flowers, considering it was getting harder and harder for her to make these trips because her hobby was turning into a business.

'You've got children?' Renata asked.

Kathleen didn't think she was allowed to do that, to ask questions. 'I don't know, do I?' she asked.

Renata placed both hands in her lap and flattened her mouth into a prim smile.

'I'm kidding. I have a daughter.'

'They're telling me you miss her. They're saying it the French way, that she is missing from you.'

Kathleen tried not to react, but Renata was ensnaring her, a little. She may have twitched.

Renata tilted her head again. Apparently, *they* were trying to tell her something.

'What. What?' Kathleen said.

And then, without preamble, Renata said these words exactly: 'You will always be left by the people you love.'

Kathleen stared at the pattern of crumbs on the tablecloth and waited for the sting to pass, the ammonia sting that shoots across the bridge of the nose just before the tears fall.

'That's a pile of shit,' she eventually said, when she could manage words. She dabbed her eyes with the embroidered napkin.

But. She didn't trust what she'd just said, that it was a pile of shit. Renata had her number; Renata was right. She was telling Kathleen what Kathleen already knew.

Now Kathleen is losing track of time. Neither she nor Yannick has bothered to change the dashboard clock with the time zones and, anyway, Kathleen doesn't know where the delineation lines are. They passed into the province of British Columbia twenty minutes after they left the hotel in Jasper this morning, around six thirty, gaining another hour. She knows this much: that in losing track of time she's actually gaining it.

Not long ago they passed the highest mountain in the country and very soon after this there was the sense that the symphony was tapering off, the mountains very quickly changing from snow-striated rock striking up into the stratosphere to much closer, steep and green. The view was like this for hours, after they turned south again, until they got close to the town of Kamloops where the landscape became smoother, the mountains kneaded down into a series of bald, folding hills.

Now, on the road out of Kamloops, Highway 5 heading

south, they climb a steep and hairy section of highway, heading bang into a black sky and the heaviest rain they've encountered on this trip.

The worse the road gets, the more Yannick apologizes for not being able to drive.

The rain lifts as they approach the top of the Nicola Valley, and for the first time since the mountains, the view opens up again and Kathleen can see beyond the flat-bottomed valley into the distance. Layers and layers of the blue, rolling mountains that she recognizes from all the times she went looking for Una. Getting both further from home and closer to parts familiar. They cross into the valley and, for a few hours, the road is dry and smooth.

By two in the afternoon, Kathleen has been at the wheel for six hours. They've joined the Coquihalla Highway, and are somewhere between the towns of Merritt and Hope, and it's raining again. Hard enough that both the rain and the spray coming off other vehicles have merged into one. The road is black; it is a river; it is fiendishly twisty. They've entered the temperate rainforest now, and the mountains are even steeper and feel closer than they did before.

Isn't it something, Kathleen thinks, how much can change in only a few hours? She says this to Yannick. He nods.

They're in a canyon. Fingers of mist tendril up the mountains, giving the impression that the mountains are floating. Mostly these mountains are wrapped in thick forest, but where it's too steep for anything to grow, there are vast, exposed slabs of rock, weeping shiny black and dark grey. Waterfalls everywhere.

Kathleen is in a state of road coma, hands bent into claws and concentrating hard, maybe a little (maybe a lot) afraid of skidding off into the blur of smoky mist and rain. She's been following the same wet smudge of taillights for half an hour, holding tight as if she's got her hands on a guide rope. They pass another of many road signs warning of rockslides.

'You okay?' Yannick asks.

'Eh?'

'The road.'

'What?'

'It's treacherous.'

'So don't distract me.'

As they get closer to sea level, to the place where Una disappeared, Kathleen finds it harder to breathe. The air is laced with something toxic and irresistible. It's wet and dark, and there's the sensation that the land is trying to suck them in when they're so close to the end. Hope is the next town but she doesn't dare take her eyes off the road, not even to read the signs, so she doesn't know how far away Hope is. The car she was following has turned off, leaving her on her own.

'Gas?' she says.

Yannick leans over. 'We're fine.'

'My fine or your fine?'

'We're fine.'

A logging truck noses up behind them and honks, long and hard. Headlights nudging straight into her eyes.

'Dickhead,' she mutters.

'Ignore him.'

'I can't go faster than this. I'll crash.'

Yannick puts his warm hand on her arm. 'Ignore him.'

The driver dances up against her, swerving into oncoming traffic and then scooting back to avoid collision. His headlights snigger into her neck.

'Look,' Yannick says. 'There's a pullout coming up.'

They pull in and the tailgater elbows past, water cascading off his high stack of timber.

'I'm sorry about this,' Yannick says.

'For godsake, please. Stop apologizing.'

'Stop telling me to stop apologizing.' He clicks his seatbelt open and tosses it off his body.

'Where are you going?'

'For a piss.' He unfolds himself out of the door, wincing.

Kathleen gives him a minute to do his business, then hops out. He's hobbling up the steep dirt track of the pullout and she trots to catch up.

'Is this a good idea?' she says.

'Good enough.'

They climb and the rain comes down. This humid, beefy air is familiar. This sticky, conifer smell, this dense, jewelled moss and rich dirt, and these queer fairy-tale trees, all familiar. Again, that sensation of being lured back down into a place out of which she's only just digging herself.

'This reminds me of those days in the woods,' Yannick says, breathing deeply. 'When we were looking for her. The smell. And these fucken trees. They're different from other trees.'

Kathleen can't help herself. She smiles.

'What's funny?' he says.

'I was thinking the same thing, that's all.'

'About the trees?'

'About this being familiar. I feel the same. I didn't expect that.'

Cars cruise by below and they continue to push upwards. There's a deep, ragged slash down the middle of the track that rushes with muddy rainwater.

'How's your back?' she asks.

'How's your tooth? How's your back? Get a load of us.'

'She would find this funny, I think.'

He nods.

'At least she doesn't have to watch us getting old.'

He doesn't say anything for a moment, and then: 'You have to let me square some of this off, Kathleen.'

She raises her face to the warm rain.

'I didn't help. I never went back there.'

They've come far up the track. Getting back down won't be easy. 'I think we should turn here,' she says.

'All that time,' he says, 'I didn't think it was up to me. I thought the only person who could bring Una back was Una.'

She turns and takes a few steps down, but it's so steep and muddy, she can't let him walk alone. She stops and looks back up and he's standing there, getting wetter. His clothes stick to him and he looks even smaller. Smaller than the small he already looks.

'I want to square it all off,' he says again.

'You're too late,' she says, and offers him the crook of her arm.

'Don't say that.'

'It doesn't matter any more,' she says, and she's smiling. She's smiling because she means it.

He doesn't seem to hear what she's said, either that or what she's said isn't what he wants to hear. He works his hands into his wet pockets and turns his head to stare into the trees. 'I did it all wrong,' he says. His strong, proud profile. Even now. Even the old hump of his shoulders. Still him.

'Look at me,' she says, stepping back up to where he is.

He looks.

She touches the scar, the one she gave him, with the pad of her thumb. She kisses his mouth. 'I'm sorry I threw that ashtray at your head. Possibly the only time in my life I've ever hit any-thing I was aiming for.'

He manages a sad smile.

She drops her hand to the side. 'We're almost there,' she says.

She can see that he's spent. He hooks his arm into hers and they hold each other up, toeing carefully back down the track, braking each other's weight to keep from skidding to the bottom.

Turns out Hope is half an hour away. Yannick was right, they have enough gas, so they don't stop.

When Kathleen told Renata the tea-leaf reader that her predic-tion was a pile of shit, Renata only smiled. Kathleen could see that her paid session was coming to an end by the way Renata sat up in her chair, distancing herself a little from the table.

'Can you see where my daughter is?' Kathleen asked, lean-ing forward, peeking into her cup. There was no liquid left and the leaves had scattered wetly up the sides. Her future looked a little like skid marks in a toilet.

Renata turned to face the window. The drizzle had become rain by then, slanted and blunt, and Kathleen could see it coming down in the reflection in Renata's glasses. Thinking about it now, though, it's not like you'd truly be able to see the rain reflected in a person's glasses.

'Can you tell me where she is?' Kathleen asked again.

Renata continued to look out of the window. Eventually she spoke. 'I don't feel her on the other side,' she said.

'Meaning she's alive,' Kathleen said.

'I don't feel her.'

This was all Renata could give, so Kathleen took from it what she wanted. Besides, she had no patience for ambiguity, even from a tea-leaf reader. Particularly from a tea-leaf reader who, in the end, charged her forty bucks for a pot of tea and an over-mayonnaised chicken salad sandwich.

Kathleen came away from that episode with three things. First, confirmation that Una was alive. Second, confirmation that she, Kathleen, would always be abandoned by anyone she dared to love, for evermore, and third, a slightly soiled napkin – embroidered.

She'd earned it.

But here's the thing. Two nights ago, when Una woke her up? When she looked for Una in the morning and nothing was there? That's not true. Standing under the hot shower, the temperature high enough to scald (to scold!) her skin, she looked for Una but what she found instead were rituals: the party, the Facebook page, the tally of missing days. The stalking of poor, recently deceased Oliver Hanratty, and the frigging candles in frigging jars. A whole lot of time lost, an emptiness filled with dirt.

Because it wasn't Una who woke her up two nights ago. It was never Una. It was only ever Kathleen, wanting so badly for it to be her.

PART THREE

The Bones Place

24

YANNICK'S MOTHER DIED an uncomplicated death due to brain cancer. This has always been the story. Unlucky.

He was thirteen years old and perched on the edge of her hospital bed when she died. His father was there too, his parents still being technically married, though for many years estranged. Mostly what Yannick thinks of when he thinks of his mother is his longing for her. He lived with his father, or his *grandmère* when his father was in the bush, and when his mother visited (and she did come plenty, she did try), when she came to see him she would bring gifts: an illustrated book of Babar the Elephant or a Nestlé's chocolate bar, offerings pushed into his hands with a desperate frazzle in her eyes, her voice pitched too high – 'For you, baby.' And then she would accuse him of hating what she brought. 'You think it's stupid,' she would say, sometimes before he even registered what he was holding.

Yannick doesn't think about this often, though he knows he was loved by his mother in a fierce and needful way. But something vital to do with mothering was stolen from her, and he has grown not to blame her for the way she was.

The point is this: he was with her when she died, so he knows the difference between someone who is gone to death and someone who is just gone. He watched her exhale her last breath, and it is true, you can see the moment the spirit, or the oomph, whatever you want to call it, leaves a body. It rides out on that last exhale, which, in his mother's case, was a committed *pfft* of the lips as if she were dismissing the whole show. With that last breath, the colour left her face. He pressed his fingers to the back of her hand, cold. His father called into the hall for someone to come, and while they waited, Yannick stared into his mother's hollow face. He was impressed, if that is the right word, by how rapidly a person can go from being alive to being dead to being a memory. Even before the elevator doors opened to take him and his father to the ground floor, his mother was a memory.

So when someone you love is missing without a trace, these distinctions get muddy. In the early days, Yannick didn't know if Una was alive or dead, and now he can't remember when he allowed the memory of the girl to replace the girl.

Too soon, though. He let it happen too soon.

They have made it to Vancouver. Arrived last night. Yannick has to give Kathleen the credit she is due – she drove upwards of ten, eleven hours yesterday, like it was nothing. They've settled into a hotel at the north end of the city, closer to the ferry that will take them back to the island. Last night, getting here in the dark, they crossed over the inlet that carves away the northern cap of the city from the rest, crossed over on a colossal suspension bridge, the lights of the city winking below, begging to be looked at.

Yannick slept okay last night. Turns out Kathleen's painkillers are pretty goddamn good. This morning he had a long shower and got dressed without too much struggle, and now he waits for her in the hotel lobby. She wants breakfast. She is also keeping him waiting.

Every time the elevator doors ping open he thinks it will be her, and it isn't, until eventually it is, and there's something different about her. Hard to put into words. He tries to capture it, this change. The way she holds her head, or a refresh to the shoulders, like pillows that have been puffed. It's been eight days, give or take, since he met her in the coffee shop and she gave him the broken lamp. She handed it over and he felt sorry for her. She was confused about the DNA sample and used the party as an excuse to leave, after only a few measly minutes in his presence. She said to him yesterday, 'Isn't it something how fast things can change?'

And how.

Here she is, waving her phone at him. 'I've just been speaking with the coroner's office,' she says. She holds open the hotel's glass door and they walk out into watery sunshine. They wander up the road looking for somewhere with a decent breakfast, and she explains that in two hours they have an appointment at an outpatients' clinic in a hospital not far from here. Someone from the RCMP will meet them there.

'Did you ask if we could go to the place? Where they found the bones?'

'Yes, I did,' she says. She stops in front of a café. 'Here?'

Yannick does not really care where they eat breakfast. They go in. They sit at a small table by the front window and there are trails of condensation sliding down the inside of the glass. The sun shines through the trails, trying its best to look pretty.

'So what did they say about going to the place?' he says.

'She couldn't tell me for sure,' she says. The menu card is wedged into a wooden block on the table and she slides it out and flips it with authority, from one side to the other, and he gets that feeling again. Something is different. 'She said it's up to the RCMP because it could still be a crime scene. But she also said, because the bones were found four months ago, she thinks it would probably be okay.'

'Four months?'

'I guess it took them that long to find us.'

'I guess it did.'

'Relatively speaking, four months is nothing,' she says, drawing a finger up a trail of condensation on the window.

A tall kid strides over to their table and nods at them coolly. Kathleen orders a coffee and some sort of artisan breakfast sandwich, and Yannick orders coffee only.

'Please eat something, Yannick,' Kathleen says.

'Those painkillers are appetite killers,' he says.

'Something small.' She reaches over and wiggles his arm.

The boy suggests a croissant and Yannick tells him fine, he will have a croissant.

'Chocolate, almond or plain?'

Yannick flicks his eyes up at the boy.

Kathleen tells the boy to better make it plain.

'There are four other families,' she says, as the waiter strides away. She tells him the other things she learned on the telephone this morning while he waited for her in the hotel lobby. The bones are at a laboratory at the University of British Columbia where they have been examined by a forensic pathologist. They were found in a provincial park in the centre of the island by a team of parks staff who were building a new hiking trail.

Yannick's coffee arrives and he drops in two spoons of sugar and stirs. He pulls at a greasy string of croissant and half the thing flakes apart in his hands. He pushes bits into his mouth and chews.

Kathleen tells him that most of the skeleton was found in one spot, and after a few weeks' search the investigators found other bones in the vicinity. The femur, which is the thigh bone, a shin bone and a section of spine, all marked by the teeth of some wild animal. Probably a cougar.

'They suspect,' Kathleen says, 'that the body was buried intentionally and disrupted by animals. Most likely scenario, apparently.'

'Buried intentionally, eh?'

'Yes.'

They look at each other, for a long time. And then the boy comes over and asks how they're doing, and Yannick turns his face to the window to stare hard at those pretty little trails of sunlit condensation, and he thinks about the watercolours, no, pencil, he would need to draw this. Exactly this.

The fella from the RCMP is waiting for them at the entrance to the outpatients' clinic in the hospital, and seems to know who they are just by the drag to their feet. He approaches as they shuffle down the hall with his hand outstretched, and introduces himself as being an investigator with something called the Integrated Forensic Identification Services. He wears a dark blue suit and tie and has thin hair for a man his age. His voice is measured and his handshake firm.

Upon meeting this man, who would have been a scab-kneed boy when Una disappeared, sweat trickles down Yannick's back, and his heart strums out of tune. Something about this investigator, in his simple suit and tie, suggests a kind of mid-level authority. It's something in the thin black hairs rising individually off his tight, smooth forehead. End-of-the-road kind of thing. A whimper. Now that they're here, Yannick would like to roll back the map; he would rather be looking out of the window of his truck at the bobbing oil derricks he saw just outside Calgary, or at the deep sky over Saskatchewan, or at the blasted granite along the northern highways of Ontario. This man has an official-looking red folder tucked under his arm, something to do with Una, Yannick is sure. Kathleen's eyes are on the folder, too.

'If you don't mind, I'd like to speak with you somewhere quiet before we go in for the blood draw,' he says. The man leads them down the hall and they push through a set of double doors, and go down another hall and turn some wide corners. Eventually, they are in a windowless office, or something like an office. An unclaimed room.

'I gather you drove from Ontario,' he says, as they sit down. A restless fluorescent light mutters above their heads. He moves the red folder from under his arm and places it on the table carefully as if it holds something fragile.

'What's in there?' Kathleen asks. Yannick can tell by her voice that she's not feeling so well, either.

'We do not want to see pictures of them,' Yannick says. He means the bones. These words have just come out of his mouth but the tone is all wrong: his lips don't seem to be working, and this is not his voice. This queer kind of wave rolls through his skull, and the room shifts under his feet. Yannick looks at Kathleen and she is the only person in the room. 'This is happening too fast,' he says.

The RCMP guy (who likely told them his name but, if so, Yannick didn't catch it) places his hands on the table, one over the top of the other. He waits to see if Yannick has anything else to say, then speaks. 'That's not what this is,' he says.

'So what's in there, then?' Kathleen asks, nodding to the folder. 'What do you want to talk to us about?'

'First, I wanted to thank you for coming all this way. It means a lot to me, to meet you.' He tells them he remembers Una's case.

'You're too young for that,' Yannick says, in a way that's meant to cajole. He tries to smile but has no control of his mouth, so it is a warped and shaky smile.

'I was a constable then,' he says. 'Just starting out.'

'Okay,' says Kathleen. 'And?'

'I would very much like to get you some answers,' he says. There's a new tear at the corner of the folder and he pinches it between his thumb and finger, making it neat again.

Kathleen nods, and in the way she moves in her chair, pushes her shoes against the floor, she becomes more solid. She, at least, is ready for the big waves.

'Hard to know what answers we want any more,' Yannick says.

'I can understand that,' this man says.

'And maybe there are no answers at all and we end up worse off than we were before you guys picked up the phone.'

'We don't make that call until it's time.'

'How do you know when it's time?' Kathleen asks. 'What about the other families?'

'This is what we know,' he says. He hooks his finger over the knot of his tie and shifts it a little. 'This person was female, aged between twenty and thirty-five years when she died. Her height was between five feet seven inches, five feet ten inches. She died between twenty and thirty years ago.'

'That's a lot of in-betweens,' Yannick says.

He nods, says that he agrees, and understands how hard this must be.

'People say that too much,' says Yannick. 'I am guilty of it myself. It's what you say when you have no idea how hard it must be. I don't doubt your sincerity, son. What's your name? Did you tell us your name?'

'Samuel Lim.'

'I don't doubt your sincerity, Mr Lim.'

'Yannick. You're being an ass,' says Kathleen.

'I am not being an ass. I'm sparing us the formalities.' He looks at Samuel Lim. 'You're just doing your job. And that's okay.'

'Are you all right, Yannick?' Kathleen says. 'We've driven a very long way,' she says to Mr Lim.

He smiles sympathetically and presses a careful hand on the folder, and explains that what he's got in there are photographs of personal items found with the bones. Actually, he doesn't say *the bones*, he says *the remains*.

'You don't have to look at these,' he says. 'But it could help with identification.'

Kathleen looks at Yannick to see if he's okay, and he nods.

The first picture is of a bra or the parts of a bra left over after it has been in the ground for two decades or more, displayed on a metal table. It was white in the long-ago, but is now the colour of the dirt it was buried in and looks like it has been dredged up out of hell. There's also a close-up photo of one of the straps to illustrate the style of the strap, which is, Lim tells them, scalloped. The next picture is of a pair of underpants in the same condition as the bra, same metal table. Clumps of dirt have fallen off the fabric onto the table and Yannick is struck by this fresh intrusion. Whatever happened to this girl once (maybe Una, maybe not), there is now this digging up, this displaying of intimate and rotting belongings on an indiscriminate metal table — it is an intrusion.

'I have no idea,' says Kathleen, scrutinizing one of the photos.

Yannick shakes his head. It's underwear, so. How could they know?

The next photograph shows a pair of shorts. They are the army-surplus kind, khaki with roomy pockets. Yannick doesn't recognize them but Kathleen says this is the kind of thing Una would wear, and he agrees with that.

Next, a T-shirt. Yellow, once. A V-neck style, and across the breast, a spray of wildflowers. It's angrily wrinkled and distorted in how it's laid out on the metal table, with the short sleeves pulled wide as if they hold arms, which they do not. It tells Yannick nothing but Kathleen picks at her bottom lip, staring at it for a long time.

'This isn't what Una was wearing that last night,' she finally says.

'No,' Lim says.

'But it looks vaguely familiar. And it's . . .' she looks at Yannick '. . . it's her thing, isn't it? Grubby old, saggy old man clothes on the bottom and something cute on top.'

'How sure are you?' Lim says. 'About the shirt? Being familiar?'

'Vaguely. Not sure at all.'

Lim pushes forward one more picture. At first, Yannick can't make out what it is, but then he sees it's a bracelet of beads, caked in soil.

'What are those beads?' Kathleen asks.

Lim flips the picture over and reads off a label stuck to its back. 'Tortoiseshell,' he says. 'Plastic.'

Kathleen looks at the picture and she looks at Yannick, but he does not recognize the beads. (Never went to visit, did he? Didn't know about any beads.)

All five pictures are laid out between them and they pull them closer – one hooked finger, tentative, on each photo's edge – across the surface of the table for a better look. These are all Una-type items, no denying it, and these are also summer clothes, which fits, but there is no proof here.

The only certainty? This is a collection of lost and unoccupied items that once belonged to a daughter, maybe his, and a long time ago these items stopped holding the shape of the person they belonged to. Una or not Una, this person woke up on the last day of her life and she pulled that underwear up over her legs and clasped that bra behind her back. Pulled that yellow T-shirt with the wildflowers over her head and slipped her hand through a string of plastic beads called tortoiseshell. This, undeniable.

An Empty, Tinny Feeling

OUR GIRL STILL has to get into town, and it remains too far a journey to make on foot, even if she weren't injured. This time, sticking her thumb out with a little less hubris, she hitches a ride with a woman not much younger than she is, driving a faded red hatchback, rock 'n' roll stickers in the back window and a whistling fan belt.

The driver is exceedingly friendly and easy with small-talk. They talk about the capricious weather. They discuss an apparent cougar sighting near town (totally out of the ordinary) from the week before. The driver tells her that she will be, the following day in fact, leaving to work for a charity in Nicaragua for two years. She's giddy with anticipation. Not wanting to talk about her own life, our girl is now furnished with all the questions she needs to fill this jalopy with chat until they reach town. She learns an awful lot about the charity organization in Nicaragua.

She gets out of the faded-red hatchback opposite a mediocre bakery, which will, in less than a week's time, be host to the crowds of people who will be searching for her high and low.

She walks around the corner to a phone booth and shoulders the awkward, folding door so that she is sealed inside, and makes a collect call to her mother, who doesn't answer, though her machine picks up the voice of the operator. She doesn't attempt a collect call to her father because he's just sent her the twenty-dollar calling card (which is in her wallet, which she thought was in her bag, but is not) and it would feel ungracious now to reverse the charges. He's not made of money.

It's five p.m.

In one hour, her oldest friend (her lingering love), her memento from home, is meeting her at a restaurant called the Nootka. She believes he will want to start something up again. It's always been that way with him and her.

She goes now to a playground across the street from the restaurant to wait for him. She might watch him go in, instead of calling out. Or she might call out, and meet him in the middle of the street. She sits on the swing and pulls off her shoes, and swings very loosely, careful of her knee, back and forth. Lets her heels drag in the dirt. She waits. Her knee throbs. Six o'clock comes and goes but this isn't anything to worry about. To get here, he's had to catch a ferry from the mainland, and then the drive is at least three hours, on roads he's never been down before. It's difficult to be accurate with a trip as involved as that.

She watches people going into and coming out of the Nootka.

She moves from the swing to the edge of the sandbox, dusty and littered with kids' stuff: a plastic shovel with a broken handle, a yellow Tonka truck, two raisins (fresh) and a handful of seashells. If she goes now, she'll miss him.

She swims the soapstone salmon in the sand and is tempted to leave it there. It seems to belong. Tempted, but no. She blows the grains of sand from its detailed grooves and pushes it back into her pocket. Pats the bulge to reassure herself of its safety.

She moves between swing and sandbox, tick-tocking back and forth, her knee getting worse and worse.

Seven o'clock, eight o'clock. The Nootka closes. The sun is

gone and the moon, a dusty purple, rises in the east, full and appearing slightly oblong.

What a day this has been. She thinks about what happened earlier, about that growing pile of animal feed cascading out of the torn bag, how her chin hit the dirt when she tried to hurdle the back of that pick-up truck. For a harmless nothing. She can laugh at herself.

She should have accepted the breakfast: her stomach now rumbles angrily.

(The man who picked her up, and his mother, will recognize our girl on the news, and in the posters slapped across their town. They will discuss together, long and hard, the wisdom of contacting the RCMP to report this encounter, considering the following factors: they could be considered suspects; the missing girl made it into town that day, regardless of whether they met her or not, so what would be the point?; the hydroponic marijuana-growing operation in the mother's basement.

They will elect to keep schtum.

Many years later the man will confess this omission to his new wife, who will frown in a way that will make him feel deeply uncomfortable. She will admonish him for his selfishness, but will agree that his input would have made scant difference to the girl's predicament.)

She laughs until the laugh dies away, and decides that the thing with the man and his mother wasn't, actually, a harmless nothing. For a few minutes there, she was genuinely scared. She ought to be more careful.

Living here at the edge of the world could almost make her weep, all this wild, exaggerated beauty. In later years, this town will be beset by tourists and microbreweries and whale-watching operations and luxurious holiday properties directly on the beach, but right now, today, it's not like that. It's a small town at the edge of nowhere, a stopping place for the working men who make their living from fish and lumber. A lot of alcohol is consumed here. Plenty of drugs. Plenty of bad judgement.

Best not to be caught out here alone, at night.

Best not to hitchhike home on a forest road, in the dark.

She makes her way to the marina, where (she was once told by a fellow squatter on the beach) you can usually find an unlocked boat-hatch, a place to spend the night if you're ever in a pinch.

It's nearly ten p.m. Her bag is snugly attached to her back and she's lost her walking stick. She walks in a slow shuffle, a crick developing in the ankle and shin of her good leg due to the compensation.

Maybe, she thinks, he'll come in the morning. Maybe he got lost. Maybe, for the first time since she's known him, he is the one saying no to her.

The hurt is an empty, tinny feeling. It's rusty and you wouldn't want to rub your finger on its edges.

She gives up on the boats after having checked only three (all hatches undeniably battened down), the pain of having to navigate the guard wires in getting on and off proving too much. She feels safe here, though, on the marina jetty. She'll stop for a while and watch the moon rising higher into the sky. There's nowhere she needs to be.

25

BLOOD IS DARKER than you think. Anytime Kathleen has had blood taken, she's impressed by its colour. How vibrantly it bubbles and gallops up the phial.

'Great veins,' the phlebotomist tells her, with a wink.

To be told this, that she has great veins, feels like a minor victory. Something useful she can do for Una, at last. Kathleen thanks the man more breathlessly than she means to.

Her dark blood swills up and down the sides of the phial as the phlebotomist writes her name on the label. He drops it into a clear bag and seals the adhesive strip at the top. Kathleen signs some papers. The bag with the phial goes into another sealed bag along with the papers she's just signed, and this is all handed over to Samuel Lim from Forensic Something or other Somethings, who's been waiting just on the other side of the door.

The photos that she's just looked at, of the dirty clothes and the bracelet – if this is Una, it means she didn't die the night she disappeared from the jetty, which is what Kathleen has always known. Possibilities begin to sprout, to circle and climb (and strangle) the latticework of Kathleen's brain like twined ropes of bindweed.

She is not getting into this again.

The last possibility she is ever going to consider lies within that plastic phial of blood. Currently en route to some other lab in some other part of the city. Samuel tells them he'll be in touch with the results in a few days.

The ferry again.

As it turns out, Kathleen and Yannick are not the first who've requested a visit to the burial site. Samuel Lim tells them some of the other families have already been. It's a queer feeling, sharing this monumental discovery with people they've never met, the sorry bunch of them claiming their small scrap until the results come back and they claim either none of it or all. They all want it and don't want it, and together, they are not alone.

Today, Kathleen and Yannick travel back to the island to see for themselves the place where the bones waited for decades to be found. If this is where Una died, or where she was brought after her death, Kathleen has to see it. Yannick was right to come. She should tell him this, this so-very-right thing he has done.

Sometime today, Samuel Lim is going to email a map showing the exact location of the site, which after twenty-two years feels like a cruel joke. A treasure map! He says there's not much to see except a newly cut, unfinished hiking trail, the laying of which, he says, has been put on hold due to the investigation.

Kathleen has left Yannick inside the ferry, sitting on a long row of seats near the cafeteria. He is depleted. She doesn't want to say that she's worried about him, but she is. She's worried that when he goes home there won't be anyone there waiting for him. What's this wife's name again? Leigh. It would be so much better if Leigh were there.

She's come out to the deck to smoke and look at the view, which is, like so much of this part of the country, enchanting. Hazy blue layers of mountains in the distance and all that. Sun glinting off the water, illuminating the haze in a surreal way. Almost paranormal. They churn past richly forested islands with inaccessible beaches, close enough to see kelp floating in serene coves. Gulls stir the sky.

It's nice. And too windy even to joke about lighting a cigarette.

Una would have stood here, right here in the wind, with her hair whipping across her face. Her gaze would have been forward, towards this island where she decided to move her life to, and she would have been over-excited and pleased with her decision. Kathleen looks to the empty space beside her and Una is standing there, face forward to the wind.

Flowers are planted, nurtured, cut and sold at market, and planted again. A well-aimed glass ashtray bursts open skin, and scars harden, and new babies are born, and teeth crumble and are pulled, skin loosens and is marked by time, hair coarsens, photos of other women's children are folded into a man's wallet and grow soft and bent with age, and are later replaced by new, more recent photos. And here is Una, unchanged.

The ferry horn clears its throat.

Kathleen has never before been allowed – allowed herself – to appreciate the charm of those mountains on the island, how, from here, they look like perfect paper cut-outs, like shadows. Never noticed before what the sun does.

The day Yannick and Sunny left Tofino, Kathleen went on Abner Francks's fishing boat so she could see these infamous hot springs for herself. The place where, as the Coast Guard supposed, Una may have been trying to get to – if there was any truth to their stolen-kayak theory. Kathleen didn't buy it, but she wanted to see the place Una had described to Sunny in the email, the one where she wrote that drivel about not feeling mothered.

Still galls her, even now.

At first, on the boat, she thought she was going to get away with it, the seasickness. She felt okay. She wasn't afraid. The water in the sound was choppy but she fixed her eyes on the horizon, which was what well-meaning boat lovers had advised her to do over the years. She breathed with intent, steadily in through the nose, out through the mouth, and congratulated herself for being in charge.

Pah. Ten, maybe fifteen minutes on board, and the boat deck dropped from under her feet, taking her stomach with it. Everything went loose at once. She was too ashamed to say anything to Abner and, besides, she was going to make this trip no matter what, so why bother? She stiffened her pulsating throat, denying what was happening, but it soon overwhelmed her and she got up from where she'd been sitting and vomited her breakfast over the side. She vomited until there was only dry heaving and the occasional, swinging ribbon of burning, yellow bile. At one point, when she straightened back up, dizzy, there was a can of warm ginger ale and a half roll of Lifesaver candies sliding around the bottom of a bucket placed under her chair. Abner Francks: merciful and discreet.

For some of the journey, they were walled in by those over-lapping islands, and for some of it they were out on the open ocean, the boat rising and cresting, then slamming down hard over massive rollers. Kathleen didn't have any space in her head to think about what it might have been like for Una, had she been out there in the dark in some rinky-dink kayak. How scared she would have been. Couldn't think about it until later, in the middle of the night, wide awake in her hotel bed.

Somewhere out in the open water, Abner stalled the boat and joined her on deck. He didn't ask how she was, which she appreciated. Instead, he pointed to a head of rocks pushing up above the surface, coughing foam, green water heaving up its sides and sighing back down. Abner gripped the edge of the boat and gestured with his chin towards the rocks.

'You should see some grey whales over there,' he said. 'In my father's day, after the hunt, they towed those fucken fish back home behind their kayaks.' He put his hand on Kathleen's shoulder and gave it a squeeze, and told her to look for a whale, that it would be a good distraction from the sickness, and he went back into the wheelhouse.

Maybe she glimpsed a looming crescent of white-spotted grey, or a flick of wet charcoal glinting in the sun. Maybe a placid half-somersault in the trough between two swells. But all she could do was bend over the side of the boat and retch.

Eventually, mercifully, a cove. Water at rest, heavy and languid as oil. They docked up, and as soon as she stepped off that godforsaken fishing boat, she felt somewhat better. Maybe a little hollow, but better. There was one boat there already, tied to a high jetty on stilts. She followed Abner down the jetty ramp and onto a well-trodden path into an otherworldly forest. Practically prehistoric. Tall, thin cedars and short, girthy, tangled ones. All types of lichen and fungi. Spongy green, wet green, hard green, sun green. Humid, deep-earth, dense smells that were new to her. The path took them up steep wooden steps to ocean vistas people travelled from faraway places just to gawp at, then down into gullies where it got dark and buggy. They didn't talk much.

They came to a section of the trail where a rickety boardwalk had been built over a bog. Halfway across, a girl appeared, coming towards them from behind a hanging fringe of moss. Her dark hair was swirled on top of her head in a messy bun, half the hair sliding out and framing her face. She wore a bikini top and baggy shorts to her knees. Healthy little paunch and bare feet. Kathleen, in an instant, imposed the beloved face and shape on this girl, the familiar bounce to her step. The space she bit out of space.

She called to her, roared to Una. As soon as the name careened through those silent trees, Kathleen knew her mistake. It was quite a blow.

She hadn't slept in weeks. Barely eaten. Her body was wrung out from the seasickness, and the forest had doped her with its overabundance and mystifying aromas. Her face went numb and her vision black and starry, then the black turned to purple. She doesn't remember falling. The next thing she saw was Abner's face and this girl's face worrying above her. They helped her to sit up, and leaned her against a tree. Abner sent the poor girl on her way and wouldn't let Kathleen go anywhere until she drank water and ate a Lifesaver candy, which was warm and sticky from being in his pocket.

The Hot Springs, when they finally made it that far, was just another unfamiliar place at the back end of an unfamiliar place, and Kathleen was feeling lost and stupid. Now that she was here, nothing was better. And Una was nowhere.

There were people, young and beautiful people, broiling themselves in these natural pots, a series of rock pots between the forest and the ocean. People floating like dumplings, steam being pulled back and forth by the wind. You could smell briny ocean, and sulphur, and wet rock.

'Dip yourself in there,' Abner told her. 'It feels good.'

They stood at the edge of the rocks. At their feet was a mess of discarded shoes and bags and clothes, watches and sunglasses tossed absentmindedly to the ground, in that way reserved only for the young and wistful.

'You might as well, since you're here,' he said.

'Nah.'

'It heals you.'

'Not much hope for that.'

'Suit yourself.'

Abner, it seemed, was unconcerned that she had no plan. That they'd come all this way for nothing. Kathleen didn't think about it at the time, not even briefly, what it might have been like for him, pulled so deeply into their undoing. Did he think about his own daughter? Did he keep her closer to home? But even more basic than that – surely there were other things he needed to do that day?

'We'll sit then, eh?' he said. 'Give that beast a chance to turn. It'll be just as bad for you going back. Probably worse. Conditions might ease off if we cool our heels a while and wait it out.'

'I don't care,' she said.

Out there, beyond where the beautiful people stewed themselves in sulphuric water, beyond the rocks, there was the great big for-ever-and-nothing Pacific Ocean. Directly below where they sat, way down, was a fault line that they say is, one day, going to slip and drag that part of the country underwater.

All that water. Kathleen felt the weight of it in her bones, and she was weary. She took a big breath and exhaled towards the unattainable horizon. That line in space which can only move away from you. The wind spat salty spray and the sun shone like it had nothing better to do, and for a second, she understood the impossible thing and it nearly beat her.

She stood up quickly and turned her back on the madden-
ing horizon, and told Abner she would dip her feet in the hot
spring after all. Which she did. It was warm and invigorating,
she could admit that much. But she wouldn't have called it
womblike.

It was worse, on the way back. It was horrendous.

Late afternoon when they'd motored into the marina, and
the sun was just beginning to edge behind another day without
Una, Kathleen stood on the jetty, weak as a half-starved kitten,
and watched Abner tie up his ropes or whatever it was he was
doing, putting his boat to bed for the night, one task at a time.
She watched him at work and planned her next steps. More
posters. Reward money. Keeping Una in the news. That long,
lonesome fight against idleness.

She doesn't now remember saying goodbye to Abner Francks.
She saw him again, on subsequent visits, but all she remembers
from the end of that day is the sight of him bent over and tying
a rope, the sun going down behind him.

An announcement. They're coming into the ferry terminal at
Nanaimo and it's time to return to their vehicles. Yannick is
not where Kathleen left him, on the bench by the cafeteria. He
had Kathleen's purse, which, at least, he took with him. Wherever it was he went.

He couldn't have got very far. Kathleen checks the cafeteria
and she checks the gift shop. She waits outside the men's toilet,
watching men go in and come out. Another announcement
that all drivers should now be in their vehicles. Foot passengers
to disembark on Deck Four.

She shoulders the heavy door to the outside deck and does
a half-lap of the boat. No one is out there and all around her is

ferry terminal: smaller boats dotted around, the open arms of an empty berth and its apparatus, and brutal-looking cement blocks rising out of the dark water, crusty with barnacles and rimmed with slick, hairy seaweed that rises and falls with the sleepy motion of the harbour. She has to get back to the truck before they lower the ramp.

The metal stairs that lead to the vehicle decks are narrow and steep, and she can't remember which level they're parked on, which side of the boat. She thinks it's Deck Two, and tries it. Recognizes nothing. Cars and trucks and camper vans are parked nose to tail with just enough room on either side to squeeze into half-opened doors. She scans for Yannick but it's just all these other people, and the parps and flashes of cars being brought to life by remote key fobs. Some people have already started their engines, chuffing bitter blue exhaust. She retreats back through the bit in the middle, the closed-off structure that houses the staircase, to the other side of the deck and recognizes a truck and trailer from when they drove on. She recognizes the family of bikes racked to the top of the trailer, and finds their truck just on the other side.

She goes to reach for the keys in her purse and remembers that Yannick has her shitting purse.

The ferry horn blares. A whistle blows twice, tight and quick. The boat shudders and sways as it nestles heavily into its berth. More engines start up. She looks at the guy in the car directly behind her, and he's ticked. He opens his window and drops his arm over the sill, pushes his head out. He can't be more than eighteen or nineteen years old.

'You got a problem with your truck?' he says.

'My friend has the keys.'

'What?'

She repeats, louder, her voice echoing.

He motions towards the front of the ferry with his palm. 'Well!' he blurts.

What can she say?

The ferry is long and curved enough that, from here, she can't see the exit ramp, but there is a sense that things are moving. A whisper of fresh air, engines getting louder.

It occurs to her that maybe something terrible has happened to Yannick. Her throat tightens and something in her drops. There are no windows and the light in the tunnel is yellow. Sick yellow. Carbon monoxide hovers.

And then he appears, comes around from the back end of a minibus a few rows over, looking bewildered.

'What the hell, Yannick?'

'Where did you go?'

'Give me the keys.'

The car in front of them begins to move. Horns object from behind. For two old farts, who've travelled thousands of kilometres, they can still move pretty fast. They scrabble into the truck and the engine rolls over with the first turn of the key, and they're juddering forward.

And all Kathleen feels is relief that Yannick is found.

26

FIFTEEN YEARS IS the greatest amount of time Yannick has ever lived in one house with the same people. This same house that is now empty, with Robin gone to university and Leigh just gone.

Back when they bought the place, when Robin was toddling around in saggy diapers, Yannick built her one of those backyard swing-sets. It had a curly slide and a teeter-totter. When Robin played on her own out in the yard, Yannick could hear the emphysemic wheeze of the swing labouring back and forth, and be assured that his daughter was where she was meant to be.

She grew up fast, though, as daughters do, and soon enough, the sun and the winters sapped the colour from the swing-set and rusted it, and the teeter wouldn't totter any more. Yannick tried to dismantle the swing-set to take it to the dump but all the nuts had rusted into the bolts and the bolts had rusted into their sockets. The poles were fused together and no amount of WD-40 was enough. So he took a hacksaw to it and hacked that swing-set to kingdom come.

He's thinking about this now because this is how his body feels, his knees and his back; the ligaments, what-have-you, the hinges, have rusted tight. Too many suns and winters. His bones have fused into their sockets and his muscles have hardened to rubber.

Kathleen. She was so geared up at him because of something that happened on the ferry, claiming he nearly caused some sort of traffic calamity, a disembarkation faux pas of the highest magnitude. Keeps asking him where he disappeared to. Keeps asking him if he's okay.

But he didn't disappear – she did. What happened was, she went out for a smoke and didn't come back. So maybe he got a little restless and maybe he wanted to go for a walk too. He tried to find her and she was nowhere. Instead, he found the ass of the boat, and stayed there a while. Hang around the rear end of a big boat like that and stare at the wake, that white-water highway, and what's inside a person's head and what's inside his heart will inevitably tumble overboard and disappear beneath the foam. Watch the wake for long enough and a pattern will be revealed, repeating without end, the water parting down the middle and folding back into itself, and at the furthest point, the white road dissolving back into the ocean like it was never there. Huh. Moon road.

Yannick is an old man. His hinges are no longer well oiled. Stand at the back of a big boat and you see its trace, and the trace dissolving, and you think about these things. How your body begins to fail you, how your last wife has left you. You think about your own white-water trace, your wake. And what you leave behind. And how all that will dissolve too. Poof. Never there.

Tonight, another motel close to the ferry terminal. Tomorrow they will get up early and drive to the site. Say it again: tomorrow they will drive to the site.

Yannick still doesn't know what to call this place. This bones place.

It's crossed his mind to knock on Kathleen's door. He would

very much like to sleep with her again, but doesn't think he can stomach the way she's been looking at him today. Nothing sexy about pity.

Better to sleep.

They leave in the morning under an indigo sky and make it to the edge of the park where the bones were found, a few hours' drive into the mountainous interior of the island. It's turned into a lousy-looking morning, dull with cloud.

Kathleen had the wherewithal to print out the map at the hotel's Reception, which Lim emailed to her last night. It's one of those satellite maps from the internet, and covers this small section of parkland. Lim's instructions say that, from the parking lot, they are to follow one of the older trails until they get to a blocked-off section where the new trail, the one that will take them to the site, begins. There will be signs where the new trail peels off, telling them not to enter, but they are to ignore these signs. The new trail has been abandoned, will possibly never be finished, because of the bones. Apparently, the hike should take them about an hour. According to whose pace, Yannick would like to know.

Lim has drawn a circle around the exact spot. His message says it's easy to find because the unfinished trail ends there, and because there is police tape tied around some of the trees. So.

'Here.' Kathleen passes a long, solid stick to Yannick. It's free of bark and smoothly blond, with a natural elbow at the top for gripping. She's been to the park rangers' canteen and she's packing two plastic bottles of water and some kind of nut-and-desiccated-fruit snack into her purse.

'What's this?' he asks, rubbing his thumb over the bent corner.

'What's it look like?'

'I meant, where did you get it?'

'Ranger gave it to me,' she says. 'Don't be proud. I'd take one myself if he had another.'

He grinds the worn point of the stick into the gravel in tight, crunching circles. It's a good height, and firm.

The trailhead map shows walks of various distances, elevations and degrees of difficulty. Tacked next to the map there is a warning sign instructing hikers what to do if they encounter a cougar. Among other suggestions: maintain eye contact; pick up small children and pets; if the cougar attacks, fight back with everything you've got as this is a predatory attack. Yannick suspects that any outcome of a cougar encounter is likely up to the cougar.

The trail they are meant to follow is marked by a yellow-dashed loop. It runs along the lower slopes of a mountain with a lake on the other side. The path to the bones is, of course, not shown on the trailhead map. It doesn't officially exist.

At first, the path is flat and hospitable, but very soon it drives upwards and Yannick is grateful for the leverage the stick provides. Kathleen walks ahead, and if the distance between them grows too big, she waits. The light is dead. The forest is pale and quiet.

They go higher, and looking down to the right, through the trees, Yannick can see the dark movement of the lake.

Kathleen is waiting for him to catch up. She asks if he's okay and he tells her she'd better not keep asking that or else.

'Or else what?' she sputters.

He walks right on past.

The trail winds upwards, steep and ridged with roots, interrupted by rocks, and they take it slow. Kathleen follows closely behind, and he supposes he cannot blame her. Big trouble for them both if his back goes again. When they reach the top of a particularly steep section she looks at him and he can tell she's about to ask if he's okay, and he sees her swallow those words in one wise gulp. They do pause, though, to share a bottle of water and eat a handful of nuts.

She pulls the map from her purse, unfolds it and holds it up. She squints at it as if she has the orienteering ability to determine where they are on the trail in relation to that scrawl on the map, the blue circle that marks the spot.

'You think you know where we're at?' he asks.

She draws her finger along the map, almost to the point where they turn onto the new, unmapped trail. 'I think we're here,' she says.

'Based on what?'

'I've been keeping track of the bends in my head.'

'That is not how this is done.'

'I'm kidding,' she says. 'We've been walking for an hour. I assume this is how far we've got.'

They hike on, he with his walking stick and she with her map. He cannot believe that after two decades of nothing, there is a map.

'X marks the spot,' he says.

She stops and eyes him.

'You could laugh if it weren't so grave,' he says.

'What?'

He attempts a chuckle, proud of his pun.

'Yannick. For crying out loud. Explain yourself.'

'We have a map,' he says. 'After all this time.'

She smiles bitterly. 'It is a lousy joke, eh?'

'It sure is,' he says.

The trail continues to climb and they soon come up alongside a barrier of yellow police tape tied between two trees. Some of the tape is still secured tight but most is torn and fluttering limply. A more permanent metal *No Entry* sign is nailed to a rough post of yellow pine.

'This is us,' Kathleen says.

'I wish that Lim guy never told us to ignore the signs,' says Yannick.

'So we could turn back?'

'Yup.'

'Yes.'

'How do you feel?' he asks.

'Mixed up.'

'Me too.'

They step off the old trail and pick their way around the taped trees onto the new path, which doesn't feel so much like a path. The dirt is a darkly rich mixture of loose stones and clods of mud. Soft and harder to navigate. The established path was packed down hard and moved with the undulations of the forest floor as if it has always been there, an old scar, the edges blending smoothly into the vegetation. This path is more like a fresh wound, slicing into the woods around it.

And it has started to rain. Yannick knows it's raining because he can hear the patter high up in the trees. The air has cooled and the rain has conjured up the smell of sawdust from the trees that were cut.

'Are you getting wet?' he asks.

'Eh?'

'It's raining but I can't feel the rain.'

'Because of the trees,' she says, waving a hand in the air like she's some kind of expert. 'Keep an eye out for the police tape,' she says.

Samuel Lim's written instructions say the spot is directly

behind the uprooted base of a cedar tree (as if the person who dug the hole used this for cover). There is also, just next to it, a boulder the size of a car and of course more police tape; these are the features to look out for. The root mound, Samuel Lim writes, is roughly the height of a person.

Yannick's heart kicks clumsily. He is thirsty but doesn't want to stop for water or, more accurately, ask Kathleen for water, in case she thinks he's weakening.

This trail is more level, cutting into the side of the mountain horizontally instead of driving up it. If it was Una buried out here, she would have walked. You cannot carry a person through this. Whoever it was, she walked. All through here. These same rocks, these trees, this same dirt. This time of year too, give or take, so it would have looked just like this; the air would have felt the same, the smell of the ground.

Something rustles in the ferns downwards from where they are. Some bird caws.

He's looking for the bright police tape; he's looking for the dark mound of earth, the root mound, the rock the size of a car. The place where this trail will abruptly, finally (too soon) end.

'We've got to be close,' Kathleen says, panting. She's got the map in front of her face. No need for a map at this point but at least it's something to hold.

Now the trail takes a dip and continues downwards, and the exasperated muscles of Yannick's lower back are giving him the last of whatever they have got to give. He takes it slow, finding rhythm and comfort in a kind of sideways shuffle. A ripple of pain at the base of his spine and he has to stop and press his forehead against the stringy bark of the closest cedar tree. The smell of sap and damp bark is so strong he can taste it.

He closes his eyes and is surprised by thoughts of his three boys. He whispers their names, Sunny and Zachary and Devon. He whispers the name of his daughter, the one who is not lost. He thinks of her, of Robin.

'There.' Kathleen's voice echoes strangely through the trees. 'It's there.'

Where she's standing, up ahead, the trail has ended. The cut they've been following opens to a clearing with piles of dirt and unorganized stacks of logs. At the far end of the clearing is the fallen tree, its root mound roughly the height of a person. There's the rock. The police tape.

He approaches Kathleen and she hooks her arm into his.

'I don't need help,' he says.

'I do.'

Rain, harder now, falls through the trees and finds its way to Yannick's neck, his shoulders. He shivers, though he is warm from the walking.

Kathleen is looking at him with a face he can't read. 'I want to tell you something,' she says, but then says nothing and looks at him a little more.

'Spit it out, girl.'

'I know I've been pissing and moaning, but this was the right thing,' she says. 'You did the right thing, bringing us here.'

Now, he is not so sure.

'We don't have to go any closer,' she says. 'If you don't want to.'

'Ach. Last few steps.'

'Come on, then,' she says.

The ferns here are knee high and so thick that the ground is lost. Not being able to see his own feet, Yannick doesn't want to break contact with the earth in case the next step is not where he expects it to be, so he considers each one, taking the next only when he's sure of the last.

And here they are. A candle and a bouquet of flowers have been tucked lovingly between the feet of one of the bigger tree trunks. The candle is in one of those tall, wine-red jars you'd expect to find in a church. The flowers' heads sag on broken necks and the petals have wilted and gone pale, and some have dropped to the ground, and the stems are held together with a pink ribbon that's not yet lost its shine.

Kathleen kneels to the flowers and rubs the ribbon between her thumb and finger and then just stays there. He leaves her to it.

Looking at the ground, it's not obvious where the digging occurred, where the actual burial site is. The earth has reclaimed this patch with sprays of young vegetation, like kids let out of school, bright green shoots and ferns and white, milky flowers. Yannick pokes holes in various places with his walking stick. He does this for what seems like a long time, before Kathleen notices and asks what he's doing.

'Looking for where they dug the hole,' he says. Point Last Seen.

'Okay.'

'You think it's okay?'

'Fuck, yes. Probably not respectable, strictly speaking, but . . .'

'I want to put my hands on the exact spot.' He moves in tight circles, poking, and there is no way of telling where the hole is and where the bones were. He moves outwards, broadening his circle. He jabs the dirt. He hits a rock or root or some other unforgiving thing, and pain shoots up his arm and straight into his back. He is sweating and out of breath and swearing steadily with the crudest expletives he can muster. He stabs and prods, stabs and prods the dirt.

'Yannick, stop.'

He is metres away from the rock, the root mound, so he

weaves back again, stabbing the ground. Tripping over his feet and tripping over the stick. Your kid does not ask much of you, does she, other than to be remembered after she's gone? He's never before allowed himself to picture what her face might have looked like the moment she knew she was going to die. That look is all he now sees as he jabs his stick into the ground. He hits a rock so squarely and perfectly that the pain shudders through his body, like a harp, like fingers are plucking his strings. He hurls his walking stick and it ricochets off a tree, landing in the dirt with unexceptional silence.

Kathleen tells him again to stop and now her hands are on his shoulders and he is so out of breath he has to bend over. The rain is cool on his hot back.

'The hole is filled,' she says. 'This is enough,' she says. She looks at him with a tenderness so rare, he has to look away. 'It will get better,' she says.

The wind moving through the trees sounds like paper, like the curled edge of his hand moving slowly over paper when he has a stick of willow charcoal nestled in his fingers.

She pushes her hair back from her face and straightens herself and squeezes his shoulder roughly. 'We should eat a little and get back,' she says, tenderness done. 'I don't want to drive in the dark.'

He moves towards the rock and pushes both his palms against it, to feel its weight, its measure, and stands in this way until his breathing slows. Cool and damp and gritty, patched with black moss and dirt, this rock knew the body that was buried here for twenty years or more. Sheltered it. Made a place for it that can be marked on a map. Yannick would like to leave something behind, but he has nothing to leave.

'Can we give her a minute?' he says.

'Her?'

'Whoever this is. I want to give her a minute. We could light the candle.'

'I don't have a lighter.'

'You have been smoking this whole time and now you don't have a lighter.'

'Correct.'

'Could you check?'

She slips her purse off her shoulder and looks through it, then drops her purse to the ground and thrusts both hands in her pockets. One hand comes out gripping something, which must be a lighter, but is not. She shows it to him: a tiny, mechanical music box, not a helluva lot bigger than a lighter.

'I found it,' she says. 'It doesn't even work.'

He takes it from her and turns it in his hands.

'I don't know why I kept it.'

'We could leave it, though,' he says, passing it back. 'To show we were here.'

She smiles. 'Yes,' she says. She goes over to where the dead flowers are, and tucks the music box in close to the red glass that holds the candle.

He again presses his hands to the rock. This enduring rock under these tired old hands. He pushes his forehead to its surface and he whispers, 'Thank you.'

27

ONE OF THE other families left a bouquet of ranunculus at the burial site. A mother or a father. Maybe a brother or a cousin or a niece who never met her aunty. The flowers were dying – no, they were dead. The sight of those dead flowers made Kathleen love, just a little, the people who put them there.

She felt safe under the dripping cedar boughs, and the earth smelt clean, and she has decided that if Una has been waiting in this place to be found, well, she, Kathleen, can sleep okay knowing it took her this long to find it.

And she is never coming back here again.

The moon rose into the dusk on the drive back. It was a full moon and took up all the space it wanted, and Yannick was morose. She asked him if he'd bothered calling any of his children to let them know he's okay. He hasn't. She told him they were worried. He said: 'They are grown-ups and they do not need to hear from me.' She asked him if he would consider taking the damn truck to a dealership or even abandoning it, and flying home with her. He won't.

But she's beyond tired now, and she cannot drive that truck another inch.

Her phone rang last night as soon as she got back into her motel room and she thought it was Samuel Lim with the test results, but the screen told her otherwise.

'Have you caught the wild goose?'

'Hi, Julius.' She was disappointed and also relieved that it wasn't Samuel Lim.

'You sound very far away,' he said.

'I am very far away.'

'When are you coming back?' he said. 'I've been to your house.'

'Oh? Why?'

'I took a walk among your beloveds,' he said. 'I miss you.'

She can't remember the last time anyone told her that. To be missed is quite something.

'The girl with the swarm of children is taking very good care as far as I can see – nothing appears to be dying,' he said. 'But what do I know? When are you coming back?'

'Are you okay, Julius?' Kathleen glanced at the clock radio on the bedside table. 'It's one in the morning for you,' she said.

He didn't say anything for a moment, but she could hear him breathing. Finally, he spoke. 'Those shenanigans at your party did a number on me,' he said. 'I don't seem to be able to recover my pluck. They're doing more tests.'

'Oh, Julius.'

'Keep your pants on. I'm fine, truly,' he said, but his voice was thick. 'Nevertheless, I would like my friend back. Soon as you can.'

She watched a red, robotic 3 on the clock radio flicker into 4. 'Soon as I can,' she said.

And today they kill time.

They find a stony beach where the grey sand is more like clay than sand, and they walk on it. The water is calm, and right here at the back of the beach is a residential road with a row of clapboard and cedar-shingled houses, very porch-y and window-y. Very ocean-front-y. The people who live here can watch the ferries coming in and going out. Kathleen imagines their lives must follow the rhythm of the ferries, the foggy blow of horns or the traffic coming off the boat.

The sky is sharp blue with low, yellowish clouds that could rain. Or not. Kids ramble about in the shallow water with plastic buckets. A tiny boy crouches at the shore, naked and bawling, sandy drool shivering from his lower lip. His entire body, every inch, is engaged in the act of crying.

Kathleen suggests going to the movies, but when they look up what's playing, nothing interests them, so they don't go to the movies.

They find little to talk about over a lunch of grilled cheese sandwiches and canned tomato soup in an empty restaurant that smells of grease and vinegar. Kathleen checks her phone for missed calls.

Back at the hotel, they take naps in their separate rooms.

Later, Kathleen watches infomercials and Yannick takes the truck to a garage to top up the oil and put air in the tyres, all that kind of thing. She must have dozed off because when she wakes the light outside her window has softened to an orangey-pink. She checks her phone. And then it rains. And then it is night.

'I cannot do another day like yesterday,' Yannick says the next morning, as they're staring into the face of another day that can only be like yesterday, unless Samuel Lim calls. It's eight a.m. and he's at her door, freshly showered and shaved. There's a blot of toilet paper clinging to his chin, held there by a drying speckle of blood.

'Yesterday was bad,' she says, standing aside for him to come in. He sits heavily on the bed, still made, the one she hasn't slept in, and hangs his arms between his legs.

'Should we call him?' he asks.

'I was thinking that.'

'Call him.'

'It's not like he knows and he's making us wait,' she says. But she calls his office anyway, leaves a message.

'I cannot walk on any more beaches,' Yannick says.

'Fine.'

'And no more restaurants.' He gets up and moves to the window, pulls the gauzy curtain aside an inch. 'You have a better view. You got the road. All I got is wall.'

Neither can she. She cannot do another day like yesterday. She cannot do this.

He goes to the little desk and pulls open the drawer. Takes out the Bible and turns it over in his hands, tests its weight. 'Same Bible,' he says, and puts it back in the drawer. He has to fight a little with his hip against the drawer to close it. He scribbles something with the hotel pen on the hotel pad, which is also there on the desk, reports that the pen is a piece of shit, then stands back and looks at the painting bolted to the wall over the desk. The painting is of nothing worth remembering.

'I have a plan,' she says, through the heat that is creeping up her neck. 'You go now, occupy yourself for a few hours because *this*,' she points at him, and gestures widely to the room in general, 'no way.'

'Kathleen, I know. I am sorry. I've never had ants in my pants so bad.'

'I know.'

'I am beside myself.'

'Let me tell you my plan.'

He stands there in the middle of the room and folds his arms across his chest, then drops them to his sides, then pushes his hands into his pockets. She wants to punch him and to hold him; she wants to be held by him. She wants to slap him and kiss him and shove him out of the door.

'I'll go and rustle up some supplies. Junk food. Crosswords. You want cryptic or normal? You want a book? I'll get you a book. I'll get you a paintbrush and some paints.'

'I cannot paint and I cannot read a book.'

'Okay, no book. Not even a crossword?'

He stares at a spot in the middle of the floor. 'Better make it cryptic.'

'You meet me back here at noon and we won't move from this spot,' she says. 'Deal?'

'What if he calls while we're apart?'

'I won't let him tell me anything if we're not together.'

'Okay, then.'

'Okay.'

They are holed up like fugitives. It's a glorious day, the sun is belting outside, screaming at them, so they've drawn the heavy curtains snugly together. Television on, some cheerless rerun dredged up from the eighties. Kathleen and Yannick take up one bed each and on the table between them, plenty of salty snacks. He balances a bag of pretzel sticks on his chest and picks them out one by one, sucking on each stick until it's a nub. He'll eat the entire bag like that, she remembers, one stick at a time.

She goes to the bathroom, and when she comes back out, the bag of pretzels has been abandoned on the bed and Yannick is at the window, peeking through the curtains.

'What are you doing?'

'Car accident,' he says.

She joins him at the window and pulls the curtain further back so she can see, and the sun bashes her eyes. Two cars. From the look of the damage, one has crashed significantly into the back of the other. Red shards of taillight glitter in the sun. Torn fragments of fibreglass bumper lie at odd angles in the road, and the front car is partway up on the sidewalk.

'You didn't hear it?' Yannick says.

'Maybe we should call the police.'

'She's on it,' he says, and points to a woman in the street with her phone pressed to her ear. An older man with very pale legs and a red face stands in the middle of the road, pulling his hands up and down his face. A younger man is circling the two cars, checking the damage.

'Who hit who?' she asks.

'I don't know,' he says.

'Hope they've got good insurance.'

Crowd, duly gathered.

'The thing about insurance—' Yannick says.

A ringing phone. Kathleen's phone. They turn to look at it, and they look at each other, and she moves to pick it up.

Samuel Lim begins with an apology.

(When Kathleen was seven years old, her parents took her to the Canadian National Exhibition in Toronto. She remembers getting drenched on the log flume, which made her cold and ornery, and eating sauerkraut for the first time. She remembers her mother slapping her hand away when she tried to pat a colossal hairy pig sleeping alone in a pen of muddy straw. Towards the end of the day, her father gave her a choice: he would buy her a paper cone of cotton candy, or a helium balloon. She laboured and whined over this for a long time, pointing out that it was meaner to make her choose than to have offered nothing at all, and he said to her: 'Well, sunshine, I can take the offer back, no problem-o.' In a crunch, she chose the balloon.

By the time they got to the car, her father's wine-red Pontiac, which was parked at the ass-end of what felt like a thousand-acre parking lot, Kathleen knew she'd made the right choice.

Her helium balloon was purple. It was secured to her chunky wrist with a silky white ribbon, like an umbilical cord. As her dad unlocked the car door, she felt the tug, the unravel, the slipping away as her purple balloon broke free and jaunced elegantly into the sky. Her mother jumped to catch the last bobbing curl of ribbon between her fingers, but she wasn't even close. Stunned, they all watched it go – what else could they do? Bodies arched, hands shielding eyes from the sun, they stood in that shimmering wasteland of hot, glinting metal, and they watched, agape. The late-afternoon sky over Lake Ontario grew bigger and bigger as the balloon grew smaller and smaller, catching the odd wind current and doing a little curtsy, a little what-have-you, a little do-si-do. Kathleen's parents quickly lost interest but Kathleen watched the balloon until it was a speck. She held her now naked wrist up to her face and wept. And she remembers this distinctly: she wasn't crying for her loss. Instead she felt sorry for the balloon, alone in all that sky.

Her father swore openly. There was a suggestion to maybe go back for another, but it was quickly decided that the hike back was too far. This only made things worse.

As her mother was coaxing her into the back seat of their Pontiac, she looked up again for her balloon and found it. It was a speck so small, it had no business being visible, but there it was. She pointed, and at first her mother couldn't see it but then she said: 'Ah, you're right, peanut, it's there.'

All the way home, along Lakeshore Drive and out of the city and past the farms beyond the eastern reaches of the city, even as the sky changed colour from late-afternoon to powdery dusk, Kathleen could see that speck of balloon. And every time she asked her mother for confirmation, her mother confirmed.

Foolish, to humour a kid like that.)

Even though it's not Una, Kathleen takes comfort in the knowledge that yesterday one of the other families was given their daughter back – their sister, their mother, their friend. This is good news, better than good. This is enough.

Yannick now waits with her for the ferry to come in. They're outside the terminal, sitting side by side on a weary bench that's missing a slat, and they're staring out at the ocean, the flat surface cut apart and criss-crossed by wind and current. The sky is washed out.

Kathleen tries once more: 'Fly home with me. We can figure out the truck. Screw the truck.'

The long drive rolls over in her mind: that tangle of teenagers in Sudbury, the goose statue in Wawa, the not-broken VW van. His glasses on her bedside table in Medicine Hat. She can't fathom him driving home alone.

'I'm not ready to go back,' he says. He scuffs the heel of his sturdy old shoe in the dirt. His attention is out there towards the horizon, and Kathleen looks at him openly, not caring if he catches her. She focuses on the black and silver stubble already surfacing since yesterday's shave, and the dear line of his jaw, still prominent under the sag of ageing skin. She would like to ask him when he's coming back, when she'll see him. She would like for them both to promise that now they can be friends again. She looks out to the water where a few sailboats waltz together. There are islands and gulls and the punchy smell of seaweed baking on the sand. The sky blooms and blooms and blooms. The questions and the promises can wait.

'That's your ferry,' says Yannick.

It's still a way off but there it is, more box-like than boat-like, rudely pushing gallons of water out of its way as it steadily gets closer.

'You better get going,' he says.

'I'm supposed to be the stubborn one,' she says, getting up.

He stands too. Pain twitches in his face. They press together in a firm hug and she taps her fingers on the back of his neck. Squints back an irritating tear before he can see.

'Go then,' she says, motioning to his truck, which is parked just a little up the road.

He winks and turns, and bends his left arm up, fingers curled, in a quiet, backhand wave as he walks back to the truck. His thoughts are already somewhere else, she can tell. She watches him get in and start the engine. Exhaust fumes cough and dissipate, and she watches him go.

Yannick is dust. Visible only in a certain light, inevitable.

She turns back towards the terminal, towards the ocean, and heaves the cross strap of her solid bag over her shoulder. It's clear enough today that she can see the coastal mountains, way the hell over there on the mainland.

Moon Road

ON THE JETTY, still.

Our girl doesn't know this, but above her there is a CCTV camera mounted on a fenced cage that houses a rack of kayaks. She's being recorded or, rather, the space in which she sits is being recorded. From time to time she roams in and out of the frame. The picture will be black-and-white, poorly pixillated and run at five frames per second, resulting in a recording that will be jittery and surreal. Uncomfortable to watch for the people who love her, who will be studying this recording, bewildered, in about a week's time.

Lost and homesick is how she feels. She's angry now that Oliver didn't come, and is mentally composing the letter she will write and send to him tomorrow. (He will, incidentally, suffer many sleep-deprived nights over the guilt of standing her up today, so guilty that he will avoid speaking about her loss with anyone, will lie to the police, will drive a car across his own front lawn to avoid our girl's mother.)

It's cold and getting colder. It's windy and getting windier. She wears only a light top with no sleeves. Nothing in her bag to keep her warm; she thought she'd be sleeping in a hotel bed tonight, with him.

But she's wrapped up in the dark. The reassuring moon. The tumble and roll of the ocean.

Across the water from the jetty are the hints of islands. Dark shapes against this night sky. Gentle, breathing humps, like lovers. The moon lights an empty, shivering road on the water, but outside that the water is black, almost not there except that she can smell it and hear it. Its rhythms, its depth and fulsome weight, wind-blown waves peaking and sighing. The pull of a strong tide, this moon and its reflection on the water. She takes all of this in, and decides it is time to go home. Not just home, to where she's been living, here, next to the beach where there are people and a fire, but back to where she came from. She never meant to leave for good.

11:17 p.m.

Behind her, amid the sound of the ocean, the shuffle and drag of something alive. She looks over her shoulder and sees movement on the jetty. Her first thought is that this is an injured bird, flopping pathetically on a broken wing. But it's not a bird, it's a shadow cast by the lights strung along posts that line the jetty, which are swinging in the wind. She realizes there's nothing there, and turns back to the water. A few more minutes pass and she hears the same noise again. Once more she looks over her shoulder. This time, she's convinced it's something more than shadow. She's not driven by a compulsion to help a stranded animal, she just doesn't like this feeling of befuddlement. Of not knowing what's in the dark with her. So she pushes herself up off the concrete and walks towards the noise, stepping outside the reach of the CCTV lens for the last time, 11:28 p.m.

She takes a few more steps, and pauses. The movement looks to her like a shadow. It looks like an animal. Now it looks like a shadow again. There but not there. She tightens her face, leans forward, trying to decipher this dark, incomprehensible flutter.

348

She senses deliberate movement and then she believes she sees a dog. She thinks it's the dog Jimi. She whisper-calls his name twice: 'Jimi. Jimi.' She hears the rapid scuffle of claws on the rough surface of the jetty, and follows the sound further down the jetty to where there are no hanging lights. No discombobulating shadows. She's worried that the dog might go over the side because even with the moonlight, it's awfully dark, and the jetty is narrow, the edge close. She walks carefully, favouring her injured leg, roughing her hands up and down her goose-pimpled arms. She calls the dog's name. This mutt was always running off and getting into scrapes, so it's not such a stretch to imagine that he would find his way down here, a manageable scamper through the woods from where he lives. She would like to return him home.

The moonlight on the water draws her attention again. The edges of the reflection look like electricity to her, a multitude of sizzling white sparks. She eyes the road of light to the moon itself, its circumference vibrating like sound.

She raises her foot in its next step and there is nothing but the sound of the ocean. Her heart beats. Her lungs expand with breath. Her eyes blink and where she expects her foot to land on solid concrete it instead plummets through air. There is nothing she can do to stop this fall into the ocean. Before she hits water, a hard knock to the back of the head on the edge of the jetty. A bolt of cold saltwater straight up the nose and down the throat and a mind too stunned and disoriented, one leg too useless, to stop this.

A high spring tide, notable for the treacherous conditions it stirs up, receives this unexpected load with indifference, carrying on its back our girl, floundering in moonlight.

28

THIS OLD MAN, this beautiful father, stands alone on the edge of a jetty in a town that's not his town. He tries and fails to cry. Though the sensation of crying fills him entirely and the muscles of his face pucker, and though his chest shudders with each intake of breath, his eyes are dry. Maybe it's the wind. Or maybe he's just tired.

In an effort to pull himself together, he watches a white and red seaplane pivot in a circle and anticipates that it will taxi and take off but all the plane does is complete the circle and stop, and then it bobs there doing nothing. This disappoints him: it would have been pleasing to watch a seaplane take off.

He wears a cotton T-shirt under a plain grey jersey and a pair of blue jeans but he's not wearing any shoes. He has a scar at the corner of his left eye, so it looks like he's smiling even though he's not. And though his hair is tied back with a rubber band, the kind you use on a rolled-up newspaper, scraps of wiry silver hair blow across his face, scratching at his dry eyes. He briefly considers clearing the hair from his eyes but instead keeps his fists tucked stubbornly in the shallow pockets of his jeans. This minimizes his frame a little, makes him seem smaller than he is.

He's sad and also burdened with a new feeling he wasn't expecting to find here. It's impossible for him to put shape to this feeling, to find its edges, to call it something, anything; it has something (everything) to do with unsettled earth, with something once resolved that no longer is.

And it's all been such a long, long time.

He's been here before, on this jetty, stood in this very spot, in fact. He recognizes the horizon, but not in a familiar way. It's not as if he could name the mountainous, forested islands he sees – and it's all islands, here on the edge of his country, an endless, shattered coast of inlets and islands – but he broadly recognizes the shapes. He hears again the ubiquitous screaming birds you would expect where the remnants of fish innards are drying on boat decks, and he hears again the soft chink of wire lanyards, reverberating like vocal cords in the wind. This wind that buffets his face is the same salty wind it was the first time he was here. This patch of ocean, the same, dotted with navigation buoys and busy with sport and commerce. Waves course heavily to the north-east, catching the wind, catching the light. He scans the water for a glint of yellow kayak, which, logically, he knows he won't see, but his eyes remember. And, anyway, logic hasn't served him up to now so he searches the water, the compulsion as involuntary as the beating of his heart. The longer he looks, the bigger the body of water grows, expanding to the size of impossibility, impossible for the eye to track one yellow fibreglass boat in all that expanding mass of water, one small boat, one suggestion of boat, one speck of boat. He remembers this.

It's like no time has passed at all.

That's the problem.

If you could see the reflection in his tired eyes, you would see the puzzle of a girl, a disheartening number of the squares left blank. He is planted on this spot and thinks about this girl, this daughter, and considers all the possibilities, all the things that could have unfolded on the final day that brought her here, right here. Point last seen.

And in the glove compartment of his truck, which is in the parking lot of the marina where he now stands, his phone rings and rings and rings. He's got people, and they want him to come home.

29

AT FIRST YOU can't see her but then she rises from behind the purple delphiniums, maybe a little stiffly. She's holding a staff hoe, the kind you use standing up, with both hands placed widely for leverage. If you look closer, you'll see the weeds she's digging, the silvery-leafed lamb's quarters and succulent purslane. She's collecting the purslane in a plastic bowl so she can steam it later, for her dinner. Maybe fold it into an omelette with green onions and cheese.

She's been away from home for two weeks and left the care of her flowerbeds to someone else, so the weeds are more abundant than they would have been if she hadn't gone, but if she's honest about it, she doesn't mind. She likes this kind of work, is content to be back on her feet, sweating, once again dirtying her work-rough hands.

This is exactly where she should be.

This is where she's always been. She travelled as far away from here as it is geographically possible to go, without leaving the country, and is glad to be back where the world feels more solid, more rooted, more settled into itself. To her, anyway. The weather is more predictable. No danger of rockslides or cougars or earthquakes. And the cigarettes are cheaper.

Slow progression as she follows the weeds up the bed until she gets to the phlox, the Miss Pepper phlox. A flower with two faces, this one. If you're looking at it from a distance, the plant looks like it has big, airy flower heads, but if you come close, you see that the heads are actually made up of dozens of tiny flowers, dark pink in the centre with round, blush petals.

She can't remember the exact spot but she knows that some-where here, buried under the phlox, is a glass jar with her daughter's infant tooth in it. She buried it just before she went away a few weeks ago, a span of time that now feels a lot longer than it was – as time, on occasion, is wont to do.

She stops for a drink of cold water from the full bottle she keeps in a kind of holster at her hip. Wipes the sweat from her forehead with the sleeve of her shirt. Ignores a horse fly and begins to dig again.

The edge of her blade hits something solid with a flat clink. This would be the glass jar. Huh, she thinks. She stops, presses her fingers to her lips and kisses them, and blows the kiss towards the dirt, lets the kiss drift off the edge of her fingers and feather to the ground. And she carries on with her work.

The Bone

On a stretch of coast several hundred kilometres north of the jetty, several hundred kilometres north of the marina, of the town of Tofino, an old bone washes up on a forsaken beach. The bone tumbles lightly up and down the shore for some time with the pulse of the ocean before a muscular wave carries it up beyond the high-tide line and deposits it there in the pebbled sand.

This particular beach is almost always windy. It's pummelled daily by deep green waves laced with white froth and is inaccessible on foot, crowned as it is by dense forest. It's populated, among many things, by puffins diving for krill. Bald eagles circling for puffins. The odd marten, deer or black bear.

The bone is human, a tibia, also known as the shin bone. It disarticulated from the rest of its skeleton decades ago, and was carried along the seabed, further and further away from the place it first sank. Eventually, the current plucked it up and slowly, slowly coddled it towards shore. This shore. The bone is salt bleached and patched with fuzzy algae, and studded with barnacles of various colours and sizes. There are deep, wandering grooves etched into its surface, almost like decorative vines, grooves that were created by the gnawing teeth of hungry crustaceans. Both of its epiphyses – its ends – were knocked off years ago, due to the wear-'n'-tear of ocean activity, and so where the marrow once was, there is now sand.

A black-bellied plover, which has been wading up and down this shoreline all morning, hunting glassy pink sand-hoppers, pauses briefly when confronted by the bone, a new obstacle on his turf. After one cursory peck, and registering zero interest, he waltzes around it with busy little steps.

If you happened upon this bone, this tibia, you wouldn't, at a glance, know what it was, so much has it changed from its original form. So far is it removed from its intended function and so much a part of the ocean now.

Una.

ACKNOWLEDGEMENTS

Thank you, as ever and forever, Clare Alexander. And thank you to the team at Aitken Alexander. Thank you to Alice Youell for getting me through the first and toughest round. Thank you so much to Jane Lawson for patiently teasing out my best. Thank you to Hazel Orme, Vivien Thompson and Marianne Issa El-Khoury.

Thank you Deborah Sun de la Cruz for bringing me home.

Thank you kindly for sharing your precious time and expertise: Gail MacKinnon at Alecto Forensics, Jason Tierney with the Metropolitan Police, Tammy Douglas and Todd Pebbernat of the Royal Canadian Mounted Police. Thank you to Chris Walker of the Royal National Lifeboat Institution. Thank you Dr Mark Skinner and Dr Richard Lazenby for the bones. Thank you kindly Thomas Kerr of the Canadian Coast Guard for your stories of salty fishermen. For the flowers, the bugs and the carpal tunnel, thank you Sarah Nixon. For the trails, thank you John Hawkings.

I would be lost and incoherent without you: Francis Spufford, Merrill Brescia and Colleen Anderson.

To Peggy Riley and Joanna Quinn, I write, always, with youse in my ear.

All the love in my heart to Eve, Ali and Kieran.

SOURCES

Many resources were consulted in the development of *Moon Road* as a wholly fictional story, but most notably, and for which I am most thankful, the following:

Highway of Tears: A True Story of Racism, Indifference and the Pursuit of Justice for Missing and Murdered Indigenous Women and Girls, Jessica McDiarmid (Atria Books, New York, 2019)

Lost Person Behaviour: A Search and Rescue Guide on Where to Look – for Land, Air and Water, Robert J. Koester (dbS Productions LLC, Charlottesville, 2008)

The Flower Farmer: An Organic Grower's Guide to Raising and Selling Cut Flowers, Lynn Byczynski (Chelsea Green Publishing, White River Junction, 2008)

The stories of the helium-balloon friendship and the blade-of-grass statistics analogy have been adapted from a 2009 episode of the podcast *Radiolab*, titled: 'Stochasticity'

Born and raised in Canada, **Sarah Leipciger** lives in London with her three children. She is Associate Lecturer in Creative Writing at Birkbeck University and also teaches at City Lit London. Her short fiction has been shortlisted for the Asham Award, the Fish Prize and the Bridport Prize. She is the author of the critically acclaimed *The Mountain Can Wait* (2015) and *Coming Up for Air* (2020). *Moon Road* is her third novel.